TEMPTATION CAN BE DANGEROUS

"This is crazy," Abby said, her tone as uncertain as she felt. "I'm not—I can't."

"No, don't say that," Matt said, his tone low and seductive.

Everything about him was seductive: his voice, his smile, his smallest gesture, the way he moved. His every nuance screamed sexuality, and steamy sex was the one thing that could make matters worse for her. Her life was already an irretrievable mess. Getting involved with a man was the last thing she needed.

He was still looking at her with that intent trying-to-fathom-her-innermost-thoughts kind of look when her resolve slipped firmly into place. He hadn't relinquished her hand. Abby let him have that much, but whether it was a lame attempt to pacify him or because she was loath to let go of his warmth and his strength, she didn't quite know. She took a deep breath and let it go by degrees while she formed her argument in her mind. "Matt, this has been nice, but I just can't."

He frowned, and Abby wondered if his libido had gotten in the way of his comprehension. "*Nice,*" he said. "It's been *nice?* What the hell is that supposed to mean?"

She thought he looked stricken, as if somebody had just told him that Old Blue, his hound dog, had died. "What were you expecting?"

He raked a hand throu
I don't know. *Fabulous,* ma
me here, Matt; take me no
conveyed his defeat, and
her hand, then closed her
gonna take shameless adva
that research? We've got a lot of ground to cover.

BOOK YOUR PLACE ON OUR WEBSITE AND MAKE THE READING CONNECTION!

We've created a customized website just for our very special readers, where you can get the inside scoop on everything that's going on with Zebra, Pinnacle and Kensington books.

When you come online, you'll have the exciting opportunity to:

- View covers of upcoming books
- Read sample chapters
- Learn about our future publishing schedule (listed by publication month *and author*)
- Find out when your favorite authors will be visiting a city near you
- Search for and order backlist books from our online catalog
- Check out author bios and background information
- Send e-mail to your favorite authors
- Meet the Kensington staff online
- Join us in weekly chats with authors, readers and other guests
- Get writing guidelines
- AND MUCH MORE!

Visit our website at
http://www.kensingtonbooks.com

AS NIGHT FALLS

S. K. McClafferty

ZEBRA BOOKS
KENSINGTON PUBLISHING CORP.

http://www.kensingtonbooks.com

*For Lina Sue Trumbull, whose beautiful
spirit outshines the brightest star.
With unconditional love always . . . Mom.*

On this home by Horror haunted—tell me
    truly, I implore—
Is there—*is* there balm in Gilead?—tell me
    —tell me, I implore!
Quoth the Raven, "Nevermore."
                    —Edgar Allen Poe, *The Raven*

Chapter One

Thomas Wolfe was full of it. You could go home again. Home was center, a safe place in a world gone insane or a life that had gone headfirst into the crapper. Home was a refuge, a place—perhaps the only place—where it didn't matter what a crashing failure you'd become.

Braking her canary yellow Jeep CJ-7 on a rise in the long, winding drive, Dr. Abigail Youngblood sat in the cool shade of an afternoon turned strangely steamy and drank in the welcome picture the old mansion made.

Dappled by the warm autumn sun shining down through the surrounding red-gold maples, Gilead Manor gleamed like a rare gem on the leaf-scattered lawn, an odd mixture of Dutch and Georgian influences. The central structure was made of salmon-colored brick. Built large and square, it had outlasted eight generations of Youngbloods, the identical gray sandstone wings flanking the original structure on either side only slightly less. There had always been an air of age and stability about the place that called out to Abby, probably because she'd had so little permanence in her own life, as David had so aptly pointed out the few times they had discussed it.

The connection and the reasons for it didn't matter as much as the fact that it existed, and that it was real, unlike her marriage, unlike the trust she'd given to the man she'd married . . . a man she'd discovered she didn't even know.

Pushing it all to the back of her mind—the arguments, David's secrets and lies—Abby breathed in the dusky autumn air, the scent of black humus and a season at its fullest, or on the verge of decay, depending on how one looked at it. God, it felt good to be home. For a moment, she sat in the middle of the drive, a death grip on the steering wheel, waiting for some sign that she'd made the right decision, that maybe, just maybe, the nightmare she'd lived for the past six months hadn't followed her home to the Catskills.

Then, as the bright leaves drifted down and the rich, ripe smell of autumn insinuated its way into her senses, she drew a shaky breath and loosened her grip on the wheel. David would have sneered at her decision to come home. *Running away from it, Abby? Taking the easy way out?*

"I'm not running away," Abby muttered defensively. "It's temporary. It'll give me a little stability until I can get my bearings, decide what comes next. There's nothing wrong with that. Besides, I'm not the one who destroyed it all; I'm not the one who took the easy way out. I'm still here, aren't I? I'm still alive, and doing my damnedest to cope. . . . Okay," she admitted, "so I'm talking to myself. I never said I was all the way there, but I'm definitely working on it."

She was working on it. Making progress, too, damn

it. After some desperately needed R and R, she would be ready to take stock, deal with her ghosts, and weigh her options, then begin to reconstruct her life from the wreckage remaining. There must be something salvageable, she reasoned. Some remaining threads she could pick up and weave into something meaningful—something productive. She was just too blind at the moment to see it.

It was good to have a plan, and it gave Abby something solid to focus on as she slipped the Jeep into gear. Yet, as she nosed it forward, a small red sports car leaped into her rearview mirror. The Corvette topped the rise doing sixty. As Abby braced herself for the inevitable collision, the driver cut out around the Jeep, flinging gravel and dirt as it narrowly missed Abby's right rear fender. The driver, bottle-blonde and nowhere near twenty-one, lay on her horn and threw an obscene salute out the window.

"This is a private drive, damn it!" Abby shouted into the cloud of dust left in the girl's reckless wake. The car continued another fifty yards past the mansion, then swung sharply left, sliding to a stop in front of the carriage house, which, having outlived its original purpose a century ago, had been transformed into a guest house.

As Abby watched in disbelief, the car door opened and the driver wriggled her way across the porch and through the front door of the guest house; amazingly, her companion turned to wave. Beth Langtry had been on the fringes of Abby's high school clique a decade ago. Yet, if the local gossip had a grain of truth in it, Beth had peaked emotionally during her junior year, and at twenty-nine still wasn't past the party scene.

Abby shook her head. Almost simultaneously, the driving beat of an old Lynyrd Skynyrd song kicked up a notch, transcending the slim barrier separating merely intrusive from utterly ridiculous.

Abby parked the Jeep beside Catherine's green Mercedes and, shooting an irritated frown at the source of the commotion, took her bags from the back. "Let it go, Abby," she said under her breath. "Just stay focused ... stay centered." She took a deep breath, blowing it out slowly, as the instructor of her rage-management class had taught her. Then another. "Home is center," she said, convinced but not quite there. "Center, right now, is everything."

She opened the door to the mansion and put her suitcase down just inside, still feeling frazzled despite her mantra. "Aunt Catherine?"

Abby didn't hear Rose's footfalls, or realize that Catherine's housekeeper had entered from the kitchen, until the older woman touched her arm. Startled, Abby jumped, her hand automatically flying to her chest, balling into a fist.

She met the housekeeper's gaze. The look of concern was there on Rose's face, just as she'd known it would be. Abby clenched her jaw and somehow managed to weather it.

She wasn't fragile, she wasn't helpless, and she'd be damned if a sympathetic look would cause her to shatter into a million tiny shards of jagged humanity.

"How you doin', Miss Abigail?"

"I'm fine," Abby insisted. "Just fine, Rose. Thanks for asking."

Rose assessed her with a single critical glance. "Fine, she says. Well, if you're so fine, then how come you look like ten miles of bad county road?"

"I'm a little tired is all," Abby said defensively. "And maybe a little dehydrated. Six glasses of spring water and a nap and I'll be as good as new."

"Ha! Skinny is what you are. Why, I've seen fence posts with more curves than you got. What have they been feedin' you at that university? Why don't I fix you somethin'? Got a fresh batch of chowder on the stove. That and a little crusty bread'll put some meat back on those bones."

Rose had been managing Gilead Manor and everyone in it for as long as Abby could remember. She knew the old mansion's every nuance, knew every detail of Catherine's life, and Abby's. She pried into their affairs, kept their confidences, and doled out advice whether they asked for it or not. Rose was a household fixture; she was indispensable. Gilead Manor couldn't manage without her, and even worse, she knew it.

The commotion outside was filtering in. The bass on the stereo throbbed in the still air, alive, oppressive, vastly irritating. Gritting her teeth, Abby raised a hand to her temple and concentrated on blocking out the sound.

"Headache?" Rose asked.

"Big time."

"Come on, then, and I'll get you a nice cup of catnip tea to go with that chowder. Patricia," she called out to her granddaughter. "Honey, Miss Abigail's home. Put the kettle on. Don't you worry, Miss Abigail. We're gonna take care of everything."

Abby drank in the feel of the old place as she followed Rose to the kitchen. It was a wonderful room, with a red-brick hearth wall and a huge fireplace. The old fireplace oven was still in excellent working condition, thanks in no small part to Catherine.

Catherine was the keeper of the Youngblood heritage, steward of the past. If not for Catherine's tireless efforts, the mansion would have been reduced to rubble long ago, since her brother, William, Abby's father, didn't give a rat's ass about saving the past for posterity.

He was too caught up in the all-encompassing process of acquiring his next trophy wife while dealing with alimony payments that rivaled the National Debt to concern himself with the preservation of the family legacy— or his own legacy, for that matter. Abby hadn't spoken to him in almost three years—not since he'd married Cecilia, wife number six and counting. He hadn't even had the decency to put in an appearance at David's memorial service. Not that she'd expected he would. He had sent flowers from Rio, along with a terse and meaningless message neatly penned by his secretary. Not that he'd disliked David. To dislike someone, one had to take the time to get to know the person. And as far as William was concerned, time was money, and sex, and power—all of which eclipsed his only daughter, and had for her entire life.

Abby hadn't really expected more from him. It was learned behavior, after all. Pavlov's dogs in reverse. And while there was no denying the fact that her father was a genuine prick, at least he was a consistent prick, and therefore he gave her few unpleasant surprises.

It was more than she could say for David.

The kitchen was filled with the fragrance of freshly gathered thyme, drying lavender, and a sweet-pungent mix of spearmint and peppermint. A shaft of mellow autumn sunlight shifted through the wavy glass windowpanes, dancing over the surfaces of the antique table and Windsor chairs.

Everything was precisely as Abby remembered it, just as it had always been. She took a deep breath as Skynyrd skidded to a grinding halt and Aretha Franklin took up where the country-rock band left off, wailing "A Natural Woman" at a decibel level Abby just couldn't ignore.

"My God," she muttered, pressing her fingertips to her throbbing temples, "is nothing sacred?"

Rose filled a Wedgewood cup with steaming water and plunked a silver tea ball into the liquid. Placing it carefully before Abby, she laid out the honey and cream. "Not to Matthew Monroe. I tried to tell Miss Catherine that he was nothin' but trouble. I told her not to have truck with any writers! But would she listen? No, sir. She said he was a gentleman who needed a quiet place to create." Rose snorted her derision. "Only thing he's created since he got here is havoc. Fiction writer, my ass. Hell-raiser's more like it. Between him and those bone diggers from New York University, we haven't had a minute's peace around this old place for almost two months."

Abby barely heard Rose's diatribe. She was stuck six sentences back. "Matthew Monroe? Aunt Catherine is renting the Carriage House to *The* Matthew W. Monroe?"

Rose half-turned, bracing a fist on her brightly flowered hip. "So, you heard of him too?"

Who hadn't heard of Matthew Wilde Monroe? He was everywhere: talk shows, tabloids, even *Oprah.* He was a media-made phenomenon, a rising star, the quintessential overnight success, and if any of the rumors were true, he hadn't handled his sudden rocket to stardom with grace, poise, or the tiniest molecule of self-restraint.

"How on earth did Aunt Catherine—" Abby broke off, putting up a hand to ward off Rose's reply. "Never mind. I don't think I want to know." She took a determined sip of the catnip tea and prayed that its calming effects would soothe the raw edges of a badly bruised psyche. Then, she ran through her mantra once more for good measure.

Center, center. Home is center. Home will ground you, Abby. Home will help you heal.

Aretha continued to wail, disrupting Abby's train of thought, annihilating her concentration. Her irritation quotient rose a notch. Valiantly she clung to her resolve and did her level best to ignore it. "Where is Aunt Catherine, anyway? Her car was in the drive. I saw it when I came in."

On the heels of Abby's query, a ferocious clanging came from the utility room, accompanied by feminine grumbling of the four-letter kind.

"Fightin' with the hot water heater," Rose answered. "They've been in a pitched battle for days. I wanted to call Amos Ledbetter over at the hardware and have them drop off a new one, but Miss Catherine won't allow it. You know how stubborn that woman can be."

Almost before Rose finished her explanation, Abby was out of her chair and headed toward the source of the clanging. She found Catherine on her knees beside the water heater, a huge pipe wrench in her perfectly manicured hand. "Blasted contrary, incontinent thing!" Catherine said, and let go with a blow.

Clang!

Having taken as much abuse as it could stand, the dripping pipe split wide open, sending a spray of water and steam shooting vertically into the air. As Catherine scooted out of the danger zone, Abby dove for the valve to turn off the geyser. When the danger had passed, she sat back on her heels to survey the mess, not to mention her aunt. "Aunt Catherine, have you lost your mind? What on earth are you doing?"

"Abigail! Dear me, I didn't know you'd come!" Catherine, seventy-six going on sixteen, fussed with the wrench, then handed it to Rose, whose dark eyes took on a wicked gleam.

"I know just where to put this," Rose said, turning back toward the kitchen and the steady pulsing beat drifting through the old-fashioned screen door.

"Tut, tut, Rose," Catherine scolded. "What has Mr. Monroe done to deserve your animosity?"

Rose gave her a dangerous look. "Other than the fact that he's been disturbing the peace around this place for nigh onto eight weeks, I can't think of a single thing! Are you gonna let me call Mr. Ledbetter?"

"Not until I've exhausted every avenue remaining," Catherine said with a sniff. Then, placing a bucket beneath the leak, she pushed Abby from the room.

"Aunt Catherine, what's going on here? I come home to find you banging on the hot water heater, and Rose complaining about bone diggers?"

"It's nothing to worry about, dear. We've sprung a leak, that's all, and Rose was referring to Professor Bentz from New York University—a friend of yours, I believe."

"William Bentz?"

"Yes, dear. A lovely man, so quiet and polite. You do know him, don't you?"

"Barely. I believe he gave a guest lecture at Sullivan late last year." She struggled to recall a face to go with the name, but it was difficult. All she got was khaki clothing—safari-chic that was ultra cliché for a professor of anthropology—and highly polished shoes. "Please, go on."

"There isn't a great deal to tell," Catherine allowed. "He brought some students down from the department to do an experimental dig. He said the findings could have historical significance, and since he put it that way, I just couldn't refuse. Besides, he reminds me of that Indiana Jones person, only not as dashing." The voice of calm, of good-natured eccentricity and studied distraction. It was precisely what Abby needed. "Come, now, and tell me what's happened. I saw the papers. Did you serve up that reporter's balls on a silver platter?''

Abby gritted her teeth. The story had been splashed all over *The New York Daily News*. It had even made the *Times*, a major coup for Albert Carr, the journalist who broke it.

And who could blame him? It had all the elements of an award-winning exposé in the making: a sex scandal at a prestigious university, a made-to-order victim, and a crusading do-gooder making accusations of a major cover-up, a role Abby had unwittingly fit to a tee. At first, she'd viewed Carr as an ally, someone willing to help her uncover the scandal, give it the attention it deserved. She hadn't been aware that she would play a dual role in the incident: that of justice-seeker and victim. David's involvement had come as a total shock. At times she still had trouble accepting it. Just thinking about it made her sick with impotent rage—rage that had no outlet. David had seen to that personally.

"Rose," Abby said quietly, pushing her dark thoughts back into the shadowed recesses of her mind, "may I please have another cup of tea?" It was a tactic she'd learned in childhood. When she didn't wish to discuss something, she quickly changed the subject. The ploy had never worked with Catherine. Her straightforward nature did not allow for evasions or half-truths, and this was no exception.

Catherine's pale brows drew down over her startlingly blue eyes. "Abigail Rowan Youngblood, tell me that you didn't let that skunk get away with printing that horrid, self-serving claptrap—"

"It wasn't claptrap!" Abby snapped. "It was true— all of it." She immediately regretted her actions, the persistent and unbearable throb in her temples matching the beat of her heart. A few hundred feet from the kitchen, a truck engine roared to life. Its driver ripped it into gear, spinning tires, flinging gravel, and stirring a cloud of dust that hung in the autumn air long after he sped away.

Even worse, Aretha started again.

Some inconsiderate, self-centered imbecile had hit replay. The pain in Abby's temples quickened, magnifying until she feared that her head would explode.

She pressed the heels of her hands to her temples.

She couldn't think about Albert Carr, or the university, or David's betrayal, but she couldn't quite dislodge the look on Lily Pascal's face, when she'd asked about the girl's bruises and abrasions, from her memory.

Lily was just a kid, a long way from home and friendless. Halfway through her first semester, freshman year on a full scholarship, she'd been so wary, afraid that any breath of scandal would mean an end to her one chance at a good education. Her inner-city background had bred suspicion deep in the girl's soul. *Go along to get along, but don't trust anyone.* It had taken weeks to gain her trust, and when at last the story of the rape came pouring out, the look of mingled fear and shame in her eyes had torn at Abby's heart.

Time and distance were supposed to heal all wounds. Yet it hadn't helped Abby get over her anger and her sense of betrayal, of shock, disbelief, then outrage. And she could only wonder whether time had been any kinder to Lily. Would she ever get over what happened to her at John Thomas Sullivan University?

Deliberately she pushed back the memories, more forcefully this time. If she thought about it now, she'd run screaming from the house, or worse yet, crumple in a nerveless heap. "Aunt Catherine, I can't talk about this right now. I just want to soak in a hot tub, and then sleep for a couple of weeks."

"That'll be a trick, since there's no hot water," Rose put in, still indignant that she'd been prevented from plying the wrench.

"You make me feel . . . you make me feel . . . you make me feel like a natural wom-an . . ."

Abby, having reached the saturation point, couldn't take any more. "God damn him," she said, shooting from her chair, stalking purposefully from the kitchen. She felt as frazzled as an unknotted piece of rope—in grave danger of becoming completely undone.

"Abigail?" Catherine called after her. "Abigail! Where are you going?"

"To kill Matthew Monroe," Abby grated out. "But don't worry, Aunt Catherine. I can always plead insanity."

"Oh, dear," Catherine said, shaking her head. "I was afraid this would happen."

Rose crossed her arms over her chest. "You want me to phone nine-one-one?"

"Report my niece to the police?" Catherine looked properly horrified.

Rose just chuckled. "I was thinkin' more in the lines of an ambulance for that writer. He's gonna need one when Miss Abby gets through with him. Unless of course, you want to bury him under the roses?"

Abby stomped across the well-manicured lawn, past the Dresden roses planted by her great-great-great-grandmother, and across the carriage house porch. She wasn't in a blind rage, like on that last horrible day with David, and she wasn't teetering on the edge of insanity. But she was going to stop Matthew Monroe from wreaking more havoc. "Center, Abby, center. Just breathe."

Aretha howled as Abby pushed through the front door of the carriage house, pausing just long enough to set her sights on a likely target. There were at least a dozen young men and women, mostly under legal age, several of whom she recognized. Caleb Abernathy was grabbing a beer from the fridge, one arm looped around Beth Langtry's bare midriff. He closed the refrigerator door, then, at Beth's urging, gave her a quick, distracted kiss, before he noticed Abby. "Hey, Doc Youngblood. How've ya been?"

Beth sent her a smile. "Hey, Abby. You got home just in time to crash the party. Come on in; have a beer. Matt's gonna put us in his next book—immortalize us. Kinda cool, huh?"

"I'm not here to join the celebration," Abby corrected. "I'm here to end it." She headed for the massive stereo system filling the entire east wall of the living room. It must have been worth a cool five grand, minimum. Abby looked it over, top to bottom. "Wish to God I'd thought to bring Rose's handgun. I'd love nothing more than to put a hole in you the size of the Ashokan Reservoir, but I suppose this will have to do." She settled for a well-aimed finger on the power button, and Aretha died a swift and merciful death.

Then she took a deep breath, repeating her mantra in her head while she retrieved the cell phone from the pocket of her forest green wool blazer. Calmly, coolly, she punched 911. "This is Abigail Youngblood. I'd like to report a disturbance. The Youngblood residence on Osgood Deane Lane, and please hurry. It looks like there may be bloodshed."

She closed the phone with a click and watched as the stream of drunken humanity made a collective dive for the exit, including Beth and Caleb. Thirty seconds later a half-dozen engines cranked to life as the party-goers

made a break for freedom. All that was left was the little
red Corvette that had almost succeeded in running Abby
off the road earlier.

Abby glanced around.

It was eerily quiet.

The party had ended, just as she'd planned. Her mission was accomplished, but as she turned toward the
door, intending to leave Matthew Monroe to explain
things to the sheriff, a deep Mississippi drawl issued
from the door to the bedroom. "Hey, sugah, what'd
you say your name was again?"

"Bobbi. Bobbi Carmichael." There was a long pause,
closely followed by an impatient sigh, punctuated by a
deep male groan.

"Bobbi. Now, how am I gonna get this big ol' thing
in that tiny little hole if you keep distractin' me?"

"I've read your books, Matt," Bobbi fairly purred. "I
know how creative you can be. I'm sure you'll think of
something."

Another pause, a surprised grunt. "God damn, that
was sneaky. Aw, shit, see what you made me do? I lost
it." His voice was seductive, full of the promise of a
genteel sexual depravity, and it drew Abby like a magnet.
She was halfway to the bedroom before she realized
what she was doing, and by that time it was too late to
back down.

Besides, she thought, she wanted him to know that
she had called the cops, that he would have to check
his wild behavior and become an exemplary tenant, or
be out on his ass.

She cleared her throat, pointedly, steeling herself for
a confrontation.

But there was only the soft rustle of movement from
the bedroom, the sound of a snap letting go and a
zipper being slowly edged down, the distinctive sounds

of a prolonged and mutual kiss. "Man, you're a fast one, and I'm sure you'd be the perfect remedy for a bad case of backwoods boredom, if I had the time to fuck around. Unfortunately, I don't. I have a deadline. And if I don't get this thing up and runnin', I'll never pull my ass out of the fire on time."

"Ah, c'mon, Matt," Bobbi coaxed. "I'm hot for you now. And wet. Here, feel."

"Damn. How old did you say you were?"

Bobbi giggled. "I didn't. C'mon, Matt. It'll be fun, and who knows? I *could* inspire you to greatness. It'll be so hot, so good, you might even want to write about it."

A cynical snort. "And I'd have plenty of time for it, too. Statutory rape carries a hefty term, and sweetheart, though the thought's temptin', I'm just not drunk enough to consider you worth the risk—not yet, anyway. Listen, why don't you grab me a beer, and we'll talk about why you *don't* want to get involved with a writer."

Bobbi flung out of the room in a huff, nearly colliding with Abby in her haste.

"Party's over," Abby said. "Try to drive more carefully on your way out than you did coming here, will you? The sheriff's on his way, and I'd sure hate to see you lose your learner's permit."

"Fuck you, egghead!" Bobbi said, slamming from the carriage house.

"Bobbi, honey, about that beer—"

Abby turned back, and there he was, leaning against the doorjamb, an empty bottle of Coors Light dangling from his sun-browned fingers. Everything about him screamed indolence, from the thick shock of sable hair that had fallen over his forehead, and which he did not bother to brush back, to the faded jeans and open long-tailed Oxford shirt he wore. But Abby wasn't fooled by the laid-back Southern drawl and "don't-give-a-good-goddamn" attitude. Behind that lean, handsome face, with its slightly arrogant nose, sensual mouth, and cleft chin, there was definite cranial activity.

It shone brightly in his eyes—always a dead giveaway, as far as Abby was concerned—eyes the shade of sun-warmed bourbon, eyes that had seen too much and, damn it all, missed nothing as they did a slow, sensuous slide from her head to her toes and back again.

Though she hated to admit it, she could see why he'd caused such a stir in the media when he'd leaped onto the literary scene. Matt Monroe had what Aunt Catherine might have termed "presence," that indefinable something that drew people to him and held them there until he saw fit to toss them aside. Abby called it raw sexuality, and it rattled her to the bone.

"Hey. You're not Bobbi," he said, sending her a lop-sided smile.

Abby felt her heat rise and tried for the offensive. "No, I'm not. Tell me, Mr. Monroe, do you always entertain with such unrestrained exuberance?"

"Exuberance?" he said. "Did you just say 'exuberance'?"

"I know most of your guests personally, and at least six of them were under the legal age for the consumption of alcohol."

He motioned toward the kitchen. "If they were drinkin', they didn't get it here. Go on, check the fridge. I drank the last real one half an hour ago. Nothin' left but *O'Doul's.*"

"Bobbi Carmichael is the daughter of the Reverend Carmichael, the pastor at St. Mark's Lutheran Church—"

"A preacher's kid?" Matt snorted. "Small wonder I had to fight to keep my clothes on. Damn near lost, too. Though win, lose—I suppose it's all in the way you look at it. Listen, I don't suppose you'd like to sit in? You're all grown up, and a hell of a lot more intriguing than Little Miss Muffet there. Is that a no? Pity, for a minute there I had a fantasy goin' on—just you and me and that little bear-shaped squeeze bottle of pure clover honey in the cabinet—"

"You really are a pigheaded, chauvinistic ass," Abby shot back. "And I'd sooner see you dead than see you naked."

She gasped at her own comment, reddening slightly, and Matt thought he heard her mumble something about "center" under her breath. Intrigued now, he watched her intently while she fidgeted in an effort to regain control of a very controlled temper. As put-downs went, the one she'd heaped on him was tame compared to a few he'd received. Not that he got that many rejections—just enough to keep him from getting bored with the whole sexual tango, enough to keep things intriguing.

Nothing like being told to go to hell to whet a man's appetite. *No* didn't always mean *no*. Sometimes it meant, "Hang around and find out." Women loved the chase as much as their male counterparts. They were just too damned stubborn to admit it.

This one definitely piqued his interest. He didn't have a clue as to who she was, but he liked the way her eyes lit up when she was in a fury. They were an odd color, those eyes, a pale green, without the gold or brown that would have classified them as hazel. Haunted eyes that shone like twin peridots in her heart-shaped face and went perfectly well with her honey-gold hair.

Haunted . . . It was strange that he should come up with that, but there it was, and the more he tried to shake the impression, the more firmly rooted it became.

His writer's instinct, comatose these many months,

struggled sluggishly to life. *Haunted by what? Or more specifically, by whom? What sort of demons could this blatantly cultured, well-educated young woman from the right side of the tracks possibly have? The pressures of being the weekly Garden Club secretary, or the vast problems that came with being a deaconess of the First Presbyterian Church?*

Matt's interest was aroused, and the wheels were turning—slowly, perhaps, but turning all the same.

How long had it been since anything had sparked his interest beyond his next case of Coors, or carton of Camels? So long that he couldn't bear to think about it for more than a second or two. Those seconds passed in uncomfortable silence and another thought arose, this one more horrifying than anything he'd ever dreamed up for his novels.

What if this prickly young thing with honey-blond hair and pale-green eyes was his muse? And when she walked out the door, his inspiration, limited though it was, went with her?

The thought made him edgy, and his edginess made him crave a cigarette. He fumbled for the beat-up pack in his shirt pocket, shoving a half-crushed Camel into his mouth before he remembered his manners and held the pack out to his uninvited guest. "Join me?"

She waved them away. "I don't smoke," she said shortly, and the look on her face said that he shouldn't either.

Perversely Matt ignored it. "You won't mind if I indulge," he replied. "After all, this is home, sweet home—however temporarily." He lit the thing and drew the fragrant smoke deep into his lungs, swearing that once the fucking book was finished he'd quit—again. He wasn't sure how many times he'd tried to kick the habit, but he suspected that it was rapidly approaching double digits. "It's too goddamned quiet in here." Feeling restless and dissatisfied, not quite sure why, he went to the stereo and hit the power button, then pushed play. But Aretha had barely crooned a single syllable when her voice died away. Frowning, Matt glanced up.

His muse held the electrical plug in one hand, a pair of scissors that had been lying on the table in the other, and her haunted eyes gleamed dangerously. "Mr. Monroe," she said carefully. "We need to talk about the terms of your lease, and set some clear and undisputed boundaries."

Matt's distracted frown deepened. "Who are you, the party police? So, did Sophie send you down here to check up on me, or what? If she did, then tell her I said that she can go to hell. I'm working as fast I can, given the circumstances."

"I don't know any Sophie, and you can party yourself into an early grave for all I care, just as long as you do it quietly." *Snip!* She cut the plug end from the electrical cord to the stereo and thrust it triumphantly into her blazer pocket.

Matt bent a look on her. "That's easily fixed, you know. There's a plug in the drawer behind you, and I can have it spliced back together before you clear the driveway."

She frowned. "I thought writers were supposed to be introverts who craved quiet and needed solitude in order to create. Don't you have an idea for a book that's burning a hole in your brain?"

"Yeah, sure," Matt said. "I'm just tearin' up the keyboard. Or at least there's a chance I would be, if I could get my computer to cooperate. It's been in a deep coma since last Tuesday."

"There's a computer store down on Main Street. Flynn's Computer Sales and Service."

"Been there, done that, didn't help much. Flynn's out of town, and though his nephew's got one hell of a sales pitch, he can't fix shit. He said my motherboard's shot, then he said Ole Lucky here was obsolete, and he tried to sell me a whole new processor. He doesn't know his ass from a hole in the ground. I just had the motherboard replaced two months ago."

"I'll admit, Daryl can be somewhat enthusiastic, but he's honest, and he knows an antique when he sees one. Maybe you should reconsider. It's not like you can't afford it."

Matt threw her a sidelong look. "What the hell would you know about the shape of my finances?"

She shrugged, and her silk blouse grew taut across her breasts, barely visible under her green wool jacket. If Matt was any judge—and he'd done his damnedest to qualify—she had great breasts. Not too big, not too small, with dusky rose nipples. The first two categories were certainties. The third remained to be seen. It gave him something to aspire to, and a reason to pry his lazy ass out of bed in the morning.

"You from around here, sweet thing?" Matt asked, his attention diverted by the mental image of perky white breasts.

The computer could definitely wait.

"You seem to know the locals on a first-name basis—first Bobbi What's-her-name, then that Flynn character."

"Can't you think of something more original than 'sweet thang', Mr. Monroe?" Abby asked, mimicking his drawl. "It's old, and it's tired, and I believe I heard you use it on another potential target not fifteen minutes ago."

He grinned, and his whiskey eyes crinkled at the outer corners. "Well, you could tell me your name, and then

I could leave off the *sweet thing*s and the *darlin*'s until we know one another better."

"It's Gertrude," Abby said. "Gertrude Scully, and I'm visiting." It was a childish, retaliatory tactic, a less-than-mature attempt at avoiding the issue and putting him off, but Abby didn't care. She had the strange need to protect herself. Matt Monroe's grin was predatory, his tactics familiar and all too predictable. In a minute he'd be asking her sign, or wanting to know where she'd been all his life, or something equally trite.

Abby's defense mechanisms kicked into gear of their own volition. She was too wounded, too fragile even to look at another man—though she had to admit, what she'd seen of this one was deliciously sexy and more than a little intriguing, in a jaded, well-worn sort of way.

"If you don't mind, I think I prefer 'sweet thing.' Now, about my computer—"

"Pardon me if I don't feel sympathy pains for your plight, Mr. Monroe, but if the scuttlebutt's even half true, you're richer than God. Daryl Flynn can have a new system out here and up and running in less than an hour."

He was shaking his dark head. "You don't understand. I wrote my first novel on Ole Lucky, and it was a mammoth best-seller. I can't break in a new system now; it'll ruin my stride, stop it dead in its tracks. I need *this* computer."

Abby was astounded. "Oh, God, this is rich. *The* Matthew Monroe, wonder-boy genius of the publishing world, is superstitious."

"Call it whatever you like, Ms. Scully," he replied, totally unruffled despite her superior tone. He headed for the phone. "You don't mind if I make a few calls? As long as my system's down, I've got more than enough time on my hands."

Abby narrowed her eyes. It wasn't like her to lend aid to the enemy, but the thought had occurred that a busy writer was in all likelihood a quiet writer. Or in Matt's case, quieter. "Screwdriver," she said abruptly, holding out one hand, palm up.

He was juggling the phone while trying to light another cigarette. "I beg your pardon?"

"I'll make you a deal," Abby said. "If you swear on your next thirty-million-dollar contract that you'll take the party elsewhere the next time you get the urge to shatter eardrums, I'll have a look at it. But I'll need a screwdriver."

"You know your way around a motherboard?"

Abby lifted her chin. "I've cracked open a clamshell a time or two."

"Well, well, well, not only does she have great tits, she's resourceful, too. I like that in a woman. My dear Ms. Scully, you've got yourself a deal." He opened a drawer, palming a pair of screwdrivers, which he offered to her, handles first. "One last question. Phillips or straight?"

Matt opened the refrigerator, cracked an O'Doul's, and pulled a face. "Pseudo beer, body condoms—the lengths to which Science insists upon going in order to suck the last ounce of joy out of life boggles the mind."

Abby was on her way to the bedroom. At the door, she paused just long enough to send a cutting glance over her shoulder to the man who sauntered after her.

Sauntered . . . She'd be willing to bet that he'd take exception to her choice of words, so she clung to it and smiled an inward smile. "How many real beers have you had, Mr. Monroe?"

"I stopped countin' before brunch, and it's Matt.

Listen, if you're gonna screw around with my computer, then it's only right that we be on a first-name basis. Why don't I call you Gertrude?" he asked, grinning a wicked, knowing grin that clearly told Abby she'd been caught in her untruth. "Or maybe you prefer Gertie."

"Are you always so suggestive, *Mr. Monroe?*"

"Are you always so defensive, so anal, sweet thing? You ought to loosen up a little. I'm beginnin' to think your bun's too tight."

Abby's hand went to her nape before she realized that she'd opted for a low-slung tail that morning instead of her usual neat chignon. Caught, she reddened. "Just because I don't simper and purr at your mindless come-ons doesn't make me anal. Damn it, where are the screws for this thing?" She groped the corners of the metal case but couldn't seat the tip of the screwdriver. "Oh, for Heaven's sake! Will you turn on the overhead light?"

"Can't. It hasn't worked in a couple of days."

"Did you try changing the bulb, *Mr. Monroe?*"

"I did. But the sparks flew, so I did the manly thing and reported it to my landlady. She promised me that she'd have a look at it just as soon as she fixed her hot-water heater."

Abby frowned, feeling ever so slightly contrite. She wasn't sure how it had happened, but things around the old place had definitely got out of hand. She made a mental note to have a serious discussion with Aunt Catherine, but that didn't help her present dilemma one iota. There was only the skylight overhead, and the afternoon was advancing, the light growing dim. "A flashlight, then? Surely, you own a flashlight?"

"Well, of course I own a flashlight. Have you ever known a self-respecting male who didn't own a flashlight?"

He fumbled in the topmost drawer on the left side of the nearby chest of drawers and came away triumphant. Abby snorted at the tiny penlight and its ineffectual beam. "Well, Gadget Man, I suppose if that's the best that you can do . . . Let's see if we can find those screws—ah, there they are. Shine the beam a little to the left—no, not there—*there.*"

Abby plied the screwdriver, removing the remaining screws that secured the case and lifting it off with the precision of a surgeon. She checked the connections one by one as Matt leaned close.

Abby could feel the warmth emanating from him, smell the faint, crisp odor of his cologne, and despite her wariness, she shivered. "You sure you know what you're doin'?" he said softly, doubtfully. "That cable looks kind of twisted."

Before she could reply, he reached around her, straightening the kinked connection with exaggerated care. "There. That looks better, doesn't it?" He glanced at her and paused.

Abby's gaze clashed and locked with his. She couldn't seem to help it. It was like the strong, irresistible pull of a magnet against steel, female to male. He had invaded her space, insinuated himself into her comfort zone without her even realizing it, and now he was close—too close for her to ignore.

"It isn't Gertrude, is it?" he said in a voice that was low and lazy and drawling. The sound of it abraded her senses, like raw silk abrading hot, bare skin. "It's Elizabeth, or Constance, or Amelia Ann, or something rich and cool and classically Puritan—so well-bred, so cultured, so lovely, like the woman who wears it."

Abby felt her stomach flutter, and a light sheen of perspiration dampened her palms, making them slippery. She lost her grip on the screwdriver and it clattered to the floor. "Allow me," he said, but he didn't move to retrieve it. Instead, he moved closer, and his eyelids lowered slightly. "God, you smell like a summer's day. I wonder, do you taste half as sweet?"

He tilted his dark head and Abby froze, caught between the wild urge to flee and the force of Matt Monroe's blatant carnality. His lips parted slightly, and Abby gasped, but she didn't move away.

She was flustered, fearful of overreacting to a situation that any competent, self-assured woman could handle with ease. But she wasn't self-assured. There were too many wounds, too many lingering doubts. She was fearful of not reacting quickly enough. She didn't want to send mixed signals, but a surge of electricity zigzagged through her, chasing along her nerves, charging her senses with an excitement that she hadn't experienced since—well, since ever. Then, just before his mouth touched hers, reality raced in, bringing with it an overwhelming sense of panic.

She tried to turn away, but Matt was quick and caught the tip of her chin, holding her steady, accessible. "Ah, no," he said softly. "Amelia-Elizabeth Ann-Constance-or whoever you are, don't fight it."

"Mr. Mon—Matt—oh, no, oh God—I—can't—I—" Abby broke off as he touched his mouth to hers.

At the same moment, the sound of running footsteps pounded over the grass and up the front steps, and a split second later a fist rattled the screen door on its rusted hinges. "Miss Abigail? Miss Abigail, are you in there?"

Abby pushed away, breaking the spell Matt had woven so effortlessly around her, hurrying from the room. Rose's granddaughter, Patricia, stood on the porch, hand poised to rap on the door frame. She had just turned fifteen, and she looked frantic. "What's wrong? Has something happened to Aunt Catherine?"

"Miss Catherine's all right, but she wants you to come home. Those students from the college—they dug up a body."

Long after his muse had left him, Matt lingered in the doorway, watching the scarlet and gold of a Catskill sunset fade over the summit of Blue Mountain in the distance. He'd cursed Sophie up one side and down the other for sending him here, despite the fact that she'd been doing her damnedest to salvage what was left of his career. Their last conversation had been heated. He'd called her a meddlesome, manipulative, bloodsucking bitch not worth her ten percent, and threatened to fire her.

She'd calmly informed him that there was not an agent in Christendom who would have an egomaniacal bastard like him as a client, and that it was only her sadomasochistic tendencies that goaded her into taking his calls at all. When the edge had worn off his temper and he could hear her again, she issued her ultimatum, giving him one last chance, throwing his career a lifeline. "Just finish the fucking book, Matt. It's your last chance. Blow it, and they'll sue to get back the advance."

He'd snorted and made some remark about the chances of getting blood from a turnip, but she had his attention. "I wish the hell it was that easy," he said, Erin's face leaping to mind.

She would have turned thirty-one on January third, if only he'd kept his distance and stayed the hell out of her life. He thought about Erin while Sophie rattled on, telling him about a friend of a friend of a friend, who owned a quaint cottage in the Catskills, the perfect place for him to finish the manuscript. He thought about his lack of enthusiasm, his dull brain cells, his lackluster turn of phrase, and the other nine hundred and ninety-seven reasons that he couldn't write, each one of which he meticulously enumerated to Sophie in a two-hour-long conversation. Yet, in the end, he'd taken her advice and headed to the Catskills in a futile attempt to avert impending disaster.

Matt sighed. The last crimson streak had faded to black, and thoughts of Erin and Sophie and a career in its death throes still nagged at him. Maybe he'd try to finish chapter one this evening, then anesthetize his brain. It was the only way he slept these days. He was halfway to the bedroom before he remembered that his computer lay in pieces across his desk.

It was too late to call Flynn's, too late to do much of anything except return to the shelter of the porch, where he fumbled in his shirt pocket for another ciga-rette. Across the lawn, mellow light spilled from the windows of the old mansion, puddling in bright pools on the leaf-dotted grass.

Dragging the last breath of smoke into his lungs, Matt flicked the cigarette's remains into the drive, then turned toward the carriage house. "Abigail," he said softly. "I should have known."

Chapter Two

"Sheriff Rhys to see you, Miss Catherine. He says it's official business. You want me to tell him you're not home?"

Catherine finished stirring her Earl Grey and placed her spoon across her Wedgewood saucer. "No, Rose. I want you to bring another place setting. I'm sure he is anxious to speak to me about Professor Bentz and his recent 'find.' That is what you call it, isn't it, dear?"

Abby glanced at Catherine. "Ordinarily. But in this case, I'd call it a nightmare." She'd gone to the dig site as soon as she'd received the news, and she couldn't quite get the image of the shallow grave and the rag-swathed bones nestled on their bed of soft, dark earth out of her mind.

For a long time she'd tossed and turned, then, near dawn, when she had finally drifted off, she'd dreamed disjointed dreams of lonely woodland graves and sexy

Matt Monroe, an incongruous mix that continued to haunt her well into the morning.

Rose reappeared with a tray bearing the requested place setting, jolting Abby back to the present. Sheriff John Rhys followed the housekeeper at a respectful distance. "He says he had breakfast down at the café, but I brought the china all the same, just in case he changes his mind." Rose plunked down the dishes one by one on the saffron-colored table linen. "All that fried food. You stick to that diet, Sheriff, and you won't live to grow no bald spot on the back of your head."

"Thanks, Rose. I'll try to remember that." John's gaze met Abby's before sliding to Catherine. Abby saw questions in his blue eyes, a flicker of sympathy, and a spark of interest that six years and a pair of equally disastrous marriages had failed to erase. It made her slightly self-conscious, and more than a little wary. "Sorry to disturb you, Ms. Youngblood," he said to Catherine. "But I wanted to stop by and let you know that the dig site has been secured, and the team will be leaving shortly. I've spoken with Professor Bentz, and he's going to move his students to a spot near the old church, if that's okay with you."

"Yes, of course," Catherine said, then clucked her tongue. "That poor young man. He must be beside himself. Abigail, we really must invite him to dinner."

John frowned. "It might be best if you wait until a later date. They're moving the last of the evidence this morning and Bentz was kind enough to lend a hand— in an unofficial advisory capacity, of course. Since he's got firsthand knowledge in dealing with this sort of thing, we thought he could be of use to us."

Abby thought she detected a hint of distaste. "There's no need to pull any punches, John," she said. "I was there last night, remember? I saw the contents of the grave." She took a fortifying sip of coffee and sat back in her chair, neglecting to add that it was a sight she would be a long time forgetting. "Have you identified the body yet?"

John shook his head. "The coroner has the remains, and Doc Marshall has the dental records. With any luck we'll get a match. DNA tests take weeks, and I'd like to avoid that route if I can."

"When do you expect the results?" Abby asked.

"Three, four days."

"That long?"

"This isn't the city, Abby. The wheels turn more slowly here."

Abby raised her gaze to John's, hoping the unsettling ache in the pit of her stomach wasn't reflected in her eyes. It wasn't every day that skeletal remains were found in Abundance, let alone on Youngblood land, a circumstance that raised a host of questions with no obvious answers. Still, she couldn't help asking. "Who did this, John?"

"I wish to hell I knew, but it's way too early in the investigation for me to even hazard a guess. When we have more information—victim profile, age, sex, approximate length of internment—we'll start resurrecting old files, checking whatever leads we can find. My deputy is working the case with me. You know Shep Margolis."

Abby knew Shep, and she didn't like him. Shep was county born and bred, so steeped in regional pride that he was suspicious of anything different or new, and if that wasn't enough, he was a bully.

"I didn't know Deputy Margolis could handle anything more weighty than traffic control," Catherine put in.

John's answering smile was tight. "It's a small department, and my resources are limited. Shep may not be in the running for man of the year, but he's observant, and he knows this jurisdiction. I thought he might have a fresh perspective.''

"If it's a fresh perspective you're after, Sheriff, I'd be more than happy to lend a hand." The statement, issued from the doorway to the morning room, sent shivers up Abby's spine. It was indecent, his talent for making every word—the simplest, most innocuous statement— seem to brim with hidden meaning. Abby didn't glance immediately up, concentrating instead on the cooling contents of her coffee cup while she studied her nonexistent nails and willed her heart to abandon its crazy stutter and resume its normal beat. Only after she deemed her senses acclimated to his presence and her reactions under rigid control did she dare to meet his gaze.

He was dressed in faded jeans, a long-sleeved khaki shirt rolled to a point just below the elbow, and well- worn cowboy boots. A tattoo of a salamander basked lazily on one tanned and muscular forearm, its tail hidden by the cuff of his shirt. *Strange,* Abby thought, *but I could swear it was smiling.*

Matt dropped a kiss on Catherine's outstretched hand, then turned to wink at Abigail. "Miss Gertrude," he softly teased. "Do you always look so delicious in the morning? Or could that flush on your cheeks have somethin' to do with the company you're keepin'?''

Catherine frowned at Abby. "Gertrude?"

"It's a long story," Abby said, narrowing her eyes at Matt. "One that doesn't bear repeating. Don't you have a computer that needs your attention?"

"I decided to go against my better judgement and compromise. Daryl Flynn will be here later this after- noon with a backup system, and he says he can rig it so

I can use my old keyboard. Flynn will take a look at Ole Lucky when he gets back. Besides, Ms. Catherine was kind enough to invite me to brunch."

"And you just couldn't resist."

It was almost an accusation. Matt smiled. The young lady suspected that he had designs upon her lithe, willowy body. And she was right. He shrugged lazily. "I couldn't very well pass up a free meal, now could I? Especially when the company's so . . ."

"Gorgeous?" she inquired flatly, suspiciously, "delectable? So gosh-darned darlin'?"

"Actually, *stimulatin'* was the word I was lookin' for," Matt supplied.

The sheriff cleared his throat. "If you don't mind my asking, just who the hell are you?"

"Matthew Monroe," Matt replied. "And you might say that murder is my business, after a fashion." He took his seat, withholding his handshake. It was an intentional slight, but he didn't care what the sheriff thought. The man had taken an instant dislike to him, and the feeling was mutual.

Matt didn't like the sheriff's clipped Yankee accent, or the way his chill blue eyes kept coming to rest on Abby—eyes that shone with a possessive light. Either he'd slept with her, was planning to sleep with her, or both. In either case, he was competition.

"No one said anything about a murder," the sheriff swiftly pointed out. "In fact, as far as you're concerned, no one said anything. You got that?"

"I went out there myself this morning, Sheriff, and I saw the body. The body of a young woman in a shallow grave. Surely you don't expect me to believe that she got there all by herself?"

"I don't give a—" John began, then, with a glance at Catherine, "I don't really care what you believe, Monroe, but I will give you a friendly word of advice: steer clear of this. You're a guest of this county, not a resident. Stick your nose where it doesn't belong and you'll wear out your welcome real fast."

"No need to mince words, Sheriff. Go on, spit it out."

The other man's eyes glittered with hostility, and it was becoming obvious his reputation had preceded him. "Gladly. Let's just say that I won't take it kindly if the details of someone else's tragedy become fodder for your next bestseller. And that goes doubly for anyone I care about."

The sheriff stood, nodding to Catherine. "Ms. Youngblood. Thanks for the coffee." When he turned to Abby, his voice softened. "Could I have a word with you privately?"

Abby sent a penetrating look Matt's way, a warning look, then reluctantly followed John from the room. When they reached the foyer, he turned to face her. "Julianne didn't tell me you were home."

Julianne was John's sister and Abby's best friend, but they'd only spoken briefly since David's death. Abby hadn't intentionally cut herself off from the world, but she hadn't wanted to immerse her friends and family in her problems either. "I haven't had a chance to call her yet. I only just arrived last night."

Rich masculine laughter drifted from the door to the morning room.

John grimaced. "So I heard. The dispatcher filled me in about your complaint, and the fact that you'd canceled it. I would have come personally, but Rachel called. John Jr. took a spill on his ATV, and I had to meet them at the emergency room."

"Is he all right?"

"He broke his collarbone, but the doctor said he'll

be fine in a few weeks. His mother, on the other hand, had to be sedated."

"How is Rachel?" Abby asked.

John sighed, and the mask of politeness he'd affected slipped a notch. "You don't want to discuss my ex-wife any more than I do. Besides, that's not why I called you out here." He dug in his jacket pocket and held up a small sealed plastic bag. Inside was a gold half-heart and chain. "Do you recognize this by any chance?"

Abby took it from him. "I have one just like it in my jewelry box upstairs." They'd all had them: Julianne, Paige Nevers, Millie Gray, Beth Langtry, everyone in her high school clique. They'd all been overachievers— even Beth Langtry—members of the drama club, the cheerleading squad, or, like Abby, academic high rollers. "Where did you get it?"

John hesitated, and in the interim the image of the lonely woodland grave materialized in Abby's mind. "Oh, John, no! Not Millie."

John sighed. "It's a distinct possibility, and I thought it best that you hear it from me. The only thing we know for sure is that the body's been in the ground for a long time."

"Millie's been missing since just before graduation." Abby frowned. "Since prom night, to be exact."

At the time, the authorities had conducted a thorough tri-county search, enlisting the help of the news media and more than a hundred volunteers. . . . And all that time she'd been right here, almost under their noses.

Abby gingerly handed back the bag and turned away from John, away from the necklace. If she stared at it a moment longer, she was afraid she'd be sick. "I really should be getting back. You'll keep me informed?"

"I'll notify you just as soon as we have a positive ID," John promised. "Abby, are you okay?"

"What?" Abby said, still coming to grips with the fact that the body unearthed the evening before was in all probability a long-lost friend. "Oh, yes. Yes, I'm fine."

Hand on the door handle, John turned back. "Listen, Abby, be careful around Monroe. I've heard about him, and if even a third of it is true, he's trouble like you've never seen."

Abby bristled. "I appreciate your concern, but I'll handle whatever comes my way, I assure you. Besides, I'm not looking for involvement—with anyone."

If John was disappointed with her declaration, he didn't show it. "If you need anything, day or night, you know where to find me." The front door closed with a soft click. Abby closed her eyes and drew a deep cleansing breath, but she felt no calmer, no steadier for it. And with each passing second she became more convinced.

Millie was dead. The necklace had confirmed what John couldn't. Someone had killed her, burying her in the woods near the heart of the estate. Abby shook her head. If she hadn't seen it herself, she would have found it too incredible to believe.

Abundance was a small community, and closely knit. Some families had gossiped over the same backyard fence for five generations, and secrets were nearly impossible to keep. Murder might be commonplace in the city, but it simply didn't happen in Abundance.

And almost a decade of intermittent city dwelling and exposure to the day-to-day violence that was an integral part of urban life somehow didn't make it any easier for Abby to accept. She was still struggling to gather the edges of her composure together when Matt materialized beside her. He had a talent for that sort of thing, and it was damned unsettling. Appearing at the most inopportune moments, providing a distraction when she needed one most.

"You got somethin' goin' with Mr. Law and Order?"

Abby stiffened. "As a matter of fact, I do. We're friends. I would explain the concept, but I doubt your Neanderthal brain could grasp it."

"Well, I'd like to believe you, but there's one small thing. When a man is that possessive of a woman, either he's *been* a part of her life, or he'd like to be."

Abby's calm, hanging suspended by a gossamer thread, disintegrated, replaced by a vast irritation and something else—a wariness unlike anything she'd ever felt before. "My relationship with John Rhys, or the lack thereof, is none of your business, so kindly butt the hell out!"

He draped one muscular arm over the newel. "No need to get defensive, Abby. You don't mind if I call you Abby, do you? Or do you prefer Abigail?"

Abby closed her eyes and counted backward from ten. *Deep breaths, Abby, deep breaths. Let the air into your lungs; feel the welcoming walls of the house reach out and wrap around you. Nothing can touch you here, not even an egomaniac who's always on sexual overload.*

She tried to slough off the anger and fill her being with a calm white light, but it was no use. She couldn't escape Matt Monroe's disturbing presence. Couldn't ignore the fact that he was staring at her, that asinine grin plastered all over his gorgeous face. Abby sighed. "Go away, Mr. Monroe," she said, opening her eyes, turning back toward the morning room. "Go write another best-seller, drink beer with the Queen Mum, or do whatever it is you do. Just do it quietly, far away from me."

"I take it you're not a morning person? Or is it all this talk about dead bodies over brunch that has you out of sorts?"

"It wasn't just any body." Abby replied softly. "Her name was Millicent Gray, and she was a friend of mine."

He blew out a low whistle. "You knew the victim?"

"Look, I really can't talk about this." She would have brushed past him, but he caught her arm in a grip that was strong and sure, and wholly unexpected. Warmth seeped from his fingers through the silk of her cream-colored blouse to bathe her skin and send delicious little prickles along the length of her arm. It was hard not to react to it, not to be drawn in by his magnetism, and only the knowledge that men like him ate women like her for breakfast helped to strengthen her resolve. Matt Monroe was poison—pretty poison, to be sure— but poison all the same. And there was no way in hell she was going to risk getting involved with him—not as friends, not as lovers.

Easy to say, hard to resist. How long had it been since a man had touched her? Eight months? Ten? Before David's death, there had been his deepening depression and her preoccupation with her work. It was only natural that she react to Matt's touch, only natural that her skin drink his warmth hungrily in.

"Abby, wait a minute," he said, catching her off guard. "Look, I'm sorry. Really."

"About what?"

"About your friend. I didn't realize—it must have sounded callous, and I apologize."

Abby nodded awkwardly, unable to force the smallest sound past the lump in her throat. It was too much. The certainty that someone had taken Millie's life, John's concern, her reaction to Matt. Then, he took his hand away, and the moment was broken.

"Listen," he said, "your aunt said the hot-water heater's broken. If you'd like, I could take a look at it."

"That won't be necessary," Abby replied, the image

of Matt with the ineffectual penlight in hand flashing to mind.

He must have read her thoughts, because he chuckled. "Okay, so I'm not so great when it comes to electronic wizardry, but I know my way around hot water, having been ass-deep in it often enough." He put up a hand, as if taking an oath. "Swear to God, I was a plumber's apprentice for two and a half years. If you don't believe me, then you can call Spence Bradley at Bradley's Plumbing and Cooling. Area code six-zero-one, nine-two-two, three-zero-four-four."

"You? A plumber's apprentice?" She laughed and realized belatedly just how good it felt.

Matt cocked a brow and grinned. "I was sixteen, on the brink of forfeiting my virginity to Miss Jean Louise Taylor, and I needed the money."

Abby held up a hand. "I do not want to hear about your sexual exploits."

"Well, don't worry. I've never been one to kiss and tell. Jean Louise broke my heart, though, just in case you're interested."

"I'm not," Abby said. Then, "What happened to her?"

"Jean Louise?" He shook his head. "It's a real tragedy. She was elected county sheriff, so I guess you and I have something in common after all. The follies of youth, and all that. So . . . let's weigh your options: you can let me take a look at this hot-water heater, or you can shower at the carriage house. Course, that option *does* have its possibilities." He groaned low in his throat. "I can see it all now: you, me, some steamy water and a loofah sponge."

Abby raised her chin, determined not to react to his baiting, or to the fact that she found him incredibly attractive. "Are you aware that such blatant flirtation

and overt sexual innuendo usually indicate a deep sense
of sexual inadequacy and self-doubt?''

His grin widening, he leaned closer, so close that
she could feel the gentle heat radiating from him, and
growled, ''Go on, sweet thing, talk dirty to me.''

Abby giggled in spite of herself and gave him a half-
hearted shove, or at least she tried to. When her hand
connected with his solar plexus, he was hard-bodied, as
solid and strong as warm granite.

''Mmm, mmm, mmm. Foreplay,'' he whispered
warmly. ''I think I'm going to like bein' your neighbor.''

''You really are a dreadful man.'' Despite some hefty
reservations, Abby succumbed and led the way to the
laundry room. She eyed him skeptically as he squatted
beside the ancient, ailing metal beast. ''Are you sure
you're up to this?''

''You might be pleasantly surprised at the scope and
complexity of my hidden talents,'' he replied a little too
confidently to win Abby's trust. He tightened the valve
that had stemmed the flow of Catherine's geyser, then
glanced around. ''Hand me that toolbox over there,
will you, Abby?''

Abby shivered at the familiarity he'd claimed without
her consent, then scolded herself mentally for the absurdity of her reaction. Matthew Monroe was just a man,
no more, no less, and while it was safer to be wary, she
was acting like an inexperienced virgin, a milestone
she'd passed eleven years ago in the backseat of John
Rhys's cherry red Chevy Blazer. Since then, she'd had
at least a half-dozen relationships, the last of which had
ripened into what she'd thought was a good marriage,
then ended in tragedy and self-recrimination.

Matt opened the lid of the toolbox and rummaged
through the contents, scattering wrenches of various
sizes over the floor at his feet. Then he gave a grunt,

that universal male signal for satisfaction, and came away with a large roll of duct tape.

"Duct tape?" Abby said. "You're going to fix it with duct tape?"

He sat back on one heel to consider her, one knee on the floor and his legs spread wide. His worn denim jeans rode low on his hips, stretching tight and leaving precious little to Abby's imagination. "You got a better idea?"

Abby tried to find a focal point as far away from his crotch as possible and finally settled on a crack in the faded wallpaper just beyond his left ear. "Duct tape is not a solution, it's a cop-out. You said that you knew your way around hot-water heaters."

"This thing must be thirty years old. It's a wonder it's lasted this long. Looks to me like the lead water main has a couple of pinhole leaks, there's a hairline crack in the elbow, and the burner's ready to go. If I wrap the main with a rag and some duct tape, it'll slow it down till your aunt can get a new one out here."

"Duct tape and a rag," Abby said tightly. "Now, why didn't I think of that?"

"Somehow I'm not surprised," he said. "You academic types are all the same. Long on brains, but sadly lacking in life strategies."

Abby stiffened. *Oh, God, he knows.* Suddenly, she felt transparent, as if every shameful secret, every failure, every dysfunctional cell in her body were right out there in the open for Matt Monroe to see and scoff at. "I beg your pardon?" she said somewhat shakily.

"Problem-solving skills. You know, common sense." He produced a neatly folded bandanna, which he molded to the pipe like a bizarre bandage, then wrapped the whole tightly with duct tape. "You may know your way around a slide rule, but you couldn't stop a leak to save your life." He tore the tape, secured the ends, and dropped the roll back into the toolbox; then, hand poised over the valve, he grinned up at Abby. "Shall we?"

Abby glared at him. "If it leaks, you'll clean it up."

Matt remained oblivious. "You up for a little wager, sweet pea?"

"Not if it involves anything of a sexual nature."

"Matthew Monroe? On a first date?" He put a hand on his chest and tried to look innocent, but he couldn't quite pull it off with those darkly golden eyes glinting impishly from the shadow of his sooty lashes. "Not without dinner and a movie first. Wouldn't want to give you the impression that my favors come cheaply."

Abby smiled; she couldn't help it. His grin was infectious, his manner so thoroughly outrageous that she couldn't possibly take him seriously, or take offense. "Are you ever serious?"

"Are you ever anything but?" he said. "Do you realize that I've known you for sixteen hours and forty-seven minutes, and that's the first time I've seen you smile. You're kind of breathtaking when you smile, Abby. You ought to do it more often. Life's too short to take too damned seriously."

Suddenly, it was David's voice, not Matt's, that echoed crazily in Abby's head. *"Let's take a drive upstate. It's pretty there this time of year. The leaves'll be turning. We can find a cozy little B and B and make love all night long."*

"I can't, David. Not now."

"Then when? Next week? Next month? Next year?"

"David, please, don't do this," she heard herself say. *"You know how important this is. This paper can either make or break my career. I can't afford to shrug it off. Please don't ask me to choose."*

She could see his face in her mind's eye, and she saw

something pass over his features: a subtle resignation, a grim awareness, as though it was the defining moment in their marriage—in his life. *"Don't worry, Ab. Asking you to choose between your job and our marriage is the last thing I'd do. Besides, I already know what your answer would be. . . . "*

The memory faded, but the residue of Abby's regret clung like a damp and cloying second skin. Matt Monroe was watching her with a slight frown creasing his forehead, and in that instant Abby had the insane urge to tell him that there wasn't a great deal in her life to smile about, that due to recent events she'd forfeited the right. She had the urge to tell him a lot of things, all of them inappropriate, all of them immediately squashed behind the protective wall she'd erected. He was staring at her expectantly. "I'm sorry. Did you say something?"

"Our wager," he prompted. "Your aunt was kind enough to allow me the use of her library, and the freedom of the Youngblood archives, but I sure could use a research assistant."

"Gee, that's too bad. I'm afraid that Rose doesn't do floors, and she doesn't do libraries."

"I like Rose well enough, but she wasn't exactly what I had in mind." He grasped the valve and grinned. "How about it, Abby? An afternoon with me, together-alone among all those dusty old books, the smell of leather and vellum surrounding us. Are you adventurous enough to risk it?"

"And if you lose, and your ingenious remedy leaks all over Aunt Catherine's floor?"

"Then I'll see that the hot-water heater and the pipes are replaced, and as a special treat, you get to go mud-boggin' with me on Saturday. Seems to me that it's a win-win proposition all around."

Somewhere deep down inside, the thought of spending time with Matt Monroe was scintillating, yet the mental image of a mop in his hands proved the deciding factor. She didn't even allow herself to think what she was risking by spending time with him. "You've got yourself a deal," Abby said.

She offered her hand and he took it, bringing it to his lips, kissing the inside of her wrist, lazily caressing the place where her pulse leaped with the tip of his tongue.

A jolt of pure heat shot through Abby at the warm roughness of him, the shameless suggestiveness of the act. Her reaction to his advances was strange, and totally out of character. She should have slapped his face, cut him with a cold and scathing put-down—anything but the tiny gasp she gave, the momentary hesitation, the indecision, the ragged sense of need that froze her to the spot.

That need was so basic, so primal, so raw and throbbing that for the space of several heartbeats Abby was hard-pressed to fight it. Then she got hold of herself, jerked away, and rubbed the tingling skin of her wrist. "Mr. Monroe."

"Matt," he corrected, opening the valve and getting to his feet.

"Matt," Abby relented, inclining her head at the small jet of water and steam that found its way around the duct tape. "There's a mop and bucket in the broom closet over there. You won't mind if I go find Rose. I'm sure she'll want a photo for her scrapbook."

"Holy shit." Matt breathed the words so softly that he was certain the young woman walking ahead of him couldn't hear him. When Catherine Youngblood had mentioned her library, he'd pictured some small, cramped room done in shades of hunter green and tan, not a cavernous, high-ceilinged rotunda.

On second glance, he realized the room was not round, but octagonal, with wide French doors and Palladian windows. Shelves filled with books stretched from floor to ceiling on the remaining walls. Rolling ladders provided ready access to the mind-boggling array of titles—at least to anyone who didn't have a paralyzing fear of high places.

In the center of the domed ceiling was an octagonal masterpiece, a stained-glass window depicting a young red-haired woman lounging in an enchanted vale with sprites and wood nymphs cunningly hidden in the foliage all around her. The rich, deep jewel tones overhead threw sparks of multicolored light onto an ancient Abusson carpet and the period furniture arranged comfortably around its fringes.

For the space of a heartbeat, Matt's only thought was that the worth of this single room could have bought a thousand tiny run-down clapboard houses on a dead-end street in Atwater, Mississippi, just like the one he grew up in, that the money Catherine Youngblood spent on light bulbs alone would keep a family of four in hot dogs, beer, and cornbread for a couple of years.

Then he checked himself, remembering that the Matt Monroe who'd struggled and scraped and worked three jobs to get through law school was a thing of the past, a ghostly shadow, gone—and for the most part, blessedly forgotten.

And he had every intention of keeping it that way.

Beside him, Abby stood, cool, blonde, and wishing she were anywhere but here. She was waiting, watching, those big green eyes gauging his reaction, and for a moment he had the strange impression that she was trying to read his thoughts. "Impressive," Matt said. "I haven't seen anything this elaborate, this extensive, since . . . well, since never." He made a slow circuit of the room, scanning titles, reaching up to pluck a volume from the shelf. "Voltaire," he said, "and a first edition at that. It must be worth a few dozen hot-water heaters." He opened the flyleaf to the faded, spidery scrawl. "For my darling Fallon, from your loving Lucien. April seventeen seventy-five." Matt made a cynical sound, somewhere between a sigh and a snort. "Lovers?"

"Hardly. She was my great-grandmother seven generations back, and he was her doting uncle," Abby replied. "Does everything in your world revolve around sex?"

"There are three common denominators around which the world and everything in it revolves," Matt replied. "Sex, power, and money. What else is there?"

Abby wished that she could refute what he was saying, yet it wasn't just cynicism; it was the truth. The ruin her life had become, and everything in it that had gone so horribly wrong, could be traced directly back to sex, power, and money. The thought triggered the anger, always there, simmering beneath the surface, and the anger boiled over onto Matt Monroe. "What about honesty, and fairness, and justice? They do exist—somewhere—or at least they should."

"Yeah? Well, not where I come from."

It was said so quietly that it barely registered, yet by some miracle, some quirk of Fate, it penetrated Abby's fury and settled into her conscious mind, slowly drawing her focus away from the shame and ruin of her recent past, giving her something to concentrate on besides her failures, her regrets. "And where is that?"

"Back beyond nowhere." He glanced up from the volume of Voltaire. "Atwater, Mississippi. It's a small town not far from the Alabama border. Two stop signs, a lot of backwater when it rains, and mosquitoes bigger than that little yellow Jeep that sits in your drive. It's a little piece of heaven, all right."

His sarcasm was impossible to ignore. It hinted at something unpleasant in his past, a crack in the smooth facade of wealthy Southern playboy that he so effortlessly affected. Abby was intrigued, though she did her best to hide it. "Bitterness doesn't become you, Mr. Monroe."

"And here I was, thinkin' we'd settled that name thing." He put the book back on the shelf and walked to where she stood. "It's Matt. And it's not bitterness. I just don't care to squander my loyalty on people, places, or things that don't deserve it, and native son or no, Atwater never did a damned thing for me."

"Somehow, I would have figured you for something more exotic," Abby said candidly.

Interest and humor kindled in his eyes. "Such as?"

Abby shrugged, wishing now that she'd never broached the subject. He was watching her closely with his odd half-smile, a smile that, despite her best efforts, sent a lightning bolt of searing warmth zigzagging a path straight to her toes. There was something about him, something dark and dangerous and completely unsettling . . . something he kept hidden from the casual observer. Abby could sense it, but she couldn't pinpoint its cause, and the possibilities tugged relentlessly at her imagination. She shrugged, suddenly self-conscious. "Something Faulkneresque, I suppose. An old mansion full of eccentrics, an alley of live oaks dripping Spanish moss leading straight up to the door. Mint juleps and long, sultry afternoons."

"Well, that's kind of cliché, isn't it? And anyhow, who the hell's this Faulkner guy?" He was joking. It was his way of avoiding what he didn't want to discuss. "What about you, sweet thing? Did you grow up in this old mausoleum, or did they ship you off to some prim and proper Yankee boardin' school to learn the finer things in life, like which fork to use first at dinner?''

Abby felt heat rise up her throat. She'd had no intention of talking about her father and stepmother, or her less than idyllic childhood. But he continued to watch her with that unwavering stare, and she couldn't seem to help answering. Besides, it wouldn't have been fair, probing into his past, then refusing to reciprocate. "Sorry to disappoint you, but I'm afraid I didn't go to boarding school. My mother died when I was seven. I don't remember much about her. Less than a year later, Dad remarried. Her name was Gwen. She was twenty years younger than my father, and we didn't like each other very much." She shrugged her shoulders, as if she could shrug away the sudden wave of vulnerability that sluiced over her. "A few years later, I came to stay with Aunt Catherine. . . ." A sigh, and her guard slipped a notch. "They didn't seem to want me around, and Aunt Catherine did."

"Yeah, well, I know a thing or two about not bein' wanted." Matt felt the pull of his past. Behind his eyes, the image of his mother flashed. She was sprawled on the sofa, her arm hanging limp, an empty highball glass dangling from her fingers. Abby must have felt the change come over him, felt him close himself off from the pain the image caused, from her. He immediately pulled himself back from the memory, locking it away. The past had nothing to do with the present. He was more than the sum total of an alcoholic mother and an old man who'd hit the skids and hadn't had the guts to stick it out. "It's good that you had someone," he said simply. "Everybody needs somebody, right?"

Who do you need, Monroe? He immediately shrugged

off the thought. He didn't need anybody. It was dangerous to need, to want, to depend on anyone.

Matt saw her frown. "Are you all right?"

"Yeah, sure. I'm fine."

Abby recognized the lie for what it was. Matt knew it. She'd sensed that something had affected him, touched him deeply, and she also suspected that whatever had passed behind his eyes in that moment of quiet had been unbearably painful.

She might have questioned him, tried to ferret out the truth, but he took a step closer, and the shock of his nearness stopped her. She caught her breath, fumbling with a lock of her hair, pushing it behind her ear then freeing it again, anything to keep from confronting her desire directly. "I don't know why I told you. It isn't my habit to bare my soul to every man I meet."

"There's the ticket, sweetheart. I'm not just any man." Matt tucked the wayward lock of hair behind her ear, tracing the line of her jaw with his fingertip. Her skin was as soft and velvety as a rose petal, and she smelled just as sweet. He felt himself leaning toward her, and was shocked that she didn't pull away.

The current that always seemed to surge between them crackled and pulsed, an electrical arc that defied time, space, logic. They were polar opposites, and Matt knew it.

Abby was cool and polished, an overly educated Ivy Leaguer with a slightly untouchable air. Matt acted on instinct, burning hotter than a shooting star streaking across the midnight sky, and racing just as quickly toward extinction.

The capacity to burn out was deeply embedded in his genetic code; hell, it was more than that. It was his fate.

A fate he'd earned.

Yet in that moment, their total incompatibility didn't seem to matter. He sure as hell wasn't looking for a lifetime commitment; hell, he didn't even allow himself to think as far as a one-night stand. All he wanted was to hold her, to feel the softness of her breasts yielding beneath their thin veil of silk as he crushed her to him, to test those peony pink lips.

"No," she said, and Matt's pulse faltered to a stuttering stop. "No . . . I don't suppose you are. You're unlike anyone I've ever met, and I never know exactly how to take you—"

He drew a ragged breath, falling back on a glib response. It was a talent he had, one that had served him well over the years and had gotten him out of more than a few sticky situations. It was strange how easily people accepted it, how eager they seemed to dismiss him as a shallow charmer. And he didn't even mind. It kept them from asking uncomfortable questions, from getting too close. Getting too close was a damn dangerous thing.

"Doesn't matter how, Abby. As long as you do." He reached for her—or at least, that was how he saw it later. At that moment, he didn't know anything beyond the softness of the woman in his arms, the stunning eagerness of her response as he backed her against the bookshelves and kissed her.

Abby was stunned. One moment she'd been fumbling for words, and the next she was running her hands over him, across his broad shoulders, up the strong column of his nape, into his hair. She opened her mouth under the carnal onslaught of his kiss, the same way a tightly closed bud opens under the bold persuasion of the hot summer sun.

There were a thousand reasons she shouldn't be kissing him, a thousand reasons she should have torn herself from his arms and walked away, but at the moment she couldn't seem to remember a single one. And then the thought faded completely, and there was only sexy, scintillating Matt Monroe, urging her up and onto her toes with a hand on the small of her back, bending slightly to bring her even closer, more intimately molded to his long, lean, muscular self.

He slanted his mouth over hers, and slipped his tongue inside to caress hers, to remind her of how it felt to have a man invade her body.

Abby remembered, and she shook like a leaf.

The hand at the small of her back slipped down, curving around and cupping one cheek of her derriere. Pressed tightly to him, Abby could feel the heat and the rigidity of his arousal, and she knew that he wanted her every bit as badly as she craved and feared the heady intimacy of the act.

Firmly entrapped between trepidation and desire, Abby found the strength to push from his embrace, but Matt caught her hand, as though unwilling to let her go. "This is crazy," Abby said, her tone as uncertain as she felt. "I'm not—I can't."

"No, don't say that," he said, his tone low and seductive.

Everything about him was seductive: his voice, his smile, his smallest gesture, the way he moved. His every nuance screamed sexuality, and steamy sex was the one thing that could make matters worse for her. Her life was already an irretrievable mess. Getting involved with a man who spoke only the language of lust was the last thing she needed. Though she was fairly certain that Matt Monroe knew his way around a bedroom, getting involved with anyone romantically was out of the question.

He was still looking at her with that intent, trying-to-fathom-her-innermost-thoughts kind of look when her resolve slipped firmly into place. He hadn't relinquished her hand. Abby let him have that much, but whether it was a lame attempt to pacify him or because she was loath to let go of his warmth and his strength, she didn't quite know. She took a deep breath and let it go by degrees while she formed her argument in her mind. "Matt, this has been nice, but I just can't."

He frowned, and Abby wondered if his libido had gotten in the way of his comprehension. *"Nice,"* he said. "It's been *nice?* What the hell is that supposed to mean?"

She thought he looked stricken, as if somebody had just told him that Old Blue, his hound dog, had died. "What were you expecting?"

He raked a hand through his dark hair. "Well, hell, I don't know. *Fabulous,* maybe. Or *earth-shattering,* or *take me here, Matt, take me now."* He sighed, a sound that conveyed his defeat, and dropped a kiss in the palm of her hand, then closed her fingers over it. "If you aren't gonna take shameless advantage of me, then how about that research? We've got a lot of ground to cover."

Abby was about to reply when Rose appeared in the doorway. "Miss Abigail," she said, fixing Matt with a disapproving scowl, "telephone call for you."

Some time later that same evening, Abby padded barefoot to the bedroom window and stood looking out at the lengthening shadows of Vanderbloon's Woods. Somewhere out there, in the world beyond the window panes, Millie's killer went through the motions of everyday life. He walked in the sunlight, he worked, and he ate, and he slept with his ugly secret kept close to his heart.

Was it someone she knew? Abby wondered. Or had it been a drifter who had taken Millie's life, someone in the area temporarily and then gone? Had it been a single, isolated incident, or was there something more sinister, more cunning, and infinitely more evil happening here?

She pondered the possibilities, her thoughts finally drifting away. The lights burned brightly at the carriage house, but Abby wouldn't permit herself to speculate on Matt's activities any more than she would allow herself to touch on the fact that he'd kissed her just a few short hours ago.

She stood staring through the windowpanes a moment longer, then left the window and climbed into the old tester bed. Tomorrow everything would be better; she would feel more firmly grounded, she promised herself. Tomorrow, she would forget all about Matthew Wilde Monroe.

As the light went out in the second-story window, a shadowy form separated from the knotted gray trunk of a large maple and stood watching the window a moment longer. A cigarette flared brightly orange, illuminating his stark features for the barest instant, revealing the hunted look in his eyes, then dying out completely as he dropped it on the ground and crushed it underfoot. Then, his compulsion satisfied for the present, Matt turned and slowly made his way back to the porch of the carriage house, where he settled into the hickory rocker he'd purchased in town, and slowly, deliberately, lit another cigarette.

Chapter Three

Amos Ledbetter owned the local hardware store and had for almost forty years. Amos was unique in that he still installed most of what he sold. His grandson, Harry, who was learning the business, was as lanky and tall as Amos was small, and as slow on the uptake as Amos was quick.

It was Harry who rapped lightly on the doorframe to the morning room just after breakfast the next day. "Miss Abigail, Granddad would like a word with you. He wants to know if you'll come to him? He's been in the crawl space, and he doesn't want to track dirt all over Miss Catherine's house."

"Yes, of course. I'll be right there." Abby drained the last of her French roast coffee and stood, secretly glad to abandon the unpleasant task of writing a letter of condolence to Millie's parents. She'd called John's office earlier in the day and talked to the dispatcher, Sarah Helmsley, who had been more than happy to pass along the news that there would be no need for extensive DNA testing. The dental records were a perfect match. The body discovered at the dig site was definitely that of Millie Gray.

The news came as no shock to Abby, yet strangely, it hit her hard, mostly due to the fact that Millie had been on Youngblood land the entire time.

Amos came backing out of the crawl space just as Abby and Harry approached the walled rose garden. Covered in dust and cobwebs, he reminded Abby of a demented elf. "Miss Abigail," he said with a courteous jerk of his head. "Nice day, ain't it?"

Abby sighed. The sun was shining, but the bank of low-lying clouds off to the west was the dull gray of an old pewter spoon, and the leaves had all gone belly-up. It would be raining before nightfall. Abby forced a smile. "Yes, nice. Is there a problem with the water heater, Amos?"

"There's a problem, all right, but not with your hot-water tank. It's top-of-the-line. Mr. Monroe, he seen to that. Nice fella. Generous, too."

Abby's smile grew strained. The mere mention of Matt's name brought back scalding memories of his tongue toying provocatively with hers, the vital heat of his hard body, the yearning to have him inside her.

"Yes," Abby said. "Yes, I'm sure it's the best money can buy, and I will be certain to reimburse Mr. Monroe and reassure him that his interference, though perhaps well meaning, isn't necessary—or welcome. As a matter of fact, I was planning to stop by your shop first thing this morning."

"Yes'm, I figured as much," Amos said, switching tactics with a finesse Abby couldn't help but admire. "The Youngbloods have always seen to their own affairs, and I can't imagine Miss Catherine'll care for some stranger buttin' into her business, even a generous one. That's why I didn't mention the foundation or the other problems to that fella Monroe."

"The foundation?"

"Umm," Amos said.

"There's something wrong with the foundation?"

Amos scratched his head, and a trickle of dust fell onto his shoulder and nestled among a tangle of cobwebs. "I told Miss Catherine last year: like us, this house is getting old," he said in his own maddeningly slow fashion. "And old things tend to settle. Just ask my wife, Mildred. I got the arthritis so bad in this here knee that I can barely walk when it rains."

"I'm sorry to hear that."

"Like I was sayin', this here stonemasonry wall's got a crack in it, and the mortar's beginnin' to fall away. It's not a good thing, not good at all. If you want, I can ask Seth Bankcroft to come take a look at it. Brick-layin's his specialty, but he's done a little restoration work on the side. I'd have him look at that wiring, too—he's got a cousin in Kingston who specializes in electrical work."

Abby's tension level soared. More problems. More headaches. More things to think about. God, how she longed just to push it all aside, do the Scarlett O'Hara thing and think about it tomorrow. But that wasn't at all like her. She'd never been one to avoid problems, and she preferred to meet confrontation dead on, even when its source lay surprisingly close to her heart. "I'll talk to Aunt Catherine and get back to you."

"All right," Amos said, "but I wouldn't wait too long if I were you. Too much rain and that wall could fall completely in."

Abby left Harry and Amos to put their tools in the truck, entering the house by the back door. Catherine was in the kitchen conferring with Rose about the week's menus. "Aunt Catherine, did Mr. Ledbetter happen to mention last year that there were cracks in the foundation?"

Catherine tasted the onion soup Rose was simmering. "Why, yes, dear, I believe he did say something to that effect. And he mentioned something about the wiring, too, as I recall."

"Did you call Mr. Bankcroft to come and take a look at it?"

"Oh, there's no need for that," Catherine began.

Rose snorted, cutting her off. "She's plannin' to fix it herself," the housekeeper said indignantly. "Can you believe that? Seventy-six years old and she thinks she's Bob Vila."

Catherine sniffed. "It isn't about age, Rose. It's about attitude. All the foundation needs is a little mortar to make it solid again. And I bought a home-repair book on wiring. I'm sure it's nothing I can't handle. This house has stood for two hundred and eighty-five years. It will stand at least two hundred more."

"Not without a lot of repairs and a great deal of money," Abby interjected.

"Might as well save your breath, Miss Abigail," Rose said. "She won't hire Mr. Bankcroft to fix that wall. She's gonna try to fix it herself to save some money— probably try to talk me into helpin' her, too. But there's no way I'm messin' around with the electricity. She won't be happy till she electrocutes herself!"

"You can't make a decent onion soup," Catherine retorted. "I somehow doubt you'd be much good at mixing mortar, and as for the wiring, it requires a cooler head than the one you can claim."

Abby frowned. "Aunt Catherine, I don't understand. Why put yourself to all of this bother when you can hire a professional?"

"Professionals cost money, that's why," Rose put in.

Catherine's crack about her onion soup had been the first volley in what was gearing up to be a full-scale war. Abby tried to block it out, but her nerves were wearing thin. "But money has never been a problem."

Catherine glared at the housekeeper, a cool warning that Rose ignored. "It is now that she doesn't have any."

Abby held up a hand to keep Rose from saying anything further; then she turned to Catherine, who was looking daggers at her housekeeper-turned-adversary. "Aunt Catherine?"

"It's a temporary inconvenience, Abigail, and nothing to trouble yourself over. I had a slight difficulty with Nathan Stant, is all."

"Difficulty, my African-American ass!" Rose put in. "He put her money in bad stocks, and when the market plunged, she lost a bundle. If that wasn't bad enough, good old Nate took the rest and flew his behind to the Grand Caymans. And she won't even try to have him arrested."

Catherine thrust out her regal chin. "I wouldn't expect you to understand the concept of loyalty, but his late father was a friend of the family for years."

Rose refused to back down. "He left you one step away from the poor house. Friend or no friend, he needs to pay for that."

Catherine would have replied in kind, had Abby not stepped between them. "Rose, I appreciate your concern, but this is something I need to discuss with Aunt Catherine—alone, please." Abby bent a look on Catherine, who tucked her lips tightly together in a thin line of disapproval. "Aunt Catherine?"

"Oh, very well." Turning, Catherine stalked from the kitchen, down the hallway and onto the airy light and shadows of the front porch. "Go on," she said grumpily, "tell me that I am a foolish old woman, too incompetent to see to her own affairs; I've said it often enough to myself these past months."

"I think we both know differently," Abby replied, studying Catherine's face closely. The years had been kind to her aunt. Her blond hair was generously shaded with silver, her skin soft and relatively smooth, and the indomitable spirit she'd always been still shone in her eyes. "Aunt Catherine, how did this happen?"

Catherine slid a look of pure disgust in Abby's direction. "It's Rose's fault, you know. Her and that damned surprise party she arranged for my last birthday. You should have seen the candles on that cake! Why, it looked like a bloody forest fire. I didn't know whether to make a wish or call nine-one-one."

Abby took Catherine's hands and gave them a reassuring squeeze. "You are *not* old."

"I was just trying to look to the future, Abigail, and the legacy I would leave behind. Though it scalds me to admit it, I ran through my inheritance almost as quickly as your father did his, restoring this old place. Obviously, there were certain aspects we neglected. At least he and I have *that* much in common! I wanted something substantial to bequeath to you, and to any children you might have someday. When I discussed the problem with Nathan, he suggested I take my remaining trust and build a new portfolio. He said that he knew of a way to make a quick turn-over. Oh, he freely admitted that there was a marginal risk involved." She snorted, a fine imitation of Rose. "Within six months, it was gone, all of it. I called Nathan to consult on how to recoup my losses, but his phone had been disconnected. It seems he'd relocated, and he'd taken the small nest egg I had left in reserve with him."

"Have you spoken with your attorney?"

Catherine cut her a sharp glance, then quickly looked away. "Tell Brisbane Coleridge that I'm incapable of managing my own affairs? Not on your life! And I don't want you talking to him either. I got myself into this mess; I shall get myself out, one way or another."

Abby sighed. Coleridge was a distant cousin, and though Catherine had felt obliged to let him oversee legal matters in the past, they had never gotten along particularly well. "Very well, then. But you don't have to face this alone, you know. I'll speak to Julianne Rhys this morning. I'm sure she'll be happy to help." Catherine would have protested, but Abby laid a hand on her arm. "Don't worry. She's nothing if not discreet."

But Catherine *was* worried. Abby could see it in her face. "You shouldn't be doing this," she said. "You shouldn't be saddled with my problems when you've got concerns of your own."

Abby's mouth curved in a wry smile. "It's kind of you not to use the words grief-stricken or neurotic. 'Concerns' sounds so much more manageable."

"Oh, horse manure," Catherine said, and somehow made the expletive sound completely appropriate. "You don't have a neurotic bone in your body. You need to rest, that's all—to rest and to take stock, decide where you go from here. You're a Youngblood, my dear, and we don't give up that easily. In a week or two, you'll be your old self again. You may bank on it."

Abby thought of all the time she'd spent, trying to build a career, a life with David. She thought of the countless hours of research, the meticulously documented data—everything she'd thrown away when she resigned from the faculty. She thought of David's suicide note, the bitter ramblings of the man she'd loved and married, a man she barely knew.

It all passed through her mind in a lightning-quick

flash, and on its heels a threatening sense of panic hovered.

Abby turned away from it. She couldn't take stock of her life; it was too painful looking back. And she couldn't be her old self again when she wasn't even sure who she'd been. The only thing she knew for sure was that she was afraid of making another mistake. Of trusting her own judgment. It was something she kept locked away in a secret place deep inside her, something she couldn't admit to anyone.

Not even Catherine.

"What I need is to focus," Abby said, determined not to let her crowding doubts close in. "I'll speak with Julianne, and then together we'll weigh our options."

Julianne Rhys owned an antique bookstore on Church Street called The Bell, Book, and What-not. It sat at the opposite end of the street from St. Mark's Lutheran Church—an appropriate location, Abby thought, since Julianne's faith was at the opposite end of the spiritual spectrum from the Reverend Carmichael's.

One relied on divine intervention to solve the world's ills, the other on a combination of age-old wisdom and practical magic. Julianne wasn't a flagrant witch, more at home in a business suit than basic black. And she hadn't hung out a shingle; the black cat curled on the corner of the hand-painted sign that screeched discordantly in the slight breeze above her doorway, and the delicate silver pentagram hanging in the window and throwing off sparks of brilliant light said it all. But then, witchcraft was her mainstay, her sideline, not her principal occupation. Suspended from the quaint old sign was a smaller one, proclaiming in small block letters: *Julianne Rhys, Attorney at Law.*

The Reverend Carmichael made no bones about the fact that he considered Julianne's shop "an abomination and a blight upon an otherwise God-fearing little town."

But ignorance was bliss, and it was obvious to Abby that the Reverend Carmichael had never set foot inside Julianne's shop.

The place didn't just have atmosphere.

It had ambiance.

The ancient brass bell attached to the front door clanged as Abby entered the shop. The building was nearly as old as Gilead Manor, and the ghosts of two centuries seemed to lurk in every nook and cranny, corner, and chimney piece, their whispered laughter gently stirring the cinnamon-scented air.

Oil lamps and candles lined the ancient mantel over a fireplace of ballast brick brought to New York from Holland in tall-masted ships, and were accentuated by recessed lighting cleverly concealed among the old oak rafters. Antique rockers flanked a drop-leaf table in front of the fireplace, adorned with delftware cups and saucers in mint condition.

The three remaining walls were lined with books, bric-a-brac, incense, and candles of various colors, sizes, and shapes.

Behind the first of two tall standing floor shelves dividing the rectangular room into thirds, the crown of a black-and-gold baseball cap could just be seen. Abby had hoped that by coming in before noon she would have the place to herself. On the heels of a trying morning, she was in no mood to make small talk, and chances were slim that the other customer was an out-of-towner. Averting her face, Abby slipped past the other patron, and at the same time Julianne's voice drifted from the back, "Be with you in a minute."

Abby ran a finger along the spine of Grisham's latest novel. Julianne's tastes had always been eclectic, and offerings by Koontz and Cornwell were tucked among leather-bound classics and crumbling volumes on the downfall of the Byzantine Empire. As Abby took a book from the shelf, Hissy, Julianne's gray-and-black-striped tabby, jumped onto the seat of a nearby rocker.

Startled, Abby sucked in her breath. Unimpressed by her reaction, the cat settled into a furry circle, tucked his nose into his tail, and fell to catnapping.

Abby glanced quickly up.

The baseball cap hadn't moved. The customer hadn't even noticed her reaction and appeared to be engrossed in the pages of a magazine.

Yet as Abby turned away, the man behind the counter let out a low wolf whistle. "My, my," he said, his voice muffled by the slick pages of a *Playboy* magazine, "look at the woofers on this one, would you?"

Cheeks burning, Abby spun back. "I beg your pardon?"

"Woofers," Matt repeated, grinning a carnivorous grin as he lowered the magazine. "Here, check this out." Before she could protest, he flashed the centerfold at Abby . . . a glossy spread of a surround-sound stereo system, complete with the largest base speakers Abby had ever seen.

Abby sighed, and some of the tension drained out of her. He'd concealed a copy of an electronics magazine inside the pages of the *Playboy* pictorial. "You know, you really are demented."

"Just protectin' my reputation," he said. "Wouldn't want anyone to get the wrong idea." He closed the magazine and, lowering his head to peer at her over his sunglasses, walked to where she stood. "What are you in for, sweet pea? Oprah's book-club selection for the month? Or the latest in pop psychology?''

Abby leaned closer, lowering her voice to a secretive tone. ''Actually, it's none of your business. And just in case you were planning to get two magazines for the price of one, the owner of this bookstore is a friend of mine, and shoplifting is against the law.''

He draped an arm over the top shelf, still grinning like a cat in a barn full of dairy cows. ''The thought never crossed my mind. But there is somethin' else I won't hesitate to steal.''

Reaching out, he teased the line of her jaw with the tip of his thumb and, his grin fading, lowered his head to kiss her. At the same moment, Julianne Rhys appeared in the doorway.

She took in the situation at a glance: their close proximity to one another, Abby's guilty flush as she jerked back. And in that instant Abby knew what she was thinking.

''You two know each other?'' Julianne asked with a bemused half-smile.

''Know each other?'' Matt began. ''Why we're practically—'' The statement was punctuated with a surprised grunt as Abby trampled his instep.

''Strangers,'' Abby supplied sweetly. ''We're practically strangers. Mr. Monroe is Aunt Catherine's new pest—I mean, tenant. He's renting the carriage house—but enough about him.''

She turned a shoulder to Matt and lowered her voice to a near-whisper. ''Do you have a few minutes? I need to speak with you—*privately*.''

Julianne frowned. ''Yeah, sure, just let me take care of Matt first.''

''That's okay,'' Matt said. ''I'd be happy to wait. In

fact, I need to have a word with Abby," he said with a wink. "It's about our lunch date."

Abby threw him a look of pure annoyance. "Would you stop? We do *not* have a lunch date."

"Sure we do, sugar. Don't you remember? You said you'd help me with my research, then you got a phone call and said you'd have to give me a rain check. Well, I'm ready to cash it in."

"I never said anything of the sort," Abby objected.

Matt went on, as though he hadn't heard. "Hmmm, let's see . . . was that before or after you tried to seduce me? It was after, I think—yeah, it was definitely after. As I recall, at the time I was in desperate need of a smoke."

Abby desperately needed some air. The atmosphere of the shop had suddenly become stifling, and she couldn't quite decide if she should strangle him or give in to the insane urge to laugh at his shameless teasing. "All right, you win. What will it take to get rid of you?"

"How about a corner booth at the café in, say, half an hour? I hear they've got a chicken quiche that'll knock your socks off."

"Half an hour," Abby agreed, "on one condition. You have to promise to leave your libido on the stoop."

"No problem." Matt paid for the magazines and the book Julianne brought from the back, and touched the bill of his baseball cap. "Miss Julianne, it's been a pleasure doin' business with you."

The small brass bell signaled his exit. Abby let go of the breath she'd been holding. She could feel her friend's steady gaze on her.

"Well?" Julianne prompted.

Abby strove for casual, but she couldn't quite pull it off. "Well, what?"

"When were you going to tell me that you're sleeping with a celebrity?"

"I am *not* sleeping with him," Abby shot back, then belatedly realized that the windows were open. Several heads turned on the street. Alfred Orr, the unemployed husband of the local gossip, paused in his daily meanderings to press his nose against the windowpane. He gaped open-mouthed at them both until Abby groaned and turned away. "Look, I didn't come here to talk about my sex life, such as it is. I came because I need some legal advice."

"Does this have anything to do with David's death?"

"Actually, it's about Aunt Catherine."

Julianne put up the "closed" sign and followed Abby into her office in the rear of the building. It was a converted closet of a room, barely large enough to house the law books neatly shelved behind the desk and a pair of leather chairs, yet sufficient for the handful of cases that came her way every few months. Abby had asked her once why she had opened a practice in Abundance when she could have gone to Albany, New York, or Philadelphia. Julianne had looked at her as though she'd lost her mind. "And leave all of this? I like it here, Abby; besides, I'm right where I'm supposed to be."

At the time, Abby hadn't questioned Julianne's certainty. In fact, she'd understood, certain that she too was on the right track—that she'd known where she belonged, her purpose in life.

But the trouble at the university had changed all that. And quite suddenly, she wasn't as certain about anything.

Julianne sat back in her chair and toyed with her amber beads. "Now, what's this about Catherine?"

Abby explained Catherine's unenviable position as

quickly and succinctly as she could. When she finished, she sat back with a sigh.

"The Caymans doesn't recognize extradition, so even if we can manage to get an indictment handed down, we probably couldn't bring the little weasel back to face the embezzlement charges. Of course, as her acting counsel, I would heartily advise Catherine to file charges, despite the possibility that he'll be a no-show."

"What good will that do? We can't recoup her losses if he's not here to face the charges in court."

Julianne pushed back her long auburn hair. "Maybe not, but it'll make it easier to grab him once he does come back. And they usually do—weddings, funerals, family crisis. I know a good Private investigator. If you'd like, I can have him look into it."

Abby said that she'd have to discuss it with Catherine, and the talk took another turn. "John told me about Millie," Julianne admitted. "You okay with it? I mean, coming on the heels of David's—"

Abby took a deep breath. "Suicide. You can say the word out loud. I promise I won't fall apart. Besides, the two hardly compare. David died because he wanted to. Millie never had a choice."

Julianne shuddered. "There's got to be a lot of negative energy associated with the dig site. Why don't I call Elda and Marlene and the girls and we can try to dispel it." Abby was about to decline when Julianne held up a hand to stay her. "Yeah, I know, you're a skeptic, and that's okay. You don't have to don a robe and join our Circle if you don't want to. In fact, I don't want you anywhere near that place until it's been thoroughly cleansed. You're in a bad place; your aura's cloudy, and evil seeks out vulnerability."

"I'm jobless, not vulnerable," Abby joked, but she

could tell that Julianne was worried by the look in her brown eyes.

"Just humor me on this one," Julianne said, her tone deadly serious. "Be careful, Abby, and don't take this too lightly. There's something really weird about this whole thing with Millie. And something tells me it's not over yet."

Abby smiled. The thought of having lunch with Matt frightened her far more than any negative vibes lurking on the grounds of the estate. "Is that the sensitive talking, the witch, or the lawyer?"

"It's Julianne, your friend, and I don't want to see anything bad happen to you."

Abby almost said that it was a little too late for that; then she stopped herself. "God, Jules, you're starting to sound like John."

Julianne quirked an eyebrow, and a secretive smile curved her lips. "Warn you away from Matthew Monroe? Not a chance. You go, girl. You could use some fun— and that one's got 'good time' written all over him."

He was flirting with the waitress when Abby entered the café. Young, streaky-blonde, and tanned, the girl reminded her of Bobbi Carmichael. For a moment, Abby watched them, wondering as Matt scrawled an autograph on a paper napkin and handed it to her as if he had a thing for big-breasted blondes.

It certainly would explain Bobbi, and the waitress, but it didn't shed a speck of light on why he continued to pursue *her*, teasing, flirting, asking her out, goading her into accepting this lunch date.

Maybe he couldn't help himself, Abby reasoned. Maybe he was just a natural flirt, born to take advantage of the fact that his grin lit up a room—or at the very least, her little corner of it.

Or maybe, just maybe, he wanted something, something she hadn't thought of, something besides the obvious.

But what?

Suspicious now, Abby approached the table, stopping just behind the waitress, who tucked the napkin inside her bra before topping off Matt's coffee from the pot she was holding. "I can't thank you enough," she was saying.

"No problem," Matt replied. He was soaking in the celebrity attention—Abby could see it—loving every adoring glance, every worshipful word, and his ego was expanding by the moment.

"Listen," the waitress said, "are you sure you don't mind coming by on Sunday? I mean, you must be really busy."

"Sunday at two. I'll be there," Matt assured her.

Cursing herself for a fool, Abby turned toward the exit. If she could just reach the door before he noticed her, he would assume that she'd stood him up. It would be a unique experience for him. It might even help build his character.

Oh, who was she kidding?

He was way beyond help.

"I can't wait to tell the kids. Brightmeyer Youth Center in Kingston, at the corner of Fourth and Elm. And Matt, thanks again."

"Any time. Abby? Hey, Abby! Wait a minute."

His voice stopped her dead in her tracks. Forcing a smile, Abby slowly turned to face him.

"You weren't runnin' out on me, were you?"

Abby latched on to the first excuse that came to mind. "What? No, of course not. I forgot my handbag at Julianne's shop."

"You mean *this* handbag?" he asked. "The one you have tucked under your arm?"

Abby's smile tightened, and in a futile effort to combat the subtle heat creeping into her face, she lifted her chin.

"I didn't take you for the type to renege on a bargain," he said softly.

Abby shrugged. "I didn't want to interrupt your . . . autographing." She slid into the booth and pointedly positioned her black leather clutch on the seat beside her.

Matt seemed determined not to notice. "I'm eager to please," he said with a flash of deep, groove-like dimples. "Or haven't you noticed?"

"Another sexual innuendo," Abby replied, fixing him with her best detached and clinical stare, "could be signs of a fixation, but somehow I don't think so. My take on it is that the subject resorts to meaningless flirtation as a method of distraction, a means of throwing the curious off the so-called scent."

"Is that just an observation, Ms. Youngblood, or is it your way of tellin' me that despite all of your token resistance, you're interested?"

Abby smiled, a little too sweetly. "That's *Doctor* Youngblood to you."

"Doctor, huh? I'm suitably impressed. Doctor of what?"

"History—colonial history to be exact, with a side order of psychology."

He grinned. "Now I'm really impressed."

The waitress returned with their orders. Matt had a

burger and cheese fries; Abby, a salad. She gave his cholesterol-laden feast a jaundiced glance. "What happened to the chicken quiche?" Then, before he could hit her with some cliché, smart-alecky line, "No, don't tell me. Let me guess. Real men don't eat quiche."

"Actually, it isn't the concept of quiche I object to," he said, completely untouched by her sarcasm. "It's the eggs. I can't quite get past the fact that they come from a chicken's behind."

"Have you considered therapy?"

"You offerin' the use of your couch—Doc?"

Abby let the question slide. If she so much as suggested an interview, he would run like a scalded hound. She considered it for a moment, aware that it might be the perfect method for avoiding his unwanted attentions, his constant come-on's, his devastating bad-boy grin. Yet despite her curmudgeonly thoughts, she was strangely reluctant to employ it.

Abby thought about that, too, but she pointedly ignored the reasons for it, unwilling to admit that she was enjoying his brash and unorthodox company, even to herself.

He was primitive, and although he was undeniably bright, he seemed to be ruled by his baser instincts. In that aspect, Abby thought, they were nothing alike. Not that she couldn't appreciate the way the black T-shirt he wore stretched taut over his broad shoulders, or see the power and beauty in his muscular hands. Abby had never thought of hands as being muscular before, but Matt's were exactly that.

His palms were thick and broad and square, his fingers long, nimble. She imagined them playing over her bare skin, touching her all over—and abruptly pulled back from her reverie.

As much to distract her own thoughts as to steer the conversation in a different direction, she tilted the book he'd bought in Julianne's shop and glanced at the spine.

"*Sexual Predators,*" Abby said. "Your biography, by any chance?"

He laughed, and the sound rippled over Abby. "It's research. You sure you don't want some fries?"

Abby smiled. "Thank you, no. You never mentioned what you're working on, or why you're here in Abundance."

He slanted her a look, his expression unreadable. "I'm flattered that you asked, but I don't talk about my work in progress. It kills the mystique. As for why I'm here, my agent thought the quiet would 'stimulate my imagination and help to nurture my creativity.' "

"Has it?" Abby asked.

It was Matt's turn to smile. "I did say that I don't talk about my work."

"Okay," Abby said. "Then let's talk about the Brightmeyer Youth Center. Do you make it a habit to visit halfway houses for troubled teens? Or did you volunteer so you could get closer to Bambi over there?"

"Her name is Shelley," he said with a smile. "Would you like a little catnip with that salad by any chance?"

Abby wrinkled her nose at him and made another stab at getting information. She was a historian in fact and a researcher at heart, and extracting information and compiling data was second nature to her. "Are you intentionally avoiding my question, or are you just naturally shy and retiring?"

"Matthew W. Monroe? Shy?" Still smiling, he held up a french fry, his gaze burning into hers. "Tell you what. I'll make you a deal, sugar. If you show me yours, I'll show you mine—figuratively, of course. How long's it been since you took off that weddin' band? And where's Mr. Youngblood?''

The question caught Abby off guard. For a moment she considered trying to evade the question, but he was watching her so intently that she was certain he would not let her off the hook so easily. "There is no Mr. Youngblood. My husband's name was David White-field.''

"Divorced?''

"No. Not divorced. He died six months ago." She took a deep breath and turned the tables on him, neatly sidestepping the offer of condolences she knew was forthcoming. "Okay, Matt. You've seen mine," she said. "Now show me yours.''

"No, I do not make a habit of visiting halfway homes for troubled youths.''

"But it's a cause that's close to your heart.''

His mouth curved in a slow, slightly self-deprecating smile. "What's the matter, darlin'? You surprised that I've got one?''

Abby slanted him a look. "Reneging on our bargain so soon?''

"I suppose I can identify, havin' been a troubled youth once. I've been fortunate. Call it my way of givin' something back.''

"That's very noble of you," Abby admitted.

"Yeah, well, don't go talkin' to the tabloids. I've got a reputation to protect.''

Abby smiled. "So I've heard.''

He finished his french fries in silence while Abby picked at her salad. "Can I offer you a lift home? It's on my way.''

Abby shook her head. "Nice try, but my Jeep is parked outside Julianne's shop. Which reminds me: I have an appointment, and I'm already late." She reached for her wallet, but Matt was quicker. He tossed a twenty on the table and stood.

Abby pinned him with a look. "You don't have any unreal expectations about what follows french fries and a salad, do you?"

"I expect you to keep your promise. Mud-boggin', tomorrow, remember? I'll pick you up at five A.M. sharp. We can watch the sunrise together, have a little breakfast, let one thing lead to another, and see where this takes us. See you then," he said, turning to leave, then turning back with a wicked grin. "Unless, that is, you'd prefer to sleep over?"

"Five A.M.," Abby said. "Is there something I should bring?"

"A tight pair of jeans and one of those cut-off tops would be nice. Trust me, darlin'. I'll take care of the rest."

He walked backward for several steps; then, grinning like an idiot, he turned, adjusting his ball cap so that the visor jutted out behind him, and whistled his way down the street.

Abby sighed. God, he had great buns.

Tearing her gaze from the sight of Matt walking away, Abby turned sharply toward the curb and ran right into Professor William Bentz, who'd been headed toward the café.

Bentz was several inches shorter than Abby, with thinning blond hair and wire-rimmed glasses that made his eyes seem to recede in his angular face, a face that would have been entirely unremarkable if not for the diagonal scar on his chin.

She'd first met Bentz at Sullivan a year ago, where he'd been invited to speak, then again, at David's memorial service. She'd thought it odd at the time that he attended, since they couldn't be called more than acquaintances, yet his expression of concern as he'd offered his condolences had been above reproach.

The impact of the collision knocked the folders from Bentz's hands, scattering papers over the sidewalk. Abby hurried to help him retrieve them. "Professor Bentz, I'm so sorry. I didn't see you."

His mouth twitched, his version of a smile. "No harm done, Abigail. Besides, it's easy to see why you were so distracted. Wasn't that Matt Monroe I saw you with just now?"

Abby handed him the papers. "It was, actually. He's renting the guest cottage on my Aunt Catherine's estate."

"How fascinating. I have one of his novels in my quarters back at the campsite. But after all that has occurred, I'm not quite sure I can work up the courage to read it." That twitch of a smile stretched the corners of his thin lips, then disappeared, and Abby shivered. "I'm sorry," he said, "I realize that I shouldn't joke about such things. How is your aunt?"

"Aunt Catherine is weathering it all quite well. But then, she takes most things in stride."

"And what about you, Abigail? You knew the poor unfortunate girl quite well."

Abby had been searching in her purse for her keys, but suddenly she stopped. "How could you know that?"

His expression never changed; he didn't even blink. "I believe Sheriff Rhys mentioned it."

He was keenly attentive, hanging on every word, but the last thing Abby wanted to do was stand on the street in front of the café and discuss the loss of a friend with a man she barely knew. She neatly changed the subject; then after a moment, she made her excuses and hurried away.

William Bentz stood for a long while outside the café, watching Abby Youngblood. Not until her Jeep was a mere speck of yellow on the horizon did he turn and go inside.

Chapter Four

The world according to Willard D. Early was a dangerous place full of crazies just waiting to catch you off guard so they could do you or do you in. Screw or be screwed, those were the rules. It had been that way all of his life, and Willard, a hard-bodied, hard-nosed ex-marine, owner of Early's Guns and Ammo, and Taxidermy Gift Shop, was determined to be on top.

Willard ran a thriving weapons-slash-taxidermy business, aboveboard *and* under wraps. If you wanted to preserve your latest kill, needed a qualified gunsmith, or were thinking of buying a stuffed squirrel for the girlfriend's birthday, or a vintage AK-47, then Willard was your man. Taxidermy was his mainstay, and his reputation was widespread. He took particular pains with his mounts, elevating the snuff-and-stuff business to the level of an art form. He'd gotten calls from as far away as New Jersey, and had even been approached by some lunatic who'd wanted Willard to stuff his girl-friend.

Willard had turned the guy down flat. Not that the concept didn't intrigue him, especially on days like this one when his ex-wife, Brenda, was harping on the fact that he was six months behind in his child support and threatening to have him arrested.

The wacko had offered him a cool eight grand for the whole deal, ten if he agreed to give her permanently perky tits, cup size double-D. But Willard just wasn't that crazy. Assuming the young woman in question was already dead, he could have been arrested for the mistreatment of a corpse at the very least, and fantasies of Brenda with an apple in her mouth aside, it hadn't been worth the risk.

Not when he was about to cut the deal of a lifetime. Throwing the bolt on the door to his shop, he drew the curtains and turned down the lights, checking all of the window locks as he ducked under the sign that warned, *"Pass This Point and You'll Wish The Hell You Hadn't,"* and headed for the storeroom in the basement.

The storeroom was a survivalist's dream. Walled off from the rest of the basement, it had double-wall construction two feet thick, reinforced with one-inch steel plate, enough canned goods and bottled water to last a few months, and its own generator. Well ventilated, it couldn't be breached with anything smaller than a tank. There was a chemical toilet, reading material, toilet tissue, and an assortment of weaponry large enough to boggle most minds and give Willard a massive woody.

With a government gone berserk with the need to control, taxes, riots, and protest marches, women's rights, and affirmative action, the world was headed to hell in a 747. The end was coming. Willard could smell it, even though nobody else seemed to be paying attention.

And when it happened, taking the rest of Abundance by total surprise, Willard Delraine Early would be ready.

He would also be richer than Jesus.

Flicking on the lights, he opened the wall safe to shine light on the six brick-size plastic bags of white powder. He hadn't told his girlfriend, Shelley, about the cocaine. He'd agreed to keep it for a friend, who had promptly kicked off from a massive coronary before Willard had the chance to hand it over to him. Willard didn't use drugs, and he wasn't stupid. The small mountain of blow in his basement storeroom meant the difference between enduring another New York winter and retiring to sunny Arizona in style, none of which Shelley would understand.

Shelley was a looker, with tits that made him stand at attention the minute she entered a room. The sex was awesome, but aside from that, they didn't have much in common. Shelley was a do-gooder on a save-the-world kick. If she found out that her lover had three kilos of coke hidden away in the basement, she might just decide to do her civic duty and turn him in, and there was no way that Willard was going to prison.

He fingered the bags, his arousal pulsing as it strained at the denim covering his hips. Nothing turned him on like the prospect of cold, hard cash. Enough cash to set him up royally in Arizona, a place where a man still had room to breathe. He'd buy himself a piece of Nirvana near the base of the Hualapai Mountains. No nosey neighbors minding his business, no cops, and the government would be lucky to find him. Willard could barely wait.

The battery-operated clock on the wall said five till nine. Shelley would be ending her shift at the café in twenty minutes. If he hurried, he'd have just enough time to grab a quick piece of ass before he met his contact, not discounting the steady knocking on the door to the shop as Willard double-locked the store-room and all but ran up the stairs, visions of Sheriff Rhys and that idiot he called a deputy waiting in the rain with a warrant.

The pounding sounded again.

"I'm comin'. I'm comin'! Jesus, I was on the shitter," he lied. "Give me a minute, will you?"

He threw the deadbolt and opened the door. The man on the other side of the threshold sucked the last puff of smoke from the cigarette he was holding, then dropped it on the gravel walkway. "The sign says you're open till nine."

"Business was slow," Willard replied. "Thought I'd close up early, meet my girlfriend. You here for that 9 mm?"

"Yeah, if it's ready."

"Good news, my friend. Your paperwork went through this morning. The permit checked out, and Uncle's satisfied that"—he turned the small stack and read the name—"Matthew W. Monroe hasn't escaped from an asylum, or popped his grandmother last week. With tax, that comes to three-hundred, eighty-five dollars and zero cents."

"Any fruitcake can get a handgun," Matt said, counting out four crisp hundred dollar bills, laying them faceup on the counter. "As long as that fruitcake's got enough cash. Hell, with enough cash, not only can you kill your grandma, you can beat the murder rap and attain celebrity status."

"Don't get me started," Willard grumbled, shoving the receipt across the counter. He watched as his customer pocketed the papers, then slipped the weapon into the inside pocket of his jean jacket. "Hey, don't you want the box for that?"

"Don't need it."

Willard grabbed his coat and turned out the lights. It was five minutes after nine. Not enough time to catch Shelley at the café. He'd have to swing by Maple Avenue and surprise her at home.

It was twenty minutes past nine when Shelley La Blanc turned the "closed" sign face-out in the café window and flicked off the lights. Marge Turner, the woman who owned the place, had come down with the flu earlier that afternoon, and rather than infect half the town, she'd asked Shelley to stay and lock up; then Marge had taken her intestinal virus home to bed. In some perverse way, Shelley almost hoped she had caught Marge's bug. It would be worth a day or two of misery to be able to pass it on to Willard. And it would be a fitting if sneaky sort of revenge for his forgetting her birthday last Friday and standing her up.

She'd already reamed him out for that one. Not that she got an apology from him, or an explanation. She still had no idea where he'd been all evening, but she suspected that he'd been busy warming his ex-wife's bed. Shelley didn't like Brenda Early. Brenda was trailer trash, all tight black vinyl pants and fake-gold fingernails. Even worse, she was greedy trailer trash, and not above putting out to Willard just to wheedle more money from him.

Shelley didn't trust Brenda, and she wasn't always sure she could trust Willard. She'd seen how he looked at the Reverend Carmichael's daughter, as if he'd like to accept the invitation in the girl's blue eyes—and he would too, if he thought he could get away with it. Yet despite Shelley's suspicions, Willard D. Early was what passed for a good catch in Abundance, and she wasn't about to let him slip from her grasp.

Shelley, an eternal optimist, knew that she could have a future with Willard. A bright future. Arizona bright. He'd been talking a lot about it lately. About selling the shop and relocating there. And she was going with him.

Hugging her oversized gray sweater closer against another gust, Shelley ran the last few yards to her Honda Civic. As she slid into the cold vinyl bucket seat and turned the key in the ignition, she could almost feel the warmth of the Southwestern sun on her face. Hot days and cold desert nights, Phoenix was as far removed from Abundance, New York, as the sun from the moon.

She glanced at her watch, the watery blue-green light of the streetlight glinting off the wide silver-and-turquoise band. It was getting late. Willard usually called or came by shortly after nine. Shelley liked to think that he was concerned that she'd arrived home safely, but she knew he was checking up—making sure she wasn't out with some other guy. All that would change with Arizona, she promised herself, turning the key in the ignition. The engine clicked but refused to turn over.

Shelley bit her lip and tried again. Nothing happened. She glanced at the instrument panel, groaning as the red indicator lights faded to black. "Come on! Not tonight. Willard is gonna be so pissed!"

Someone rapped on her window, and Shelley nearly jumped out of her skin. Heart stuttering a crazy, nerveless beat, she fumbled for the lock, and at the same time the tip of the cigarette flared a bright orange through the rain-splattered glass of the driver's door. "My God, you scared me!"

"Car trouble?"

"I think my battery's dead. Listen, I really hate to ask,

but I need to get home. Do you think you could give me a lift?''

Matt sat up, his heart pounding. Drenched in a cold sweat, he glanced around the bedroom. The computer screen on the state-of-the-art backup system he'd had installed the previous afternoon shot pinpoints of white light at random on the black screen—a poor simulation of a twinkling, star-studded night sky, and the only illumination in the otherwise darkened room. A cigarette had burned to cold, gray ash in the ashtray by his elbow, and the stereo had moved on from Aretha to Don Henley. . . .

It was all very familiar, his current reality. Yet dread twisted his insides into knots while he blew out a shaky breath. "Get a grip, Monroe. It was a nightmare. It was only a nightmare.''

It didn't matter what he said, how much reason he injected into the moment, the image of the woman lying naked and still on the sand-colored carpet, her pale skin translucent in the soft glow of the overhead lighting, had been too real, too vivid to slough off easily. With freeze-frame clarity, he saw himself on his knees by the body, felt the combination of shock and horror that came as he realized that beneath the blood and the bruises was Erin, his fiancée. . . .

"A nightmare,'' Matt muttered. "Christ. It was only a nightmare.'' But that was only half-true. The image wasn't some bizarre scenario his subconscious mind invented out of habit or boredom or whatever. He'd lived it.

Matt sat with his face in his hands, the horror of finding Erin playing out in his mind again and again. The 9mm lay on the desk, inches away from the keyboard and ashtray. He reached for it, his fingers closing over the textured grip. He could end it so easily: the nightmares, the restlessness, the self-loathing. He could put the shiny chrome muzzle between his teeth, and he wouldn't have to face any of it ever again.

Christ, it was tempting. Matt thought about it while the minutes ticked by, thought about the soft black nothingness, silent and inviting that awaited him. It was an escape, a way out, but if he took it, Karl would win, and he couldn't let that happen. He'd already given up too much of his life to Karl Jensen. His vision, his hope, his ambition, his career, his ability to believe in anything, to trust: it had all gone into the ground with Erin. The sick bastard had seen to that.

Matt lit a cigarette, trying not to dwell on the fact that he was still shaking. The nightmares were periodic. He wasn't sure why it had so taken him by surprise. It was always right there, lurking in the dim recesses of his unconscious mind, reminding him that as long as Erin's killer remained somewhere out there, he would never know peace again. Maybe it was no more than he deserved.

He'd helped Karl kill her, through his unmitigated arrogance, his inattention, by believing his own press, buying into his reputation—and he was every bit as responsible for putting an end to her life as the hand that had plied the knife.

Matt snorted, flicking off the power, shutting down the computer and wiping out his file. Then he headed to the bathroom for a cold shower.

Tomorrow he would have to write the chapter again, squeeze out every stubborn syllable, but at the moment, he couldn't summon the will to give a flying fuck.

* * *

It was raining when Abby left Gilead Manor the following morning, and though the wind had ceased to gust out of the northwest, water dripped from every leaf and branch. Cued by the twin red taillights at the carriage house, she walked to the edge of the porch and waited. A few heartbeats later, Matt's truck stopped in the drive.

It wasn't exactly the sort of transportation one might expect of a best-selling author-slash-superstar. In fact, with its chipped paint and a serious ding in the passenger door, it seemed better suited to some of the less-than-affluent locals, men who preferred the company of white-tailed deer, black bear, and wild turkeys to neighbors—who hunted, fished, and frolicked in the mud for recreation. A short, ironic laugh escaped Abby as the passenger door swung open, and almost simultaneously she recalled the purpose for this outing.

"My, my, you look good enough to—"

"Don't even say it," Abby warned.

He ignored her and grinned. "Make a man's mouth water. Need a hand up?"

Abby eyed the hand he held out to her. She hadn't forgotten his electrifying warmth, or the effect it had on her. "Thank you, but I've had some experience, and I think I can manage." Grabbing the overhead doorframe, she stepped onto the running board, then hopped onto the seat and shut the door.

The grin he gave was electrifying. "And here I was, hopin' to be your first time."

Abby bent a look on him, her most stern don't-act-up-in-class look, usually reserved for less-than-studious students. "I thought we agreed that you were going to leave your wisecracks and innuendos at the carriage house."

Matt pulled a face. "Baby, you don't know what you're askin'. The wisecracks and innuendos are part of my charm, a large and inseparable part. In fact," he said, leaning closer, his tone secretive, "Without my smart mouth, I'm dull as an unsharpened pencil. Though it shames me to admit it, and if you breathe a word I'll swear it's a lie, deep down, underneath all this good-times-and-fun facade lurks the heart of a man who's all work and no play."

It was Abby's turn to smile. "Now I'm definitely interested. When do I get to meet this guy?"

"If your luck holds, never." He smiled, but it wasn't the fifty-watt, good-natured grin he usually plied with such devastating accuracy. This time there was something behind it, something barely hidden, and Abby had the strange impression that what he'd just said lay very close to the truth. Too close for his comfort—or hers. As she watched him, he clenched his jaw; his muscles flexed. She could feel his tension, pulsing and ebbing like a dark riptide, and she could only wonder what lay behind it.

"Are you sure you don't want to cancel?" Abby asked. "You seem distracted."

He patted his shirt pocket, seemingly to assure himself he had his cigarettes, and the mask he normally wore fell neatly into place. "And let you get away, when you're here in my truck and lookin' so damned sexy? Not a chance. Buckle up, sweetheart. It's gonna be a hell of a ride."

They took the highway west of town, past the highway shed, then cut a sharp right onto a narrow dirt road. Well, maybe the word "road" was a tad optimistic, Abby thought. In reality, it was two tire troughs with a strip of grass and shin-high weeds growing right up the center. More a cow path than anything.

Its apparent disuse didn't deter Matt, however. If the speedometer was correct, then they were doing sixty-three miles per hour, about fifty miles per hour too fast for conditions.

The old-growth timber was long gone from this area, replaced by thick woods crowded with underbrush. Maples, oak, and balsam fir encroached so closely on the rutted track that the branches met overhead, forming a leafy tunnel through which they recklessly hurdled.

The truck plunged into a pothole at a mind-numbing rate of speed, sending a plume of water and mud hood-high on either side, then fish-tailed for several yards before the knobby tires caught and dug deep once again. Leafy branches slapped the side windows, leaving bits of verdant debris clinging to the damp glass.

Abby tensed, preparing herself for a collision. "For the love of God, would you slow down a little?"

Matt just laughed. "Slow down? Darlin', I live for speed."

"It seems to me that *live* is the key word here, and while you may have a death wish, I have responsibilities—" Abby let out a high-pitched shriek as Matt whipped the steering wheel hard to the right and sent them skidding through a break in the trees at a phenomenal rate of speed. The truck spun and skidded, bounced and rattled down the steep hill, headed directly for the creek.

"Oh, my God," Abby cried. "Are you insane? You're going to kill us both!"

Matt just laughed. "C'mon, Doc, live a little!"

He was loving it. Abby could see it in his face. The exhilaration that came with an adrenaline rush, the wild pumping of his heart, the sharpening of all his senses that came from the unconscious awareness that every breath he took might well be his last.

Abby felt it, too, and it terrified her. The skin of her arms prickled alarmingly as the creek water splashed onto the running boards. It threaded its way in a thin brown trickle into the cab, and the fine hair at her nape stood on end. Then, in a flash, the water receded and they were climbing again . . . up and up and up, leafy branches snatching at them as they topped the rise and came to a sudden, shuddering stop.

Matt killed the lights, turned off the ignition, and half-turned to face her, his arm draped over the back of the seat. "You hungry? How about some breakfast?"

"Breakfast?" Abby repeated, breathless. *"Breakfast?* You really are insane. In fact, you really should be institutionalized before you kill someone!"

"No need to overreact. I was in control the entire time." Matt opened the sliding glass window behind the seat and retrieved a wicker basket from the covered toolbox at the front of the bed. Placing it between them on the seat, he closed the window and leaned closer, his carnal mouth curved in the barest of smiles. The light in his amber eyes was the light of knowledge; his expression revealed his intent. He meant to seduce her into lowering her guard, abandoning her defenses, to tempt her into living life on the edge just as he did. But Abby was keenly aware that a little knowledge and a lot of temptation could be a damned dangerous combination.

"Admit it, Abby," he said smoothly. "Your heart's pounding. The blood's singing through your veins. You can feel every nerve, every cell in your delicious, sexy self. You feel alive—keenly alive—maybe for the first time in your entire life."

Abby would have denied it if he hadn't put a finger to her lips, lowered his voice to a silky whisper, flipped down her visor mirror, and said, "Look before you answer. See that blush on your cheeks? The light in your eyes—they've lost that haunted look, and they're brimming with emotion, with life."

"They are brimming with fury," Abby insisted, but for an instant she couldn't help staring at her own reflection, at the not-so-subtle changes he artfully pointed out.

She looked wild.

Her hair had escaped its ponytail and lay loosely on her shoulders, framing a face that was a study in pastels: pale green eyes rimmed with spiky black lashes, and a hint of angry rose on her cheeks. Matt was right about one thing: she hadn't given David or the mess her life had become a moment's thought since she climbed into the cab of his pickup truck. She hadn't thought about the ignominious death of her career, and there had been no room for feelings of frustration and impotent fury in the face of impending disaster.

"See how beautiful and alive she is," Matt said softly, his breath warming her ear as she stared into the mirror, and he stared at her. "Does she take your breath away? I swear, she stole mine the moment I saw her, and I haven't had sufficient oxygen since."

"Maybe you should stop smoking," Abby replied, but inside she was warm to the point of melting.

"I have stopped," he said, "at least a dozen times, and don't change the subject. I believe we were discussing how lovely you are, and the fact that you take my breath away."

Abby's pulse did a strange little hop-skip that made her feel as breathless as he claimed to be, and it had nothing to do with cigarettes.

At that moment, she was intensely aware of who and what he was, of her own shaky position. Two centuries ago, he would have been labeled a libertine and a seducer of women. But in Abby's world, he was a danger, plain and simple, and she privately thought he should have come with a flashing yellow caution light around his gorgeous neck.

"Is that why you dragged me out here, in the middle of nowhere?" she asked, struggling to hold onto her skepticism in the face of his full-frontal assault upon her senses. "So that you could ply me with compliments? What comes next? Do we mysteriously run out of gas?"

"Christ. Give me credit for havin' a little more originality than that." He sighed. "I invited you to share my Saturday mornin' because I like you, and because you intrigue me, and because I'm strangely compelled to try and solve the mystery behind those big green eyes."

"There's no mystery," Abby insisted. "No intrigue, no secrets. Nothing to be solved."

Matt watched her intently for a moment, saying nothing. He had unfastened his seat belt and he sat facing her, his right arm draped over the back of the seat. Abby should have felt threatened. Instead, she felt only the magnetic pull of his fingertips.

It was strange, and a little frightening, that he could be inches from her and she could still feel him, as though he touched her on something other than a physical plane. The interior of the truck was warm, comfortable; nevertheless, Abby shivered.

"There's another reason I brought you here," he said, still using that soft, low voice. It was almost as if he were sharing a confidence, imparting a salacious secret, and despite her doubts, her reservations, Abby was mesmerized. "C'mon."

He opened the driver's door, took the basket, and held out his hand. The simple expectancy in the gesture was strangely compelling. He never doubted for an instant that she would come to him, trust him. Abby glanced over her shoulder at the passenger door; then, with a sound like a shivery sigh, she slid across the seat. "This had better be good, Monroe."

He took her hand and led her along a rocky wooded path. The sky was lightening by degrees, but the world still seemed bleak, completely denuded of its color and vibrancy, a monochromatic study in stark shades of black and gray. The rain had stopped completely. Still, water dripped from every leaf and branch, ran in runnels down tree trunks and snaked in trickles over the uneven surface of the gray boulders hulking here and there amid the balsam fir and mountain laurel, remnants of an age of ice, snow, and constant upheaval.

Upheaval Abby understood. She'd struggled to deal with it her entire life. Her mother's death, her father's neglect, her move from the Connecticut house to Gilead Manor. She refused to list the rest of it, didn't want to think about everything she'd lost, had cruelly torn from her life, or simply thrown away.

It was too unnerving. Far too complicated.

And following Matt's lead was easy by comparison.

Matt was easy.

Easy to look at. Easy to be with.

Maybe, easy to fall for.

He didn't want a relationship, and he wouldn't have expectations, so she wasn't likely to disappoint him. And he wouldn't make demands, beyond the obvious.

Julianne had been right about one thing: Matt Monroe was a good time waiting to happen. But could he happen to her, if she let him?

The notion was intriguing, and downright scary.

The wooded path petered out at a rocky outcropping overlooking the creek bed below, but it was the sound of rushing water that caught Abby's attention. Rushing, spraying, falling, tumbling over itself in a roiling, bubbling effort to reach Esopus Creek—Murderer's Falls. . . . Abby hadn't been here in years, and she'd never been here when the dawn was breaking.

"Kind of pretty, isn't it?" Matt said beside her, his tone low and thoughtful. "I come here sometimes when I need to get away. I kind of like the way the water sprays over the rocks. It's so clean, so cold, so free. Nothin' holds it back. Makes you forget all about deadlines— or dead friends, for that matter. And all you have to do is let go, give yourself to the moment."

Somewhere in his twisted logic was a grain of truth. In searching it out, Abby forgot to be offended. "You make it sound almost easy."

He shrugged noncommitally, dropping the moss-colored wool throw he'd draped over one arm onto a large flat rock. "Yeah, well, for some folks it gets easy. Distraction is my drug of choice. Has been for almost four years. Hell, you could say I've made a career of it."

"Four years is a long time to be distracted," Abby said, watching him closely. His dark, handsome face gave no hint of what he was thinking, and she could only guess at what sort of thoughts were flitting behind his amber eyes. Like huge cloud banks floating stealthily across a clear blue sky, those thoughts cast shadows over the darkly golden depths, sending an inexplicable chill through her.

"Feels more like a lifetime," he admitted quietly.

"You never mentioned what you did before."

"You mean between my brief stint as a plumber's helper and my current fling with infamy? There's a reason for that. It's a subject I do my damnedest to avoid."

"But you must have done something," Abby persisted. "Everyone does something."

He sprawled on the right side of the throw and gave a short, hard laugh. "Yeah, I did somethin'. I took money from the rich, and swallowed their bullshit and their lies. I twisted the truth to my advantage, and I was damned good at it. But mostly, I fucked Lady Justice."

"You? A lawyer?"

"You surprised by that? Lawyers and writers have a great deal in common. We both make a livin' out of twistin' the truth to our advantage. But that was another lifetime, so long ago, so far removed from now that I don't want to remember. How about you, sweet thing? You've got your doctorate, but I don't see you pullin' down a nine-to-five."

She took a deep breath. "I used to teach history at J. T. Sullivan University."

"Red, white, and blue-blood," he murmured. "Appropriate. But you said 'used to teach.' What? You couldn't get tenure?"

"Nothing as simple as that," Abby said, a thread of strain lacing its way through her voice. She shied away from the subject. She didn't want to discuss the fact that she'd walked away from a viable and promising career, nor would she lay herself open to Matt Monroe's casual, cynical inspection.

He was watching her closely. She could feel his gaze touch her face, her eyes, her cheeks, her lips, and linger there. A fragrant steam wafted into the cool morning air, soothing, familiar, and sweet. He'd opened the thermos. "Green tea, honey and lemon," she guessed. "You're very intuitive."

"No. I'm resourceful and shameless. I bribed Rose's granddaughter, and she gave me a list of your favorites. Scones and black raspberry jam. I made it myself."

"Liar," she accused. But it coaxed a smile from her, and some of the tension eased from her voice. Matt made careful note of it. Observing the changes in Abby was rapidly becoming one of his favorite pastimes. "Okay, so I bought it at one of those little specialty shops in town. I should get points for aimin' to please, don't you think?"

"You *did* go to a great deal of trouble." She shot him a sidelong glance. "I hope you don't have any unrealistic expectations about what follows breakfast."

"Sweet, prickly Abby," Matt said. "I want the pleasure of your company. Nothin' more. And here you were, thinkin' I was a shallow, self-servin', manipulative cad whose sole interest in the company of women is for sexual gratification. Your guilt at this moment for misjudgin' my character must be a terrible burden."

She laughed now, and it was genuine and full-throated. Matt felt a strange electrical surge in his chest. He wanted to lay her down and kiss her, right there in the cool, damp, just-breaking dawn. He wanted her filling his arms, wanted her sweet essence flooding his senses.

God, he wanted to lose himself in her, to drown in her. He wanted it so badly that it hurt to restrain it, to fight down the impulse to be everything she imagined and feared him to be.

He wanted it—wanted Abby, more than he could remember wanting anyone since Erin.

The two had so little in common that it would have been ludicrous to mention their names in the same breath. Erin had been as gypsy-dark as Abby was fair, and she'd loved him, trusted him, admired and cherished him—and look where it had gotten her.

Abby didn't trust him, and she sure as hell didn't love him—and Matt was glad of it.

It sure as hell was safer that way.

His wariness, however, didn't stop him from reaching

out and taking the thermos from her, from setting it aside so that he could brush back the shining strand that caressed the curve of her cheek, from slipping his hand beneath her hair to cup her nape, to urge her closer. This time when he kissed her, she didn't even gasp. She just held very tense and still for the space of a startled breath; then she reached up and explored his face with her fingertips.

Matt was startled by the cool caress of her fingertips playing over his cheek. He half-expected her to realize her mistake and pull away; he even anticipated the sense of loss that would flood him when she did, but strangely, it didn't happen.

Instead, she leaned into him, her hand slipping down and coming to rest at the juncture of his shoulder and throat, her fingers curling around his nape, threading through his hair. And then he was pressing her back on the throw, one hand freeing the buttons of her blouse, the other tangled in her dark-honey hair. He kissed her until the tension inside him was so tightly coiled he thought he would die of it, and then he left her lips for the softness of her throat, the sweetly scented valley between her breasts. She smelled like a sun-warmed spring woodland, like lily of the valley, trilliums, and greenery. "Matt," she said, in a voice that was half moan, half breathy whisper, "I don't think this is the time or the—"

"No, no, no. . . . Baby, don't think," Matt replied, unhooking her black silk bra in front, freeing her breasts. "It's too dangerous. Just go with it."

Abby knew it was terrible advice, yet it was exactly what she needed to hear. Matt was an aphrodisiac. His nearness heightened her senses, drew her so strongly that she could feel him even before he touched her.

Sex with him would be a life-altering experience, one

that, in this moment of absolute weakness, she just could not resist. Maybe it was the heat of his mouth on her skin, or the way he touched her with such surety. Maybe it was her fury at David for betraying their marriage, her trust, then abandoning her instead of facing the truth. Maybe it was a fine way to get revenge against his memory. Or maybe she just needed to prove something to the world, to herself. In Matt's eyes, she was just a woman he wanted to be with, not someone ready to shatter at the slightest start. He didn't think of her as fragile, and maybe she wasn't. At the moment, she certainly didn't feel fragile. She felt hungry, and needful—greedy, even. Greedy for Matt Monroe.

She gasped at the way he worshiped her breasts. No one she'd been with—and there weren't many—had ever paid such minute attention to detail. He pinched one nipple gently, rolling it between thumb and forefinger until it grew hard and more keenly sensitive, capturing the other to sate his oral fixation while Abby watched.

She couldn't help it. Couldn't seem to stop staring at him, even though she masked her fascination with him through the cover of her lashes.

She would not have thought it possible for a man to be so virile, so handsome. Caught up in the moment, his face had lost the look of jaded amusement he usually wore. His expression was strangely intent, as though this moment negated all others, past and present, and the act of pleasing her was the most important thing that he had ever done, or would ever conceive of doing.

It was incredibly erotic, strangely moving. It was also the secret behind Matt's allure, that certain unconscious something that made him so intriguing, so sexy, so hard to resist; and Abby could only drink him in and wonder where it would lead. He didn't keep her guessing long.

He abandoned her breasts and unbuttoned the waistband of her jeans, inching the zipper down. She felt
the heat of his mouth grazing her waist, nearly cried
out as his tongue delved into the shallow dip of her
navel. The simple act held unbearable intimacy for her,
and Abby had to look away.

"Pretty, self-conscious Abby," he said, pressing a kiss
on the pale skin of her abdomen, then rising above her.
"You can't bear to look at me, and I can't seem to tear
myself away from you." Their faces were inches apart
as his hand slipped into the gaping waistband of Abby's
jeans, but he'd barely brushed her skin when the heavens opened and it started pouring down rain.

"Great timing." Matt took his hand away, glancing
at the sky. He could hear the deluge intensifying, a
sound like rushing wind in the treetops, and knew their
window of opportunity had just slammed closed. Abby
was already zipping her jeans, hooking her bra and
buttoning her blouse . . . and maybe it was just as well.
Better to stop now, before he said something he would
come to regret, something neither of them would ever
believe.

Abby was recapping the thermos as Matt grabbed up
the basket and throw, but the thermos was wet, and her
fingers slipped. The lid flew from her grasp, ricocheting
off a rock and bouncing into the underbrush along the
wooded path. As Abby bent down, reaching out to part
the weeds, Matt tugged on her arm. "Leave it," he said.
"C'mon! You're gonna get soaked."

"I saw where it went," Abby countered. "It'll only
take a second."

Matt was amazed at her tenacity. It was just a lid—
not a big deal in the greater scheme of things. He could
afford to get another, or at least he thought he could—

in all truth, he hadn't glanced at his bank statement in months.

Abby reached for the cap but dropped it again. More determined than ever, she shoved aside a hemlock bough that brushed the ground, then fell back onto her lovely ass with a terrified scream. She gained her feet so fast, Matt could have sworn she bounced, and then she put herself behind him. "Oh, God," she said shakily. "Please, tell me that I'm seeing things."

Matt brushed back the hemlock branch, and the air went out of his lungs in a rush.

Lying on a bed of pine needles, her manicured hand with pale-pink nail polish stretched out toward him as if in a silent plea, was Shelley La Blanc, the waitress from the café. Her face was bruised and bloodied, her eyes wide, staring. "Jesus," he said; then he grabbed Abby's arm. "C'mon. We'd better call the cops."

Chapter Five

It was the damnedest thing Shep Margolis had ever seen, and during his eighteen years in the Abundance Police Department, he'd seen a hell of a lot: women beating their husbands, men slapping shit out of their wives, a slew of bar fights, teen runaways, and even a wife who had taken one too many shots to the head from her abusive husband and decided to even the odds with a twelve-gauge shotgun. But in Shep's opinion, the half-naked body of Shelley La Blanc lying exposed to the cold mid-morning rain eclipsed it all.

Shep told himself that it was the personal aspect of the case that got to him. Shelley had served him his morning coffee Monday through Friday for almost eight years, and he'd become as accustomed to her good-natured baiting as he had to her smile. Privately, he'd always thought that Shelley was wasting her time at the café, and wasting herself on Willard D.

Everybody knew that gun-toting Willard was a little crazy. It was a mystery to Shep, what Shelley had seen in him.

Shep shook his head, watching as the crime photographer finished his shots, and James Johnston, director of the local funeral home and county coroner, zipped her into a black body bag.

Shelley had been especially nice to Shep lately, making sure he had enough sweetener for his coffee, topping off his cup every few minutes, encouraging him to linger at the café. He'd been almost convinced that she'd been getting ready to dump old Willard, and Shep had planned to ask her to the Pumpkin Fest himself if that happened.

Now she was dead, brutalized, and Shep knew that whoever had put the bruises on her face and body before wrapping the ligature around her neck had been one cruel son of a bitch.

Jesus H. Christ.

Who could have imagined that something like this would happen, especially to a nice girl like Shelley?

The whole thing put Shep in a lousy mood, and it didn't do much for his acid reflux, either. He reached in his uniform pocket and popped a few antacid tablets. It also didn't help that she'd been discovered by an outsider—even if he was accompanied by Dr. Youngblood.

Shep had a real problem with outsiders since the country chic crowd had discovered the quaint rural charm of Abundance and taken over the town. They'd bought his mother's house right from under him, shooting his future clean to hell. He'd always figured to inherit when the old gal passed on, and the fact that she'd sold out and used the profits from the sale to relocate to Florida didn't help much in the grand scheme of things.

With the sale came major change, and suddenly going home had taken on a whole new meaning to Shep. The new owners had opened a novelty shop, The Auld Corner Cupboard where they sold fancy embroidered hand towels, gourmet sauces and cooking gadgets, lamp shades, wall hangings and Amish quilts, and fancy little things that weren't of any real use to anybody.

Shep hated outsiders. And even more than that, he hated progress.

Turning his back on the scene, he leaned against the cruiser's right front fender, a yellow legal pad in one hand, a pencil in the other, liking the picture he made, if not his reason for being there.

"You say you and Doc Youngblood were out in the woods at the crack of dawn, on a rainy morning, for a picnic?"

Matt shook a cigarette out of a beat-up pack and shoved it between his lips, then paused as he realized his matches were wet and he didn't have a light. The deputy didn't offer one. "That's what I said, Deputy."

"You expect me to believe that you were out for a picnic on the coldest, wettest damn day of the year, and you just happened to pick the spot where Shelley was murdered?"

"Call it dumb luck; call it coincidence," Matt replied irritably. "I really don't care what you call it. It's what happened."

"How long you say you've been in town?"

"Since the second week of August. I rent the carriage house on the Youngblood estate. Now if you don't mind, Ms. Youngblood's had a hell of a shock, and I'd like to take her home."

"As it so happens, I do mind," the deputy said. "In

fact, I mind very much. You have any objections to my having a look inside your vehicle?"

"Not if you have a warrant," Matt replied irritably. "No? Then I guess we're through here."

The deputy seemed to settle in upon himself, folding from his comfortable leaning posture into a dissatisfied slouch. He almost looked deflated, as if somebody had pulled a plug and let the air out of him. Matt didn't know what Margolis's problem was, and he didn't really care. He just wanted to take Abby home, to have this day end.

He was worried about her. Not that they were emotionally connected or anything. They weren't, and he had no plans in that direction. He'd just wanted a distraction, some conversation maybe, to see where things led. He hadn't planned on their promising morning turning out as it had.

And the fact that the victim was the girl from the café was more than a little unnerving. He'd made arrangements to meet her at the youth center tomorrow. But she wouldn't be going there ever again, and neither would he.

Matt sighed. There was nothing he could do to help Shelley, but he could get Abby away from the red-and-blue strobe of the police cruiser and the unpleasant memories and the questions. He could take her home, make sure that she was okay.

Margolis was still taking notes. "I suppose you can go. Just make sure you're available to answer further questions, should they arise."

"Don't tell me, " Matt said. "Let me guess. Don't leave town."

Margolis tipped down his glasses to glare over the top. "You know, boy, you're a real pain in the ass. A genuine tack on the chair of life, and I can do without your sarcasm. It's been a bitch of a day."

"There's one thing we can agree on," Matt said, turning an angry shoulder to the older man. "I don't like this any better than you do."

A few yards away, Abby huddled in the smoky warmth of Matt's jean jacket and wondered what he was saying to Shep Margolis. Abby had never liked Shep, but then, Shep wasn't exactly easy to like. He was a genuine throwback. A small man in a big car with a siren and flashing red and blue lights, and a mind so narrow it couldn't accommodate anything that even remotely resembled an unbiased opinion. Thanks to Shep, the municipality had narrowly escaped a lawsuit backed by the American Civil Liberties Union for racial profiling. The case, as Abby recalled, had something to do with the distribution of a controlled substance. Someone in the county had been pushing drugs, and the plaintiffs in the lawsuit, John and Lamont Johnston, had been roughed up, hauled in, and held for twenty-four hours on the basis that they had "contacts" in the city. The Johnston brothers' "contacts" turned out to be an aunt who was caring for their grandmother, who'd been stricken with senile dementia.

The Department had settled out of court, a hefty sum that had effectively blown the budget for the fiscal year. Because Shep had wide-reaching connections, he'd kept his job—just barely. The mayor had promised, however, that if the deputy allowed his personal prejudices to interfere with his civic duty again, he would be fired on the spot. The incident was enough to make Abby wary where the deputy was concerned. Forgetting about John Rhys, Abby strained to make out what Matt was saying. From his tense expression, she suspected the exchange wasn't exactly pleasant.

"Abby? Abby, would you try to stay with me?"

John Rhys's voice, brimming with impatience, jerked Abby's attention away from Matt. "I'm sorry, John, I guess I didn't hear you. What did you just say?"

"Could you stay with me for just a few minutes, please? I'm just as anxious to conclude this as you are to get back to your date."

There was sarcasm in the sheriff's tone. Abby hugged the jacket to her, as if it could serve as a shield against an unpleasant reality, as well as against the damp mist rising off the falls. But the denim couldn't erase from Abby's mind the knowledge that the body of the young woman being bumped along on a gurney over muddy and uneven ground was someone she knew, any more than it could deflect John's disapproval of her choices. "He's not my date," she said, hating the urge to defend herself to anyone, especially John.

They had been friends since high school—closer than friends during the summer of their senior year, just before college, but it hadn't lasted, and they'd drifted apart. Over the years, there had been a few Christmas cards, a brief conversation or two about inconsequential things, but there were no strong feelings beyond friendship, nothing to warrant John's bristling every time he came within two hundred feet of Matt. She found his sudden possessiveness off-putting. In fact, it was downright adolescent.

John's expression lost all of its official detachment. There was no more politeness, no more pretense. "You're alone with Monroe, out in the woods at daybreak? Do me a favor, will you? Don't insult my intelligence."

"Then at least have the decency to return the favor," Abby snapped. "And while you're at it, drop the big-brother act. You're not going to turn this into a pissing contest, John Rhys. I told you what happened. Now, if you don't have any further questions that pertain to your investigation, I would like very much to go home."

"Just how long have you known him?"

The question was coldly, angrily spoken. It caught Abby off guard, summoning up emotions she did not wish to deal with: anger that a man she had known all her life and whom she considered a friend would suddenly question her judgment, suspicion about where this was leading, and a thread of half-submerged fear that he might just be justified in having reservations about her recent choices.

"What's that supposed to mean?" Abby shot back.

"Humor me. You owe me that much. How well do you know him, Abby?"

"I don't have to answer that," she said, her voice low, feverish with fury. "And I don't owe you anything. I'm going home."

"Because you don't *want* to answer it, or because you can't?" John demanded.

Abby turned away, but John wrapped one large hand around her upper arm, holding her fast. Abby looked down at his hand, then up into his rugged face. "Let go of me."

"Someone has to say it," he went on, his tone low and urgent. "And it might as well be me. You've made some bad choices in the past. David was a self-involved, overly educated ass who didn't deserve you—"

"Damn you," Abby said softly. "This has nothing to do with David, and you have no right!"

John's grip lessened, and some of the anger left his voice. "Maybe not, but I care about you, Abby. I always have. And I can't just stand by and watch you get hurt again. Tell me you know Monroe, *really* know him—his past, what he expects from you, what he's capable of—

and I'll back off, but I'm begging you, don't fall into his bed without at least knowing who the hell you're sleeping with."

Abby hit him, hard, and the sound of her palm connecting with his cheek echoed like a pistol shot in the relative stillness of the wooded clearing. She flinched when Matt's hands settled protectively on her shoulders. "Hey. You all right?"

"She's fine," John answered. "Or she will be, once she comes to her senses about the company she's keeping."

"The lady can make her own decisions," Matt said. "She doesn't need you to think for her, but that's part of the problem, isn't it, Sheriff? *She doesn't need you,* and that realization's chewin' you up inside."

John took a half-step toward Matt, who flatly refused to give ground. Abby spun, pushing against Matt's chest. She just wanted to leave this place and never look back. "Matt, please. I want to go home. I just want to go home."

Matt put his arm around her, pulling her close to his side as they walked to the truck. "You have any further *legitimate* questions, Sheriff, you know where to find me."

John's voice rang out stubbornly behind them. "Just remember what I said, Abby! Remember what I said!"

John had begged Abby to remember that she knew next to nothing about Matthew Monroe. That he was a virtual stranger. And in light of all that had happened that morning, she could hardly forget that fact. They finished the drive back to Gilead Manor in a more sane and less deadly fashion than when setting out that morning, and in an awkward, uncomfortable silence.

Several times Matt made some comment, a half-hearted attempt at conversation, but Abby's monosyllabic replies made for rocky ground, and nothing lasting took root. By the time they reached the long gravel drive that led to the mansion and carriage house, the tension between them was palpable.

Matt made the turn onto the gravel lane, pulled off onto the grassy skirt, and stopped the truck, turning off the engine. "You're awfully quiet. Mind tellin' me what's wrong?"

Abby's voice was laced through with sarcasm, but it was the tautness of it, the perceived ache in the words that deepened Matt's frown. "What do you suppose is wrong, Monroe? Two murders in less than a week, and I knew both of them. Pardon my pique, but it isn't every day that I stumble onto a dead woman. God," she said, then forced herself to calm down with deep, even breaths. "Look, I know I'm being overly emotional. It's a temporary upset, that's all, and I'll deal with it. Millie's death happened a long time ago, and I didn't really know Shelley all that well—"

She broke off abruptly, but the unspoken words hung heavily between them. "But I did," he said quietly.

She looked at him, a chilly glance that said it all. "You said it, not me."

Matt's demeanor changed. She could feel him withdraw, as if he'd moved behind an icy wall. Even his voice was softly cold. "Maybe you'd like to tell me what your friend Sheriff Rhys had to say back there?"

She turned her face away, staring out the passenger window. "It's not important," she said.

But it was more than important to Matt. It was crucial. The morning had held such promise. They had gotten closer than he'd imagined they could in so short a time, and it had felt better than he ever dreamed it could.

He didn't know where it would lead, but he was certain of one thing: for the first time in a long time, he'd had his finger on the pulse of something good, and he couldn't think of a worse way for it to end. "Lemme see. Did he by any chance remind you that I was new in town, that you know nothing about me?"

"He's concerned, that's all. And in retrospect, I have to admit that some of his concerns have validity."

"So, you thanked him by slapping his face? Kind of an odd custom, even for a couple of Yankees."

She closed her eyes, as though trying to shut out his voice. "Please, just take me home."

Matt reached out, intending to offer whatever comfort he could, but as his fingertips brushed her face, she flinched away. There was fear in her eyes, wariness, suspicion. Fear of what? Of him? "If you won't drop me at the door, then I'll walk back!" She clawed for the door handle, and he gave her what she was desperate for, slamming the truck into first gear.

They rode the rest of the way down the drive in silence. Abby grabbed for her purse but couldn't seem to hold onto it, and its contents spilled out over the floorboard. Matt reached down at the same moment she did.

He scooped up her wallet, lipstick, compact, and various items, depositing them safely inside her bag. Then, she was out of the truck and vaulting the steps to the porch. He watched as she opened the door and flung inside the rambling old house, half-expecting her to hesitate, to flip him off, something. Hell, she didn't look back. Not even once.

* * *

"How dreadful for that poor girl's family!" Catherine said. "I can't even imagine what they must be feeling just now."

"She didn't have much family to speak of, from what's been said," Rose added. "Just an elderly aunt over near Woodstock. I'll contact the Baptist Ladies' Auxiliary, and see if there's anything we can do to help."

Catherine nodded. "I'm sure it will be appreciated." She patted Abby's hand. "Good heavens, first the dig site, now this. What on earth is happening to our lovely little town?"

"It's a dreadful coincidence," Abby replied. "Nothing more."

It had to be a coincidence.

Anything else was unthinkable, and way too far-fetched.

"If you don't need me for anything, I think I'm going to lie down for a while. I have a thundering headache."

Catherine's concern showed on her face. "Dear me. Rose, do we have any aspirin?"

"It's on my grocery list. If you want, I can ask that writer if he's got some. He probably keeps plenty on hand, for hangovers. God knows what else he's got in his medicine cabinet."

Abby held up a hand. "There's no need to bother him with this, really. I think I have some in my purse." She offered a halfhearted smile to both women, kissed Catherine's cheek, then made her way to her bedroom, where she peeled off her clothes and put on her gray sweatpants and her oldest, most comfortable sweater. A half-glass of water sat on the night stand. Head throbbing with every beat of her heart, Abby opened her purse, and froze.

Lying half-hidden beneath the checkbook and keys

was something she did not immediately recognize. Frowning, she lifted it out.

It was a woman's watch, silver and turquoise, partly encrusted with mud and sporting a shattered crystal. It wasn't hers, but there was something chillingly familiar about it. Something she couldn't quite put a finger on. She'd seen it before. Or one just like it. She was sure of it. But where? And how had it gotten into her purse?

That last moment in Matt's pickup truck flashed in her mind. Her bag and its contents scattered over the floorboard, Matt's strong hands beside hers as he helped to put it all back.

The watch must have been lying on the floorboard of his pickup, and had been scooped up with her checkbook, nail file, and keys, and accidentally placed in her purse. It was a wonder she hadn't stepped on it.

Yet that didn't explain whom it belonged to, or why it seemed vaguely familiar. Abby's grip on the watch tightened as a snatch of another mental image came to mind, Matt talking to the waitress in the café the previous day, smiling up at her as the left-handed girl poured coffee into his cup.

Abby closed her eyes, but she couldn't seem to block out the scene. With nightmarish clarity, she saw Shelley's wrist, encircled by a turquoise-and-silver watch just like the one she was clutching—a watch that had to have been in Matt's truck this morning, just hours after Shelley's murder.

Abby picked up the phone on her nightstand intending to call 911, hesitated, then placed the receiver carefully back in its cradle, John's warning that morning about what Matt—a stranger—might be capable of, ringing in her ears.

* * *

The rain had ended in late afternoon, but the air was damp and chilly. A gust of wind shook the leaves of the old maple, liberally spattering Abby and the young man walking beside her down the garden path with icy droplets.

Catherine had invited William Bentz to dinner to express her concern for his well-being and that of his students after the shock of their recent macabre discovery and the events that had rapidly followed. The students would be understandably rattled, and as a direct descendant of the town's founder, Catherine considered it her civic responsibility to do what she could to put their minds, and Professor Bentz's, at ease.

With dinner successfully concluded, and his hostess properly thanked, Bentz surprised Abby by asking to see the rose garden. Catherine's roses were renowned, and had garnered the attention of horticulturists worldwide. It was a passion that William Bentz shared.

"It's too late in the season to enjoy the full effect of the garden," Abby said, glad for the warmth of her chocolate brown wool slacks and pale gold chenille sweater. "Many of the warm-weather roses have ceased producing long before this."

Bentz paused to admire the old-fashioned floribunda that grew by the garden wall. "I'm certain it's breathtaking at the height of the season, but summer is an illusion—even for roses. Everything thrives in warm weather, from the most delicate flower to the lowliest weed. But autumn," he said, elevating one finger to stress his point. "An advancing autumn presents a real challenge. The rains are harsh instead of nourishing, the chill is bracing, and the sunlight short-lived. Life is fleeting, and like the world in which we live, only the strong will survive, or the cunning.''

Abby slanted a look at him. She wasn't certain whether it was the sudden gust of wind that swept through the hollow or the company she was keeping, but she was suddenly quite chilled.

"The floribunda is hardy. Its beauty and prolific nature has earned it a revered spot in the garden. But look at the vine growing atop the garden wall. *Atropa belladonna.* Deadly Nightshade. It isn't wanted; it isn't welcomed—in most places it isn't even tolerated. Yet it has cunningly found its way through a crack in the stone, where it thrives, as strong as the rose, perhaps more worthy of life because it hasn't been pampered and pruned. Yet, in time, it will wither too.''

Abby frowned. "What are you saying, Professor Bentz?''

"William, please. There's no need for formality. After all, we are colleagues.''

"Very well then, William. You sounded so cryptic just now.''

"Did I? Then I must apologize. I wouldn't wish to put you off. I was merely pointing out that beauty can be found in dying, as well as in living, that one does not need to see the garden in full bloom to appreciate its attributes.'' He glanced at his watch. "Dear me. Look at the time. The evening has quite gotten away from me. I really should be getting back. May I walk you to your door?''

"No,'' Abby said, too quickly, too adamantly, then presented him with a halfhearted smile to soften it. "No, actually, I think I'll linger a few moments more. The air is so fresh after a rain.''

"Don't stay too long, then. You wouldn't want to catch cold.''

Abby watched Bentz leave by the ornate wrought-iron gate and stood listening to his footsteps as they faded and the garden grew silent and still once again. As his engine hummed in the near distance, a voice issued from the deep shadows of the garden wall. "Is he for real?"

Abby checked a startled scream, but she couldn't seem to convince her heart to slow its racing. "Damn it, Monroe, must you do that?"

"Do what?" he asked, rising out of his comfortable slouch on the rustic iron bench, emerging from the shadows.

"Lurk about in the dark," Abby replied, "waiting to pounce. It's a lethal habit, and if you're not careful, you might just give someone a heart attack." She was calming by degrees, noticing the splotches of moisture on the shoulders of his jean jacket.

As always, she couldn't dismiss the breadth of his frame, his sinewy strength, his blatant sex appeal, or the notion that he'd been enduring the damp and the raindrops for quite some time, waiting, hoping to see her. "What are you doing out here?"

"Besides enjoyin' the garden?" He grinned. "I was waitin' for you to get rid of Old Khaki Pants, so that we could be alone. Listen, you're not thinkin' about goin' out with him, are you?"

"Don't be ridiculous," Abby said. "Professor Bentz and I are acquaintances, nothing more."

"Glad to hear it. Not that a weenie like him would give a man much competition, but he sure as hell gives me the creeps."

Abby concurred silently. Yet she said nothing to Matt, reluctant to flame the huge bonfire that was his vanity. The memory of Shelley's watch was also quite fresh in her mind—fresh, and vastly unsettling. "Speaking of competition, I thought I heard you leaving last night. It must have been around eight or eight-thirty. Were you meeting someone?''

He glanced up, amused, but there was the barest touch of wariness in his warm amber eyes. Or was she imagining it? ''Now, why does that seem like a loaded question?''

''Why won't you answer?'' she smoothly countered. ''Is there something you don't want me to know?''

He shrugged, moving closer, his steps slow, deliberate. ''My comin's and goin's aren't much of a mystery. I went out for a pack of cigarettes. A two-pack-a-day habit's hard on a man. Now it's your turn to fess up. What's really goin' on here?''

''Nothing,'' Abby said evasively.

Matt was staring down at her as she said it, close enough to smell the fresh, woodsy scent of her perfume, and every atom of his being seemed to strain toward her. He ached to reach out to her, to take her in his arms and finish what they'd started that morning, before their world exploded. That ache had drawn him here, to wait and watch from the deep shade of the garden, willing her to appear, and amazingly, she had. ''Don't ever consider writing fiction. You're not a convincing enough liar to pull it off.''

''But you are?''

''Baby, I excel,'' Matt said with a snort. He thought of all the times he'd talked about giving up his practice back in Jackson, of lightening his case load, doing more pro bono work, something a little less high-profile, a little less risky.

He thought of the hundred or so times Erin had called him on his total lack of legal ethics for defending the bottom-feeders of life's cesspool and for helping them to walk. Even worse were the times he'd brushed off her fears concerning that last case, the "it'll be all right, sugar"'s that were scorched into his brain.

Abby shivered, drawing his notice, putting an end to his internal litany of regrets. "Don't you ever wear a jacket?" he asked distractedly, taking his off, carefully placing it over her shoulders.

Abby pulled it closed at the front, savoring the heat of his body that permeated the denim, the sweet, beguiling smell of tobacco, spicy cologne, and Matt that teased her senses.

"I didn't plan on staying out so long," she admitted.

"Sometimes it's better to act on impulse. Too much thought can be confusing, and weighty contemplation is a poor damned substitute for a little action. You look like you could do with a little action. I know that I sure as hell could."

Despite her concerns, Abby smiled. Behind the act, behind the suggestiveness and the jokes, lay something else, something deadly serious. She wasn't sure just what it was, but she could see that it bothered him more than he would ever willingly admit, and she sensed that tonight he was reluctant to face it alone.

It was one thing they had in common, one thing she understood: an aversion to facing past mistakes and regrets. Abby knew it was crazy to linger. She should avoid him, avoid any messy entanglements. And any involvement with Matt was bound to get sticky. Yet gazing deep into his troubled eyes, she found herself unable to resist despite the danger he represented.

"I don't know about the action, as you put it. But I would enjoy a cup of coffee. You do have coffee, don't you?"

Matt smiled. "Do I have coffee? Does France have truffles? Does Bourbon Street have transvestites? Does—"

Abby laughed, allowing him to take her hand and lead her through the garden gate and across the yard to the carriage house. "I'm pretty sure I grasp the concept."

"You look as if you could use some help."

"No. Seriously, I've got it covered."

Matt methodically rifled the kitchen cabinets, peering behind boxes of cheese crackers and Grape Nuts, month-old doughnuts, and half-eaten bags of potato chips. Abby marveled at his persistence. He didn't admit defeat, and he didn't lose his sense of humor, even when he ran out of cabinets.

"Don't tell me," she said. "Let me guess. No coffee?"

"I'll lay in a fresh supply first thing in the morning." He picked up a box from the counter top, and held it out to her. "How about some Grape Nuts? It's only fair to warn you, though: I'm fresh out of milk."

Abby smiled. "It's probably for the best, anyway. The caffeine would only keep me awake—" She broke off, realizing how mundane she'd sounded, how ridiculous. She would be lucky if she slept at all, considering. "I really should be getting back."

She turned to go, but Matt stopped her. "Abby, wait."

Two little words, spoken so quietly she almost thought she'd misheard, yet with enough power to stop her in her tracks. She half-turned toward him. Unsure what he expected from her, what she wanted from him, Abby held her breath.

At the same time, Matt held out his hand.

Her pulse jerking out oddly uneven beats, Abby looked into his face. She wasn't sure what she expected to find there, but it wasn't the naked emotion she saw in his whiskey brown eyes, the yearning stamped on his handsome face. Her heart thudding against her ribs, she reached out, entwining her fingers with his. She couldn't seem to help herself. She could no more resist him than she could have stopped breathing.

With a torturous slowness, he brought her into his arms, fitting her soft body against his hard one. "I don't want you to go."

"Matt." It came out as a breathy whisper that sounded nothing like her. Abby turned her face into his throat, but she couldn't hide from him, and she didn't have a prayer of keeping her feelings to herself. He knew very well the effect he had on her, and he was pitiless when it came to using her attraction to him to gain his own ends.

Sliding his hands down her spine, he fitted his palms to the curve of her bottom, urging her against him so that there was not a shred of doubt left in Abby's mind that he wanted her.

She could blame it on animal attraction, on sheer insanity, maybe even on a hormonal imbalance, but whatever the cause, she wanted him, too. So much so that when he grasped her waist and lifted her onto the counter top, she didn't even protest, just waited for his next move.

She didn't have to wait long. Gaze locked with hers, he unbuttoned her cardigan sweater and unhooked her black lace bra in front; then, reaching behind her, he found the small plastic bear filled with honey. "You aren't serious," Abby said with a small nervous laugh.

"I've never been more serious in my life." As she watched, he drizzled the golden liquid over the nipple of one breast, then over the other. It was cool and sticky, unbelievably erotic. "Not that you aren't sweet enough already," he said, dipping his head and taking one sweetened peak into his mouth, rolling the other between his fingers. Heat sluiced through Abby as she watched him, the urge to follow his lead proved more than she could resist, and before she could stop herself, she'd found his fingers and slowly took their sticky sweetness into her mouth.

It got his attention. He left off his play to breathe a stunned curse, then, extracting his fingers, dove in for a long, deep kiss. "Give it to me, darlin'. Give it all to me. You know you want to."

He was already unbuttoning her waistband, sliding the zipper of her woolen slacks all the way down, enticing Abby with little nibbles into easing them off. He caressed her through her black lace panties, teasing her, then taking them off. Then, gently, he began to touch her, caressing her warmth and her wetness, his touch persuasive, seductive, deliberate.

"Come closer," she whispered, "closer." She grasped his shirtfront, working the buttons down, fumbling in her eagerness to lay him as bare to her touch as she was to his, as accessible, as vulnerable. She pushed the last one through its hole and urged the cotton off his shoulders, gasping slightly as it hit the floor.

He was beautifully made, his broad shoulders and chest well muscled and deeply tanned. A light dusting of coarse, dark hair shaded his pectorals, curling slightly over his breastbone, narrowing to a thin line as it reached his flat middle.

Abby ran her palms over him and listened to his soft curse as he faltered in his attentions. She'd gotten a reaction, the reaction she craved, but it wasn't enough. Nearly as determined as Matt was, uncharacteristically, almost as bold, she moved to the waistband of his faded jeans.

The metal button was easily freed, his fly opened, and everything the infamous Matthew Monroe had to give, impressive in its full glory, was revealed to her. "Oh, my, does Oprah know about this?"

Matt just chuckled; then, with a low half-groan, he opened the drawer beside her and took out a small round foil packet. A few heartbeats later, he parted Abby's knees, wrapped her in a steely embrace, and bringing her to the very edge of her precarious perch, he eased into her soft, wet warmth.

Now he took her mouth, kissing her with that same maddening deliberateness, delving into her as their bodies joined in heated, furious union, man and woman, as different as bright day and dark night, coming together in a rhythm as ancient and eternal as the dawn of time.

Abby couldn't ever remember wanting anyone more than she wanted Matt. But this was deeper than just physical hunger. It was as if the same compelling force that had driven her into his arms was hurtling them toward a stunning completion over which she had little control, and she could only cling to him, burying her face in the hollow of his throat as it burst full and blindingly bright upon her.

Oh, dear God, what had she done?

What had *they* done? Abby silently amended.

The afterglow hadn't even begun to dim when reality sank in, and she saw herself as she must have looked, wantonly spread out on the kitchen counter, like some bizarre sexual side dish. She actually groaned aloud at the thought. John had begged her not to fall into bed with Matt until she knew him better, and she hadn't. The breadbox at her back was a grim reminder that she hadn't even made it that far.

Matt was settling back to earth, too. The tension was

gone from his muscular frame, and his breathing was not as ragged. In a moment, he would feel the need to say something, something he thought she would want or need to hear. Something that would kill the moment, compound her guilty remorse, underscore the fact that this had been nothing more than the heat of the moment, a loss of control, a mistake—things Abby already knew and couldn't bear to have him affirm.

"I really do have to go," she said, extricating herself from his embrace, climbing down from the counter.

"But we're just gettin' started," he protested. "There's a lot about one another we have yet to discover. Important things, like which side of the bed you prefer, and whether or not we're compatible on a semi-temporary basis."

"Some other time, maybe," Abby said. "It's been fun, but I *really* have to be getting back. You understand." This was total insanity. They were wrong for each other. She didn't understand him, and she didn't want to. And he could never understand her. Not in a million lifetimes. Women like her did not get involved sexually with men like him.

It was just plain asking for trouble.

And trouble was one thing she had plenty of.

He'd seduced her, sending logic and reasoning right out the proverbial window. Her behavior had been out of character, so un-Abby-like that its potential ramifications terrified her.

They hadn't given a thought to the awkwardness that would follow, and worse than all of that, Matt was going to do everything he could to deny her a dignified escape. She could see it in his eyes as he reached for her, and her heart skipped a beat.

"Yeah, sure. I understand." He let her go reluctantly. "Will I see you tomorrow? Maybe we could do a little research, and we can go to dinner after. Miss Catherine mentioned a tunnel of some sort under the house. Maybe you could help me sift through the archives.''

"I'll get you the documentation," Abby replied, more to herself than to Matt, "but I can't go to lunch with you tomorrow." She bit her lip and lied like hell. "I have a previous commitment. Besides, I think that at this point it might be better if we don't make any plans.''

No expectations.

No commitment.

It was safer that way.

With her clothing in place, she would have slipped past him and made a clean exit, except that Matt caught her arm.

"All right. All right. At least let me walk you home.''

It was risky for him to be trawling for prey so soon after, but walking with her, talking with her, being with *her* triggered the compulsion, and the compulsion was incredibly strong—especially given the knowledge that he'd held her life in his hands with every breath, that he could have easily ended it anytime he chose.

Knowledge was power, and power got him off more effectively than any willing whore ever could. Not that he would lower himself to have dealings with a prostitute. His taste was more refined than that, as Abundance was about to discover.

It was the day after, and he'd calmed a little, become reflective after setting his plan into motion. He should have been satisfied, complacent. He always was, after. Yet doing the waitress hadn't taken the edge off. She'd been too easy, not presenting much of a challenge for an experienced and dedicated predator like him. She'd tried to put up a struggle, but he'd practiced his craft and honed his skills for so long that she had never really had a chance of survival.

There had been a moment, though, during their time together when he'd allowed her to think that she might live. From the cover of his ski mask, he'd watched the hope spark in her eyes, then abruptly die as she realized she'd been wrong. And as he snuffed the life from her, he'd thought of Abby Youngblood.

He cruised the length of Highway 28 until he saw the lights of Phoenicia, then turned around and headed back to Abundance. Not a single hitchhiker. The urge to kill rode him hard after leaving Abby, and as he grappled for control, he told himself that it didn't really matter, that the anticipation made the act all the sweeter. There would be other nights, other opportunities, soon enough.

Chapter Six

John Rhys's day had been a long one and it still had no end in sight. Sarah Helmsley, the dispatcher, had been sending him disapproving looks all afternoon. Sarah was bugged because of his ex-wife Rebecca, who called every fifteen minutes like clockwork, caught in the midst of yet another full-blown neurosis attack. Since John wasn't taking any calls, Sarah had been stuck with the thankless task of shoring up Rebecca's shaky nerves without leaking any of the details of Shelley's murder.

The phones had been ringing since just before daybreak. A day had passed since the body was found, and the station was already a madhouse. If this kept up, he'd have to contact the temp agency over in Kingston and hire someone to help answer the phones. Since the police department was already over budget, the mayor would no doubt be spastic.

John was at the coffeepot getting his hourly refill when the phone began its bleating. With the volume turned down, and Sarah's sweater piled on top of it, it sounded like a sheep with the colic. Sarah put the heels of her hands against her temples, propped her elbows on the desk, and glared at him. "It'll die down soon. Hell, everybody's already called at least twice."

"This had better be my boyfriend, Harold Lee, telling me he just won the lottery." Sarah picked up the receiver. "Sheriff's Department, Sarah speaking, how may I help you?" There was a slight pause. "Oh, hi, J. T. How are things down at the paper?"

"I'm not in," John said, taking his coffee to the interrogation room. Willard D. Early slouched at the table, the ladybugs buzzing the bare overhead lightbulb casting weird shadows on his shaved head. "You want some coffee, Willard?" John asked. "Or maybe a sandwich or something?"

Willard glared at John. "If it's all the same to you, Sheriff, I'd like to go home."

"Home to your apartment above the shop, or home to Shelley's?" John asked casually. "I hear you were at her house last night. In fact, isn't that where Deputy Margolis picked you up this morning? You tie one on before you went to see her?"

A shrug. "I had a couple of beers while I was waitin' for her."

"You pissed off at Shelley, Early?" Shep put in. "She happen to mention she was plannin' on dumpin' you?" Until now, Shep had been silent, just watching, one hip on the table, his overly shiny black shoe swinging back and forth, back and forth. He hadn't taken off his Ray-Bans, and Willard's face suddenly loomed large in them as the bigger man came out of his chair.

"You know, you've got a hell of a nerve, Margolis. And for a couple of quarters, I'd wipe up the coffee the sheriff spilled with your necktie." Shep's thin lips flattened even further, and his lower jaw jutted out, a sure sign of impending trouble. John put his Styrofoam cup in Shep's hands. "Take this out and dump it for me. It's gone bitter. Maybe if you spell Sarah at the phones she'll make us a fresh pot."

Shep balked, reluctant to miss out on the questioning. "Maybe I'd better stay here. He could be trouble."

"Everybody knows that Willard hates authority, cops, the government, the I.R.S., F.B.I . . . he even hates the school crossing guards, don't you, Willard? But he's not stupid, and he's not being charged with anything—yet. Shep? The coffee?"

Shep went out, but he sure as hell wasn't happy about it, and he was grumbling when he left the room. "Now, why don't you tell me about last night?" John suggested.

"There's nothin' to tell," Willard said.

"Deputy Margolis found you at Shelley's house this morning. Since we have it on record that Shelley put in a full shift yesterday, it seems obvious you let yourself in."

"She gave me a key." A shrug of his beefy shoulders. "Look, I didn't do nothin' to Shelley. I was waitin' for her to come in after work. We were gonna get it on, you know? I must've fallen asleep on the couch waitin' for her."

John sank into the chair across from him. He didn't believe in the intimidation angle of standing at all times while the suspect was forced to sit, of getting in their faces. Those were Shep's tactics, and though they had their place, it wasn't here. "You two been getting along lately?" The question made Willard a little tense. The muscles in his arms flexed, and a vein in his neck stood out. " 'Cause I heard from Mrs. Brimley next door that you and Shelley had a knock-down, drag-out just last week."

He shrugged. "So we fight, sometimes. She was pissed because I forgot her birthday, and she thought I was two-timing her. Shit, I thought she was gonna cut my balls off. Shelley had a temper when she got worked up."

"Were you cheating on her?"

Another shrug. "Maybe. So, I get a little on the side. It's not exactly a crime."

"You ever knock her around?" John asked. "Like when she mouthed off too much about it?"

"I don't hit no women."

"Funny, that's not what your ex-wife says." Willard got a little strange after that. He was quiet, warily so. John's antennae went up. He wasn't getting anything of any use from Willard, and he wouldn't with him clamped down so tightly. "I got these back this afternoon. How about taking a look at them for me?" John plunked a folder down in front of the big man in such a way that the crime-scene photos came spilling out, graphic shots of Shelley's half-naked body. The bruises, the ligature marks, the blood smears. When Willard cursed and looked away, John shoved them toward him. "Look at her, Willard. Take a good, long look. Did you do this to her?"

Willard dove for John's wastebasket, where he hunched, puking his guts out while John watched in disgust. "Shelley," Willard sobbed. "Oh, God, Shelley."

John handed him a paper towel. "That's all we need from you today. Clean yourself up, then get the hell out of here."

Shep, hovering in the doorway with two fresh cups of coffee, was slack-jawed as Willard brushed past and all but ran from the room. "You're letting him go? Well, now, I've seen everything."

"I'm lettin' him go because he didn't do it," John

affirmed. "If we try to hold him, he'll have an attorney down here and in our faces so fast it'll make your head spin. Funny thing, but the law takes a dim view of persecuting an innocent man."

"Shee-it," Shep drawled. "Willard D.? Innocent?"

"Trust me on this one, Shep. Willard didn't have anything to do with Shelley's death."

"Whatever you say, boss." Shep set John's cup on the table, pushed his aviator shades a little higher on the bridge of his nose, and walked stiffly from the room. But his deputy's dissatisfaction was nothing compared to what John was feeling.

Willard's reaction had told him more than six hours of intense grilling could. The photos had shocked him, and no one could feign such a violent reaction. Willard hadn't savagely beaten Shelley, hadn't killed Shelley in a fit of rage and dumped her body in the woods, but somebody had, and without any answers, without a clue to who could be responsible for the girl's murder, John had a huge problem on his hands.

As John sat staring morosely into the cooling cup in his hands, a silent procession of five dark-robed figures walked single-file across the back lawn of the Youngblood estate. Matt, barely able to believe what he was seeing, put the half-finished bottle of beer on the porch and followed at a respectful distance. In the grassy field that bordered the creek, they stopped and slowly formed a circle. Then, while the quartet began to chant, their priestess tipped back her head beneath the full hunter's moon and began the call to quarters.

The ceremony was rich with symbolism and the poetry of ancient words and fluid motion. When it ended, the redhead walked to where Matt stood waiting. Julianne

Rhys's face was animated. In fact, it was strange, but she seemed to be lit from within. "We don't often have an audience," she said. "Unless, of course, one of Reverend Carmichael's flock decides on a little moonlight reconnaissance."

"I saw you crossing the lawn," Matt admitted, "and thought I'd investigate. Literary curiosity and all that. Never know when somethin' like this might be useful, and I like to do my research." He motioned to the trio, two of whom were departing. The third, completely cloaked head to foot, threw a glance in their direction, then seemed to hesitate. "This a regular gig?"

"Every full moon," Julianne replied. "Catherine generously offers us the use of the estate. She's open-minded, and that's more than I can say for some people in this town. It's also important to have our privacy."

"It's an intimate gatherin'," Matt observed. "I would have expected something larger, something a little more . . ." He searched for the right word.

"Gothic?" She laughed. "I prefer to leave the drama and shock value to others. Simple solutions for simple everyday problems, and some that aren't so simple." It was a cryptic comment, and Matt could only wonder what she meant by it. "As for the intimacy of our circle, there are usually five of us, but Joan's on vacation, Marlene has the sniffles and tonight we had a stand in. J. T.? Honey, come on over here. There's someone I want you to meet."

The tallest member of the robed quartet complied with a shrug, tossing back his hood as he approached, offering his hand. "Jed Langtry, and it's not a regular gig as far as I'm concerned—at least not until recently. It was the only way I could convince her to join my bowling league."

Julianne leaned into J. T., kissing him teasingly.

"Admit it, you're glad you came—or at least, you will be. Honey, this is Matt Monroe."

"Jesus," J. T. muttered, shrugging out of the robe. "I'd heard you were in town. It's a pleasure to meet you—a real pleasure!" Langtry shifted gears so smoothly, Matt never even saw it coming. "This is really ironic. Your name came up in conversation today. Listen, is it true what they're saying? Did you really find Shelley La Blanc's body?"

"J. T. is editor-in-chief of *The Ashokan Sun*," Julianne explained. "I have a feeling we already know what Matt's answer will be. Besides, we really should be going. I've got an eight-thirty appointment. Early to bed, early to rise, talk sweet to me on the way home and you might just get lucky."

J. T. might have argued, but the promise shining in the brown eyes of the voluptuous redhead convinced him, and in a moment they had faded into the deep shadows of the tree-shrouded drive. Matt glanced back at the still, dark waters of the creek, then at the lights in the upstairs windows at Gilead Manor.

Abby was awake, despite the fact that it was almost midnight. He tried to picture her curled on her bed with a book in her hand and reading glasses perched on her nose, but all he could see was the way she'd looked as she'd unbuttoned his shirt earlier, her face taut with a need she hadn't anticipated, or welcomed. A need she hadn't quite been able to control.

Did she feel it now?

Did it pull as relentlessly at her thoughts as she pulled at his?

Or had she dismissed him from her mind, from her life, as easily as she would shrug off an overdraft of her checking account?

Matt snorted at the thought. *Like she's ever been over-*

drawn in her entire life. The Youngbloods were the first family of Abundance—of Ulster County, and they came from old money. She hadn't grown up poor, as he had; she'd never known what it was like to hate her life so badly that she would do anything—lie, cheat, or manipulate—just to break free of it.

Matt couldn't quite forget. The past haunted him. It always had. And no matter how successful, how wealthy, how powerful he became, it was always there, just a stone's throw away. The stench of the old neighborhood after a hard summer rain was impossible to forget: the smell of garbage and squandered lives, of too much alcohol, too many drugs, not enough hope.

It took a hell of a lot of willpower to crush those memories on a night like this. He'd clawed his way out, and swore on everything he'd seen and detested that he'd never look back. Three jobs and a hefty scholarship he'd worked his ass off to get had gotten him into Ole' Miss. A ruthless streak and a one-track mind had taken him to the top of his class. Law school was the one place where grades took precedence over the size of your bank account, or who your granddaddy had chosen to marry.

Matt shook off the past long enough to light a cigarette. Abby wouldn't know what it was like, wouldn't understand the things the other half had to do just to live, and he sure as hell wasn't about to enlighten her. But the simple fact remained that they couldn't be less compatible, more opposite.

Women like Abby didn't date men like him, let alone do the wild thing on the kitchen counter with them, and they both knew it. He'd seen the panic in her eyes. It was the reason she'd been so hot to get back to the mansion afterward. She'd realized her mistake, and she couldn't wait to put it behind her.

"That makes two of us," Matt muttered as he flung open his truck door and got behind the wheel. "I can't wait to cut loose from this goddamned hick town."

Abby kept busy for the next two days. It was a purposeful sort of busy, meant to keep her thoughts from straying outside the boundaries of her comfort zone. The trouble was, that at this point, most of what was occurring in her once well defined life seemed to be occurring outside her comfort zone, a fact she didn't like and did not intend to tolerate a moment longer.

Promising herself that she would be strong, that she would not succumb to Matt's dark charm a second time, was easy enough in the daylight when there were dozens of distractions to keep her occupied.

It was when darkness fell over the fields and hollows, and quiet descended in the Catskills that Abby's thoughts turned to the dark-haired Southerner, to seduction, and blissfully, sinfully sweet surrender. Unable to resist, she relived every moment, remembered every whisper, imagined that she felt his touch, and was tempted to seek him out. He would not turn her away, and Abby knew it, knew that he would revel in her weakness, rejoice that in her confusion she turned to him. Matt was selfish, and he was sexual, and he wouldn't care what involvement with him cost her, as long as her interest stroked his massive male ego.

Controlling her more disastrous impulses wasn't easy, but Abby did her best not to let thoughts of Matt intrude. From Tuesday morning until late afternoon, she went over Catherine's financial records: bank statements, legal fees, all remaining sources of possible income, not to mention the household expenses.

The news wasn't good.

The rent from the carriage house would not even cover the household expenses, let alone pay the real estate taxes or fix the crumbling foundation and repair the wiring.

To complicate matters further, Delbert Eastbrook, an entrepreneur from Soho, had made Catherine an offer of forty-five thousand dollars that very same morning for the old stone Congregationalist church, which sat at the very edge of the western boundary of the Youngblood estate. It was not a great deal of money compared to all that Catherine had lost, and it couldn't keep up the old house for long. One more reason, in Abby's opinion, not to accept the deal.

The idea of selling off even a section of the estate rankled. Not only was the church a local landmark with great historical significance, the charming old structure had played a large part in the history of the Youngblood family. During the Revolutionary War, Draegan Youngblood, Abby's ancestor, a spy with Washington's Army, had taken to the pulpit by day, preaching to the townsfolk, while at night he rode the countryside in search of a British operative. His masquerade had been a daring one, and in the end, he not only captured the spy, he won the heart of Fallon Deane, Abby's grandmother seven generations back. In the two centuries since, countless Youngbloods had been married in the quaint chapel, or laid to rest in the churchyard.

"Selling it," Catherine had said with a sigh an hour before, "would be like selling a piece of our heritage, like selling a part of my soul. It pains me no end that because of my gullibility it has come to this." Then, Catherine had gone out to Fallon's rose garden to walk and to reflect.

Abby sighed, still bothered that their brief conversation had robbed her aunt's step of its characteristic elasticity, that her shoulders suddenly seemed to sag beneath the weight of her problems.

If the truth were known, Abby's spirit sagged a little too. The thought of the old church sporting a wide veranda decorated with silk seasonal flags and dotted with redwood lawn furniture, tacky welcome candles in the windows, and a parking lot made her a little sick.

"There has to be some way to come up with the money," she said softly.

Closing the account books and rearranging the papers in a neat and accessible pile, she picked up the phone and dialed her accountant. Then she called Seth Bankcroft for an estimate. Aunt Catherine would be furious, but it couldn't be helped. She'd given the bulk of David's insurance money to Lily Pascal's family, but there was just enough left to do a portion of the needed repairs.

It might go against her aunt's grain to accept Abby's help, but it was better than the alternative, and Catherine and Gilead Manor had given so much to her over the years: strength, stability, a sense of belonging, love; it was only right that she give something back.

Her forward march on the old house's restoration filled Abby's afternoon hours, and while she discussed the details of the work with Mr. Bankcroft, there was no room for thoughts of impetuosity, of honey bottles and unrestrained, mind-numbing passion. Yet as evening drew near, thoughts of Matt invaded her solitude and refused to be budged.

The urge to pick up the phone and dial the carriage house just to hear his voice was strong, and it didn't help that Catherine was off to a civic meeting, or that Rose was headed home for the night. With nothing and no one to distract her, there was a very real danger that she would once again end up in Matt Monroe's strong arms.

She considered toughing it out; then, she decided to do the next best thing. She'd go see Julianne, perhaps the only person in Abundance who could help her regain her perspective.

The streets of the town were deserted: no children on bicycles, no older couples lounging in the shadows of their porches, taking in the evening breeze. The windows of the corner market were lightless, and the "closed" sign showed clearly on the door of the café. The supper crowd had evidently opted to stay home. It was the difference between small town-life and life in the city. Shelley's tragedy wouldn't be forgotten, ignored, or shrugged off as the price one paid for having the world just outside one's stoop.

Murder was anything but commonplace in Abundance, and the residents of the closely knit town did not take losing one of their own lightly. John Felix, who owned the corner market, was turning the key in the lock as Abby walked by. "Miss Abigail," he said, tugging the brim of his ball cap, then hurrying to his house on the other side of Main Street.

The lights were still on at the Bell, Book, and Whatnot, even though there were no customers to be seen. Abby stepped inside, and the chimes affixed to the door jingled pleasantly.

Hissy perched on the counter by the cash register, contentedly licking one white-tipped paw, while his mistress turned over another card just inches away. "Company coming," Julianne said. "And I didn't even see it. I must be slipping."

"Anything interesting in there?" Abby asked, moving

to peer over her friend's shoulder at the tarot cards. "Some tall, dark stranger about to sweep you off your feet?"

Julianne smiled, putting down the deck and meeting Abby's gaze directly. "There's a stranger all right, but he's untrustworthy, and a darkness travels with him."

"Darkness? Are you serious? Or are you practicing for your booth at the Pumpkin Fest?"

Julianne frowned down at the cards spread out before her. "I wish this was a stage show. It would be a whole lot easier to look at. Death, chaos, destruction, upheaval, and grief. I don't like this, Ab. I really don't like this."

"Death, chaos, destruction, upheaval," Abby said. "You could be talking about my life." She tried to make light of it, but the truth was that Julianne's mood was contagious. "You aren't kidding, are you? You really see something there?"

She turned over another card—the nine of swords. It symbolized death, failure, utter despair. "Whoever this guy is, he's packing some heavy-duty evil."

"Who is it?"

"I don't know," Julianne replied. "I wish I did, but the cards are never that specific. I can tell you one thing, though. This is only the beginning."

"Have you talked to John about this?" Abby asked quietly.

"Doubting Jonathan?" She shook her head. "My big brother doesn't exactly share my beliefs. We may have the same gene pool, but we don't think alike." She put the cards away and, bracing her palms on the counter, fixed Abby with an inquisitive look. "How are things between you and that fine-looking novelist these days? Did he tell you I ran into him the other night?"

"Actually, I haven't seen him," Abby replied. It wasn't

quite a lie, she told herself. After all, she *hadn't* seen him—in several days. "Why? Did he drop by the shop?"

"He saw the Circle forming at the manor and came to watch. He's open-minded. I'll give him that much." Julianne didn't even flinch when the cat leaped onto her shoulder. She crooned his name as she turned her face toward him. Hissy responded by touching his nose lightly to hers and purring loudly. "So ... have you slept with him yet?"

"It's odd, but I have the strongest craving for a cup of tea," Abby said suddenly, hoping her friend would take the hint and change the subject. She had come here in hopes of finding an hour or two of pleasant, friendly distraction. The last thing she wanted was to talk about the very subject that had driven her from the estate—and his close proximity—in the first place.

She settled into the rocker near the delftware. Seeing the opportunity for a little gratuitous stroking, Hissy jumped down to wind his sleek body around Abby's legs, meowing and purring by fits and starts in the hope of getting her attention. Abby reached down, lifting him onto her lap while Julianne watched her and patiently waited.

Finally, her patience ran out. "You haven't seen him," she prompted, plugging in the electric teapot and setting out a small tin of Earl Grey. "Does that mean you *haven't* seen him? Or that you *aren't* seeing him?"

Abby sighed, speaking to the cat in an unnaturally high falsetto that she reserved for nonhumans and children under the age of three. "And I thought that by coming here I would be getting away from Matt Monroe."

Julianne's brown eyes narrowed. She opened her mouth to comment, but the phone rang, saving Abby from having to answer yet another uncomfortable question.

"Are you sure?" Julianne said into the receiver. "Okay. Thanks, Stooley. I'll be right there."

Abby's brows dipped in concern. "Stooley? As in Stooley's Bar?"

"It's Beth. She's at the bar, and Stooley says she's up to her nose ring in trouble."

"Beth Langtry? I didn't think you two traveled in the same circles these days—" Abby winced. "Pardon the pun."

Julianne shrugged, grabbing a lacy, fringed wrap lying over the back of a nearby chair. "We don't, usually. But J. T. had business in Albany. It's an overnight thing. And I promised I'd look out for her while he was away. Besides, I feel sorry for her. It's hard being emotionally stunted. Beth may be growing older, but she's never grown up. I think it's a latent fear of her own mortality."

Abby heard her assessment, but was still marveling over her mention of a promise to J. T. Langtry. J. T., Beth's older brother, published the local newspaper, running the entire operation out of a storefront across town. He was also very handsome in a Kenneth Brannagh sort of way. "J. T.?" Abby said. "I thought you two didn't get along."

"We don't—always. But there are some things we've come to see eye to eye on."

"Such as?" Abby prompted.

But Julianne wasn't giving anything up willingly. "Can we talk about this later? I won't be more than a half hour. Just long enough to kick Beth's butt all the way to my car. Can you wait? Or should I call you?"

As Julianne grabbed her purse and car keys, Abby put Hissy off her lap and stood. "Are you kidding? I'm coming with you. You might need a little backup."

Julianne lowered her head and peered at Abby from under her brows. "Backup, huh? Ever been in a fight?"

Abby shrugged. "There was that time in third grade when Jimmy Peterson took my lunch money."

"And how did you handle that?"

Another shrug, this time a little sheepishly. "I gave it to him. Okay, so maybe I'm not pugilistic material, but I minored in psych. If we get in a tight spot, there's an excellent chance I can reason our way out of it." She frowned at her friend, who merely snorted. "I'm coming with you, Julianne. No more arguments."

"You can't reason with a room-full of drunks, Abby, but maybe you can help me get through to Beth. Someone has to make her see that she's wasting her life, not to mention the fact that she's hurting J. T."

Stooley's Roadhouse Bar and Grille was on Highway 209, halfway between Hurley and Abundance, and the only tavern within a ten-mile radius of the town. Even on a week night it did a booming business, which had always astounded Abby. But then, she'd never quite understood the allure of dimly lit, smoke-filled rooms where the music was too loud, and the company either overly giddy or sullen and morose.

When Abby and Julianne walked in, the juke box was belting out Steve Earle's redneck anthem "Copperhead Road" at an ear-splitting decibel level, while a pair of twenty-something women in crop-tops and tight jeans busily fed it quarters, arguing heatedly over the next selection. A trio of regulars perched on the red vinyl stools at the mahogany bar, nervously keeping an eye on the small group of newcomers at its opposite end through the swirling haze of blue smoke.

Madeleine Stooley kept a close eye on them too, and

only the loner hunched over a pile of papers at a corner table, a pair of empty Coke cans on the table and his back to the room, seemed oblivious to his surroundings. Stooley's no-nonsense gaze met Abby's, then slid to the group of bikers in the corner. Beth was there, dressed in a top that was far too tight, the neckline dipping down to show an embarrassing amount of cleavage, complete with a small tattoo of a union jack on the inner curve of her right breast, a souvenir from a rock-and-roll ex-boyfriend from Sheffield. Her leather skirt rode ridiculously high on her thighs as she flopped onto a biker's lap and planted a huge kiss on his bearded mouth.

Abby choked back a gasp. He was a mountain of a man, with an ear bristling with gold hoops, and wearing more black leather than a herd of Hereford cows. As he bent the willing Beth backward over his lap and buried his goateed face in her cleavage, his hand riding up under her skirt, his three companions hooted loudly.

"Oh, my God," Abby and Julianne breathed in unison.

"J. T.," Julianne said. "You owe me big-time for this one." She turned to Abby. "Listen, if this gets too heavy, call John. But tell him I said to come personally. If Shep shows up, he's liable to start World War Three." She grimaced and took a deep breath. "Wish me luck."

But before Julianne had taken more than a step, Abby pushed in front of her, clearing her throat. "Beth? Oh, thank God. We've been looking all over for you. Beth, you're coming with us. It's time to go home."

Beth pushed up on the big man's lap, her fingers entwined in the oiled dark curls cascading from under a bright red dew-rag. "Abby? Abby Youngblood? Is that really you?" She giggled wildly. "Anal little Abby in a bar? Christ, get me another beer, will ya? I think I'm seeing things."

"Abby's right," Julianne put in. "You shouldn't be here, Beth—"

"No?" Beth said with a bitter laugh. "And where should I be? At home, helping J. T. proofread that miserable little four-page rag he calls a newspaper? Drinking herbal tea at the What-not, or cochairing the garden club with Abby? Give me a break! And while you're at it, get off my neck, Julianne. I need room to breathe! Go back to your bullshit little lives and leave me the hell alone."

As Beth turned back to her biker, the door flew open and a small knot of women entered, headed by a platinum blonde with too much mascara, and black matte lipstick. She took one look at the passionate display in the corner and launched herself at Beth, dragging her off her biker boyfriend's lap, giving her an enormous shove.

Beth stumbled back, latching onto a fistful of bleached hair as she fell backward into Abby. Abby grabbed Beth, putting a hand out to stop the blonde in midswing. "Wait! Wait, please. This is all a dreadful misunderstanding."

"That's right," Julianne put in, trying to step between them. "Our friend's a little drunk, and a whole lot stupid, and she's going to apologize right now. Aren't you, Beth?"

Beth looked at Abby, then at Julianne, then down at the hank of blond hair she was clutching. "Yeah, sure. Sorry. I didn't know he was taken," she snorted as she held out the hair. "I think this belongs to you, too."

Screeching obscenities, the biker's woman shot a wicked punch at Beth, narrowly missing Abby and knocking Julianne out of the way. Abby stumbled back, catching her foot on the leg of a barstool and falling headlong into Matt's arms. "A little out of your element, aren't you, Doc?" His tone was lazy, his voice unexpected, and shivers rippled over Abby.

"I'm—helping," Abby said. "Or at least I thought I was."

"I can see that," Matt replied. The bartender was on the phone calling the cops, but by the time they arrived, the girl on the bottom of the two-woman pile would need a gurney. "She a friend of yours?"

A jerky nod. "Yes—Julianne! Oh, God. Where's Julianne?" She fixed on her friend, who was in the midst of a heated argument with the platinum blonde's companion, and tried to break away from Matt. At the same time, a dispute erupted among the locals over who was winning, and a beer bottle whizzed past Matt's left ear. "Jesus Christ!" Matt dove for the cover of the bar, taking Abby with him. "Stay down and don't move!" he yelled.

Abby grabbed his sleeve. "Where do you think you're going?"

"To see if I can't get her the hell out of there before she gets somebody killed."

The bartender hung up the phone. Julianne's shouting match had progressed to shoving. The second biker chick threw a punch, and the redheaded bookseller-slash-lawyer caught her wrist and, spinning, flipped the girl over her shoulder, pinning her to the floor with a knee in the center of her back.

Matt grabbed Abby's friend around the waist, but as he dragged her off the blonde, she pulled back for one last right. Her elbow caught him in the eye. The room exploded in a hail of black and white that kind of looked like the screen saver on his computer—tiny pinpricks of white on a field of black. He shook his head, feeling the numbness recede and a hellish throbbing take its place.

He'd taken a few punches in his time, but he couldn't

remember anything that hurt quite that much, probably due to the fact that he was appallingly sober. He tried to shake it off. The blonde was already up and rounding on Abby's friend.

In an instant, it would start all over again. Still holding the struggling, half-drunken combatant, he swung her around, out of reach, and held up a warning hand to the advancing blonde. "As much as I'd love to see you two lovely ladies go at it at some other time and place, I need my other eye for that pile of paper over there on my table, and this is one cat-fight that's over."

"It's over when she's out cold," the blonde countered.

"I said, back off!" It was just enough to bring the bikers out of their chairs. Matt cursed under his breath, shoving Abby's friend toward her and Julianne. The nine millimeter was in the glove box of the pickup, and he had a strong suspicion that they weren't going to give him the opportunity to retrieve it. Besides, all he needed at this point was a few days in jail and a nice little fine to totally screw up his life. "Look, boys, I don't want any more trouble than I already have. See that lady behind the bar? Well, she just called the cops. You really want to be here when they arrive?"

For one tension-filled moment, Matt thought he was a dead man—or at the very least, a broken one. The big ape in the black leather vest and nail-studded leather pants glowered at him. "Hey. Don't I know you from somewhere?" he demanded in a voice as gravelly and deep as a growling dog's.

"If we'd met, I think I'd remember," Matt said.

"Hey, I know!" the ape said. "I saw you on *Oprah!* Yeah, that's it! You're that novelist—fuckin' yeah," he said, half-turning to his buddies. "It's Matthew Monroe." He seemed inordinately pleased with himself, and even feigned a punch at Matt's midsection. "Hey, man. Love your books."

"Thanks. I think."

"No, I really mean it. *Kiss Of The Hellcat* was fantastic. I got so caught up in it, I couldn't put it down. Made me late for my job at Wendy's the next morning. My boss was so goddamned pissed at me, he had me scrubbing the toilets for a week. Come to think of it, you damn near got me fired." He lowered a glare in Matt's direction, then laughed abruptly. "Hey, don't sweat it, man. I was just kiddin'. I don't need that shit-bag job anyway. My old lady's a physical therapist. She makes the payments on the Harley. Keep up the good work— oh, yeah, and man, you'd better do something for that eye. Put a steak on it, or get yourself some tequila. Personally, I'd go for the booze. It won't do shit for the swelling, but in an hour or two you won't feel a goddamned thing."

They turned and filed out of the bar. Matt let go of the breath he'd been holding. His face throbbed. The girl with the short dark hair who'd started this whole fiasco sidled over to hook an arm around his middle. "Poor baby," she crooned drunkenly. "Did I really do that? Well, I got somethin' that'll fix it right up."

"Some other time, maybe," Matt said. He was looking at Abby, who was doing her damnedest to ignore him. "If you'll excuse me."

The girl blinked stupidly; then it dawned on her. "You're with Abby?"

"He is now," Julianne said. "I'm taking Beth to J. T.'s farm. He's supposed to be home later tonight. If I'm very, very lucky, I may be there for breakfast. Matt, would you mind terribly giving Abby a lift home. It's on your way, and my hands are a little full at the moment. Abby, I'll bring the Jeep by tomorrow."

Julianne led the girl out the door and into the cool autumn night. The fight had been cleared away, and one of the regulars was righting the red vinyl stools while Madeleine Stooley swept up broken glass, grumbling to herself. Matt and Abby faced one another.

She wouldn't look at him, and he had no inclination to look away. "Doc? You need a lift?"

She glanced at the door, then back at him, crinkling her nose prettily at the picture he made. "It appears that I do, but if you don't mind, I think I'll drive."

Chapter Seven

Abby pulled up in front of the carriage house, and turned off the engine. The lights were on downstairs at Gilead Manor, and the front porch light burned brightly, Catherine's concession to recent unsettling events. It was a short walk across the lawn, and despite the discovery of Millie's body, despite Shelley's murder, she wasn't afraid.

She felt safe here. She always had. And then there was big, strong, dangerous Matt, looking more provocative than he had a right to in a black Aerosmith T-shirt, jeans with a gaping, thready hole at the knee, and an eye that was almost swollen shut. Despite all of that, Abby didn't open the door. Instead, she grasped one of Matt's hands and placed the keys in his palm.

Touching him was her first mistake.

Not pulling away immediately was her second.

Instead, she folded his fingers inward, over the keys, then cupped his hand in hers. He was watching her expectantly and seemed to be trying to gauge what she might do next. It was a crazy thought, but Abby imagined that he was holding his breath.

The moment was as unsettling as it was compelling, as natural as it was strange. "You didn't have to step between them back there," she said to break the tension. "But I'm glad that you did. As you may have guessed, Beth has—uh—some problems."

"You two been friends long?" he asked, his voice lazy and warm. "She doesn't exactly seem like the type you'd hang out with."

Abby raised her brows. "Oh? And what 'type' would I hang out with?"

"Oh, I don't know," Matt replied, "librarians, church deacons, maybe a burned-out writer or two."

She smiled. She couldn't help it. He had that effect on her. "We've been friends since grade school, though in recent years we lost touch and went in different directions."

"It's easy enough to see why. Somehow, I can't picture Abigail Youngblood throwin' herself at Hell's Angels wannabes, or generally tearin' up the bars, although you certainly seemed to handle yourself well enough tonight."

Abby laughed. He held up his right hand, the one she wasn't holding. "Swear to God. I couldn't have gotten this shiner without you, and to show you how grateful I am, I'm gonna invite you in—for coffee."

"You bought coffee?"

"One whole pound. Well, actually, it's like thirteen ounces. They cheat on those things, you know. I hope you like French roast."

"You're paying attention. I'm flattered." It had been meant as a joke, but he took it seriously. Abby could see it in his face.

"Yeah, I guess I am," he said softly. "But only to you, Abby. Only to you." They both paused, as if to catch their breath, then slowly he moved to kiss her. The truck seat creaked. Their lips met and clung. It was an oddly tender kiss. Surprisingly so, and not at all what she expected from Matt. Gentle at first, it gradually deepened. Abby settled into his arms, turning slightly, slipping her arm around him as her breasts molded to the hard planes of his chest, but she couldn't get quite close enough. She hitched up on the seat in an effort to change that, and their cheekbones collided. She felt his sharply indrawn breath, and pulled back with a wince. "Oh, Matt. I'm so sorry. Is it very painful?"

"A little," he admitted, then, when she bent a look on him: "Okay, a lot. But I'm pretty certain it'll be just fine after a good night's sleep." He opened the door and turned back to take her hands in his. "Come with me, Abby. Stay with me." He bent to kiss her lips, lightly, lingeringly. "Be with me."

Abby caught her breath. "I don't think that's wise. This is the last place I should be. We're not terribly well suited to one another. Tonight just proves it. Besides, I'm not looking for a relationship. Not with you or with anyone."

"Neither am I," he assured her. "Neither am I. But you have to admit, we made a pretty good tag team. I didn't hit anybody, and neither did you. I'm not askin' you for a commitment. Just spend the night with me."

Abby shook her head. "You aren't listening to me."

"Sure I am," he insisted. "You want me—you want *us*. You're just not ready to admit it."

"I only went to Stooley's because Beth was in trouble, and I thought Julianne might need help to get her out of there. Like you so aptly pointed out a moment ago,

I'm more comfortable at the historical society than I am at Stooley's Roadhouse."

He brushed a thumb across her lower lip. "You know, you've got the sexiest mouth I've seen in a long time, and I'll bet you don't even realize it."

She frowned. "That's so transparent, Monroe. Don't even try to change the subject."

"I'm not," he said. "It's a viable argument, important to my case, and very, very pertinent to your objection. Your lower lip's strongly molded, sensual and erotic— one might even go so far as to say carnal."

"Matthew Monroe, what does this have to do with what happened at Stooley's?"

"I'm gettin' to that," he said softly. "Now, as I was sayin', your bottom lip—sexy, yeah, very much so; but its mate's the one that keeps me up at night. It's a shade thinner, perhaps, definitely a lot more vulnerable, a perfect cupid's bow, and perfectly intriguing. One lip that's strong and carnal, the other more reserved, more conservative; opposites, yet they complement one another so well that no one could ever say they didn't belong together. Kind of like you and me, if you think about it."

"I'm not vulnerable," Abby insisted, a trifle defensively. "I wish people would stop saying that."

He held up a hand. "I never suggested you were. We're just different, that's all. Different isn't bad, Abby, it's just . . . *different*. And if you promise not to invite me to the historical society luncheon, I won't ask you to Stooley's. Deal?"

"You really are—"

"Crazy. Yeah, I know. It's what makes me so damned irresistible. Crazy's dangerous, and dangerous is sexy. Especially to nice, well-bred ladies like you. It's the allure of forbidden fruit, you know? So, what'dya say? You gonna give in to your wilder impulses and come have a bite of my apple? I'm the original no-commitment man, and you know you want to."

Leaning in the open door, he kissed her, a long and searching kiss that swore she had nothing to fear, nothing to be wary of; and when he released her, Abby could barely catch her breath. She knew what came next. And even before he spoke the words, she knew what her answer would be. "C'mon, be with me, baby," he said softly. "Stay with me."

"All right. I'll come in, but just long enough to look at that eye," Abby replied, and she meant it, but a kiss at the porch steps and another at the door left her will in tatters. Matt opened the door and led her inside, but he didn't turn on the lights. Instead he leaned in to take her mouth again. Abby gave a delighted little gasp at the roughness of his tongue toying with hers, pressing even closer. Then he reached down, lifting her, his hands cupped beneath her derriere. Abby didn't need any more encouragement. She wrapped her legs around his lean middle, growling low in her throat when hard and eager met the almost desperate need to be filled.

There was something wild in her, a part of her she was only just beginning to realize even existed. Too long suppressed and ignored, it sprang to life only when she was in Matt's presence, in his arms. As he carried her to the sofa and they tumbled as one onto the overstuffed cushions, Abby unleashed the uninhibited wildness in her spirit and let it have its head.

Matt felt the change in her, but he didn't stop to question it. He didn't give a damn about its origins, and he wasn't one to overanalyze. The only thing that mattered to him was that she had changed her mind, that the bleak emptiness of another night alone was now filled with the promise of Abby. She was a light in his eternal darkness, the bright spot on a dim, boredom-filled horizon. She had the capacity to distract him, and he hungered for the forgetfulness, no matter how long it lasted. When they were together, he didn't think about deadlines, or agents, publishers, psychopaths, or regrets.

There was only room for Abby in his conscious mind. Her softness, the sweet way she resisted, then threw caution to hell and surrendered it all. It always took some convincing, and he loved that in her. She made him work for it, and the fact that it didn't come easy kept him interested.

Abby wasn't just hard to get. She was hard to hang on to, as illusive as the shuddering climax she would bring to him at the end of their lovemaking. There, and then gone, leaving nothing but a bittersweet memory. She always left him gasping for breath, already anticipating their next encounter, wondering if and when it might happen. That he couldn't quite manage her, couldn't quite figure her out, made her all the more fascinating, like a Chinese puzzle—something to tickle his brain when he was away from her, just as surely as she tickled his libido in moments like this one.

The sofa was one of Catherine's cast-offs, circa nineteen-seventy. It had a broken spring in the left cushion, and it was a bit short for what Matt had in mind, but he tried to ignore it and concentrated on pulling off Abby's camel-colored cashmere sweater. He worked it slowly up over her rib cage, kissing each tantalizing inch of her that he unveiled, drowning in the scent of fresh lavender that clung to her skin. She was so perfect, so lovely, so impatient.

She was already reaching for him, running her small hands under his shirt and into the waistband of his jeans. "You asked me that first day if I wanted to see you naked," she whispered. "Well, the answer is yes. I want to see all of you, Matt. I want to feel all of you. I want my hands on your skin."

And then she sat up and, placing her palms on his shoulders, eased him back onto the cushions. She was methodical once she gave herself up to the act, single-minded. She took off his boots, and then peeled off his T-shirt, giving as good as she'd gotten from him, kissing his belly and ribs while he resisted the urge to hurry her. Trying his level best to be patient while her palms skimmed his shoulders, his pecs, and followed a heated path to the metal rivet closing the waistband of his oldest pair of Levi's.

Matt held his breath as she unzipped the zipper and parted the fly on his jeans, hooking her fingers in his belt loops, sliding the denim down over his hips. She gazed at him; at the clear indication that he wanted her, needed her, then, slowly, she raised her gaze to his, and he saw naked desire reflected in her pale-green eyes—a desire so intense, so profound that it burned with a clear, unextinguishable light. She struggled with it, he knew, but she couldn't win. It was too strong, too all-consuming.

"I hate this," she confessed in a moment of total candor. "I hate that I have no self-control when I'm with you, that I can't resist you. God, why can't I resist you? I know it's wrong for me—*you're* wrong for me. But in moments like this, I just don't care."

There was no anger in her voice, just a lingering trace of sadness at her inability to control her desires. Matt took her face in his hands, his thumbs caressing the downy skin of her cheeks. "Pretty Abby. Do you really want to spend the night alone? That's what this is all about, isn't it? You don't like the quiet any more than I do. Quiet leaves too much time to think, so let's don't, shall we?"

She refused to confirm what he already knew. She didn't have to. Her eyes said it all. There was a loneliness in her that Matt sensed and understood, even if he didn't know its cause. She'd lost someone, and she'd been deeply hurt by it. Now she was one of the walking wounded. Just like him. And like him, she didn't want to face the night alone.

Where was the harm in that?

Instinctively, he knew. The danger lay in getting too close, in getting involved. Caring for someone meant opening up, letting them in, being vulnerable. Something he sure as hell wasn't about to do.

She might not know it, but with him she was completely safe, at least from an emotional standpoint, because Matt Monroe could not afford the luxury of caring about anyone. With a psychopath out there, possibly keeping track of his every move, it was just too damned dangerous. After Erin's tragedy, he'd sworn that he would never make the mistake of getting close again. And it was one vow he fully intended to keep.

Abby's internal battle was brief. The grace and the beauty of her surrender took Matt completely by surprise. With a sound like a sigh, she bent down, closing her eyes as she kissed him—at first a light nuzzle through the silky fabric of his bikini briefs, then, sliding them down, she took him fully into her mouth.

Matt swore softly as the wet heat of her kiss enveloped him. Whatever he'd expected from her, it hadn't been this: a forfeiture, and at the same time a claiming.

He immediately recoiled from that thought. Abby Youngblood, staking a claim on his body? The notion was just this side of ridiculous.

It was hot sex. Give and take. Mutual pleasure.

Adult recreation.

Nothing more, and there was no reason not to take

full advantage of it. No reason at all. *Full tilt,* that was his motto, his approach to life. Live while there was still breath in your body, and when an opportunity like this one presented itself, give it three hundred percent. Sliding his hand under her chin, he interrupted her play with a dangerous smile. "We've got the whole night ahead of us. I'm not in a hurry, darlin', are you?"

Still riding the high tide of passion, Abby sighed. He urged her up off the sofa, guiding her to his bed, where he peeled away her slacks, her black bra and lace panties. Then, kneeling on the mattress, he pulled her down with him, and Abby's introduction to mutual seduction began.

It wasn't as if she were a virgin. And she wasn't inexperienced. She'd had a few affairs, and she'd been married to David for three long years. But there was not a doubt in her mind that she'd never been with anyone like Matt.

Men tended to be selfish and driven when it came to the sexual act. David had been reserved, even in bed, and he hadn't liked oral sex very much. He'd had issues concerning trust, with giving over the control of his sexual satisfaction to someone else, totally letting her into his fantasies—something she hadn't understood until much, much later. David's fantasy world had been a dark, depressing place.

Abby didn't like to admit that their sex life hadn't been satisfying, but she'd always felt the restraint and had taken it as an unspoken criticism. She'd secretly suspected that she'd done something wrong, that somehow she wasn't woman enough to please him, and she'd privately mourned the lack of true intimacy in their marriage. It had left deep scars, but there was no denying that Matt was nothing like David.

Totally uninhibited, Matt had a way of looking at her,

of watching her with that smart-assed predatory grin that clearly conveyed what he was thinking; and what he was thinking was usually X-rated. In an odd, unexpected way, he made her feel confident—sexy, even. It was brand-new, that feeling. And it was just heady enough that Abby didn't want it to end.

Intimacy didn't frighten Matt Monroe in the least.

In fact, he embraced it fully, lying on his side and gathering her close against him, guiding her knees apart and initiating the long kiss. A moment of shock, of adjusting to and accepting the wet roughness of his tongue as it abraded and explored the most sensitive part of her; then, Abby relaxed, taking him into her mouth again.

She'd always imagined it to be like this: the desire to give every bit as intoxicating as the need to receive; the even exchange of intense physical pleasure almost too great to be borne in silence; the sanctity and beauty of their love-making too beautiful, too precious to be spoiled with mere words. Even as his own pleasure was steadily building, Matt seemed attuned to the changes in Abby's breathing, the rapidity of her pulse, and the tenseness in her muscles. Carefully, with practiced ease, he choreographed her complete surrender, then, moving to face her, sank into her quaking flesh and lost himself inside her.

Matt was sleeping soundly, one arm flung above his head, and his right cheek buried in his feather pillow. In sleep, he lost that jaded, well-worn look he worked so hard to cultivate. His face was relaxed, his expression open, and instead of being someone who wanted nothing more than a little recreational sex, he became someone with feelings, dreams, and desires. Someone who could be hurt.

Abby didn't want to hurt him. And she didn't want to risk being hurt by him, either.

In her slim experience, the morning after was the worst. Too much affection, not enough, the wrong word spoken at the wrong time, could make things very uncomfortable. And with two fragile egos right out there in the open, waiting to get trampled, the wisest course of action seemed to be a swift and silent exit.

Tiptoeing around the bottom of the bed, she gathered her clothing, dressed hastily in the living room, and walked quickly out, closing the door softly behind her. Forgetting what had occurred in the carriage house just a few short hours ago, the aggressiveness she'd displayed with Matt, and the wonderful way he'd reciprocated, was going to be a damn site harder.

The shops opened at ten A.M., and by twelve it was citation heaven for Shep, who eyeballed the rear end of a Ford Taurus, then jotted down the number on the license plate. "Two feet over the line restriction. That's a major violation in a town with a serious parking shortage." He shook his head and clucked his tongue. "Ten-dollar fine or a day in court. Good thing these outta-towners have deep pockets."

The influx of tourists was at peak this time of year, a steady stream of blue-haired ladies and their polo-shirted escorts who trampled the townsfolk's lawns and generally disregarded the God-given right for a man's home to be his castle, or his town to be his fortress.

Sunday before last, the Reverend Carmichael had talked about the Plagues of Egypt down at the First Presbyterian Church. Watching a tour bus pull up in front of the town square and a steady stream of elderly humanity trickle out in the street, Shep slipped the citation under the windshield wiper and prepared to move on. Old Pharaoh hadn't had a whole lot over on Abundance with that horde of locusts, he thought smugly. Only the pests he was dealing with ate funnel cakes and drank cappuccino.

Shep grunted as he moved onto the next vehicle, a black Chevy four-by-four with mud spatters on the side panels and a ding in the passenger door. The owner had nosed it as close to the bumper of the car ahead as was possible. There was barely a hand's width between the shiny red trunk of the Taurus and the truck's bumper, and the truck was still three feet over the line in back. If the owner had been local, Shep might have walked on, ignoring this blatant violation of his interpretation of the Abundance parking ordinance. But he recognized the truck, and its owner wasn't a local. He wasn't even close.

Flipping the page on his citation pad, Shep had just poised the pen to jot down the license number when a flash of pale blue caught his eye. It was fringe of some sort, dangling from the bottom of the door, and it seemed vaguely familiar. Without hesitation, he opened the truck door and freed the designer scarf. It had somehow fallen onto the floorboard and, lying forgotten, had become caught in the door.

"Damn careless," Shep muttered, lifting the bundle of cashmere out. "These things cost a freaking fortune." He knew because he'd bought one just like it for Shelley last Christmas. Same color, too. The department store hadn't had the deep blue he'd been looking for, the blue that would have matched her eyes, so he'd settled for baby blue instead. Cautiously, he lifted it to within inches of his face. It had an earthy smell to it, the smell of wetness and mud; yet under that, still detectable, was the faintest trace of Shalimar perfume.

Shep arrived at the station with lights flashing and sirens screaming. It was ten-thirty in the morning, and John was already halfway through his third pot of coffee. Julianne had been harping at him for two years to switch to decaf, and lately Doc Fife had chimed in, claiming that when taken in excess caffeine was bad for the stomach, bad for the heart. At the moment, it was also the only thing that was keeping him upright.

After eighteen hours' worth of coroner's reports, interviews with Shelley's family and friends, a long conversation with Millie Gray's mother, who was adamant about the immediate release of Millie's remains despite the fact that forensics said they needed more time, and trying to catalog and confirm every moment of Shelley's last day—where she was, whom she had spoken to—John was working on his last fully intact nerve. Painfully aware that when he returned home, his answering machine would be flooded with frantic calls from Rebecca, he was dragging his feet about leaving, and the last thing he needed was Shep on a testosterone overload.

John met the car in the parking lot, and as his deputy shoved it into park, he made a thumbs-down motion, indicating that he kill the lights. "Either you go easy on the lights and the siren until things simmer down, or I'll have Rufus disconnect them. Folks around here are jumpy enough without the dramatics."

Shep hit the switch and got out of the car. "Bad day, huh, boss? Well, it's about to get a whole hell of a lot better."

He shoved what appeared to be a pile of pale-blue cashmere at John. "What? You found a shawl?"

"I found Shelley's shawl," Shep corrected, "and it was hangin' out of a vehicle over on Main."

John lowered his head over his coffee. It was getting cold. In fact, it had a small circle of fine white milk scum forming in the center of the cup that resembled a full moon, and the odd thought came to him that his seeming inability to manage more than a sip or two from each cup before it turned rancid might by Juli-anne's subtle way of "helping" him to cut back. "Come again?"

"It was hangin' out of a vehicle over on Main—"

"And you appropriated it? Without a warrant? Shep, do the words 'illegal search and seizure' mean anything to you?"

"It's evidence, John!"

"How do you know that? Does it have her name on it?" John turned back to the station house, dumping his coffee on the ground in disgust as he went.

Shep followed. "I bought it for her for Christmas. It's still got her perfume on it. Shalimar."

"Any number of women wear Shalimar, Shep, includ-ing my ex-wife."

"Okay, but how many of these fake Pashmina things have you seen in Abundance?" Shep demanded, hold-ing out the pile of blue. "We're not exactly the height of fashion around here. Fact is, in order to find it, I went all the way to Albany."

An uneasy silence followed. Shep's quiet belligerence was like an icy wall between them. John felt for the man. He really did. He knew that Shep had been sweet on Shelley. Hell, half the town knew it. The only person who hadn't known it, or acknowledged it, had been Shelley.

"It's Shelley's, for Christ's sake," Shep said. "The least you can do is haul that writer's ass in here for questioning."

John stood silently for a moment, the news that the

scarf supposedly belonging to Shelley had been found in Monroe's truck settling on his stomach as poorly as his tenth half-cup of coffee. Abby wasn't going to like this, but a part of him did. It was no secret that he didn't like Matt Monroe, and he didn't think that Abby had any business spending time with him. In fact, their involvement, if the rumors were true, had "potential train wreck" written all over it. Abby, unfortunately, couldn't see it. Or wouldn't. "You win," he told Shep. "I'll get an affidavit to Judge Ross to impound the vehicle. We'll send Rufus, but you go with him—and Shep?"

"Yeah, boss?"

"Put that damn thing in the evidence locker. If Monroe had anything to do with Shelley's death, I don't want him walking on a technicality. By the book! You read me?"

Abby had gone to bed just before dawn, certain she wouldn't sleep a wink, and well into the morning woke to the smell of freshly baked apple turnovers and feelings of profound regret.

She could barely believe that she had set out last night looking for healthy distraction and ended up in Matt's bed. And a long, hot soak in the old claw-foot tub filled with lavender-scented water didn't help to erase the mortification she felt each time she thought of the carriage house.

What in God's name was wrong with her? She'd always been the embodiment of self-restraint. She'd never been much of a party girl and had avoided people who were. To this day, she didn't indulge in more than the rare social cocktail, and a kiss at the door had been the rule more than the exception for a first date. She'd never doubted for a moment that she was more academic than exciting, an assistant professor not greatly inclined toward stimulation of the noncerebral kind.

She'd even been accused of being dull a time or two, and she'd had to admit that there was a very good possibility that the accusation might be based on a grain of truth. Abby's idea of a good time was to put on her favorite sweats and curl up with a copy of *A Portrayal of Women Throughout History* on a Saturday night.

She was far too logical, too analytical, to be considered a dreamer. She wasn't given to thrill-seeking, or reckless behavior, and she didn't take risks—or at least she hadn't until her return to Gilead Manor. Until she met Matt Monroe.

There was no logic in any of this, and no matter how hard she tried to analyze it, no matter how she reasoned that Matt was nothing more than a welcome distraction from her current unsolvable problems, it didn't excuse her total disregard for propriety, or her complete lack of self-restraint. She knew better. She knew that an affair with someone like Matt could only end in a ton of self-doubt.

Doubt. It was the last thing she needed to compound, the one thing she'd lived with day in and day out since discovering the truth about David, and his involvement in the sexual assault on Lily Pascal.

Involvement. What a lame way to put it. He'd raped her, and then he'd threatened, bullied, and manipulated her into keeping his dreadful secret.

Even worse, Abby had never suspected.

How could she not have suspected? How could she not have known?

It made her furious just to think about it, to speculate on what David had been thinking. What had driven him to commit such a horrible act on an innocent girl? What went through his mind during those last weeks, when she ranted on about breaking the code of silence at the university? About seeing to it personally that there was some sort of justice for Lily Pascal.

Abby climbed from the tub, wrapping a towel around her. She might as well just resign herself to the fact that there would always be questions where David was concerned. He'd seen to it. The morning the story broke and Lily put a name to her attacker, David put a gun to his temple and ended all hope that Abby would ever have the answers she desperately needed.

No answers.

No closure.

An endless sea of speculation, a river of self-doubt.

Even worse, David's death had also been the death of her ability to trust.

She'd married him thinking she knew everything there was to know about him, yet she'd never seen his dark side, never guessed that she was living a lie. Given the mess she had made of her life, how could she possibly trust herself to make the right decisions?

The mirror clouded with steam from the draining tub. Abby used the heel of one hand to wipe it away. "Matt isn't David," she insisted. "And this isn't serious. In fact, it isn't anything more than a momentary infatuation—a harmless, temporary distraction."

The woman in the mirror remained doubtful, and nothing Abby said, no argument she made, seemed to convince her.

With Catherine already gone, Abby opted for something less formal than breakfast in the morning room, and joined Rose in the kitchen instead.

"Morning, Miss Abigail," Rose said, lifting a pan of

muffins from the oven and placing them on a small serving tray. "How'd you sleep last night?"

"Fine, thank you."

"You gonna join me for breakfast?" Rose asked, reaching for an extra plate. "There's plenty of muffins."

Rose sank into a chair opposite Abby. "I'm glad to see your appetite's come back. There's clover honey in the condiment dish. Put a little on that muffin. It's good for you."

The comment caught Abby midswallow and she nearly choked on her muffin. Given the events of the past few days, she was fairly certain that she would never be able to look at honey as wholesome again. "I think I'll pass."

She helped herself to a cup of coffee, reluctant to give up her seat by the window. From this position, she had the perfect view of the French lace floribunda. The bush was large and in a fit of sporadic late-season blooming. Beyond its dark, glossy leaves, beyond the old stone wall, was Matt's beat-up truck and the corner of the carriage house, slightly fuzzy in her peripheral vision. *Center, Abby, center. This is foolish, Abby, foolish.*

It was almost certainly self-destructive.

She wasn't looking for love. Wasn't interested in a relationship of any kind. What, then, was she doing?

She thought about it rationally, thought about everything that she was risking.

Just thinking about him triggered an odd little quiver low down in her belly. Abby frowned, reaching for a second muffin. It had to be hunger. There was no other logical, reasonable explanation for this physical response. The justification made her feel a little less moody, a little less doomed, a little more optimistic.

All she needed was a substitute distraction, something to fill her days and nights with, something to keep her from thinking about Matt. Seth Bankcroft and his cousin were coming by this morning to look the house over and give her an estimate on the foundation and the wiring. Figuring out where to get the money for the needed repairs should effectively occupy her thoughts for the next few days.

Patricia craned her neck to one side to stare out the window. "Isn't that Mr. Vanderhorn's tow truck?"

"Why, I believe it is," Rose said. "And he's hooking it up to that Matt Monroe's truck. Miss Abigail, is there anything else you need? If not, then I think I'll just step out into the yard. I could do with a little fresh air and sunshine." Rose chuckled.

Abby didn't answer. She was half in, half out of her chair, mesmerized by the scene taking place beyond the garden wall. Rufus Vanderhorn's tow truck was backing toward Matt's rear bumper. A mere three feet away, Vanderhorn got out of the truck to set the tow bar. As he stepped back and turned toward the driver's door, the carriage house door opened and Matt barreled outside, his angry shout carrying over the yard and into the manor kitchen. "Hey! Goddamn it, that's my truck! What the hell do you think you're doin'?"

"Followin' orders, that's all. Are you Matthew W. Monroe of three forty-six Osgoode Dean Lane?"

"I own that vehicle, and you aren't takin' it anywhere."

"Tell it to the sheriff, mister. I've got orders from Sheriff Rhys to take this vehicle to police impound."

As the words left Rufus's mouth, Abby dropped her muffin and ran.

Matt didn't give a good goddamn about John Rhys or police impound; the only way this upstate rube was taking his truck was over his cold, dead body. He could blame it on a sleepless night, the unaccustomed feelings of regret about having taken advantage of a vulnerable young woman ... a woman who confused and confounded and perplexed him.

If pressed exceptionally hard, he might even admit that he had felt a little cheap and rejected when he woke to find her gone, and wondered if she'd even hung around long enough for the afterglow to fade. He could point to any number of things, including the fact that Erin had bought him that truck as a birthday present a few years before her death, but the plain, hard fact was that nobody was taking his truck.

In the time-honored fashion of men who had lost all sense, he grabbed Rufus's arm and jerked him around, but before he could do more than pull back his fist, the black-and-white belonging to the sheriff's department swung alongside. "I wouldn't do that if I were you," Deputy Shep Margolis advised, setting his parking brake and getting out of the cruiser. He had a half-eaten sausage-and-egg muffin in one hand, and his old-fashioned 38 in the other. "He givin' you grief, Rufus?"

"No more'n usual. What is it with these rednecks and their pickup trucks? You'd think I was tryin' to make off with his grandmother, for Christ's sake."

"You'd better damn well have a warrant, Deputy," Matt said, cursing as he noticed Abby fumbling with the rusty latch on the garden gate. His morning was headed into the toilet, and he didn't want Abby in the middle of his ongoing conflict with the local sheriff's department.

Margolis smirked. "I've got more than that, Monroe. I've got orders to bring you in for questioning. Up against the car."

Matt snorted. "You go to hell."

As Margolis cocked his weapon, Abby came flying full

tilt across the driveway. Matt glanced up and swore. "Get back in the house, damn it!"

Determined to make the most of his distraction, Margolis hooked the toe of his shoe on the front of Matt's boot and at the same time gave him a shove. Matt fell, his left cheekbone colliding with the hood of the black-and-white. Then, as he grunted in pain, Margolis grabbed his arm, forcing it up behind his back, clamping the cuffs on his wrists.

"Shep, stop it! Let him go."

"Doc Youngblood," Shep said, touching the lip of his cap. "Sheriff Rhys wants the pleasure of Mr. Monroe's company down at the station house. Looks like I'm his escort."

"What has he done?" Abby demanded. "You can't detain someone without probable cause—can he?" She shot a questioning look at Matt, who winced.

"Not unless his goal in life is to be immersed in a very long, expensive lawsuit."

"You want probable cause, Monroe?" Margolis said, getting in Matt's face. "How about if we start with refusing to cooperate with a murder investigation, then throw in a little disorderly conduct on the side. That work for you, Doc Youngblood?"

"Shep, this is insane and you know it," Abby insisted.

"Go home, Abby," Matt ground out. "And stay out of this."

"Sounds like good advice," Margolis told her. "I'd listen, if I were you."

"I'll call Julianne," she promised.

"No need. I've already got a lawyer." Matt ground his teeth. She wouldn't listen to a damn thing he had to say, and he knew it. She'd do whatever the hell she pleased, just like last night. Just like always. And it rankled like hell that while she was too damned good to spend the night in his bed, she seemed to feel the irresistible urge to be ass-deep in the middle of his problems. He wanted her, but he didn't need her. He wouldn't need anyone ever again. It was just too damned dangerous. "Go home, Abby!"

"I am not going home!"

"I said go home, damn it!" Matt shouted, his voice as cold and cutting as the steel bracelets clamped around his wrists. "It's my life and my problem, and I don't need you or anyone else to help me deal with it."

Chapter Eight

Matt watched John Rhys take a seat on the edge of the table at which he was slouching and calmly light a cigarette, but he didn't offer Matt a smoke. It was strategy, and a lame one at that. This small-town badge had it somewhere in the back of his caffeine-saturated brain that by denying him petty privileges, like trips to the can, or cigarettes, or by risking overexposure to the one-hundred-watt lightbulb that dangled overhead, he could somehow break him, make him admit to things he wouldn't tell his own mother. Matt's mother had never been one to inspire a son's confidence, and Rhys's transparent tactics just made Matt irritable.

They'd forced him to empty his pockets when he'd entered Abundance Elementary School, a small red-brick building that, two decades after the last class bell had sounded, served as the headquarters for the sheriff's department. Confiscating and cataloging his belongings was a routine precautionary measure. Yet since all he'd had on him at the time was fifteen dollars and thirty-three cents, a pack of smokes, and a half-used book of matches, there was little chance that he would attempt to buy, bribe, or burn his way out.

"We can sit here all night if you like," Rhys said in a calm, even tone. "Or, we can have a little heart-to-heart and you can go home."

His calm was a practiced calm.

Rehearsed, one might say. It was meant, Matt was certain, to reassure him that he wouldn't be in any trouble as long as he was a good boy and cooperated with the nice policeman. It was also a huge crock, and Matt wasn't buying it. "Anybody *ever* believe that line, Sheriff? Or is this the first time you've got to try it out? I don't expect you have a lot of big-time crime around here. Just small stuff: petty theft, maybe some shoplifters at the hardware store, some enterprising young buck caught with a field of marijuana. Must be a real kick for you and your deputy now that you've got a murder investigation on your hands."

Rhys flicked the ash of his cigarette onto the floor. A few grayish-white particles drifted onto the table, half an inch from Matt's left elbow. "Like I said, we can stay here all night if that's what you want."

Matt shrugged. "Oh, I don't know. I kind of like it here." He shot a glance at the bare bulb overhead. "It reminds me of home."

"Did you know Shelley La Blanc intimately?" Rhys asked.

"About as intimately as I know you, Sheriff. I saw her at the café a couple of times, and we talked a little. She seemed like a nice kid."

John took a drag on the cigarette and blew the smoke in Matt's direction. "You sleep with her?"

"No. Why? Did you?" Matt strove for a casual tone,

but it was damned hard, considering. He knew the drill well enough, but it was the first time he'd been on this side of the table in anything but an advisory position. And he sure as hell didn't like it.

"You want to?" Rhys persisted.

"Frankly, Sheriff, I didn't give it much thought. Not that it's any of your damned business. Did you ask me down here just to see if I'm gettin' any, or is there some point to all of this? I don't usually give interviews, you know, and I never talk about my personal life. You never know when someone's gonna to misconstrue something you say—twist it around and use it against you. I've found it's best to avoid that kind of thing whenever possible—like now, for instance."

John Rhys crossed his arms in front of his chest. Matt had known a few guys like him in high school, solid family background, good reputation. The guy everybody liked. The football hero who screwed the class slut on the sly while dating the valedictorian. Matt hadn't liked any of them. It was plain to see that Rhys didn't like him either, but he didn't really give a shit.

"Would you like to call your lawyer?" the sheriff asked.

"No, but I would like a smoke. Deputy Fife took my Camels and my matches. Maybe if you gave him a raise, he could afford his own cigarettes."

The comment seemed to push all of Rhys's buttons at once. His calm shattered like a pane of glass in a hurricane. He leaned down into Matt's face, and his blue eyes got tiny pinpricks of furious light in them, as if they were lit from behind. "Damn it, Monroe, I've got an eyewitness who says she saw Shelley talking to a man that fits your description the night she was killed. The witness says Shelley got into this suspect's pickup truck, and she wasn't seen alive again. A black truck with a noticeable dent on the passenger-side door. Unless I miss my guess, I'd say it was the same truck we pulled into impound a while ago, and this was found inside."

He got up and, with two quick, angry steps, reached the scuffed metal filing cabinet. He opened a drawer, reached inside, and tossed a plastic bag on the table. "That's Shelley La Blanc's shawl. You want to tell me how the hell it came to be inside your truck? Or maybe you'd like a little time to think it over, like a day or two in a holding cell."

"You mind?" Matt asked, picking up the bag. "Cataloged as evidence, even though my truck just went to impound half an hour ago. Your deputy plant this—I mean, *find* this, by any chance?" Matt tossed the bag to Rhys. "Nice try, Sheriff. I'll tell you this much, though. I took Shelley home that night. She said she had car trouble and needed a lift. And she wasn't wearin' anything like that. She was wearing a gray sweater. Still had her name tag on it."

"You admit to being with the victim prior to the murder?"

"Like I said, I took her home, and that's what your witness saw. Last time I checked, givin' somebody a ride home wasn't a felony. Shit, it's not even a misdemeanor." Matt snorted. "Now, I realize that I just effectively shot your day in the ass, and I'm not even gonna apologize. Consider it thanks for draggin' me down here."

"Why the hell didn't you tell me this before?" Rhys demanded.

"I would have if somebody had thought to ask me," Matt said. "Besides, you've been itchin' for somethin' you could slap me with ever since Abby came back to Gilead Manor. Makes me wonder how much of my bein' here has to do with Shelley, and how much of it has to do with the fact that Abby doesn't seem to know you exist."

It was a casual observation, but it must have hit home, because Rhys lost it. He came off his perch, grabbing Matt by the shirtfront. Matt, working on his own short fuse, shot out of his chair, wrapped his hands around Rhys's throat, and shoved him against the wall. When Julianne Rhys appeared in the doorway, Matt let him go, stepping back.

Julianne raised an eyebrow. "Since I happen to know my client isn't stupid, I have to assume this attack was provoked. Big brother, I'd like to have a few choice words with you in the hallway."

"Stay out of my way, Monroe," Rhys warned quietly. "And stay out of trouble. If you have so much as an unpaid parking ticket, I'll make you wish to God you'd stayed south of the Mason-Dixon."

Matt relaxed, but he didn't unclench his fist. "That all, Sheriff?"

Abby watched from the doorway as Matt shrugged off the incident, but John continued to stand, fists balled at his sides. He wanted an altercation; she could see that. And she could only wonder what had been said in the moments before she and Julianne arrived. Yet she was also aware that part of his tension had to do with her presence—a notion that took hold and refused to let go. She walked into a room, and any trace of self-control John possessed instantly disintegrated. It was a dangerous circumstance—for him, for her, for Matt. She'd thought she was doing the right thing coming here. Suddenly, she wasn't so sure.

Matt nodded to Julianne, but he wouldn't look at Abby. "Thanks," he told the attorney.

She smiled. "We're siblings. He expects me to give him a hard time."

Abby exchanged glances with Julianne. Julianne cleared her throat. "If you'll excuse me, I need to talk to my big brother."

She went out, and Abby was alone with Matt. It didn't help to ease the tension. She hadn't brought her handbag, and she didn't seem to know quite what to do with her hands. Finally, she shoved them deep into the pockets of her charcoal tweed blazer. "Are you all right?"

He refused to meet her gaze. "Go home, Abby. You don't belong here."

"Oh, and *you* do?"

"That's not what I said."

"You're being questioned in connection with a murder investigation. Matt, this is serious."

He ran a hand over the back of his head, and the gesture was full of impatience. "Don't you think I know that? Look, it's my life; I'll handle this my way."

"Why do you have to be so infuriatingly stubborn?" Abby tried to drag out her mantra but was too frustrated to employ it with any success while she was so busy seething. "If what I just witnessed is any indication of what went on here, then 'your way' just doesn't appear to be working."

"When I want your help, your interference, I'll ask for it." His voice was soft but cold. And she had to resist the urge to take a step back. This wasn't the man whom she'd fallen into bed with last night. The one she'd regretted leaving this morning. He wasn't tender. Or sensitive to her feelings. In fact, he was so cool, so remote, that she barely recognized him.

While she marveled at Matt's duality, and her own capacity for stupidity, John came over and, taking her by the arm, urged her away. "Leave him be, Abby," he said, but what he meant was "let him rot."

Abby jerked away from John. Her reluctance to have him touch her had all the impact of a blow to the solar plexis. He flinched, then seemed to recover, his jaw hardening. "I want to talk to you—alone," he said, steering her out of the room.

"I know what you're going to say," Abby told him, "and I am not in the mood."

"I warned you about him, Abby. I told you he was trouble. I told you to stay away from him."

"He didn't kill Shelley," Abby insisted. "And you know it."

"I don't know it, and neither do you."

John remained implacable, hellbent on believing that Matt was responsible, but Abby knew better, or at least she thought she did. "For God's sake, John! I'm not an imbecile, and I don't need you to take care of me! Don't you think I would know if he was capable of something like that?"

"You're not stupid, Abby, but you're also not using your head. Monroe's up to his eyeballs in this mess. Don't you think it's kind of strange that he breezes into town and all of a sudden bodies are popping up everywhere?"

"You can't blame him for Millie's death," Abby argued. "He was nowhere near Abundance ten years ago, and he's not a murderer."

John's expression was hard. "Okay, maybe he didn't have anything to do with Millie's death, but he's still no innocent. In fact, there's a Pashmina shawl stashed in the evidence locker that belonged to Shelley. It was found hanging out of the passenger door of Monroe's truck."

"Found? By whom?" Abby demanded. "Shep? You know as well as I do that Shep can find evidence even where none exists. The whole town knows it. Everything

Shep does is suspect, John. He's bigoted and narrow-minded, and he hates everyone who wasn't born in Abundance. Admit it; you would have fired him years ago if it hadn't been for the fact that your ex-wife is his sister."

"This isn't about Shep," he said flatly. "It's about protecting you. You don't know what's good for you these days, and you're blind to what's bad. Somebody's got to save you from yourself, from him."

Abby looked at John, really looked at him, and for the first time in years, she saw him clearly. "Oh, God. Is that what this is? Jealousy? You're trying to keep Matt away from me, and you'll use anything at your disposal—including your badge—if it will give you a second chance."

She shook her head, a little sick at how he saw the world, and her. "I'm not weak, John. I can think, and think clearly, and I can make up my own mind about who I want to see, and who doesn't interest me. I'm going to say this once, and I hope to God you never make me say it again. You're a friend—or at least, I thought you were. There's nothing else. There is no us. What we had was over a long time ago."

"For you, maybe," he said; then there was no time for more as Julianne stepped into the hallway.

The night advanced and the moon, now two days past its fullest point, illuminated the clouds from behind, giving the sky the appearance of a furrowed field. He glanced at his watch. It was half past three, and except for a few insomniacs mesmerized by the gray-blue glow from their television sets, the residents of the town had gone to sleep. No one saw the dark-colored vehicle roll silently along the streets. No faces peering from the windows, no curtains drawn back by a curious hand. Not a single barking dog, or even a cat to cross his path.

It was his hour. The night belonged to him, and it was a time of stunning silence.

He took his time prowling the streets, only half-hearing the whimpers from the cargo bay. It was almost as if the sounds of primal fear were absorbed through his skin instead of his ears. He already felt the closeness to the girl that he always felt. He had chosen her, claimed her, but he didn't own her yet.

She wasn't a part of him.

They hadn't bonded.

But they would.

And when he finished with her, she would become a glittering part of his dark repertoire, a part of the essence of what made him what he was: the hunter, the predator. He would relive this night again and again. It almost made her immortal, but she was too frightened, too weak, too easily manipulated to realize it.

The lights were on at the old elementary school. Deputy Margolis was just getting out of his car, scratching the left cheek of his buttocks as he half-turned to watch the dark vehicle pass. Margolis raised a hand in a half-hearted wave while the girl whimpered.

The deputy didn't know.

And he would never guess.

No one would. He'd fooled them all. Even Abby.

Late the next day, J. T. Langtry showed up at the police station. John invited him into his office and offered him the bitter dregs at the bottom of his coffeepot, but that was as far as he was willing to go. J. T. was Julianne's problem, not his, and though the possibility that she might decide to jump the broom and make

184 S. K. McClafferty

him his brother-in-law demanded a certain level of politeness, he didn't owe the man a straight answer. Things were bad enough around here. He wasn't about to compound his problems by being misquoted in J. T.'s paper.

"Sure you don't want some coffee?" John asked, settling behind his desk and placing his Styrofoam cup in the center of the blotter. It upset his rhythm and his concentration to have it off to the left or right. With J. T. in a chair directly in front of him, and the steam from the cup curling in the air between them, he just might get to finish it before it turned to acid.

"So that's what you're calling it these days. Thanks, but I think I'll pass. So, how are the kids?" J. T. propped one ankle on the opposite knee. He was striving for casual, but John wasn't buying it and J. T. knew it.

"They're fine, considering, but you didn't come over here to talk about John Junior's algebra."

"I was hoping to kind of ease into it." He made a scooting motion with one hand, then shook his head. "Blame it on your sister. She gave me hell the other night for trying to squeeze an interview out of our local celeb."

At the reference to Matt Monroe, John grimaced. J. T. shook his head. "Another score, and I wasn't even trying." He sighed, squeezing the bridge of his nose between his fingers. "Julie, honey, I'm sorry, but your way just isn't working. All right, gloves off. You know I'm going to be a genuine pain in your ass until this whole thing is over. I don't really like it any more than you do, but it's my job."

"J. T.," John said. "This really isn't a good time."

"Any suspects?"

"No comment."

"Funny, your sister says there are. In fact, she couldn't

say enough about your bullheadedness. She also said that Shep's 'innate capacity for narrowness' was rubbing off on you."

John tilted his head down to give J. T. a disgusted look. "Thank you for sharing."

"So, you're denying that Matt Monroe was brought in for questioning in the murder of Shelley La Blanc? And that you've got Willard D. under constant surveillance?"

The question caught John midsip; he swallowed too quickly and nearly choked. "God damn it!" he said, setting the cup down again. "Shep! Shep, get your ass in here!"

Sarah, the dispatcher and receptionist, stuck her head around the doorframe. Sarah was five-foot-nothing, brunette, and weighed in at ninety-three and a half pounds. Her voice was small, almost elf-like. "Shep's out on patrol, Sheriff. You want me to get him on the radio?"

John sighed. "I specifically told him not to hound Willard," he muttered, then pointed a finger at J. T. "That's off the record, you hear me?"

"Sheriff?"

"It's John, Sarah," he said. "And no. Don't call him. But I want his scrawny ass in this office the second he gets in."

"Will do, sir." Sarah popped out as lightly as she'd popped in.

"Sometimes I think I should send Sarah to the Academy and let Shep man the phones. It'd be a damn sight less hassle." He jabbed the same finger at J. T.

"Yeah, I know. It's off the record." J. T. jotted something on the notepad he was holding. "Since you obviously have no intention of giving me specifics, why don't we speak in generalities. You've already identified the remains found on the Youngblood estate. Do you feel

that the murder of Millie Gray and Shelley's death are
in any way connected?''

"No connection. Unequivocally. That, you can
print.''

"One last thing. Did you find any damning evidence
in Monroe's pickup?''

"No comment, and unless you want coffee, we're
done here. I have things to do.'' But John clenched his
jaws at the inquiry. There had been no surprises, given
the fact that Shelley had been a passenger in the truck
on at least one occasion. Monroe had covered his
wealthy behind, and that fact burned John.

Though he didn't feel inclined to inform J. T., he
would be releasing the vehicle from impound the next
morning. Reluctantly. He had no other choice. Monroe
had admitted to taking Shelley home the night of the
murder. Any defense attorney worth his salt would take
that admission and build a mountain of reasonable
doubt from it. Even with the shawl, John knew he
couldn't touch him, but it didn't stop him from wishing
it were otherwise.

While J. T. fired questions at John and John gave
his best, most emphatic "no comment," Deputy Shep
Margolis was in the middle of conducting some serious
business in the parking lot of Stooley's Roadhouse. Shep
knew that he was bending the rules a bit, but he'd been
bending the rules for years and people had come to
expect it of him. John sure as hell wasn't about to repri-
mand him for it.

John had filed for divorce from Shep's sister, Rebecca,
and he still walked softly around Shep. Not that Shep
held a grudge. Rebecca was his sister, but she was also
a raging neurotic and had always been something of a

whiner. He couldn't really fault John for leaving her, and it wasn't as if he'd abandoned her to shack up with some hot little nineteen-year-old. He just couldn't take any more of her "episodes."

What Shep did fault John for was his naïveté when it came to the job. It had been damn near a week since they'd found Shelley's body, and almost two since they'd found Millie Gray, and they still had two empty holding cells at the station. Hell, it wasn't as though they didn't have suspects. He'd dragged two of them in this week alone, and John released them as quickly as Shep found them. One of these two guys was guilty as sin; Shep could smell it. Monroe had had Shelley's shawl in his truck, a fact that stunk to high heaven. And then there was Willard.

One brief conversation, a mess in the waste paper basket, and John had declared him as innocent as Jenny Caswell's three-month-old baby girl.

Shep wasn't as easy. And he sure as hell wasn't buying it.

The crying and pretending to be sick at the autopsy photos could very well be an act. Shep had known guys who could practically turn their stomachs inside out at will. It was a handy talent to have, to avoid an exam, or to dodge a murder charge.

Willard was from Syracuse; he was a weapon-monger who hated the government, and there was a rumor going around that he had red-and-white striped grease rags around his shop that looked suspiciously like the American flag. If that wasn't enough, there was his connection to Shelley, and the fact that he was acting funny. Jittery and nervous, always looking around, darting little glances. Like a fox who'd been in the henhouse, or a man who had something to hide.

John had ordered Shep to lay off Willard, and in

188   S. K. McClafferty

Shep's mind, that was exactly what he was doing. He
hadn't harassed him unduly; he hadn't so much as spat
in his direction. He just happened to show up in the
places Willard frequented. He parked the cruiser in the
wide spot on the berm a hundred feet from Willard's
shop and place of residence, trawling for speeding
motorists, ignoring the fact that Willard lived on a dead-
end street. He ate in the same out-of-the-way restaurants,
even when he was off duty, at the same time Willard
did, and he usually showed up at Stooley's to sit in the
parking lot and scan the trickle of customers streaming
out into the deepening dusk for underage drinkers.

Shep took his job very seriously, and if he knew anything, it was how to get results. "A little pressure, and
somebody'll crack," Shep muttered to himself, watching
as the door swung open and Willard stumbled out.
"Bingo." Shep had parked in the third row, toward the
back of the lot. It was Wednesday, league night in the
bowling alley, and the place was packed.

Willard emerged from Stooley's and paused long
enough to glance around. He had a creeping sensation
along the back of his neck, just inside his collar. It
felt as if someone ran a cold finger along his skin. He
immediately thought of Shelley. Was she trying to tell
him something? Jesus, he missed her. He didn't think
it would be this bad. He'd been intending to dump her
all along, but somehow, her dying had affected him. It
was weird, but he almost felt as if he'd been cheated.
And in a way he had.

When Shelley died, the last shred of security had been
ripped from Willard. Not only had he lost Shelley, but
the opportunity of a lifetime was rapidly slipping from
his grasp. Fucking Shep Margolis watched him night
and day, and when Shep wasn't watching him, Willard
suspected someone else was. His buyer, spooked by Wil-

lard's newfound popularity, had headed south to the city, leaving Willard as high and dry as a beached whale. And almost as doomed.

He had three kilos of blow in his storeroom that he wouldn't use and couldn't sell, and all it would take was for Shep to convince Sheriff Rhys to get a warrant, and Willard wouldn't see the light of day for the next thirty years, if ever.

He'd thought about flushing it, but he wasn't quite that desperate, and the thought of all of that cash going down the shitter made him nauseous. He couldn't bag it and push it himself. It was too damned dangerous. Too much potential for disaster.

Willard had a real dilemma on his hands, and if that wasn't enough, his bladder was about to burst. He thought about going back inside to the restroom, but it seemed like too much effort, so he opened his fly near his Malibu and pissed on the ground beside the left front tire. At the same time, someone behind him kicked on a floodlight. With his dick in one hand, Willard raised the other to shield his eyes, half-turning to face the glare. Too late, he realized it was the beam from a flashlight, and Shep Margolis grinned from behind its halogen halo.

"You know, I do believe that's called indecent exposure. Be so good as to put your hands up on the roof of your car, but put that thing away first, will ya? Wouldn't want to embarrass Sarah when I haul your sorry ass in."

For over an hour, Matt had dug through the documents Abby had given him concerning the labyrinth of tunnels that were rumored to run under the Gilead Manor. The catacombs had served various purposes over the years, including as a stop along the Underground Railroad during the years immediately prior to the Civil War.

The facts Abby had provided had promise, and he might have been able to find a use for them if he could just sit still long enough. In his present mood, he couldn't have strung two words together to save his life, let alone make any real headway on the manuscript.

Sophie would be incensed that he was sloughing off yet again. His excuses wouldn't mean shit as far as she was concerned, and his publisher was just about out of patience with his promises. It didn't matter that his current block was very real. Getting hauled off to the local lock-up had a way of putting a damper on a man's week.

He hadn't spoken to Abby since she dropped him off in front of his door the day before. He was still a little put out over her running out on him earlier in the week. He'd told himself a million times since that he was being irrational, but it didn't lessen his anger. Why should it matter to him that she'd gone home before dawn? She'd saved him the awkwardness of promising he'd call, hadn't she? And saved herself the obligation to pretend to believe him, even when they would both know it wasn't so.

Truth was, he wasn't much for telephones. He had a cell phone, but he didn't carry it with him, and when he did carry it he refused to turn it on. It was just another avenue for Sophie to keep tabs on him, and it was something he resisted. He hated feeling as if he was on a short leash.

For what seemed like the ten-thousandth time, Matt caught himself staring out the window at the canary yellow Jeep and wondering about Abby. He told himself it was stupid and self-defeating, totally out of character, yet he couldn't seem to help himself.

He just couldn't stop thinking about her. Great sex tended to do that to a man.

Ms. Catherine's Mercedes was conspicuously absent, and he knew for a fact that Rose had gone home for the day. He'd watched her leave with her granddaughter Patricia more than an hour ago.

Abby was alone at the mansion.

Why did that realization bother him so much?

Matt scribbled a few notations on a scratch pad, then sat back to read them. There was a kernel of a plot twist there somewhere, but he was too bored or too restless to pursue it.

On the way to the fridge for a beer, he paused by the window. Had something moved in the inky shadows near the mansion?

He stared harder. Great. Now he was seeing things.

The night was overcast and might as well have been moonless, and Catherine had flaunted convention, refusing to mar the mansion's aged ambiance by installing one of the dusk-to-dawn lights so popular with home owners these days.

Matt frowned, unable to ignore the crawly sensation on the back of his neck. He tensed, but nothing happened. He was just about to crack his beer and tell himself that he needed to get a life when he caught sight of it again, the dark silhouette of a man crouched near the shrubbery growing close by the library windows. Inside the library, the slim form of a woman passed by the windows.

Abby.

Jesus.

The figure moved closer to the glass, the dark ski

mask that covered his face highlighted by the light that spilled from the library. Matt didn't wait to see what came next. Dropping the beer, he slammed from the carriage house and sprinted toward the mansion.

Abby fled to the library, seeking distraction. She'd been home for almost two weeks, and she was no closer to getting her life together than she had been when she'd arrived. She really should work on updating her résumé, start concentrating on where she wanted to go from here. She could always apply to another college, but after the scene she'd made on her last day at Sullivan, storming into Dean Howard's office, accusing the governing board of a cover-up, demanding an open investigation of the attack on Lily Pascal, and due to the fact that she had already leaked information to the press, she couldn't exactly expect a glowing recommendation.

She could always apply to her father. There was a chance he could pull some strings and get her a position, despite the mess her life had become. He would love helping her out. He had always preferred parenting by proxy. He wouldn't have to do anything; he wouldn't have to talk to her, to listen to her problems. Just order his secretary to call in a favor or two, and he could play the benevolent daddy. Abby cringed at the thought. She hated the idea of asking him for anything.

But there was no denying that she would have to do something, and soon. Seth Bankcroft and his cousin were coming in the morning to begin the repairs, and she still hadn't informed her aunt Catherine. She had enough money in her savings account to replace the worst of the old wiring, and to tide her over for a few months, but it wouldn't last beyond that.

Abby worried at a hangnail with her teeth as she paced in front of the library windows. Life at the moment was unbearably complicated. *Everything* was complicated these days.

She was worried about Catherine and her financial problems, worried about how her aunt would react when she learned that she had decided to begin repairs to Gilead Manor on her own, and then there was Matt.

She tried not to think about the incident at the police station, yet she couldn't seem to think of anything else. If there was even a shred of truth in what John had alluded to, then Shelley's wrap had been discovered in Matt's truck.

Shelley's watch.

Shelley's wrap.

Abby squeezed her eyes shut, her thoughts a confusing whirl behind her closed lids. John thought that she was a fool, blinded by lust, unable to think rationally.

And maybe he was right. She hadn't told anyone about finding the watch. Not even Matt. Why was she delaying? What was she afraid of?

Did she really believe on some level that Matt was somehow involved in all of this?

She shook her head, but she couldn't quite dislodge the thought. She'd often thought that he was hiding something. That she'd sensed some dark undercurrent swirling just beneath his jokes and sexual innuendos. Something he didn't want to think about, let alone discuss.

But was he capable of such brutality?

There must be some mistake, something she couldn't see. Matt was uninhibited and maybe even a little self-destructive. But he wasn't a murderer, no matter what John said.

She shook her head again, walking to the bookshelves

to stare unseeing at row upon row of books, old and new. He was sexy. He was charming. And he liked adventurous sex. But that didn't make him a killer. She took the watch out of her pocket and stared down at it. She'd been on the verge of going to him all evening, of demanding the truth, and only the prospect of where any contact between the two of them might possibly lead kept her from it.

Abby paced from the bookshelves to the divan, but as she passed by the French doors, a strange sensation came over her, an acute prickliness at the base of her neck. The fine hair on her forearms stood on end—an instinctive fear response. Fight or flight. It was primal, reactive. Her body was trying to tell her what her mind was slow to accept.

She was being watched.

Someone, or something, was in the dark beyond the French doors, looking in.

The child in her wanted to dart behind the divan, to hide, and forcing herself to approach the French doors instead required every ounce of courage she possessed. It took several seconds for what she was seeing to register. The cold and emotionless eyes looking in seemed to float in a sea of unrelieved black. Then, she saw the narrow slits of paler flesh that ringed them.

It was a ski mask. He was wearing a ski mask.

Fear froze Abby to the spot. Stunned, she held her breath, watching, mesmerized as his black gloved hand reached for the door handle. The inside knob slowly turned. Abby's breath stilled in her throat. Somewhere beneath the heavy thud of her heart, she heard footfalls, rapidly pounding toward the house. Someone running.

The prowler heard it too, and tensed, but his gaze remained locked with Abby's, a startled breath and a few fragile panes of glass the only things separating them. . . . Then, realizing the danger, he spun, melting back into the darkness, leaving her with the chilling impression that she had looked into those eyes before.

But where?

Then, the door was flung wide, and she was in Matt's arms.

Chapter Nine

"Are you all right?"

Abby nodded. "I'm okay. He tried the knob, Matt. Another minute and . . . Thank God you're here."

For a moment she clung to him, intensely glad for his strength, his nearness, unwilling to let anything intrude that might spoil it. Then she pushed back, and he didn't even try to hold on to her. Abby was surprised at the wave of disappointment that washed over her. "I'm sorry. I guess I'm a little more shaken than I realized."

"Yeah, well, that's understandable. Maybe you should sit down."

"I'll be all right. Just give me a minute." She crossed her arms under her breasts, then uncrossed them, pushing her hands deep into the patch pockets of her oversized sweater. "How did you know to come?"

Matt flipped the latch on the doors, locking them, then ran a hand through his hair. She wasn't the only one who was agitated. He couldn't believe how close the prowler had come to getting in. How close it had been to happening again. Erin, Abby—different, the same, both involved with the wrong man, for love, for lust . . . but he was linchpin, the draw. If it weren't for him—he broke off, unable to complete the thought. "I happened to glance out the window, and thought I saw something. Did you get a look at him?"

"I couldn't see his face. He was wearing a ski mask, a dark color. Dark ski mask, dark clothing, leather gloves."

"This guy means business." Matt picked up the phone on the end table.

"What are you doing?"

"I'm calling the cops. This town's going to hell and the sheriff's department is wastin' their time detailing my truck." He put the receiver to his ear, then just as quickly put it back on the cradle.

"What is it?" she said, watching him closely. "What's wrong?"

"The line's dead." He headed for the door, and Abby seemed to realize what he had in mind. "Don't suppose you forgot to pay the bill?"

"You're not going out there?"

"I'm just stepping out to have a quick look around, that's all."

"Can't it wait?" she said. "My cell phone is on the desk. I'll call John and have him send someone over."

"It'll only take a minute," Matt said. He didn't want to tell her that he didn't trust Rhys and Margolis not to make a mess of things when they got here, that the guy they were looking for was a lot more intelligent than either of them. He also needed to ascertain whether the wires had been damaged, or deliberately cut. And then there was the chance that the guy was still out there, waiting, watching—a chance he might be able to get his hands on him, and if it turned out to be Karl he'd make damned sure that this time he wouldn't walk away.

Abby watched him go, but he could tell she wasn't happy about it. Sheriff Rhys was off duty, but Shep Margolis came to rattle the bushes and poke around with his flashlight, then stood in the foyer glaring at Matt while he pronounced that the phone wires had pulled loose from the house and there were no visible signs of the prowler Abby claimed to have seen. Then a call came in on his car radio, and he adjusted the belt under his slight paunch. "You sure you want to report this incident?" he asked. "It won't set well with folks around here if it turns out to be a publicity stunt."

Matt snorted. "You'd love that, wouldn't you, Margolis?"

"Sure would. I'd love anything that'd make you look like the conniving snake you are." He made for the door, muttering, "Outsider."

As the door closed on his retreating figure, an awkward silence settled between Abby and Matt. "You don't have to stay," she said suddenly. "I mean, I understand if you have work to do."

Matt shrugged. "It's too early. I do some of my best work after midnight."

"I've noticed." Abby smiled, but the smile quickly faded. "I've seen the carriage house lights from my windows."

Matt moved to the French doors, where he stood looking out at the darkness. He couldn't get the image of the prowler crouched in the bushes out of his mind, and he felt restless and edgy. He wanted to punch something—*someone*. He wanted a smoke. "You mind?" he asked, taking out a cigarette. When she shook her head, he struck a match and drew the nicotine into his lungs.

Abby hugged her arms. He could see that his mood

was affecting her, but he couldn't seem to help himself. "You're killing yourself with those things," she told him, and another voice echoed somewhere in the dark recesses of his memory. Erin's voice:

"You're killing yourself with those things; you know that, don't you, Monroe?"

"Yeah, I know."

"They cause more than just cancer: things like sexual dysfunction in lab mice, reductions in desire, lower sperm counts. . . ."

He'd been seated in the posh leather swivel chair in his office. In one swift move he pulled Erin down and onto his lap, slipping his hand under her skirt, finding the heat of her.

"You complainin', sugar? Or merely having charitable thoughts for those poor little mice?"

"I'm being selfish. I want you to outlive your youthful hairline; I want you to have a chance to get paunchy and farsighted, forgetful and old; and I want to have babies, Monroe—our babies. . . ."

Matt shook off the chilling effects of déjà vu.

He wasn't in Jackson, and Abby wasn't Erin.

So, why did he have this creeping feeling that the nightmare of his last days with Erin was about to happen all over again?

The thought occurred, and he shook it off, too. *It will not happen again.*

Abby wasn't Erin. They weren't as closely connected. But that didn't mean that Karl could distinguish between something that was purely physical and something deeper. Or that he would care. "I'm surprised your aunt doesn't have a security system in this place. Big old house like this makes an easy target and ought to be protected."

"She didn't think it was necessary, and it hasn't been—"

"Well, it is now," he said softly. "I don't know who this guy is, but I know one thing. You aren't safe here."

Abby shook her head. "He had his hand on the knob. The door wasn't locked. He could have come in at any moment, yet he didn't even make the attempt until just before you frightened him off. And I had the distinct impression . . ." She paused, frowning.

"What impression, Abby?"

She lifted her head and met his gaze evenly. "That he wanted to frighten me. He looked at me as directly as I'm looking at you now, and then slowly turned the knob. He could have come in at any moment. He could have taken me by surprise, or rushed in and overpowered me, but it wasn't his intention. It was like he wanted to gauge my reaction, to see what I would do."

"To some people, fear is an aphrodisiac," Matt said softly. "They start small, probing for your one weakness, your vulnerability, and when they find it they twist the knife, just to see what the hell you'll do."

Abby laughed, but it wasn't genuine; it was half-hearted and awkward. "You sound like you speak from experience."

Matt glanced up. The cigarette had burned down to within an inch of his fingers. He ground it out in a nearby ash tray. "Yeah, well, I suppose you could say that in a way I've lived it. It's what I do—crawl inside people's minds."

Abby had thrust Shelley's watch into her sweater pocket when Matt first entered the house. Now, the cold of the silver band seemed to burn her fingers. Matt still stood by the French doors. There was more than just a few feet of worn carpeting separating them. There was a chasm of misunderstanding, suspicion, and doubt. "How did Shelley's shawl get into your truck?" she asked quietly.

He glanced up, his expression closed off, wary. "How'd you know about that?" he countered, then laughed. "Don't tell me. Sheriff Rhys . . . and I bet he tried to convince you it was out of concern. He thinks you're involved with the wrong kind of man. He thinks you've lost your perspective. That you're so mixed up with me that you can't think straight. Is there any truth in that, Abby?"

"You don't like John," she countered. "Why should you care what he thinks?"

"I don't have to like him to see that he could be onto somethin'. And I'm thinkin' that might be the reason you didn't stick around the other night. Is that it, darlin'? You afraid this thing between us is gettin' out of hand?"

Abby tensed, raising her chin defensively. "You never answered my question. Why was Shelley's shawl in your truck?"

He watched her for a moment or two, perhaps judging what he wished her to know against what he refused to own. Then he gave her what she wanted, but coolly, and on his own terms. "Be damned if I know. She was wearin' a gray sweater when I took her home." Then, when she didn't speak, "Yeah that's right. I gave her a ride home the night of the murder. She said her car wouldn't start; she needed a lift, and it was rainin'. Deputy Margolis claims to have found a Pashmina shawl belonging to Shelley in my truck. Maybe he's tellin' the truth. Maybe he's lyin', and it's a plant. But if he did find it, I don't have a clue as to how it got there."

"What about this?" Abby asked, unsure if she believed him. She retrieved the watch, holding it out. "Do you recognize it?"

He stepped close, accepting the watch she held out to him. "Shelley had one just like it. Where'd you get this?"

"It was in my purse when you dropped me off the day of the pic—the day we found Shelley."

"How did it get into your purse?" he asked, then stopped. "Oh, now, wait a minute. You don't think that I had it."

"My purse spilled over your floorboard just before I got out. We both bent down to put it all back. It must have gotten mixed in with my checkbook, compact, and keys."

"And you thought that maybe I killed Shelley and decided to keep it, and just sort of left it lyin' around for someone to find."

"I don't know what to think," she admitted.

He handed the watch back to her. "No matter what you may think of me, I'm not that stupid. Besides, Shelley had it on her arm when she got out of my truck," Matt insisted. "I saw her glance at it under the street light." He ran a hand through his hair, clearly agitated. "Who knows about this?"

"No one."

"Of course not," he said. "If you'd shared this information with the sheriff's department, we wouldn't be standin' here discussin' it. I'd be in jail right now on a trumped-up murder charge." He paced back to the windows and turned. "Why'd you hold back, Abby? Why didn't you give him the watch? It's not like you haven't had ample opportunity."

Abby shrugged, on the defensive now. *Because I want to believe in you. Because I need to believe in you. Because if*

I'm wrong, I will never trust my judgment again. Aloud, she said, "I needed to hear it from you." She waited, almost holding her breath.

"There isn't much to hear, actually. I took her home around nine. She got out of my truck, glanced at her watch, waved, and I drove back here. That's all there was to it." He stepped close, close enough that she was forced to look up to meet his gaze. "Look, I can't explain how her things got into my truck. All I can say is that someone must have put them there, because I had nothing to do with it."

"But who?" Abby questioned. "And why? Why would anyone want to put Shelley's belongings in your truck?"

"The killer, the sheriff, his deputy? I don't know. As to why, that's anybody's guess. To make me look bad, maybe? To scare you off."

Abby shook her head. "John would never do something like that."

"What about Margolis? You going to tell me he's above that kind of thing, too?"

"There have been accusations," Abby admitted. "But why would he want to frame you for something you didn't do?"

Matt sighed. "Because sometimes, baby, that's what cops do. The longer it takes for them to apprehend a suspect in this case, the more inept they'll seem. If you think it doesn't happen, just watch *Sixty Minutes*. Death row's full of innocent men. And then there's the self-serving part. Whoever catches Shelley's killer is bound to be hero material. And if the actor happens to be an outsider, then so much the better. No one ever wants to believe that the guy down the street is capable of killing their daughter. It blows the illusion of security bred in small towns. It's always more comfortable, more believable, if it's someone they barely know.

"The monster you don't know is easier to accept than the one that you do," Abby finished for him.

There was a noise in the foyer, the rattle of keys, the turn of a lock. "Abigail?" Catherine called out.

Abby glanced at the open doorway. "In here, Aunt Catherine." When she glanced back, Matt had crossed to the French doors and let himself out. He paused a fraction of a second to glance back—a look that cut her to the quick—then he disappeared into the deep shadows on the lawn.

Abby moved to latch the doors, releasing the breath she'd been holding, to touch the chilled glass with unsteady fingers. "I may be crazy," she whispered, "but I believe you."

"Abigail?" Catherine said from the doorway. "I heard disturbing news about a prowler. Are you quite all right?"

Abby faced away from the glass, away from the night and Matt. Somehow, she managed a reassuring smile. "I'm fine," she replied. "Just fine." But in reality she was far from it.

Willard made bail the following afternoon. The charge was a misdemeanor, and the bail was so low that it was a joke, but Willard wasn't laughing. Shep Margolis had it in for him, and the deputy was just persistent enough to dog him until he uncovered something that would stick. Shep was lounging by the water cooler when Willard reclaimed his wallet, watch, and his pocket change. Shep's aviator sunglasses hid his gaze, but Willard could feel the smaller man's eyes burning into his back as he hurried down the hallway toward the exit. "See you 'round, Willard," Shep said.

Willard kept on walking.

It was the longest afternoon of Willard's life. He called his friend Ziggy and begged a lift to Stooley's to pick up his wheels. Then he returned to the shop, careful to travel well within the speed limit. He couldn't be too careful with Shep Margolis out for blood. When he was safely inside his shop, he turned the "closed" sign out on the door, double locked the doors, and headed to the basement storeroom.

It was half past midnight when Willard lifted the shade on the front window and surveyed the yard and the street in front of his place. The yard was deserted except for a raccoon that perched on his garbage can. The animal glanced at Willard as he killed the lights and stepped outside, a zippered athletic bag tucked under one arm. Perceiving him as a nonthreat, it went back to rocking the garbage can in a clear attempt to purloin a midnight snack.

Ignoring the animal, Willard stuffed the bag under the driver's seat and got behind the wheel. Vander-bloon's Woods had been absorbed by the Youngblood estate a century and a half before, and Catherine Young-blood's efforts over the past forty years had kept it largely untouched. Aside from a few hikers and a fanatical jogger or two, no one ventured near Vanderbloon's Woods. The old folks around the area who were second-generation superstitious claimed that the woods were haunted. Willard had dismissed the stories as local folk-lore. The Catskill residents were full of it, and he had better things to do than to buy into local bullshit. Yet, as he parked the car on the lonely dirt road and moved into the woods armed with only a flashlight, he couldn't quite suppress an involuntary shudder.

He told himself it was just the pressure of having three kilos of dope he couldn't sell. Nothing had gone right for him since Shelley's death. He was headed down the tubes; he could feel it coming, and there was only one way he could think of to get out of this scrape without a felony conviction and a lengthy prison term.

Deflecting branches with one hand, he pushed deeper into the woods, the wet carpet of fallen leaves slick underfoot. The branches rattled and shivered overhead, scraping against one another, creeping Willard out. The path wound along adjacent to the road, then dipped into a steep-sided ravine. It was far enough away from the road to avoid detection, yet easy to find when he was ready to retrieve the goods. Willard made a sweeping arc with the flashlight. Nothing around, no one to see. He crouched down, took a small trowel out of the bag, and started to dig.

The earth was soft, unusually soft. Relief flooded him. With the dope buried, he would be able to breathe a little easier. Then, when things settled down, he'd come back and get it. It was his Arizona money. Not exactly a fortune, but enough to get that little place at the edge of the desert. Just thinking about getting out of this hellhole made Willard's pulse kick up a notch. He dug a little faster, but he'd only taken a scoop or two when the trowel met with resistance. The obstacle seemed too spongy to be a tree root, not hard enough to be stone. Willard tested the earth with the trowel, but it seemed to run the whole length of the area where he was digging. "What the hell?" he muttered, picking up the light and shining it on the ground near his feet.

A long patch of mottled blue-white showed through the rich black dirt, half-obscured by the long red tendril lying half across the rounded marblelike curve of one naked shoulder.

Willard scrambled back, dropping the flashlight, but he didn't stoop to retrieve it. He couldn't get far enough away, fast enough. He stumbled like a madman through the underbrush, branches whipping at his eyes, his breath a terrified wheeze in his throat. He was doing eighty-five miles an hour with his valves knocking when he ran the stop sign down on Main, and the lights of the black-and-white popped into his rearview mirror.

Shep chased him three miles past the town limits, running him to ground when his engine blew. Smoke poured out from under the hood of the Chevy Malibu. As Shep approached, the 38 in his hand, Willard D. put his head in his hands and rocked back and forth in the driver's seat. "You got a serious knock in that engine, boy. I'd have somebody look at it if I were you, if ever you dig out from under."

An hour and a half later, John Rhys was facing down another sleepless night in a string of sleepless nights. He stood in the middle of Skunk Town Road and watched the forensics team carefully unearth the body of the young woman, wishing that he were anywhere but here. Shep was leaning against the driver's door of the patrol car a dozen feet away, keeping half an eye on Willard Early, who slumped in the back seat like a boneless thing.

Willard had sworn a few hundred times on the way to Vanderbloon's Woods that he'd stumbled on the body while trying to hide three kilos of cocaine in the woods. Spurred on by the constant, unrelenting pressure of Shep's surveillance, Willard had been desperate to dump the goods until things cooled down.

His story carried the ring of truth, and judging by the level of his upset and the pallor of shock Willard wore, John was inclined to believe him. It didn't ease Willard's predicament, however. He was in a hell of a lot of trouble. Possession of a controlled substance with intent to distribute, unlawful flight, speeding, reckless

endangerment, and resisting arrest. Shep had enumerated each charge with an undisguised glee a while ago,
and John was just grateful his deputy had maintained
a little decorum and refrained from doing cartwheels.

"Looks like they got her loaded up, boss," Shep said,
"along with three bags full of dirt. Tapes are up to
cordon off the area, and we're ready to fly. Guess we
better get our drug kingpin to lockup. Wouldn't want
to risk losin' him, him bein' so slippery and all."

"Take him on ahead, and Shep . . ."

Shep adjusted his hat and straightened his glasses.
"Yeah, I know. By the book. No worry, boss. I'll treat
him so damned good, he won't ever want to leave."

John set up roadblocks at both ends of Skunk Town
Road. There were no houses along the lonely stretch,
and in reality, it was little more than a shortcut to a
state road three miles away. In fact, only the locals knew
it even existed. The correlation wasn't lost on him. Whoever had killed and buried the girl Willard D. had found
had been familiar with the area and had been confident
that he wouldn't be discovered, and even if he'd been
seen here, chances were that no one would have questioned him for it.

They were either dealing with a local or with someone
who had made it his business to learn the countryside.
The thought was far from comforting. Not only did the
location of the dump site indicate that this was not an
isolated incident, there was a damned good chance that
this lunatic was operating in home territory, a place of
safety and comfort. For days, John had been living with
a coil of tension in his belly, and the fact that his job
had just gotten a whole lot harder didn't do anything
to lighten the load.

* * *

By the time Abby's coffee was brewing the next morning, the news of the grisly discovery on Skunk Town Road was everywhere. "Skunk Town Road?" Catherine said. "Why, that's only a half mile from here cross-country. Do they have any idea who the girl was?"

"They haven't released her identity yet, pending notification of her next of kin." Abby watched the drip, and as soon as there was sufficient coffee in the pot, she pilfered a cup. She needed a jolt this morning, something to fortify her. In fact, had she been so inclined, she would have added a jigger or two of something stronger.

"Vanderbloon's Woods is on Youngblood land," Catherine said angrily. "How dare this maniac turn it into a graveyard! Something has to be done about this, Abigail."

They had gathered in the kitchen, disdaining the formality of the morning room. The kitchen provided a closeness, an intimacy, that they all desperately needed right now. Rose was at the stove, filling the bone china teapot with boiling water, adding Catherine's favorite loose-leaf tea and a few spearmint leaves. Catherine rose so abruptly from her place at the table that she nearly toppled her chair. Rose glanced at Abby in alarm. "Now, Miss Catherine," Rose said. "Where do you think you're going? You haven't even had your breakfast yet."

"I'm going to see John Rhys, that's where I'm going!" Catherine shot back. "This can't be permitted to go on. My ancestors founded this town—I can't simply sit here and allow it to be torn apart."

"What are you gonna do? Catch that man yourself?"

"If I have to, yes," Catherine said emphatically, her blue eyes alight with indignation. "Don't you understand, Rose? It's no longer safe here. Not for you, not for me, not for Abigail or Patricia. Not for our friends and our neighbors. This situation is intolerable.''

Abby lay a hand on Catherine's arm. "All right. If you insist on going, then I'll go with you. But you do realize that John is doing everything he can to keep the town safe, don't you?"

Catherine nodded. "John Rhys is a good man, but he's ill equipped to handle this. I fear that we all are."

There was a rattle and bang as a truck pulled into the drive, the double slam of the doors. "What on earth?" Catherine said, peering out the window. "Why that's Seth Bankcroft. What is he doing here?"

Abby shot a glance at Rose, who rolled her eyes and stepped back, out of the coming fray. "I hired Seth to repair the foundation," Abby admitted, "and his cousin to rewire the oldest section of the house."

"Abigail Rowan—"

"Aunt Catherine, I love you, but it's decided. We can't go on like this, and neither can the mansion. Please, it's my home, too. Just this once, let me handle it."

"Let John handle it. Let you handle it. It seems I have little position left in this town, and no authority in this household." Catherine's troubled glance slid from Abby to Rose; then, without another word, she swept imperiously from the room.

Abby sank into her chair as Rose sat down across from her. "She'll get over it, Miss Abigail. It's you I'm worried about. Are you sure you can do this?"

Abby sighed. "I have a little money, but not nearly enough."

Rose stirred two lumps of sugar into her tea. "I've got some bonds put back. I'd be happy to help if you'll let me. Though Miss Catherine and I don't talk about such things, we're close—like sisters, almost. We sure do fight like sisters. And I love this old place. I just can't imagine Abundance without it."

Smiling, Abby reached across the table and gripped Rose's hand. "She couldn't manage without you. And neither can I, and I thank you for your offer. It's more than generous. It's heartwarming, but I'm afraid I can't accept it. I'll find a way to fix this. I just have to."

The Reverend Carmichael was in John's office when Abby arrived an hour later. "You owe it to the community to look into it, Sheriff."

"I am looking into it, Reverend," John replied. "In fact, looking into it is all that I've been doing since Millie Gray's body was found two weeks ago. And as soon as you vacate my office, I will get back to looking into it."

"Perhaps if it was someone other than your sister, you would take this threat to our community a bit more seriously."

"I'm going to try very hard and forget that you said that, Randall. Now, if you don't mind, I have work to do." When the minister made no move to leave, John thrust a finger at the doorway. "Get the hell out!"

The Reverend Carmichael barreled from the room, nearly colliding with Abby in his rush for the exit. Abby watched him go, then turned toward the office and its sole occupant.

"Is this a bad time?" She paused, half in, half out of the room. She felt uneasy about being here, and from John's posture she guessed that he felt it too. There was a coolness in his demeanor, a certain way he held his jaw. He was angry with her, disapproving of the way she was conducting her life, the choices she was making.

That there was no logic behind those choices—no real thought, just emotions, just need—didn't help matters.

He let out a long breath, and some of the stiffness went out of him with it. "You're always welcome here, Abby. You know that. I wish I could say that for everyone, but there are people in this town who seem intent on pushing all of my buttons." He shook his head, reaching for his coffee. It was cold, and it looked more like pond scum than anything palatable, but he took a gulp anyway, grimacing.

"What's wrong with Reverend Carmichael? He seemed upset, and I could have sworn I heard him muttering something about goats when he brushed past me."

John ran a hand over his blond hair. He looked rumpled, and if she was any judge, he hadn't slept. "I suppose you've heard the news?" Then, at her nod, he continued, "Randall seems to think that Julianne and her friends have something to do with this."

"Julianne? You're kidding." Abby sobered. "You're not kidding."

"He thinks the killings are some sort of ritualistic sacrifice—Satanic shit. I'm so pissed, I couldn't grasp it all. But so help me, if he takes this to his pulpit, I'll attend my first service just to knock his goddamned teeth down his throat."

Abby smiled. "Well, I confess, I never liked Randall Carmichael very much. He's a pompous windbag who's overly enamored with the sound of his own voice. He's never seemed irrational, though. Maybe he'll come to his senses and realize how wrong he is."

"He's a lit match, Abby, and I'm sitting on a powder keg. That kind of insane talk could lead to anything. Folks are jumpy. I've already had three people in here this morning demanding that I make an arrest or resign, and it's not even ten o'clock." John picked up his cup, then set it down again. "You didn't come here to discuss Randall Carmichael, so why are you here, Abby? You come down to plead for Monroe's truck? If you did, then you're wasting your time. It's being released this afternoon."

Abby pushed her hands into the pockets of her mole-skin jacket. "Did you find what you were looking for?"

"If you mean, did I find enough evidence to build a case against him, the answer's no. That doesn't mean that I believe he's not mixed up in all of this. I just don't have enough proof to take it to the district attorney."

"Matt isn't a killer," Abby insisted.

"What brings you down here, Abby?"

"I'm here because Aunt Catherine is concerned. Three murders, and two of the victims have been found on the estate."

"Two recent victims, and you can tell Catherine I'm doing all I can."

"John?" someone said from the hallway. "I've got that dirt you asked me to dig up on Matt Mon"—J. T. Langtry faltered when he stuck his head into the room and saw that John wasn't alone—"roe. Maybe I should come back later."

"You really are out of control," she told John; then she rounded on J. T. "Is the paper doing so poorly that you've resorted to digging up gossip?"

"It's back issues of the *Jackson Herald*, Abby. So totally legit that it doesn't even constitute innuendo." J. T. shrugged. "I was just doing a friend a favor. It's some pretty interesting stuff. You really should have a look at it. Not every guy you date's got a murdered girlfriend."

John took the file from J. T., and J. T. couldn't get out of there fast enough. "Erin Louise Thompson, twenty-five, was found murdered in the apartment she shared with fiancé and fellow attorney Matthew W. Monroe. . . ."

He handed the hard copies, printed from microfilm, to Abby. Abby took them. There were two photographs. One was of a beautiful dark-haired young woman with serious dark eyes and a Mona Lisa smile. The other was a photo of Matt getting out of a limo. He had a long-stemmed white rose in his hand, and he was wearing a very expensive suit and dark glasses. His expression was somber, as befitted a man who had just lost the woman he loved. Abby crumpled the papers and dropped them into the wastebasket. "Are you satisfied?" she asked.

John's expression was hard. "Don't expect me to be remorseful. I'm not. You have a right to know."

"Know what?" Abby demanded. "That his life was destroyed?"

"They investigated him, Abby. Oh, for Christ's sake. Wake up!"

"I don't have to listen to any of this!" She stalked from the building, pounding down the steps to where her Jeep was parked. It was a rare autumn day, the sunlight so golden that it gave everything it touched a hint of the surreal. The air was heavy with the intoxicating scent of fallen leaves. Abby had put the ragtop down that morning, intent on wringing whatever pleasure out of a stressful day that she could. When she noticed that the passenger seat was occupied, warmth puddled in the pit of her stomach.

He'd been relaxing, his boots propped negligently on the dash, but when he saw her coming down the steps, he straightened, tipping back his ball cap, tipping down his sunglasses to peer over the top. "Hey, darlin'," he said with a grin. "Nice day for a ride."

"It certainly is," Abby agreed, hopping into the driver's seat, fastening her belt, and turning the key in the ignition. The engine responded immediately. She jerked it into gear, and as they spun out of the gravel parking lot, Matt let go a whoop. "Wohoo! All right! Where we headed, sweet thing?"

"I don't know and I don't care, as long as it's far away from here." Abby reached the edge of town and headed west. She never exceeded the speed limit, but today she didn't give a damn about the rules. She pushed the pedal down and let the heady rush of soft autumn wind take her fury.

Chapter Ten

Abby and Matt spent the afternoon at the Ashokan Reservoir. Nestled among the mountains, the manmade lake provided drinking water for New York City and was roughly the size of Lower Manhattan. By the time they parked the Jeep and walked down to the water's edge, clouds were beginning to gather. Sunlight found its way through the rents in the blue-gray sky, the hazy shafts drawing water vapor, glinting diamond-bright off the dark ripples of the lake.

Matt whistled his appreciation. "My God. This place is almost as pretty as you are."

"Save the flattery, Monroe," Abby said, hugging her arms. There was a bit of a chill coming off the water. Tipping her face up to it, she felt the last of her anger swept away, but nothing could touch the pall left from her latest confrontation with John, or the sobering news of the morning.

"You want to tell Ole Matt what's botherin' you?"

"They found another girl last night. They say she'd been beaten, then strangled, like Shelley."

"Jesus Christ."

"You hadn't heard?"

"I'm not exactly a fan of the mornin' news."

"She was in a shallow grave off Skunk Town Road. It's close to the estate. In fact, Aunt Catherine owns that section of land. Feels like an emerging pattern, doesn't it?"

"Three bodies, one a decade old, doesn't necessarily make a pattern. It's a wooded area, isolated, a logical choice for someone lookin' to discard somethin' and not get caught." Matt was silent for a moment, then casually asked, "That why you were at the police station this mornin'?"

Abby nodded. "Aunt Catherine is understandably upset. I went to John's office to ask if something could be done."

"And you came out pissed," he surmised. "Now, why do I get the feelin' your mood has somethin' to do with me?"

Abby didn't answer, and for a long while they just stood, staring out over the water at the sinister ridges that flanked the lake, the whimsical play of bright sunlight on dark water. "This has always been one of my favorite places," she admitted. "I used to try to bring David down here, and he always resisted. He said he was allergic to fresh air and sunshine, and he had a fear of deep water; his idea of a weekend outing was a drive upstate in an air-conditioned car."

"Sounds like my kind of guy," Matt said, his voice laced with quiet sarcasm.

Abby smiled ruefully. "I thought he was my kind—introspective, gray-at-the-temples sort of distinguished, a man with a keen intellect—but as it turned out, I didn't know him very well at all."

"You never mentioned how he died," Matt said.

"There was a girl, a student at the university. David and I were both on faculty at Sullivan, and Lily was a freshman in my class. She was a pretty girl, very bright, but never very outgoing. Halfway through her first semester, she started missing class. Her grades plummeted. Concerned, I sought her out. When I saw the scrapes and bruises on her face, I knew that something terrible had happened. She was reluctant to discuss it, but I was relentless, and she finally admitted that someone had assaulted her sexually. It wasn't until I blew the lid off the scandal that I discovered that David was responsible for Lily's attack. My own husband. Before I could confront him, he shot himself."

"And you blame yourself," Matt surmised.

Abby turned to face him, and the wind off the water blew a strand of honey-colored hair across her cheek. "What David did to Lily was unforgivable, but I've always known that I was partly responsible. He was my husband. I should have seen it coming. I should have known what he was capable of doing."

"There are dark places in everyone's mind, Abby. Thoughts we can't face in our most truthful moments, let alone admit to. Course, that doesn't kill the guilt, does it? The deep-down gut feelin' that somehow you could have guessed, that if you'd just been payin' attention you could have prevented it."

"I suppose so," she agreed.

"Evil isn't always apparent," he said. "You have to look below the surface to see it."

Abby watched him pick up a few flat stones and bend to skip them over the silvered surface of the lake. He wasn't referring to her, or to David. He was talking about himself, about his fiancée, but he didn't offer any further insight, or volunteer anything, and Abby didn't feel that she had the right to ask. They'd shared a passion, but there were places in Matt's life where she felt she had no right to trespass, lines she dared not cross. Some things were just too personal, too painful, to share with a virtual stranger.

"I suppose you're right," she agreed. "The aftermath is always hardest to face, though I'd certainly like to think this nightmare has an end."

Matt turned to face her. "We talkin' about your husband? Or the fact that they've unearthed another victim?"

Abby shrugged. "Both, I guess. What kind of person does this sort of thing?"

"Statistically speaking, a white male, usually between twenty-five and forty."

Abby laughed, a rueful sound. "That narrows it down to about one quarter of the population of Abundance."

"Yeah, but the white male Sheriff Rhys is looking for has one thing that separates him from the crowd. He doesn't have a conscience. He can take a life, do things that would make a hardened criminal shudder, shake up an entire town, and still sleep like a baby. A sociopath is like a puzzle with one of the pieces missing. He's the mechanic with a wife and four kids who works on your brakes, the grocer's kid brother, the guy down the street . . . or he could be standin' next to you at the shore, skippin' stones across the lake. It's impossible to tell these freaks from anyone else, and that's what makes it so damned chilling. Serial murder is some serious shit. Rhys is over his head with this one, and if he has an ounce of sense, he'll set aside his arrogance and get someone up here from Quantico."

The clouds were closing ranks, crowding out the sunlight, turning the water an ugly greenish-black. Robbed of the golden light, the day lost its charm, and Abby was suddenly chilled. His comments put her on edge, bringing back the unease of the early morning, and as they made the short drive back to Gilead Manor, his words refused to leave her.

John was competent enough as a small-town sheriff, but he didn't have the knowledge or the experience to deal with a serial killer, and he was just bullheaded enough to avoid asking for help from an outsider. Abby feared that it didn't bode well for Abundance anymore than it did for her peace of mind.

It was the kind of night that swallowed up the headlights, driving visibility down to nearly nothing. The cool, damp air created just enough fog to blanket the hollows, drifting low around boulders, concealing the protruding roots of the balm of Gilead trees and mountain laurel scattered near the dump site at Murderer's Falls. The atmosphere couldn't have been any eerier for what Matt had in mind if he'd written it himself.

Crouched behind a fallen log a dozen yards from the spot where he and Abby had discovered Shelley's battered body, Matt listened to the stillness. He chose the first dump site for purely logical reasons. The heat would be on the most recent location. The cops would be more likely to show up in that area, combing the woods for clues. Shelley's death had become old news in light of their most recent discovery.

He knew it, and the killer knew it, too. The guy they were looking for was organized, an expert at covering his tracks. Karl planned every move beforehand. He selected his victims, and he'd scorned opportunistic killers who chose their victims at random as being amateurs, unskilled. Karl was an expert in the art of control, manipulation, murder, but he did have a killing flaw. He couldn't seem to resist the lure of a chance to bask in his own brilliance. That was how he'd gotten charged with the murder of Suzanne Collins, a Jackson secretary and his last known victim. An off-duty police officer had spotted him at the scene, which had aroused his suspicion. A search of Karl's residence had produced enough evidence to net him a spot on Death Row, had Matt not uncovered the fact that the officer involved had been accused of evidence tampering years before.

Karl was a creature of impulse, and he was unspeakably arrogant. His IQ was in the high 150s, but he hadn't been able to resist the urge to return to the scene of his triumph any more than he could resist the compulsion to take a macabre trophy or two. With a killer of Karl's magnitude, compulsion ruled, and Matt could only hope that he made the same mistake tonight.

The luminous dial on his watch said eight-fifteen, but it was dark as midnight, and he felt as though he'd been there all night instead of just an hour and thirty-five minutes. His jeans were wet to the knees from fording the creek on foot, and there was an annoying squishiness in his boots. He'd been so still for so long that an owl had perched on a limb a foot or two above his head and to the left of the path, its beyond-the-grave *who, who, who* lending a faint touch of Hollywood-like cliché to the creepiness of the scene.

"Be damned if I know," Matt muttered, "but it looks like we're about to find out." Sinking lower behind the log, he listened to the scuff of approaching footsteps on the wooded path. A twig snapped under pressure a few dozen yards away, and slowly a slim figure emerged from the mist and the darkness. Dressed in dark clothing and wearing a knit cap, it was armed with a butt-kicking-big metal flashlight. Matt flattened himself on the wet ground as the beam of light skimmed over the log, skirting the clearing behind him, then settling on the tall hemlock that marked Shelley's woodland grave.

Matt tensed as the figure turned; then he struck, launching himself at Shelley's killer. He'd played a little football in high school, but this was without a doubt his best sack ever. In a single, fluid motion, he took the guy down. The air went out of his opponent in a pained grunt; the flashlight went flying, but that was as far as his victory went. His target was too small, too hard to hang on to, impossible to pin. He turned and he twisted as Matt grappled for the gun in his waistband. Slippery as a trout caught with bare hands, he managed to turn just enough to aim the pepper spray.

Matt ducked, but not quickly enough, and a fine misting of the liquid fire caught him squarely in the face. "Aw shit!" Clutching his eyes he staggered back, sitting down abruptly on the log, dragging his muddy sleeve over his streaming eyes and burning cheeks.

"Matt?" Abby said, crouching beside him. "Oh, my God, Matt! Are you all right?"

"Shit no, I'm not all right. You almost fuckin' blinded me."

"I'm sorry," she said. "But you shouldn't have jumped me like that! What was I supposed to do?"

He squinted at her, but she was nothing more than a watery blur. "I don't know, but a simple 'Stand back, I've got pepper spray' might have been nice."

"What are you doing out here, anyway?" she demanded.

"Seems to me that I might ask you the same question." Matt gulped air, assessing the damage. An inch higher and she would have laid him flat. As it was, he wouldn't be able to find his way back to the truck without running into a tree or drowning himself, let alone manage the drive home.

"The same thing you're doing, apparently. I'm staking out the dump site."

"You're tryin' to get yourself killed, you mean," Matt countered. "Do you have any idea the risk you were runnin', comin' out here alone, after nightfall?"

"I can defend myself," she insisted.

"With pepper spray? For Christ's sake, Abby!"

"It worked well enough on you," she said, turning her head to listen. "Did you hear something?"

Matt didn't answer—just jumped up and, grabbing Abby and the light, dove behind the large deadfall.

A few seconds later, a staccato burst of male laughter floated from the same wooded path she'd so recently traversed. Matt put a finger to his lips to silence her. She frowned at him but took the hint and flattened herself beside him.

Another flashlight beam, much smaller, more ineffectual than Abby's—a pen light, Matt decided—preceded the two young men into the clearing.

Abby gripped her flashlight in one white-knuckled hand, the pepper spray in the other. As Matt slipped the sleek 9mm from the waistband of his jeans, she hit them with the bright beam. "Holy shit!" the taller of the two said, putting up his hands to shield his eyes. "Oh, Jesus God, Jamie, he's got a gun! Aw, man, I told you this was a fucking dumb idea!"

"Shut up, man," Jamie whined. "Just shut up! Look, mister. We didn't mean to interrupt you and your girlfriend. It was an accident, honest."

"You boys want to tell me who you are and what you're doin' out here? Oh, yeah, and be careful to keep your hands in plain sight, will you? I'm in the middle of a cryin' jag here, and liable to empty my clip at anything that moves."

"There's no need for that," Jamie said. "Honest. We didn't mean any harm. We just thought we'd come out here and have a look around. This place has been all over the news."

Jamie's companion nodded. "Rancid and Willy bet us a fifth of Jim Beam that Asshole here didn't have the guts. I came with him for proof. We're supposed to take back a piece of the ribbon." He indicated the yellow crime scene ribbon, broken and hanging in streamers from the branches of the hemlock. "You're gonna let us go, aren't you? The prof is gonna bust a fuckin' vein when he finds out."

As if in a bizarre play, a familiar narrow figure chose that precise moment to emerge from the fog. "There you are," William Bentz said to his protégés. "Abigail," Bentz said with a tight-lipped smile. "I'm surprised to find you out here, and in such dangerous company." His glance slid to Matt, to the pistol where it lingered.

"You can put it away now," Abby said. "Matt? You can put the gun away. It's Professor Bentz."

"What are you doin' out here, Professor? And don't tell me you came to stake out the dump site. I'm not about to buy that one twice in one evenin'."

Bentz remained untouched by Matt's sarcasm. "I should think that would be obvious."

"I guess you don't understand the rules. I'm the one with the gun, and I've got a very limited supply of patience. That means you get to humor me."

"If you must know, I came to escort Mr. Potts and Mr. Adams back to their quarters," Bentz said. "Now, if you are through terrorizing my students, we'll vacate the area and allow you to get back to whatever it was you were doing before we arrived. Gentlemen . . ."

Abby edged up to stand beside Matt. "Matt, will you please put it away?"

This time Matt bowed to her request, watching as Bentz turned and followed his charges back into the fog. Then he took her hand. "C'mon, let's get the hell out of here. This place is rapidly becoming a tourist attraction. It's time to use Plan B."

Abby frowned. "Plan B?"

"I'll let you know when I think of it."

Abby was in the morning room when Julianne arrived the next day. She was wearing her lawyer clothes, a smart brown suit of blended silk and a creamy shirt with rounded collar and French cuffs. Abby remembered business casual. She had a closet full of it in storage in the city. She just didn't have a great deal of use for it these days, she thought, glancing down at her faded jeans and NYU sweatshirt. With her hair pulled back in a tail, and only mascara and a touch of gloss, she could have passed for Cinderella a few days before her fairy godmother arrived on the scene.

Abby refolded the loan application she'd requested from Citizens' Bank, and slid it under the empty plate meant for an English muffin. She didn't have much of an appetite and had settled for coffee instead. Julianne pulled her sunglasses down to peer over the top. "Breakfast of champions?"

"Not hungry," Abby replied, taking a sip of her coffee. "And before you comment on my laid-back appearance, I had a late night, and I'm not up to anything more stylish this early."

"Late night, huh?" Julianne said with a smile. "Anyone I know?"

"I'm going to pretend I didn't hear that." She wasn't

in the mood for girl talk, and she wasn't about to share the disastrous events of her evening. She remained convinced that staking out the dump site had been a good idea. It just hadn't yielded the desired results. The killer was still out there, still operating under a cloak of anonymity.

Julianne opened her briefcase and took out a file full of papers. "Well, since you're in an uncommunicative mood, I suppose I have no choice but to have a cup of tea and get down to business. Is Catherine in? I think that she should see this."

Abby took her coffee to the intercom and flipped the switch. "Rose? Have you seen Aunt Catherine? Julianne Rhys is here to see her."

"Seen her?" Rose's voice came through from the kitchen. "As a matter of fact, I spoke to her just before she left for the airport."

Abby's grip tightened on the bone china cup. "Airport? I don't understand. She didn't mention any plans."

"Well, it looks like she's only speakin' to one of us," Rose replied.

Abby squeezed her eyes shut. "Did she happen to mention where she was going?"

"She said she was going to Saint Croix to see Mr. William."

"She went to see my father?"

"Yes, ma'am. Tell Miss Julianne I'll bring her some tea and scones, two sugars, one cream."

"Thank you, Rose," Julianne called out.

Abby turned off the intercom, then refilled her cup from the service on the huge old sideboard and sank into her chair with a sigh. "So," she said as lightly as she could, "what's in the folder?"

"Surveillance photos of the flying orangutan who

absconded with your aunt's money. He came back to New York for his nephew's bar mitzvah."

"Did they get him?"

"They were this close." Julianne held up a finger and thumb an inch apart. "The detective I hired to tail him got caught in a speed trap. By the time the cop finished writing him up, our guy was long gone."

Abby put down her cup. "Shep?"

"Who else?" Julianne wrinkled her nose. "Is that smoke I smell? I've never known Rose to burn the scones."

"Oh, God," Abby said, jumping up and sprinting into the hallway. "Fire! Oh, my God. Mr. Chin?" Smoke poured from a little-used room in the oldest part of the house to lie in black billows near the ceiling. "Mr. Chin?"

Dominic Chin, Seth Bankcroft's cousin, sprayed chemical foam on the flames shooting out around an electrical socket. "It's all right, miss. Everything's under control. There's a short behind this wall. Good thing this happened while I was here. Otherwise, this whole place could have gone up in smoke." He coughed. "I'll just open a few windows, let that smoke out. Then, I'll reroute the wires and tear out that box. Gonna be a big job, but we'll get it fixed up good as new."

Rose chose that moment to appear in the doorway. "Oh, my Lord, what have you done?"

Mr. Chin was nonplussed. "No worry, ma'am. Everything's under control."

"Funny," Rose snorted, darting a glance at the ceiling. "It doesn't look like it's under control." She turned to Abby. "Miss Abigail, there's two men on the front porch with a box full of tools. They say that writer, Matthew Monroe, sent them to install the new security system. You want me to send them away? They say it's paid for."

Julianne grinned. Abby just groaned.

By the time Mr. Chin was finished for the day, the power had been turned off to the oldest, unused part of the house, the security system was up and running, and there was a faint taint of smoke and an eighth of an inch of plaster dust on everything.

It had been a bitch of a day, and it wasn't over yet. Not only had Catherine left Abby to manage the household in her absence, she'd dumped her civic responsibilities directly into Abby's lap. There was an emergency meeting of the town council at the civic center, and Catherine's presence was expected. The Youngbloods had always been involved in the community. As a direct descendant of the town founder, Catherine felt that she had a responsibility to its citizens. And Abby had a responsibility to respect Catherine's wishes, even if they weren't exactly on speaking terms at the moment.

Catherine would get past her anger, her hurt. Abby wasn't as sure that the town could survive the trauma of the murders. The civic center was a converted church on Jeeter Road. Volunteers gathered there every morning to prepare a hot, nutritious meal for the area's homebound elderly, and on Tuesday and Thursday evenings for bingo. Council meetings were held on the third Wednesday of the month, this night being the exception.

When Abby arrived, the parking lot was full, and she saw more than one pickup whose gun rack was bristling with firearms. With the discovery of the most recent victim, Victoria Lane, the alarm had gone out. Ms. Lane, a tourist from Granville, New York, had been staying with friends at The Dutch Treat, a local bed and breakfast. Her disappearance and murder sent a shock wave through the town. The message was clear. No one was safe in Abundance, and with the arrival of Wendy Harkness, a reporter from WKNY News, along with an onlocation crew, there was no hope of containment.

Abby pushed through the crowd and into the building. The meeting was already in progress. Conrad Lindman had the floor. A bluff man with thinning sandy hair and a perpetual tan, Lindman had been the first in a long line of ambitious transplants to buy up local property and capitalize on the town's quaint atmosphere. Five years a resident, and he still wore an air of Los Angeles. "Sheriff, I don't think you realize the seriousness of this situation. September and October are our biggest months. If we shut down, we lose vital revenue, and if we lose revenue, the community loses, too."

"No one is suggesting we close down," Mayor Wilson hurriedly interjected. "Isn't that right, Sheriff? The Pumpkin Fest is a long-standing local tradition, and we will continue on as we always have."

"Sheriff Rhys?" J. T. called from the second row. "Have you considered consulting outside sources to advise you with this investigation, such as the federal authorities?"

"The sheriff's department is doing everything possible to solve these crimes, and I'd like to assure everyone that there is no need for panic," Mayor Wilson replied.

"But don't you agree that three murders in as many weeks calls for unprecedented measures?" J. T. persisted.

"Two incidents. The first unfortunate victim was killed more than a decade ago, and her death is completely unrelated."

"How do you know that?" His voice was unexpected, and it sent a delicious wave of warmth through Abby. She hadn't seen him since the stakeout the night before. She'd half-expected him to follow her home, to ask her in, but he hadn't. He'd made the excuse that he needed to see Stooley about some beer, and then he needed to do some work on the manuscript. Work before sexual gratification? It didn't seem like Matt, and she was beginning to wonder if on some deep level, he wasn't still angry with her for taking the easy way out the last night they were together.

Mayor Wilson shifted uncomfortably, searching the crowd for his questioner. "It's been ten years since Miss Gray disappeared. The odds of the same deviant being responsible are astronomical."

"You're not dealing with an ordinary deviant, Mayor," Matt insisted. "You're dealing with a man on a mission; call it a bizarre hobby. These killings aren't random acts. It's all he thinks about, and though I hate to admit it, the sheriff's right. Why expose your neighbors to that kind of risk? If you're foolish enough to go ahead with a public display, I guarantee your boy will be there. Whether he chooses to strike or not is anybody's guess, but I sure wouldn't want to chance it."

Shep Margolis stepped up to the microphone, crowding Mayor Wilson out. "Maybe you know so much about this 'cause you're the one we're lookin' for."

"That an accusation?" Matt asked. " 'Cause it sounds like slander to me."

Mayor Wilson covered the microphone with one hand, the resulting discordant screech drowning out his comments to the deputy. His smile when he turned back was oily and self-serving. "With all due respect, Mr. Monroe, you're here on a temporary basis, and though we certainly value your input, in a month or two you'll be gone, and we'll still be here. Abundance isn't a large metropolis. Our tax base isn't wealthy. Miss Youngblood, if you please?"

He waved Abby to the front, but nothing she could say lessened the confusion. "I agree with what Matt and Sheriff Rhys had to say. The Pumpkin Fest *is* a long-standing tradition, one which my family has always sponsored and participated in, but no amount of monetary gain is worth risking the safety of the citizens as a whole."

"There won't be any risk," the mayor quickly interjected. "I intend to see to it personally that every safety precaution is taken, including extra security. Folks, be sure and see Gerry Addler to purchase your tickets for the haunted hayride, on sale after the meeting," the mayor said, then flicked off the microphone.

The meeting was over.

As the crowd dispersed, Abby moved toward Matt. She intended to thank him for lending his voice to the proceedings. He was near the back of the room, deep in conversation with J. T. At the same time that Abby approached, a curvaceous brunette paused to smile up at him. As Abby watched, the young woman leaned in to kiss his cheek, her breasts conveniently pressing against his arm. She said something, and he laughed, gently squeezing her shoulder.

Abby didn't need to see more. Feeling a little sick, and angry at herself for her reaction, she changed directions, following the flow of the crowd into the night, away from the confusing rush of emotions threatening to overwhelm her.

How very adult, Abby, she thought. She had no room in her life for jealousy. It wasn't as if he were seeing her exclusively. They weren't even dating, officially. In fact, they weren't officially anything, and that was precisely what she had wanted. What she had insisted upon.

No expectations, no strings.

It worked for her.

And it was obvious that it worked for him.

She pushed past the entrance and the crowd fanned out, heading in small knots of two, three, or more to cars and pickup trucks. Abby's Jeep was in the third row, under the dusk-to-dawn light. She opened the door, and found a small package waiting on the driver's seat. She picked it up. The size and shape of a jeweler's box, it was wrapped in gold foil and topped with a snow-white bow.

What kind of man brought one woman to a council meeting, and another a gift? Abby snorted. Matt did. When she thought about him and the leggy brunette, it took every ounce of willpower she had to keep from throwing the box out the window. But, she unwrapped the paper and opened it instead.

One gold, bow-shaped earring lay on a bed of black velvet. The diamond chip in the center mount winked a cool, brilliant blue in the watery glow of the overhead street lamp. Staring down at it, Abby frowned. One earring? It was an odd gift to give someone, even for Matt—unless, of course, he had the other and expected something for it in return.

The brunette emerged from the building, followed by J. T. and Matt, who chose that moment to glance up. Their gazes locked across the gravel parking lot. He started toward her, but the last thing Abby wanted in that moment was any attempt at conversation. Placing the box on the passenger seat, she climbed behind the wheel and started the Jeep. Matt broke into a trot. "Abby! Damn it, Abby, wait!"

She left him standing in the dust of her rapid depar-ture, his hand in the air as though he could call her back. And then there was nothing but the dim red glow of her taillights and the warm jet black of the rural night.

Matt balled his raised hand into a fist, and slowly let it fall back to his side as the Jeep taillights shrank to a dot of red in the night, then winked out altogether when she topped a distant knoll and dropped over the other side. "You're losin' your touch, Matthew," Wendy Harkness quietly observed from beside him. "I don't think Girlfriend was interested." Her perfectly practiced diction had melted away the moment she'd spoken to him, and her honeyed voice was heavy with the inflections of her native southern Alabama. Except for the accent, Wendy Harkness, anchorwoman for WKNY News, bore only a faint resemblance to the Willetta Mullins Matt had known in college. At some point during his senior year, they'd shared a brief one-nighter, then parted friends. They'd always shared common ground. When they'd met, Willetta had been just as hungry, just as ambitious as he. She'd have stopped at nothing to kick free of the memories of six kids squeezed into that tar-papered shack and the kiss of her old man's fist when he came home drunk, which was almost every night.

"She's interested, all right," Matt said, "but she fights it harder than anyone I've ever seen—even me."

Wendy smiled. "Still a heartbreaker, aren't you?"

"Shit, who you tryin' to kid? You don't have a heart any more than I do."

Wendy laughed. "Yes, and it's a damn sight safer that way. Now, how about that on-camera interview?"

Matt was so damned steeped in thoughts of Abby that he barely heard the question. He was going after her. With any luck, he'd catch her before she had a chance to barricade herself inside that fortress she called home. "Some other time, darlin'. I need to see a Yankee woman about a Mississippi hound, and I'm afraid it just can't wait. See you 'round."

Jeeter Road intersected Osgood Dean Lane and Route 375 to Hurley. Little more than a one-track tar-and-chip road, it received little to no maintenance by township or state crews, and it closed to traffic each winter. Abby usually avoided Jeeter Road. Cutting through a deep, tree-shaded hollow, the road was lonely and unpopulated, but it would slash five minutes from her drive back to the mansion, and tonight that seemed extremely important.

Half-expecting headlights from Matt's pickup to appear in her rearview mirror, she glanced up often, but the road remained black as a stagnant pond ahead and behind. A hint of the warmth from the previous afternoon continued to linger. She'd replaced the ragtop, but the window was down. She had just passed Devil's Rock, an outcropping of stone that slightly over-hung the road, when a gust of night air came rushing in, carrying with it a sound the likes of which she'd never heard. Following the path of the noise, Abby looked to the left, and at the same time, a large buck sprang from the road bank, launching itself directly into the path of the Jeep.

With a startled scream, Abby whipped the wheel to the right, onto the berm, but the shoulder was soft and she lost control. Everything happened so fast. She braked frantically, and the Jeep went into a skid, careen-ing down a shallow embankment, plummeting up and over, and coming to rest astride a fallen log.

Too shaken to do more than rest her forehead on

the cool leather grip of the steering wheel, Abby closed her eyes, wondering if her heart would ever calm its furious pounding, or if it would simply stop. Slowly, by small and nearly immeasurable degrees, she regained her equilibrium and leaned out the window to assess the damage.

The trunk of the tree was just large enough to prevent the two front wheels from touching the ground. The Jeep wasn't equipped with a winch, and even with four-wheel drive, she wouldn't be able to budge it. Unbuckling her seatbelt, Abby plucked her purse from the floor and dug through it for her cell phone. She turned it on, and the screen lit up, with the words *"No Service"* prominently displayed.

Abby switched it off in disgust. The hollow was too deep, the sides of the cleft too steep to maintain a signal. There was nothing else left for it. She climbed carefully out of the stranded vehicle and started to walk. She was so shaken that just reaching the road took several minutes. Her muscles quivered, her legs almost refusing to support her. She clambered up the steep embankment and onto the road, marveling at the totality of the night.

She'd never realized before that black was not just black. The state of lightlessness was graduated. The sky overhead was studded with pinpoint stars and seemed rich and deep and three-dimensional, like velvet, but it was not the same deep shade as the forest that flanked both sides of the road. Even the lightless track Abby followed was its own shade of bleak, and after a few times of bumbling into potholes, she quickly learned to distinguish the darker holes from the dark road.

She concentrated so fully that she wasn't sure when she first noticed the noise. For a while, it seemed to teeter at the very edge of her consciousness, or perhaps it was simply that she did not want to hear it. Acknowledging the deep rustle of the underbrush a few yards from the road's edge would make it more real, infinitely more frightening. Yet after a few minutes, Abby could no longer ignore it.

As she continued to walk, it dragged a bit behind, growing louder, more determined. The hair rose on her forearms, and the skin at her nape crawled. Abby stopped, facing the noise, trying to determine if it was animal in origin, or human. "Who's there?" she asked. A human voice usually gave an animal pause—even a predatory animal, and there were plenty of those in the area, though attacks were so rare as to be almost nonexistent. "Is someone there?"

The noise stopped, and she had the queer impression that whatever lay hidden in the underbrush was listening even as she listened. She took a step, then two, and the dry leaves crackled, twigs snapping, the sound of heavy breathing. Whatever it was, it was following her, struggling to keep pace with her, step by step, yard by yard. A frisson of fear so acute that it blocked rational thought shot through Abby. Terrified, she broke into a run, hearing a thin animal wail rising behind her. Inhuman and horrible, it was soon blocked out by the thunder of her heart in her ears, and the rumble of an approaching vehicle. As the pale-green glow of the halogen running lights topped the rise behind her, Abby turned, holding up her hands in desperation. A second later, Matt pulled up beside her, and she opened the truck door and threw herself into the cab.

"Jesus, Abby, what the hell happened?"

"I'll explain later," she said shakily. "Just go. Matt, please. I want—to go home."

"All right. All right. Calm down. I'll take you."

As the truck taillights faded to a dim red glow, the

underbrush rattled heavily again, and a young woman, battered and beaten and so bloody that she hardly looked human, crawled to the edge of the bank and rolled into the ditch. It had been a freaking miracle that she'd managed to escape him, that she'd pried the ligature loose from her neck and crawled away into the woods, but that was where her good luck had ended.

Someone had been in the road; Beth wasn't sure who, but help had been so close, and she couldn't speak, couldn't swallow, could barely breathe. She'd tried to follow. She hoped that J. T. would figure that out.

For the first time in her life, she'd really tried.

And when her salvation had started to run, the pitiful wailing sound that she'd made, the only sound her bruised larynx would allow, had terrified even her.

The sound of hopelessness.

The purr of the truck engine had faded, but someone else was approaching from the opposite direction. Beth lifted her head as the headlights came into view. The vehicle stopped. The driver's door opened. And as his crepe-soled work boots came into view and she clawed at the dirt, silent, agonizing tears congealed in Beth's ruined throat.

Chapter Eleven

"You want to clue me in on what happened back there?"

They were sitting in the truck outside the mansion. Abby had insisted on returning home despite the fact that Catherine was away, and she would be there all alone despite Matt's suggestion that a night at the carriage house would do her raw nerves a world of good. It wouldn't accomplish anything to try and explain to him that she couldn't allow herself to cave in to the fear that was gripping the town, that she couldn't bow to the hysteria. It was a matter of pride, of strength, of proving to herself that she was perfectly capable of standing alone. He would never understand her motives.

Abby shrugged, making an effort to keep her tone light. "A deer jumped off the bank, and I swerved to miss it. When my right front tire hit the shoulder, it started to slide, and I couldn't stop it."

"You didn't clip the deer?" Matt asked.

She shook her head. "He was really moving. I guess he was as freaked by the noise as I was."

"Noise? What noise?"

It echoed in her mind in that moment, like the tormented bellow of something in terrible pain, hoarse and unearthly.

Abby shuddered. She couldn't help it.

"It was unlike anything I've ever heard," she said. "It came from high on the bank, in the thick underbrush. When I turned to look, the deer jumped into my path, and the rest, as the cliché goes, is history. I tried my cell phone, but I couldn't get a signal in so remote an area, so I got out of the Jeep and made my way back to the road."

Matt didn't miss much, and the fact that she was holding something back came clearly through. "That's not all, is it? There's more."

She hesitated, clutching her keys, as though she needed to hang onto something. For a fleeting instant, Matt considered asking her to hang on to him, thought about assuring her that she could depend on him to be there, to be strong; and then the moment was gone, the opportunity lost. "I know it sounds crazy, but I think it was following me, or trying to." She laughed a shaky laugh. "This conversation is beginning to sound like the ramblings of a madwoman. Anyway, I don't think I've ever been so glad to see anyone as I was to see you. It almost makes up for the earring."

"Earring? What earring?"

"The earring you left in the Jeep. I suppose you have the other one?" Then, when he didn't answer: "It was in a jeweler's box, wrapped in gold paper with a white bow. I found it on my seat where you left it. Come on, Matt, this isn't funny."

"I'm not laughin'," Matt told her. "Baby, I didn't go anywhere near your Jeep tonight. In fact, I didn't even know you were at the meeting until the mayor called you to the microphone."

"But if you didn't leave it there, then who did?" A vertical line materialized between her straight brown brows, a clear indication of her upset.

Matt's stomach clenched. "I don't know. I suppose it could be some sort of joke." He reached out, tracing that worry line with his thumb, easing it away. "You really should try and get some rest. Why don't you change your mind and come on home with me. I'll fix you a nice hot cup of tea and take my time puttin' you to bed. In fact, if you like, we can take turns. I'll tuck you in; then you can tuck me in; then . . ."

"I think I get the idea," Abby said. "But I have to decline. I need to be here. Thanks again."

"No problem. If you hear anything even remotely weird, or you change your mind, just call." Matt thought she'd lean in and kiss him, but she didn't. She just slid off the seat, closing the truck door and turning to climb the steps to the porch. He waited until she'd unlocked the door and disappeared inside before he went home.

On nights like this one he hated being alone. Maybe he should give Willetta a call and invite her to come by and reminisce over a couple of cold ones. Then, almost as soon as the thought occurred, he dismissed it. It wasn't Willetta he wanted, not Willetta he needed. It wasn't Willetta who was constantly in his thoughts.

Matt flicked on the lights and went into the kitchen. On his way past the fridge, he grabbed a beer, then picked up the phone. He didn't bother with Jimmy Liebowitz's office. The detective was never in this late in the evening, but Matt had his cell phone number.

On the third ring someone picked up. "Liebowitz."

242 *S. K. McClafferty*

"Jimmy? It's Matt Monroe. What'dya have for me?"

"Hey, Matt. How's the book comin'?"

"Book?" Matt snorted. "What book?"

"Don't kid a kidder. You're probably finished already."

"Shit. Don't I wish. I'm pretty much stalled." Matt took a large swallow from the long-necked bottle. "You dig up anything on Karl Jensen?"

"Actually, your timing's impeccable. This just came in an hour ago. There's no way Karl can be your man. Turns out the dirtbag was arrested in Montreal two months ago—attempted murder. For once, his good time got away, and get this, she's the niece of the freakin' prime minister. U.S. authorities are itchin' to extradite, but the Canadians aren't givin' him up, and they can't agree to terms, so for now he's stuck." There was a crackle, and a pause. "Matt? You still there? Ah, these damn cell phones."

"I'm here," Matt replied. "Listen, you sure about this?"

"Positive. He was carryin' an American Express card with his freakin' name on it, and the photo they faxed down matches the one you gave me." Jimmy chuckled, and the chuckle ended in a two-pack-a-day death rattle. "American Express," he said, once he could breathe again. "Get it? Guess he should have left home without it."

"Thanks, Jim. I owe you one." Matt hung up the phone, his theory about Karl operating in Abundance blown to hell and back. If Karl Jensen had been in a Canadian jail for the past two months, then he couldn't be responsible for any of the killings, and he wasn't targeting Abby.

But if it wasn't Karl, then what the hell was going on? Who'd killed Shelley? And who put her belongings in his truck? Then there was the attempted break-in at Gilead Manor and the murder of the jogger. Then, tonight, someone had left Abby a present, a single earring, gift-wrapped, in her Jeep. But was it a gift? Or was it a trophy? A bid for attention by a very warped individual?

Matt shook off the thoughts, but he couldn't quite shake the residual feeling of disquiet brought on by the phone call to Jimmy.

The whole damned situation left him feeling unsettled. He couldn't sit still, and being inside just made him feel trapped. Even worse, Abby's rejection had left him with a sense of vulnerability that was strange and unwelcome.

He'd always been able to maintain at least a sham control over his relationships with women in the past. There had been a few who'd been a good time and little else, a handful who'd expected a damn sight more than he'd ever intended to give and who'd been disappointed when they didn't get it, and one or two who just got off on being seen around town with a celebrity. But blondes, brunettes, and redheads, sophisticates and barfly-waitress types, no one had ever messed with his head or played his emotions like this one keyed-up, highbrow, out-of-work history professor.

She took playing hard to get to new, unthought-of levels. She was a complete puzzle, a paradox, sexy but anal, aggressive yet resistant. She liked being with him, but she wasn't about to admit it—not even to herself. She wanted him, but she fought her baser urges until there was no fight left in her. In a moment of weakness, she would come to him, but Matt didn't know whether he liked being her vice, her bad habit. It had occurred to him more than once that he could put his time to better use, that there were women out there who were every bit as fascinating, every bit as intriguing, and far more willing, if only he could stop obsessing about Abby long enough to let them find him.

Disgusted with her and with himself, he went out onto the porch and, leaning against the support post, lit a cigarette. "You're wastin' your time, Monroe," he told himself. "She didn't exactly leap at the chance to spend the night with you, even in a purely platonic, protective sort of fashion."

He drew the smoke in, then released it on a low, irony-filled laugh. Who the fuck was he trying to kid? They weren't capable of anything that was even remotely platonic, and that was a large part of the problem. And this emotional tug-of-war was wearing on him.

She seemed to want time for things to cool off. Well, maybe she was right. Getting the brush-off was just as bad as lying awake thinking about her. If it were a toss-up, he didn't know which one he'd choose. One last glance across the leaf-scattered lawn, and Matt turned and went inside, closing the door on the real world. If he couldn't have what he wanted, there was always the manuscript.

Yet as midnight came, his resolve began to wear thin. He'd made good progress through the late evening hours, but the writing had left him strangely dissatisfied, and that dissatisfaction was a gnawing hunger deep inside him, in a place he couldn't even name.

Darkness didn't help.

Everything got worse after dark: colds, flu, the craving for a cigarette . . . loneliness.

He shook his head, then shook another smoke out of his battered pack. He'd quit once the book was finished, for real this time. *Loneliness?* he thought, wandering back outside. Now, where the hell had that come from?

He didn't have time to analyze it. He was too distracted by a blur of movement in the shadows of the mansion. Matt tensed, cigarette poised in midair. . . . Then, as the shadowy figure took on feminine proportions, he dropped it on the step and crushed it beneath the toe of his boot.

She took her time about crossing the lawn, and he wondered idly if she was suffering under the oppressive weight of the same impulses with which he'd battled throughout the evening. Wanting him, knowing that she shouldn't, fearing it would only lead to disappointment in the end.

They were so different that it was downright scary. She was coolly analytical; he was impulsive. She thought, pondered, weighed her options; he reacted. Their only claim to common ground was this burning desire he couldn't quite fathom and couldn't seem to fight.

Coming out of nowhere, it had hit him squarely between the eyes and knocked his world for a loop. He tried to resist its magnetic pull, but it was impossible. The more he tried to stay away from her, the deeper and more intense the craving for just one kiss, one word, one look. He couldn't sleep, and though he chain-smoked, tobacco was a poor substitute for what he really wanted.

Needed. He needed her, and it occurred to him as he watched the sheer, pale-green gown billow out around her long, shapely legs, that if he could only be certain she felt the same way, his world, his life, would take on the iridescent sheen of near perfection.

Heart lodged just below his Adam's apple, Matt watched her progress across the lawn. He'd failed to turn on the porch light, but a mellow glow filtered through the living room windows. She paused in the halo of it, her face and hair and throat bathed in gold, her small breasts and perfectly slim silhouette visible beneath the filmy fabric.

Matt held his breath as the silence played out between them.

"I changed my mind," she said softly.

"I know," he replied, resisting the urge to reach for her, to open his arms. Tense, he waited, holding back as she came to him, fitting her body against his, taking his face in her hands . . . kissing him deeply.

His tension surprised Abby, but it didn't stop her. The only thing that mattered in this moment was Matt. Matt's hands on her body, insistent, demanding, edging up the pale-green silk of her gown, sliding his hands inside her panties. It felt good, welcome, exciting, but it wasn't enough.

She wanted him. She wanted all of him.

She ran her hands down over his shoulders and chest, down to the waistband of his jeans. She would have freed him right there on the porch if he hadn't caught her hands in his. "Not here," he said, then dipping slightly, he caught her and lifted her into his arms.

Matt kicked the door closed and hit the light switch with one shoulder. Maybe she could lose herself more easily in the darkness, he thought. Maybe if the moment was right, if everything was perfect, she would forget her reservations and stay the night.

It was what he wanted more than anything, to hold Abby through the night, to know even in sleep that she was close and safe, to wake to her kisses instead of waking alone.

His bedroom was shadowy and intimate. The curtains were drawn, and the skylight overhead showed the slow dissipation of the clouds, the gradual emergence of the thin sliver of the crescent moon, her heavenly crown a spreading circlet of glistening stars. Pausing beside the bed, Matt took Abby's mouth in a long and leisurely kiss and, releasing the arm that supported her legs, he let her body slide slowly down the length of him.

Reaching up, she caressed his stubbled cheek, breaking the kiss and pulling back just long enough to look into his eyes. "I shouldn't be here," she said softly, her tone bemused, sexy. "Why can't I stay away?"

"Why do you want to?" Matt asked.

"Because it's not logical," she told him, but he was certain she was only trying to convince herself. "It's impulsive, and it makes no sense—I'm never impulsive."

"Your body, your heart, your mind—they're all tryin' to tell you somethin'. Why won't you listen?"

"I can't listen. My blood rushes so hard in my ears, I can't hear a thing." She leaned into him, her hands seeking out the waistband of his jeans. She had loosened the metal button from its mooring in the darkness of the porch. Now she slowly edged the zipper down. Then, with his hunger revealed to her, she unbuttoned his shirt and, bending close, kissed the place on the curve of his throat where his pulse hammered out a heavy beat.

She had to know how she excited him.

She had to know that if she left him now, he would break into a million needy little pieces. It was his greatest fear, and he hated her for it. He hated that she could have him any time, any place, any way she liked, but he couldn't have her, couldn't hold her, couldn't touch her—not the same way she touched him.

She didn't leave, though. She just kissed him while tracing her fingertips over his skin, a feathery touch, teasing, light, so provocative. Matt's pulse was heavy and slow. Christ, he wanted her, but she wasn't about to negotiate or compromise. She wanted to be with him, but only on her terms, and he was starting to realize that her terms had too many variables. Grasping her hands, he held them still between them. "Why'd you come here, Abby? For once, just level with me. What do you want from me?"

"Just you," she replied. "Nothing else, nothing more. No expectations, no strings, remember?"

"I remember. You remind me so often. How the hell could I forget?" Still holding her hands, he urged her back onto the midnight blue velvet coverlet and, planting one knee beside her, leaned in to tease the sensitive skin of her throat. "You want me," he said. "But how do you want me? You want me submissive, pliant, aggressive?" He pinned her hands between them, kissing her roughly, then pulling back the smallest bit, far enough to look into her eyes. "Or maybe you'd like me to make love to you like I mean it, then you can get up and walk away?"

"You're angry."

"Not angry," he countered. "I'm just tired of playin' this game." Matt wouldn't have thought it possible that he would turn down sex with no expectations whatever. Instant gratification, slam, bam, see-you-later kind of ecstasy, forfeited for the sake of his wounded masculine pride. Yet somehow, he sensed that he was about to, and even while his libido screamed that he'd better think twice before acting rashly, he plunged right on ahead, like a bull crashing through a crab apple thicket, heedless of the thorns. "This good for you, baby?" he asked, sliding a hand down to cup the source of her heat, his voice soft and low. "Or was there somethin' else you had in mind?"

"You *are* angry," she accused. "I thought you wanted what I wanted. I thought we could keep it simple."

"What you mean is that you thought I'd service you. Good old Matt, always ready for a quick, hard fuck, that right? Libido in overdrive? Just pay me a visit. Hell, you don't even need to make an appointment. I take walk-ins. And before I can light up that post-sex cigarette, you'll be back home at the mansion, showerin' away the memory. Thanks for the offer, sweet thing, but tonight I'm just not in the mood. Why don't you try again tomorrow—that is, if you don't have anything better to do?"

She had the grace to look stricken, and Matt could see the deep flush that flooded her face even in the dimly lit room. He wished to Christ that she would hit him. He would have preferred the shock of a slap in the face to this absolute certainty that he had just reverted to the lowest life form on the planet—to the slow, uncomfortable burn of the frustrated pride that wouldn't allow him to apologize or to take back any portion of what he'd said. To his credit, he released her and stood. "C'mon," he said softly. "I'll walk you home."

But Abby didn't wait for him. She ran from the room and across the yard before he could stop her, not slowing until the front door at Gilead Manor had slammed shut. Matt stood on the carriage house porch for a long time, staring in her wake; then with a defeated sigh, he went inside for his keys.

It was Friday night, and Stooley's Roadhouse was jumping. Saturday night was the night for the dance band, when couples young and old poured in to drink and dance, but Friday nights drew a whole different kind of crowd.

The young county bucks, their pockets full of quarters

for the jukebox and their wallets full of bills, would be looking for excitement, along with the usual truck drivers and a handful of iron workers home from the jobs in the city, and a biker or two. Shep gave the parking lot the once-over, then went inside for a Coke. If there was gonna be trouble, it was certain to happen at Stooley's on a Friday night.

The earsplitting thump of the jukebox was overridden by conversation and drunken laughter, and occasionally punctuated by the ring of a ball striking pins, and resounding cheers somewhere in the back. Shep looked around, sidling up to the bar. "Coke," he told Stooley, "no ice."

"You here to hang out, Shep? Or just to wet your whistle?"

"Man's got a right to buy a Coke," Shep said. "Besides, it's time for my break."

"Then you'll be leavin'? That's good, cause you bein' here's bad for business."

Shep lowered his head slightly. "You remember who broke up that fight Friday a week ago?"

Stooley planted a hand on her hip, the dish towel she gripped dangling, and gave him the same hostile stare. "You can bet I remember who started it."

Shep snorted, but he gathered his can of Coke and his glass and headed for a table. "I see there's a piece of land for sale right near here. Got a mind to use my IRA to start a little place, somethin' like this one only classier. Now, that would really be bad for business."

"Go on and do it. I'm not worried. You'd be shut down within a month. What? You didn't hear? We took a vote while your back was turned, and you won. You're the most hated man in this county."

Shep was about to put down his glass on an empty table when he saw Matt Monroe at the far end of the bar and abruptly changed directions. Luck was on Shep's side. The stool next to Monroe's was empty. Halfway there, he bumped into William Bentz. Stooley had pulled the tab on the Coke can, so that when they collided, the soda splashed out onto the professor's black wingtip shoes. Shep pretended not to notice. He didn't like Bentz much.

"Professor," Shep said. "I sure hope you drive better'n you walk."

Bentz ran a clean white handkerchief over his wing-tips, sopping up Shep's offending dribbles. "Deputy Margolis." He flicked a chilly glance at Shep from behind thick glasses.

"You send those college boys home?" Shep persisted. "We got us a maniac runnin' around in case you haven't heard, and if you keep 'em here, you do it at your own risk." The professor straightened and walked crisply out, not bothering to answer Shep's comments. "High-falutin' educated city-bred asshole," Shep muttered, sliding onto the stool beside Matt.

"There anybody around here you *do* like, Deputy?" Matt wondered, signaling Stooley to set him up again— two shots of Glenlivet whisky and an ice-cold beer.

Shep bent the pull tab back to a forty-five degree angle and filled his glass to within an eighth of an inch of its rim. "A few, but you can bet you ain't on that particular list."

"Sounds like an exclusive club," Matt said, downing his whiskey and chasing it with the Coors. "I don't do so well with exclusive."

"Trouble in paradise?" Shep sipped his soda, then chuckled. "Can't say as I'm surprised. The Youngbloods are quality folk. Been here as long as this town has. Figured she'd see through you sooner or later. Can't help bein' curious, though. What'd you do, boy? She catch you cheatin', or she finally figure out what you really are and run for her freakin' life?"

"What I am?" Matt repeated. "And what might that be?" He could feel it coming. He'd been downing whiskey shooters for half an hour, and the booze was just starting to kick in. He had a pleasant burn in his gut, and his temper was hanging by a thread. Shep Margolis would be all it took to push him over the edge.

Margolis toyed with his glass, widening the condensation ring on the counter as he twirled the glass in slow, methodical quarter-circles. "Why, a lady-killer, of course. The genuine kind." He swung his head around to face Matt, grinning under his dark glasses. "How many you do so far? Countin' your fiancée?"

With his evening in tatters and nothing to lose, Matt brought back his fist. He caught Margolis in the mouth, knocking him right off his stool and onto his ass, splitting his lip and loosening his gold tooth. The whole bar went still as Shep reached for his pistol. "Go on. Say you're not gonna come along peacefully. I need somethin' good to cap off my week, and drilling a hole in you too big to plug would pretty much do it for me."

J. T. Langtry entered the bar as Shep led Matt out in handcuffs. J. T. watched them go out, then turned to Stooley with a questioning look. Stooley shrugged, wiping out glasses and putting them back in the overhead racks. "He hit Shep. Right in the mouth. Knocked him clean off his stool. He's in a lot of trouble right now, but the next time he comes in, the house will stand him a round. I've wanted to see somebody do that for as long as I can remember."

"Guess I'd better call Julianne and tip her off. Looks

like he's going to need counsel." J. T. reached in his coat pocket and retrieved his cell phone. "Madeleine, has Beth been around?"

"Your sister?" Stooley considered the question, then shook her head. "Can't say that I've seen her in a couple of days. Listen, J. T. If he needs bail, you tell Julianne to let me know. We'll take up a collection."

No one understood the complexity of what was currently happening in Abundance. No one seemed capable of looking beyond the boundaries of their pathetic little lives long enough to see that he was close to ending one phase and beginning another. It had all begun years before with Millie Gray.

He'd been inexperienced then, a novice in the art of killing. Millie, a chance encounter in a young man's life, had been his first taste of true power, and the experience had so thoroughly frightened him that he'd convinced himself that it was a single occurrence, an accident, a fluke. Frightened, yes, and fascinated him, too. He hadn't been able to forget about Millie. Though her flesh was fodder for the worms, she'd lived on in his thoughts, and she'd died many times since that long-ago death.

In the deepest, most profound part of his being, he'd held a freeze-frame picture of her terrified face. He'd remembered and marveled at the sound her breath made when it left her body that last time, like the air escaping a bicycle tire suddenly gone flat, and how the light had bled out of her eyes. And as an interested observer, his most profound regret was that Millie's life had ended so precipitously.

By the third anniversary of her death, the compulsion had become too strong to ignore. Hundreds of miles from Abundance, at a small private college in Virginia, a nineteen-year-old coed disappeared. He took his time with Melba Duggan, a pretty little blonde with a space between her teeth, and he learned a great deal from the experience.

The ease of Melba's abduction and death gave him wings, a strange sense of purpose, a renewed infatuation with death and dying. During the daylight hours, he studied the art of deception. He found the perfect guise in the straitlaced student, an ordinary young man. At night, he expanded his knowledge, honed his methods, experimented to his heart's content.

After a few successes, the fear of discovery lessened. He had a talent for invisibility that few could claim, and his instincts for avoiding detection were somewhat extreme. He instinctively knew when it was time to move on. And he owed it all to Millie Gray.

Millie had taught him about life and death. But it was a chance encounter with Dr. Abigail Youngblood who'd inspired his greatest triumph, his return to Abundance. His homecoming was a tribute to Millie Gray and to the town that had revealed to him his life's mission.

A single light burned at Gilead Manor. A slim feminine shadow passed by the curtained second-story window. Abigail was awake. Did she know he was watching, waiting, biding his time until the perfect moment arrived? Her moment.

Abby was different from the others. She was more than just a victim. She was his crowning achievement, the perfect adversary. But would she play the game, or would she forfeit? As he watched, the light winked out. He'd have to bide his time, wait and see. Patience and observance, he knew, were the keys to victory.

The dark-haired bitch had almost gotten away tonight. When he discovered Abby's Jeep in the ravine, he had been aware of just how close he had come to losing out. It should have given him pause, made him pull back from his plan. Yet curiously, it didn't, almost didn't count when the game was murder, did it?

Chapter Twelve

There were forty-eight ceiling tiles in the six-by-eight cell. Matt had counted them two dozen times in the past hour, and he knew every speck of fly shit, every water stain, every dimple by heart. He knew by now the sound of Shep Margolis's footsteps, since the deputy stopped by the holding cells to gloat every few minutes. Margolis had a carefully measured tread, but there was no fluidity to his movements. He set his foot down with almost military precision, and Matt surmised that Margolis had either been in the army or had a burning, unfulfilled desire to be.

Rhys walked more quietly, but he was stressed—wired, almost. As if he was constantly working off a caffeine overload or, like Matt, badly needed a cigarette. It showed in his pacing, in the strain in his voice as he argued with his sister, Julianne, over her "star client." A few minutes later, Rhys turned the key in the lock and opened the door to the cell. "He's all yours," the sheriff growled, "but if I were you I'd get myself a better class of client."

"I could say the same about your deputy," Julianne shot back.

Rhys glowered at Matt as he retrieved his belongings, all but strangling his coffee cup as Matt followed his high-heeled, trench-coated attorney to the door. "You might want to add a jigger of Jim Beam to that cup," Matt offered. "It'll help take the edge off those caffeine jitters. Oh, yeah, and just for the record, if you want to stop this bloodbath, you'll look for outside help. The resources you've got ain't gonna cut it." He glanced at Shep, who scowled at him over an ice bag.

Rhys downed the dregs of his coffee and, grimacing, crushed the cup, tossing it in the waste-paper basket. "Just stay the hell out of my way, Monroe. Give me cause to arrest you again and I'll bury you so damn deep, it'll take a backhoe to dig you out."

Julianne's car was in front of the station. "If you can drop me off at Stooley's, I'd appreciate it," Matt told her.

Julianne faced him over the hood of her classic red-and-white Thunderbird. "What do you suppose your blood alcohol level is right now? Or the likelihood of Shep picking you up for a DUI if you even think about getting behind the wheel tonight?" She paused to take a deep breath. "Why don't you give me your keys? I'll drop you off at home, and J. T. and I will bring your truck by in the morning."

Matt handed her the keys. "You doin' anything later tonight? Want to get married?"

She gave him an arch, jaded look that must have been part of her legal repertoire. "Aren't you asking the wrong woman that question?"

He made a noise that conveyed his disgust—with himself, with Abby, with the whole situation.

She let him slide into the passenger seat before she hit him with the full barrage. "Is that what this was about? You had a fight with Abby and decided it would be a wise move to self-destruct by getting shit-faced and punching the most belligerent man to ever hide behind a badge?"

"Self-destruction's somethin' of a hobby of mine," Matt replied. "I guess you could say it's what I do." His head was starting to throb, and he wasn't in the mood for a lecture, but that didn't stop Julianne.

"Well, maybe you should rethink your options. Everyone knows what a loose canon Shep is, but quite frankly, so are you. Get a grip, Matt. Take up sky-diving if you want chills and thrills, or better yet, just stay home and write."

"Thanks for the counseling session. Is there a separate fee for that? Or is it part of the package?"

"For you, it's on the house." She let him out in front of the carriage house. "Do me a favor, will you? Call Abby and try to straighten things out between you."

Matt waved her off, then slowly mounted the steps and went inside.

Calling Abby to straighten things out was completely out of the question. What ailed their relationship couldn't be fixed. He'd sprawled on the sofa after Julianne left, unable to return to the bedroom without seeing Abby's stricken face, but he hadn't slept. By the time the sun came up, he felt like a caged animal, too restless to withstand another moment inside the guest cottage. Maybe some fresh air would clear his head.

He wasn't sure what drew him to Jeeter Road. It could

have been that the quiet on the sun-dappled back road was so complete that the dew dropping off the turning leaves sounded loud as it collided with the forest floor, or it could have been that last night just wouldn't leave him.

A bright splash of canary yellow revealed the location of Abby's Jeep. If the deer had left a trail when it jumped in front of her and bounded over the hill, then Matt couldn't find it. He glanced at the angle of the skid marks and followed their projected path to the opposite side of the road.

She had mentioned a noise. Something strange and animal-like. She'd said that she glanced back, and the instant she took her eyes from the road, the deer had jumped from the same general area into her path.

Matt walked on for a few more yards, but he didn't spot anything out of the ordinary, so he decided to retrace his steps back to the Jeep. Gaze to the ground, he'd only progressed a yard or two when something unusual caught his eye.

The leaves in the shallow roadside ditch were deep and, in one spot, disarranged, as though something had been dragged through them for a short distance. A few spatters of the red-brown color of rust were visible here and there. Matt picked up a leaf and looked closely at it. It was easily scraped away by a fingernail. He frowned at the dried specks on his fingertips.

Blood. Dried, and hours old.

Abby had described the noise she'd heard, before reluctantly admitting that she'd felt that whatever had been on the road bank had been trying to follow her. Giving in to impulse, Matt stepped down into the ditch, then climbed the bank. The story there was the same. Something had been dragged along the narrow shelf. Something large from the looks of it. Something heavy.

The black woodland loam showed through the trough in places, the leaves bunched and smeared with blood. Then all at once, a precipitous descent, as if it had jumped or fallen into the ditch.

As he reached the road once more, a shaft of sunlight broke through the leaves, reflecting brightly off a thin strip of gold half-buried on the soft mud of the shoulder. Matt bent to take a closer look as the sunlight flickered on the bright metal again, then, reaching down, he dug it out of the dirt.

An earring shaped like a bow, with a diamond chip in the center.

Matt stared down at the footprint clearly embedded in the mud not a foot away from where whatever it was that had tried to follow Abby had rolled into the ditch, the same place the earring had been dropped. A man's work boot with a pebbled sole and low heel.

Matt stared down at the print. He sure as hell didn't like what he was thinking, but he didn't have time to do anything about it. A rattle and crack of a heavy metal frame and poor shock absorbers signaled the approach of Rufus's tow truck. Matt stood, palming the earring as the vehicle came into view, followed by Julianne's T-Bird a short distance behind.

Rolling to a stop, Julianne leaned out her window. "Well, if it isn't my favorite client, and he appears to have recovered from his night on the town."

"Julianne," Matt replied, glancing at Abby, who got out of the car to watch Rufus position the truck, then amble over the embankment to hook it to the bumper. With the Jeep in neutral, it only took a few anxious moments to winch it backward off the log and onto the road.

Rufus got down on his knees to peer at the frame. "You got a dent in the oil pan, but otherwise it looks okay. You want me to haul it down to the shop? I can hammer that dent out, and it'll be just like new. But it should run like it is with no problem."

"I'm only a couple of miles from home," Abby said. "I think I'll chance it."

"I'd follow you home," Matt offered, "but I don't have my truck. Hey, lawyer lady, you still got my keys?" She tossed them to him.

Matt caught them in midair, slipping them into the right front pocket of his jeans. "Any chance you can give me a lift?"

"Love to, but I can't," Julianne replied. "I have an appointment and I'm already late, but I'm sure Abby wouldn't mind some company, would you, Abby?"

Abby looked tense and uneasy, and Matt knew that she would have preferred a boa constrictor for a passenger to him.

"Why are you here?" she asked, then realizing how angry she sounded, she softened her tone. "If you were planning on catching a ride to Stooley's, Jeeter Road is a poor choice. It doesn't see much traffic."

Matt shrugged, resting his hands on his hips, elbows slightly crooked. "I was just clearin' the cobwebs. Julianne was supposed to bring my truck by some time this mornin', but it appears I've been stood up."

"She means well," Abby allowed, climbing in and settling behind the wheel. "But I could live without her eternal matchmaking."

"What can't you live without, Abby?"

The question came out of left field, catching her in the sternum and stilling her breath. "What kind of question is that?"

"The impulsive kind." He searched her face for a

moment, then looked away, and Abby had the queer feeling that he'd been disappointed by what he didn't find there. "Forget I asked."

"What did you find back there?" she asked as she signaled the turn into Stooley's gravel parking lot and slowed to a stop. She hadn't said a word during the short drive, and neither had he.

He fished in his shirt pocket and held out his hand. Abby stared at the earring lying in his palm, but she didn't touch it. "This one, and the one you found on your seat, they're the same, aren't they?"

Abby met his gaze. "How did you know?"

"Call it a hunch," he said. "That noise you heard last night. Think about it, Abby. Are you sure it was an animal? Is there a chance, even a remote chance, that it could have been human?"

The implications of what he was suggesting were too huge, too horrible to be believed. Abby rejected it, pushed it away. "No. No, I'm sure of it." But was she?

"It's a possibility that the earring left for you was a trophy," he told her, "something he took off his last victim—possibly while she was still alive. If I'm even close to being right, then you could be in a whole lot of trouble." He paused, his hand resting on the door handle. "Maybe it's time you thought about following Catherine's lead and goin' away for a while. Take a short vacation. Soak up some sun."

She must have been in a mild state of shock. It was the only reasonable explanation for this sudden urge to take his hand, to try to seek a common ground they could never find. She was suddenly chilled, and she didn't want him to go, didn't want to admit that he was her warmth, her sun. She felt more alive when she was with him than she had in more years than she could remember, but her pride wouldn't permit her to reach out to him. Not after the cruel things he'd said. It didn't matter that his accusations, so soft-voiced, so hurtful, had their basis in truth. "I can't leave," she said. "I just can't."

"No, I suppose not." He gave her a level look, dropped the earring in her palm, and got out of the Jeep. Abby watched with a growing sense of dissatisfaction as he walked to his truck, but he didn't glance back, didn't even seem to care that she was there.

The cool dimness of Stooley's was a welcome relief. Stooley glanced up as Matt walked in. "Well if it isn't the man of the hour. What are you drinking? Because I'm buying."

"Coffee, black," Matt answered, parking on one of the stools.

"You got it." She placed a cup on a saucer and put it in front of him, filling it with steaming black coffee. "Didn't figure you'd see daylight for at least a month or two. Ol' Shep was pretty mad. You knock something loose, and he forget to press charges?"

"I've got a good lawyer," Matt replied. "And she's got connections. Listen, Stooley, what d'you know about Shelley La Blanc, and that other girl that was killed?"

Stooley poured herself a coffee and creamed it until it was too pale to recognize. "Shelley was an okay girl. Hard-working, too. She used to come by here every now and again looking for Willard."

"Willard?"

"Her boyfriend."

"Oh, yeah," Matt said. "Big guy. Deals in guns and ammo."

"Among other things," Stooley said, sipping her coffee.

"What about the other one?" Matt wondered. "She ever come in here?"

"Not as I would remember," Stooley replied, "but then, we get a lot of out-of-towners. Could have been that she was here and I didn't notice. Exactly what is it you're looking for?"

"Crepe-soled shoes," Matt muttered into his cup.

If there was a connection between the two victims, Matt couldn't see it. Shelley was a local, the other girl a tourist. Shelley had worked as a waitress at the little café in town, and Victoria Lane had just graduated from NYU a few months before, had landed a position at a brokerage firm in the city, and had decided to celebrate with a few days in the country. Word had it that she'd gone out jogging late one afternoon and didn't return.

No connection, few clues if any, and Matt couldn't get past square one.

There had to be a common thread, something that tied the women together, a theme.

One was a blonde, the other a redhead, but the photo of Victoria Lane in the most recent edition of the *Ashokan Sun* didn't reveal a great deal beyond the obvious.

There had been no mention of signs of a struggle being found outside Shelley's house. Her boyfriend had been inside when Matt dropped her off, supposedly asleep on the couch. Yet he hadn't heard anything, which meant one of two things: the boyfriend was lying to protect his own ass, or Shelley had known her killer. That likelihood set his teeth on edge, but he knew the odds of it being a stranger abduction were slim to none.

This guy knew the area. He belonged here. Catskill residents had a long-standing tradition of resisting change of any kind. They preferred their lives to ramble on undisturbed, uninfluenced by the outside world. Outsiders caused a stir. They trampled the lawns and asked stupid questions, and were unintentionally rude to the villagers. They were tolerated by most but detested by a few, and by one in particular with whom Matt was familiar.

Not so surprisingly, when Matt emerged from Stooley's a short time later, the sheriff's department's cruiser was parked just behind his truck, almost bumper to bumper. Its driver was sipping a milkshake through a straw.

"Mornin', Deputy," Matt said, approaching the black-and-white. "Great day to be alive, ain't it? I was just about to leave, but I'm feelin' kind of sociable. What say we go back inside and I'll buy you a cold one?"

"Fuck you, asshole," Shep replied. "I don't drink with suspects."

"Instead of a beer, how about a burger and fries?" Matt suggested.

Glowering at Matt, Margolis eased up on the brake. The cruiser drifted forward, its bumper colliding forcefully with the truck's. "Oops. Guess I forgot to put it in park."

"See you around, Deputy," Matt said, heading back to the truck. Margolis tailed him all the way home, giving Matt the high sign as he parked the truck, and the black-and-white rolled slowly past.

Gossip was always rife in a small town, and Abundance was no different. Word had it that Shep Margolis had been in love with Shelley, and that Shelley had barely known that Shep was alive. Unrequited love was as old as mankind, but was it also a motive for murder?

Matt sank onto the sofa, propping his boots on the coffee table. He could recall feeling lousier, but not in a very long time. His head ached and felt three times its normal size, and there was a tenderness about his eyes that he vaguely recalled from previous hangovers.

To make matters worse, the muddle of the murders wouldn't leave him.

Margolis was a throwback, a dedicated, card-carrying ass, capable of railroading someone he didn't like right into a jail cell, but Matt just couldn't imagine him killing a woman.

These killings were especially brutal, and the type of cold-blooded, unreasoning rage needed to commit that kind of act just didn't fit the calculating, manipulative deputy. Besides, he wore black wingtips. Come to think of it, Matt had never seen him out of uniform, and he strongly suspected the deputy slept in police-issue pajamas.

Besides, why would Shep target Abby? He didn't seem to have any overt fascination with her. In fact, he'd displayed a great deal of respect for the family. As much as Matt would have loved to be able to pin something on the deputy, it just didn't fit what he was looking for.

Rejecting Margolis as a suspect put him back at the beginning. If not Shep, then who?

Men who killed for thrills often began displaying the classic precursors in adolescence, or even childhood . . . fire-starting, cruelty to animals, chronic bed-wetting well beyond childhood. They often began small, their misdeeds escalating as they perfected their craft. It was all about honing skills, acting out, and reliving the dark fantasy—scratching the unnatural itch. It seemed odd that nothing suspicious had been reported until quite recently, unless he counted Millie Gray's disappearance and death.

Millie Gray had been discovered first, and then Shelley and the Lane girl, and in such rapid-fire succession that it almost seemed that Millie, and not Shelley, had been the catalyst that set this whole thing in motion.

It was a strange thought, so strange that he immedi-

ately dismissed it. The odds that a dig site would be set
up on the exact spot where a young murder victim had
been buried a decade before were so astronomical as
to be unbelievable.

The Pumpkin Fest was an age-old tradition in Abundance, originating in the dark days after the Revolutionary War, when the citizens of Ulster County were
struggling to get back to self-sufficiency and the simple
plenitude of rural life.

Life in the village of Abundance had changed since
those early days, but the changes weren't the drastic
changes two centuries had brought to the country's
great metropolises. The differences between past and
present were more subtle throughout the upper reaches
of the Hudson Valley and the mountain towns to the
west. Satellite dishes now dotted most lawns, and there
were dirt bikes and sport utility vehicles instead of horses
and wagons. Most of the backbreaking labor of the old
days was done by machines, and a growing portion of
the economic base of the village lay in tourism instead
of on the area's family farms.

One thing that hadn't changed since the post–
Revolutionary War period was the Pumpkin Fest. It was
designed to celebrate the harvest, and was a little like
Thanksgiving, only without the turkey and football. With
a huge bonfire, a sumptuous feast, dancing, and revelry,
it had its ancient roots in rural England and Holland
and, more important, in the annals of the Youngblood
family history.

Thanks to Catherine's generosity when it came to her
private library, Matt had done his research, and he was
aware that a representative of the Youngblood family was
expected to crown the Oak King and Chrysanthemum

Queen. It was a longstanding tradition, and tradition was not just revered in the small rural town—it was damn near law. With Catherine Youngblood out of town, there was no one left to officiate but Abby.

Several days had passed since her accident on Jeeter Road, and they'd barely spoken. Matt holed up in the carriage house, delving into research about the town and the catacombs, the entrance of which remained a secret despite numerous attempts to decipher the script, some of which was almost illegible. He had a hunch that the old passageway had opened into the mansion at one time and had been sealed off, but he couldn't locate any documentation to prove his theory correct, and the truth of the matter remained tantalizingly elusive.

When he wasn't poring over the faded, spidery scrawls of countless Youngbloods, he was busy pretending he was on a roll with the manuscript while he smoked cigarettes, watched old reruns of *Northern Exposure*, and thought about Abby.

The knowledge that she would be at the Pumpkin Fest troubled Matt. Abby would not admit to being impulsive or reckless, but she was deluding herself. A rational woman didn't venture to a dump site armed with a flashlight and pepper spray and nothing else, and showing up at his door wearing nothing but a sheer negligee didn't exactly speak well for her restraint.

What if she decided to do something stupid? Like launching a new phase to her investigation, driving lonely roads after dark, or setting herself up as a potential target for their own resident headcase?

He'd thought about calling her and offering his services as an escort, but he didn't think she'd want to be anywhere near him, and he doubted that his already bruised ego could handle another rejection. In fact, he thought about chucking the whole thing and heading off to Stooley's for a little avoidance therapy. Still, if the killer was still in the area, he wouldn't be able to resist taking part in the festivities, or at the very least observing them. Guys like Karl got off on their anonymity, their ability to disappear in a crowd, to blend in with and be indistinguishable from normal people.

Matt had made a fortune researching and writing about serial killers, and historically it was almost always the nice, quiet guy down the street, the handyman with a lisp who lived with his mother, or, in Karl Jensen's case, the Wall Street wizard who murdered young women instead of playing tennis or racquetball. Serial killers were a subspecies—soulless, not quite human— and this one seemed to be turning his focus to Abby.

It was more than that, Matt thought. He had the eerie impression that he was watching her. Maybe watching them together.

It would certainly account for Shelley's belongings being planted in his truck. At first it had thrown him off, and he'd thought that he was the focus. But what if the murdered girl's scarf and watch had been put there for Abby's benefit instead of his? Just like the earring being left in her Jeep? He'd known about the council meeting. He'd known that she would attend. And he'd known about their affair. It was almost as if the creep had a window on Abby's life, on their relationship, which seemed to indicate that he had access to the estate. He felt comfortable here, familiar with the grounds and the house, and maybe even with the Youngbloods.

Matt thought about John Rhys. He was welcome at Gilead Manor and familiar with the area. He was also familiar with Abby, but his stress at the council meeting was evident. The murders had turned his town on its ear, and he wasn't taking it lightly. His haggard appearance and rumpled uniform were also clear indications that he wasn't sleeping.

Serial murderers slept like babies.

No conscience, no worries, no regrets, no signs of insomnia.

Few other people visited the estate on a regular basis, except for William Bentz. Catherine had invited Bentz to dinner on several occasions, before Abby had returned to Gilead Manor and after. And his encampment-cum-dig site was within a quarter-mile of the estate. "Shit," Matt muttered. "Dig site, dump site." Maybe Millie Gray had been this psycho's first victim. But how did the professor fit in to all of this? Had finding Millie's body been a coincidence? Or something more sinister? It would help to have more information.

Millie, a friend of Abby's.

And Matt had seen Bentz at the café where Shelley worked.

Matt picked up the phone. "Jimmy? It's Matt. Listen, I need you to check someone out for me."

A minute later he hung up the phone, grabbing his jean jacket, heading for the door. Abby was going to have an escort this evening whether she wanted one or not. But as he stepped onto the porch, the yellow Jeep sank over the knoll and disappeared down the drive. Matt ran into the drive, shouting her name, but the Jeep never slowed. Prevented from playing the part of a good watchdog, picking her up at her door, observing her every move, hanging on her every word, and hoping for some sign that she wanted him, he did the next best thing: he jumped in the pickup and followed.

He was a quarter mile down the road and eating Abby's dust when the *thump, thump, thump* of the flat became too loud to ignore. Cursing, Matt steered the truck onto the grassy shoulder and jumped out to survey the damage.

Two long diagonal cuts scored the left front tire, three on the right. The spare was done for, too. He kicked the tire, wondering how he'd gotten this far. Knowing in his gut who had done it and why. His faceless, nameless adversary had plans for this evening—plans for Abby—and he didn't want a complication like Matt thrown into the mix.

Down the road, a small cloud of dust sprang up and a rattletrap Chevy Nova on its last legs rolled slowly into sight, a blue-haired lady at the wheel and her equally elderly companion in the front passenger seat. Stepping into the road, Matt put on his best, most engaging grin, muttered a prayer, and stuck out his thumb.

Abby hadn't been terribly enthusiastic about attending the Pumpkin Fest, but she *was* grateful for the escape it provided. The mansion didn't feel much like a haven these days. Even the new security system Matt had foisted upon them didn't make her feel safe. At night, the aging structure was alive with the creaks and groans so inherent in old buildings, and nothing could keep her from dwelling on Matt, or reliving her foolish choices.

She hadn't spoken to him in several days, other than the morning he'd given her the earring he'd found on the side of Jeeter Road. Even then, their conversation had been stilted and brief, and she got the unshakable feeling that he was holding back, holding himself at a polite distance from her.

She wasn't sure why she was surprised by it. She'd known it would happen, a cooling off after that first initial heat. She'd anticipated it—had been anticipating it from the very beginning.

So why did it bother her so much?

Their relationship thus far had been fairly straightforward and honest. It was based on mutual lust, and they both knew it. Yet Abby felt dissatisfied.

It was ridiculous, and she knew it. She couldn't expect him to become something that he clearly wasn't meant to be. In fact, she shouldn't have any expectations where Matthew Wilde Monroe was concerned. Expectations bred false hope, and hopes were too easily dashed. When hopes got dashed, people got hurt, namely her.

As Julianne had once pointed out, Matt had " 'good time' written all over him." He wasn't the sort of man a woman could spend companionable evenings with; he wouldn't enjoy long walks or quiet conversation.

In fact, there had never been anything subtle or quiet about their mutual attraction. It had been instantaneous, powerful, earthshaking, and she should be relieved that it was coming to a close. It *was* coming to a close, Abby thought as she parked the Jeep and made her way to the village green, and any day now this longing to see his face, to hear his voice, would begin to fade.

During the past three days, she'd had moments of weakness, moments when her absolute focus on the problems of the house, and her prospects for the immediate future, receded into the background; when she'd gone to the French doors of the library and grasped the knob, painfully conscious of the lights at the carriage house and the small space of driveway and yard separating them.

Then she would realize her mistake and force her attention to other things, such as the ongoing quest to find Aunt Catherine's missing funds, the foundation wall that was currently being repaired, and locating the elusive link between Millie's death a decade before and the other murders.

Sleepless, restless, she'd tried every angle and arrived at no solid conclusion based on evidence and known facts. She'd even consulted Sam Creekside, the local district magistrate, a friend and colleague who taught criminology at the college. If there was a connection among the three crimes, she just couldn't see it.

Small temporary booths had been constructed in single file on the village green. The ladies' auxiliary from the Baptist church were selling fresh homemade apple butter beside a couple of teenagers offering face painting to the local children. Grotesque masks and outlandish costumes were everywhere in honor of approaching Halloween. A boom box blaring heavy metal music competed with the local bluegrass quartet until Shep Margolis came along, silenced the underaged competition, then once again took to warming his backside by the bonfire. He gave a grim nod in Abby's direction but let her pass by without comment.

Julianne occupied the last booth. She was decked out in full regalia. Heavy silver bracelets graced both wrists, and a coronet of oak leaves and chrysanthemums crowned her auburn hair. A pentagram gleamed against the snowy white of her ankle-length robe. A huge hot-pink foam-rubber hand with a painted eye in its palm waggling back and forth on a spring marking the booth as a palmist's provided comic relief.

"Hey there," Julianne said as Abby approached. "Here to have your fortune told? You can't beat my rates, and it's for a good cause. All of the proceeds go to the Old Wiccans' Retirement Home in Stockbridge."

Abby smiled but kept her hands in the pockets of her brown tweed blazer. "I think I'll pass. I have enough trouble with the present; I think it might be safer to let the future take care of itself."

Julianne arched her brows and pulled out her best Hungarian accent. "Hmm, I see a tall, dark stranger ... very handsome, very charming, excellent turn of phrase—"

"Very complicated," Abby corrected. *"Too* complicated."

"But really good in bed."

Abby felt the heat flood her cheeks. "I think I'd better go," she said and started to turn away, but her friend was quicker, and out of the booth in a flash.

"Not so fast," Julianne said. "How did it go?"

"How did what go?"

"You gave him a ride to get his truck. Did you patch things up?" Julianne bent a look on her. "I hope you aren't foolish enough to let this one go. It's obvious he's crazy about you."

"Nothing is obvious—or easy—where Matt is concerned," Abby allowed, "and if you don't mind, I would rather not talk about it."

"Life isn't easy, girlfriend," Julianne replied. "It's designed to be complicated."

Abby was relieved to change the subject. "Everything okay between you and J. T.?"

Julianne shrugged, and her oak-leaf circlet caught the ruddy glow of a dying sun. "He's worried about Beth. She's pulled another disappearing act. He went down to John's office this morning to file a missing-persons report. I tried to tell him it's nothing to worry about. I mean, it's not like she hasn't done this sort of thing before—"

"But?" Abby prompted.

Julianne's face took on a strange, faraway expression, and Abby felt a chill. "It's just that I had this weird dream. It was like I was stranded somewhere. It wasn't just dark; it was creepy dark; and I was terrified. I felt— strange, very heavy and hurt, and it was hard to breathe. Someone else was there, but I couldn't see them. It was horrible—and it felt like—like I was seeing it all through someone else's eyes." She shrugged, as if to shrug it off. "I keep telling myself it was just a dream, but some- how I'm not convinced."

"Abby? Abby, what's wrong?"

Julianne's voice seemed to come from a distance, and Abby felt as if she'd been plunged into an icy bath. "Hey, are you all right?"

Abby shook it off. "What? Yes. Yes, I'm fine. It's just that—I'm not so sure what you described was just a dream." She dug in her jacket pocket and held out her hand. The earrings nestled in her palm caught the sunlight, winking evilly.

"Where did you get those?" Julianne asked.

"The other night, when I came out of the council meeting, there was a gift-wrapped package in my Jeep. One of them was in it. Matt found the other one along Jeeter Road." She broke off, unsure whether to go on.

"There's more, isn't there?" Julianne asked, holding the earrings protectively in her palm.

"While I was stranded—I wasn't alone. There was something in the underbrush. It moved when I moved, and it seemed to be following me. I thought it was an animal, but Matt asked—he asked if I was certain it wasn't human. He said it looked as if something had been dragged through the leaves." Abby watched as Julianne put a hand over her mouth. "They belong to Beth, don't they?"

Julianne nodded. "Oh, Abby, I've gotta find J. T."

Fred Wilson, the mayor, was waving frantically at Abby. "If you want, I'll come with you," she offered.

"It's probably better if I tell him," Julianne said. In a moment, she was lost to the crowd. With Julianne gone from sight, and her mind full of thoughts of Beth Langtry, Abby turned and ran right into a recurring nightmare—dark ski mask, dark clothing . . . the faint but unmistakable odor of alcohol. Abby stumbled back, shrugging off the black-gloved hands.

A terrified scream lodged at the base of her throat; she stumbled back.

"Doc? Hey, Doc, are you okay?" As Abby watched, stunned, the figure reached up and snatched off the ski mask. It was Caleb Abernathy. Abby sucked in a startled breath and exhaled shakily, her heart beating with a sickening heaviness. "Doc?"

"What?" she said, putting a hand to her temple. "Oh, God, Caleb! You gave me a fright."

Caleb spread his arms wide, thumbs up, a gesture of triumph and ingenuity. "Cool costume, huh?"

"With so much tension in town, you might want to rethink your choices," Abby told him once she could breathe normally again, "and Caleb—go home and sober up."

The mayor was about to burst a vein when Abby reached him. "We've got problems, big problems. Bobbi Carmichael is nowhere to be found, and I tell you this confidentially—my Edna talked to the reverend's neighbor this morning. She didn't come home last night."

"Maybe she's staying with a friend," Abby reasoned, unsure where this was leading.

Mayor Wilson seemed about to explode. "Bobbi is last year's Chrysanthemum Queen! Last year's queen always crowns the incoming queen! It's tradition."

"We can break with tradition just this once," Abby assured him. "It'll be okay, really. Try to calm down."

The mayor nodded. "Thanks, Abby. We're lucky to have you here."

"I'll be over here when you need me," she said, heading for the far side of the gazebo. From the spot she chose, apart from the crowd, she had a clear view of the village green dotted with booths and rapidly filling with people, locals and tourists. She studied each face; then, realizing what she was doing and whom she'd been hoping to see, she directed her attention elsewhere, and in that instant caught sight of a dark-clothed figure lurking near the rear of Julianne's booth. He was still wearing the ski mask, and courting real trouble if Shep caught sight of him.

Abby didn't want Caleb to catch any more flack on her account. She was embarrassed enough over the incident as it was. She glanced at the stage, then back at the figure ducking behind Julianne's booth. Mayor Wilson was just getting warmed up, and worth at least ten minutes of officiating and introductions. It wouldn't take long to send Caleb on his way, or to confiscate that damned ski mask. In fact, the mayor would never even know she was gone.

The Chevy Nova had barely ground to a halt when the back door opened and Matt stepped out. "Ladies, my undying gratitude."

The Oaklevy sisters sang out in unison, "I'll bet you say that to all the girls." Giggling, they waved as they drove off.

Matt shook his head. Two blue-haired, look-alike seventy-year-olds in pink poodle skirts and blue-framed cat-eye glasses, who spoke and talked in unison and were headed to a fifties dance contest at the local tavern.

For a moment there, he'd thought he'd stepped through the Nova's back door and into the Twilight Zone. But it was just one of the novelties of life in rural communities like Atwater, Mississippi, and Abundance, New York.

Folks like the Oaklevys were largely untouched by the dawn of the twenty-first century. Most were just hard-working people who took their kids to Little League and mowed their grass religiously on weekends. A few innocents chose to live in the past, and at least one man among them had found the taking of lives an absolute passion.

He could look for a white male, between the ages of twenty-five and forty-five, with low self-esteem and a barely suppressed rage, which might very well include a good portion of the population of Abundance and the surrounding area . . . or he could locate the man's chosen target and try to prevent the disaster he suspected was coming.

Rose and her granddaughter, a gawky teen with a metal-edged smile, were buying funnel cakes at a booth. Rose saw him coming and stuck out her chin. "Um, um, um. Looks like Abundance has hit the big time, or maybe you're doing research to see how the other half lives—you know, decent, honest, hardworkin' folk."

Matt nodded. "Nice to see you, too, Rose. Hey, Patricia. Either of you seen Abby?"

"Last time I saw Miss Abigail, she was talkin' with Julianne Rhys. Must have been fifteen minutes ago."

"Which way?"

"Over by the candy-apple stand."

"Thanks."

Rose furrowed her brows as he sprinted off. "You best watch that one! If she gets wind that you're up to no good, she'll turn you into a toad."

Matt threaded his way through the crowd, rapidly scanning each face, hoping to find Abby quickly. It was a quarter of seven. It would be getting dark soon, and darkness could cover a multitude of sins.

Shelley's killer operated at night. It had been approaching eleven when she was killed, and it had been dark when Abby's prowler had tried to break into the house as well.

Catching sight of a redhead in the crowd, Matt abruptly changed directions. "Julianne? Hey, Julianne!"

The woman turned. She was gaunt and freckled, and her bright-blue eyes were alight with inquiry. "Oh, sorry," Matt said. "Wrong redhead."

He pushed through a narrow rent in the crowd, sidestepped a half-melted ice cream cone, and ran right into Caleb Abernathy. "Hey, bro," Caleb said. "How's it hangin'?"

"Caleb, have you seen Abby?"

"Doc Youngblood? Yeah, as a matter of fact. Last time I saw her, she was over there. She has to do her bit and announce the king and queen. Hey, no need to rush off. A few minutes and it'll all be over."

"Yeah, that's what I'm afraid of," Matt said. "Listen, if you run into her before I find her, keep her with you, some place in the open, and wait for me. For God's sake, whatever she says, don't let her go home alone."

"All right, but I kind of doubt she's gonna want to hang out with me after the thing with the mask."

"Just do it," Matt ordered.

The master of ceremonies droned on about the sense of community that had outlasted fire and flood and, after more than two centuries, was still alive today. Matt could only think that a monster had stolen into their midst. He had struck at least twice and gotten away with it; unless someone stopped him, he would strike again.

The crowd had gathered close to the gazebo on all sides, but there was no sign of Abby. Then, across the small sea of faces, he caught sight of a familiar strait laced figure: tall and willowy, with honey gold hair spilling onto the shoulders of a classic tweed blazer. She was on the other side of the crowd, hurrying away from the gazebo toward the palmist's booth and the man waiting in its shadows.

"Caleb?"

Caleb Abernathy froze in the shade of Julianne's booth—a strange reaction, Abby thought. "Caleb, it's Abby Youngblood," Abby said, grasping his arm, but the instant her fingers brushed his sleeve she realized her mistake.

The man was smaller than Caleb, more wiry, and he brimmed with a tension that laid-back Caleb wasn't even capable of. She had a mental flash of spare flesh, a thin build beneath the night colored clothing, and stumbled back as he turned to face her.

Abby's shock lasted just long enough for her gaze to clash with his, for her to realize that she gazed into those same cold, emotionless eyes. "It's you," she said softly, her mouth dry and her heart beating with sickening thuds. Sweat dampened her palms, crept along her arches inside her Bass fringed-tongue loafers.

"Pretty Abby," he said, his voice hoarse and whispery.

Somewhere in the background, the mayor's nervous laugh erupted over the loudspeaker. "First we misplace Miss Carmichael, then misplace our presenter—probably stepped out for an iced tea. Donnie, would you locate Ms. Youngblood?"

The man in the ski mask cocked his head, listening, but he never took his eyes off Abby. Cold as a raw February wind, they bored into her, ferreting out and fondling her fears, claiming an intimacy she could not fathom and did not wish to understand.

Abby swallowed hard. The bluegrass band took center stage and started up a howling rendition of "Blue Moon of Kentucky," nasal and heavy on the mandolin.

Would anyone hear her if she screamed?

He took a step closer, one hand clenched into a fist. Abby stepped back, but her foot tangled with the tie-downs that held the booth in place, and she fell. As she tried to push herself up, he advanced in a crouch; then his head jerked up, and he pivoted on the balls of his feet and ran, with Matt a few yards behind him.

Abby picked herself up and brushed the dead leaves and twigs from her tweed coat while Mayor Wilson fidgeted beside her. "Oh, my goodness. This can't be happening—not during the Pumpkin Fest. We've never had a presenter accosted before, and in broad daylight. Abby, are you all right?"

"I think so," she said, then nodded. "Yes. I'm fine."

A few moments later, a winded Matt came limping back and, without a word, threw his half-empty pack of cigarettes into the trash can. "I lost him. He jumped a fence and headed for the woods. Where's Margolis? Maybe he can get some dogs down here or somethin'."

It was Julianne who answered, her voice subdued and her face pale. "Shep's with Mrs. Florin. She was walking her dog and the dog stumbled onto something. I just called J. T. They think it's Beth."

Mayor Wilson drifted away to cancel the evening's events while Julianne gathered her cards and her crystals and prepared to go home.

Matt stood alone with Abby. "Two close calls in one

week, Abby. You're hard on a man's heart. Damn good thing I've got a spare."

Taking her hand, Matt poured a pendant and gold chain into her palm, still warm from his touch. "He didn't get clean away. A. R. Y. Abigail Rowan Youngblood. It's yours, isn't it?"

Abby raised her gaze to his. In that moment, he was the only one she could truly trust, the one person she depended on to be there, and for the split second when she was forced to face that reality, it scared her almost as much as coming face to face with a cold-blooded killer. "It was in my jewelry box, in my room at Gilead Manor. He was in the house, Matt. He was in the house."

Chapter Thirteen

Julianne Rhys turned the key in the lock of The Bell, Book, and What-not and ran the remaining few yards to her car. She flicked a glance at the rearview mirror. The car ahead was parked too close; but the driver of the midnight-blue Chevy Suburban parked in the space behind had been considerate and had given her plenty of room to maneuver. She shifted the Thunderbird into reverse, turning the wheels sharply, and at the same time, a black-gloved hand came from behind and closed over her mouth. Too startled to do more than gasp, she glanced up into the mirror, into the eyes of a killer, and slammed her foot onto the accelerator.

Abby glanced at the portraits on the library wall, dark with age, wondering if he had stood where she was standing, staring up at her ancestors' faces. Did he touch the spines of the books in the library? Take them off the shelves? Did he handle her possessions, her clothing, her perfume, the wedding band she'd taken off her finger months ago?

Just knowing that a monster of that caliber had set foot in the old house prompted feelings unlike any she had ever entertained. She felt threatened, violated, furious that he would dare to breach the boundaries of her home. She thought of Catherine and Rose, of Patricia, every one of them in danger. And the question kept surfacing in the midst of those dark thoughts, like tiny methane bubbles in a dank woodsy pond: *why?*

Why enter her home?

Her bedroom?

Why take her locket?

The answer loomed in the shadowy recesses of her mind, too frightening to contemplate, too horrific to confront directly. Abby danced around it, just as she danced around her feelings for the long-boned, well-built Southerner who lounged in the doorway to the library, a cup of black coffee cradled in one palm.

He'd been quiet since returning to Gilead Manor, uncharacteristically so, sipping his coffee while he watched her methodically check every lock and draw the drapes. When she'd finished, she went to the closet and glanced inside one last time, just to assure herself it was unoccupied. He'd already checked every inch of the old house, from attic to crawl space, but he didn't chide her or remind her of his thorough search; he just let her have the ritual, anything to give her a measure of security. As if anything truly could.

"Silly, I know," Abby said aloud, chafing her hands together as she walked to the divan and sank down. "I just can't help wondering: do you think he sat here like I'm doing now? What do you suppose he was thinking?" Then, almost as quickly, "You don't have to answer that. I'm better off not knowing." She was quiet for a moment, very still, and the tension between them lay heavy in the air. In the interim, she sighed, a sound brimming with impatience. "The earring I found in the Jeep belonged to Beth. He took it from her and left it for me, just like you said. I'm his target, aren't I?"

"I wish I didn't think so," Matt admitted. "But I can't ignore it. For a while I thought that I was the connection, but now I'm not so sure. What if you were supposed to find the watch and the shawl?"

Abby shook her head. "That doesn't make sense. If he was leaving Shelley's belongings for me, he wouldn't put them in your truck, unless—"

"Unless he'd been watchin' you," Matt finished.

"Watching us," she murmured. "Oh, God." She covered her mouth with her hand. The thought made her slightly nauseated.

"With the attempted break-in, the earring, and what happened tonight, it's the only thing that makes sense. Are you sure it was the same guy who tried to get in here before?"

"I'm positive," Abby replied. "At first I thought it was Caleb Abernathy, but when he turned and I looked into his eyes, I knew."

"I figured he'd be there, but I sure as hell don't get the ski mask," Matt admitted. "Nobody knows who he is, so why risk it? Why draw attention to himself? Unless he wanted attention, your attention, and that was the only way he could be certain you'd notice him?"

Abby shivered. She couldn't help it. The thought of someone observing her comings and goings was every bit as invasive as his intrusion upon her home. How much did he know? she wondered. How much had he seen? She glanced at Matt. He'd put down the coffee cup and was leaning against the doorframe, his hands shoved deep into the front pockets of his jeans. Aloof. Untouchable.

She closed her eyes, wishing it were otherwise. She wanted his warmth, needed the escape she found in his arms, yet she was afraid to reach out, wary of letting him know. They were on shaky ground, and she had no idea how to change that. Even worse, she wasn't altogether sure she wanted to. Nothing had changed. She was still the same person, with the same problems, the same insecurities, the same deep fear of vulnerability, and the need to shield herself from being hurt. And Matt still represented a very real danger to her.

"I can stay if you want me to," he offered. "Down here, I mean. All I need is a comfortable chair. I don't sleep much these days, anyway."

Abby smiled, a halfhearted attempt at gratitude. "That's kind of you, but I'll manage. You've done far too much as it is."

He pushed away from the doorframe and came toward her slowly. He'd taken his hands from his pockets. "Don't I know it," he said, reaching out to touch her briefly. His fingertips skimmed her cheek—a light touch, full of regret. Then, lowering his hand he reached back and took the 9mm from the waistband of his jeans. "If you won't accept me, then maybe you'll accept this." Taking her hand, he pressed the pistol into her palm, then turned and walked slowly out.

A few seconds later his truck engine sprang to life. Faced with the prospect of another night of lying awake listening to the creaks and groans of the aging mansion, Abby picked up her keys.

The Bell, Book, and What-not was closed, but the lights were on at Julianne's house on Euclid Avenue.

John was sitting on the porch steps, smoking a cigarette, but it wasn't a leisurely activity; it was hurried and agitated. He sucked in another dose of nicotine, then dropped the butt onto a small pile of butts by the azalea bush at the corner of the porch steps. The porch light was off, and the moon was too new to provide much light, but it didn't help to hide the fact that he was rumpled and worn, and that something was terribly wrong.

"Doc Fife's with her," he said.

"Doctor Fife? What is it? What's happened?"

He lit another cigarette and blew out a cloud of soft gray smoke. "He grabbed her. He was waiting in her car, outside the shop, and he grabbed her."

Abby glanced at the house. "Oh, God. Is she all right?"

"She's a little bruised, and pretty shaken."

"She has a right to be shaken," Abby allowed. "But so do you. John, I'm worried about you."

He laughed, a short bark of a sound, filled with derision. "Shit, Abby, why pretend? You haven't given me more than a passing thought since you came back to Gilead Manor. You've been too busy chasing Monroe." He paused long enough to suck in another puff, his eyes narrowing against the smoke. "What is it about guys like him? Where's the draw? Is it the bad-boy fantasy? Or is he really that good between the sheets?"

Abby stiffened. "I'm going to try and take into consideration the fact that your sister had a very close call tonight and that you're worried about her. Go home and get some sleep. You can't do your job strung out on cigarettes and caffeine."

"I don't need sleep, Abby," John told her. "I need you." He got to his feet and stood facing her. Abby was afraid that he would try to keep her there, but he didn't.

Instead, he raked his fingers through his short blond hair. "Tell Julianne I'll call to check on her in an hour or two." He started down the sidewalk. In less than a moment, he was gone.

Abby recognized the diminutive, dark-haired Dr. Elizabeth Fife, Abundance's new physician. Dressed in a classic trench coat and carrying a medical bag, the GP pressed a vial of pills into Julianne's hand. "It's a mild sedative, just in case you have trouble sleeping. It's often the case with this kind of trauma. And if you have any problems—"

"I'll call," Julianne put in. "Thanks, Elizabeth."

"You're welcome." Doc Fife, as she was called by most of the townsfolk, snagged J. T.'s arm. "Try to get her to listen, and no more excitement for at least twenty-four hours."

"I'm not leaving her. As for the listening part . . ." J. T. shook his head. "That, I can't guarantee. C'mon. I'll walk you out."

The two departed together. Abby grasped her friend's hands. "Are you all right?"

Julianne took a deep breath, exhaling on a shuddering sigh. "Elizabeth says I'll be fine in a day or two." She brushed back her hair, and Abby saw the deep-purple bruise on her throat.

"Oh, God," Abby gasped. "Did he do that to you?"

"It looks worse than it is. When he put his arm around my neck, I floored the accelerator." She laughed, but it was nervous-sounding, on the edge of control. "I broke the grille on the SUV behind me and lay on the horn. John says it probably saved my life."

Abby slipped an arm around Julianne's waist and led her to the living room sofa. "Can you talk about it?"

A quick nod. "All I could think of was getting to J. T.'s place. I knew he'd take Beth's death really hard, and I thought if I could just be there ... I climbed into the car, turned the key in the switch, put the car into reverse, and that's when he grabbed me. He must have been crouched in the back seat, waiting for me to come out of the shop."

"You said 'he'," Abby said quietly. "Did you get a look at him?"

Julianne shook her head. "Just his eyes. I glanced in the rearview mirror. They were cold and empty, like he was nothing more than an empty shell—no heart, no soul."

John knew Abby was right, even though it galled him to admit it. He'd been running on raw energy for days, living on coffee and cigarettes and making do with two or three hours sleep. Not only was he feeling as touchy as an exposed nerve, he couldn't keep it up much longer. His plan when he left Julianne's was to return to the station and start reviewing the preliminary reports on the discovery of Beth Langtry's body, but as he passed Raccoon Hollow Road, he decided against it. A few hours wouldn't make a great deal of difference to anyone but him.

Picking up the microphone, he radioed dispatch. Sarah had ended her shift at eleven, so Shep answered. "Ten-four, boss. How's it goin'?"

"Quiet," John said. "I was planning to come in, but I've changed my mind. I think I'll go on home and try to get some sleep. Can you hold down the fort by yourself?"

"Got it covered, boss. You go catch some z's. Everything's under control."

"Call me if anything out of the ordinary crops up; otherwise, I'll see you at seven."

"Ten-four. Over and out." The radio crackled, then fell silent. The house he was renting was a few miles out of town. He'd never been much of a country boy, but it was one of the few places he could actually afford on his salary minus spousal and child support. It also had a great view of Woodstock Mountain, and the kids seemed to enjoy getting away from the constant clatter of lawn mowers and through traffic that was so much a part of life in a small town. Without giving it a thought, he turned down Raccoon Hollow Road. The night was clear and starting to turn colder. He'd take the long way home and hope that by the time he arrived, he'd be too exhausted to do anything but sleep.

He reached the halfway point and had started to think about whether he had anything remotely edible back at the house when he noticed the Chevy Suburban parked near Hound Dog Bridge. It was backed into the weeds, its broken grille and missing headlight facing the road.

John braked the Blazer, looking back, then slowly pulled off onto the side of the road. The beam from his flashlight illuminated the broken grille and revealed the scuff marks the color of Julianne's Thunderbird on the bumper. It was the vehicle Julianne had slammed into. She'd been too shaken up to get the license number or look for the owner, and by the time John arrived on the scene, the vehicle was long gone. Cupping his hand to his mouth, he called out, "Hello? Anybody there?"

No answer, and no one around.

He walked around to the tailgate. He glanced at the license number, then shone the light inside the abandoned vehicle. The cargo area was carpeted, and the carpet looked wet, as though it had been freshly scrubbed. John walked around to the driver's door, shining the light through the windows. Stuffed between the seats was a canvas bag. John opened the door, and as he reached for the bag, its contents tumbled out: black sweatshirt, black pants, black ski mask, duct tape, and several lengths of nylon rope.

He was closing the driver's door when the scrape of a footstep on gravel sounded behind him. John spun in a defensive crouch, but days without sleep had taken their toll on him, and his reflexes were sluggish. The lead pipe caught him above his left eyebrow, and he went down like a sack full of stones.

John's assailant stood for a moment trying to decide what to do. He would have liked to take his time with the disposal of the body, but the sheriff's presence had come as an unwelcome surprise, and he had no way of knowing if he had called for backup, so there was little time left to him.

Bending, he grabbed his victim's wrists and dragged him to the middle of Hound Dog Bridge. It seemed to take an eternity. The sheriff was quite a bit larger than he, but a growing sense of urgency lent him the strength to complete the task, and at last he crouched, panting, above the waters of Stony Creek. Swollen from recent rains, the creek would finish what he had started, and by the time someone found the body, he wouldn't be recognizable, let alone breathing.

Pushing and pulling, he maneuvered the limp form of John Rhys up and onto the low steel guardrail, then, with a shove, sent the sheriff of Abundance tumbling into the dark, cold waters of the creek.

In a neighborhood where everyone knew everyone else and where a stranger's presence never went unnoticed, speculation as to who was responsible for the women's deaths ran wild.

Mercy Langdon, ironically named since she was such a merciless scold, told everyone who would listen, and some who wouldn't, that Uley Giles was responsible. "I saw the way he looked at the La Blanc girl," she said slyly. "And that newspaperman's sister too—" She broke off, and the harrumph she gave said it all.

Sue Brindles was adamant that it was extraterrestrials, and the Reverend Carmichael turned a jaundiced and unforgiving eye toward Julianne's shop and hinted that the evil turned loose upon the town had its roots in ungodly practices.

Matt had harbored his own suspicions early on about who was responsible for tearing the town apart, but with Karl Jensen in jail, his theory was useless and he was without a likely candidate. He spent most of the day talking to the locals, gleaning whatever information he could. He covered the same tracks the sheriff's department had covered in the days following Shelley's murder and the discovery of the two subsequent victims, and he pried what little information he could out of Sarah, the dark-haired dispatcher, about Millie Gray.

It was just a hunch, since he hadn't found any hard evidence, but he couldn't shake the feeling that Millie, and not Shelley, had been the same killer's victim number one. It was definitely a long shot, but to Matt's way of thinking, it was the only thing that made sense. What he couldn't figure out was motive.

Why unearth a victim who had never been found? Why refocus attention on an investigation gone cold?

It was a hard fact that the longer it took to solve a crime, the slimmer the chances became that it could ever be solved. Every police department had its share of case files gathering dust in a box in the basement or back room, and he was sure the Ulster County Sheriff's Department had Millie Gray.

But if the warped bastard who offed Millie had gotten away with the crime, why call attention to it in so gruesome a fashion? Alerting the authorities that he was still in town, still conducting his grisly business at will, would turn up the heat and make life damned uncomfortable. So why risk it? Why call attention to himself?

All of the bodies had been found within a ten-mile radius. That was a tight area to operate in, especially with the beefed-up patrols. Yet he had continued to kill, as if oblivious to the presence of the sheriff's department. Or disdainful of them.

Was that it? Had he honed his skills to the point where he felt he couldn't be caught?

But four murders didn't make a career. Which meant that he was either unbelievably arrogant, or there were more than four.

A lot more. Just not in Abundance.

"He hasn't had any victims here in ten years," Matt murmured. "I'll be damned. Our boy's come home."

Yet unearthing him proved a great deal more difficult than arriving at the scenario that may have led to the killings. The only homegrowns who'd been away for a decade and then returned were the Reverend Carmichael and Denise Stemple, who had moved to California and recently returned to care for her father, who had Alzheimer's; and neither one came close to fitting the requirements.

Matt half-sat on Sarah's desk. "So, why's it so quiet around here this morning?" he wondered.

"You probably shouldn't sit there, Mr. Monroe," she said lightly. "It might be against regulations." She took a bite of her muffin, washing it down with green tea. "Shep went to check on the chief. He was supposed to come in at seven, and he never showed up. It's not like him. Especially, since . . . well, you know."

296 S. K. McClafferty

"Listen, Sarah," Matt said. "You know anyone who's been away and recently come home?"

"To Abundance?" She rolled her eyes. "In all honesty, the people who go away usually don't come back. Unless, of course, you can count the professor."

"Professor? Abby's professor?"

"Professor Bentz. He's a native New Yorker—State, I mean, not City. I don't think he talks about it, but I could tell by his accent. I heard him ordering down at the café. He's there every morning when I stop in for one of Marge's killer muffins. It has to do with the vowels. It's diluted, but still there, so I guess he's been away for a while—probably off digging for bones, or whatever it is an anthropologist does."

"Yeah, I guess so," Matt replied automatically, unable to shake off the sudden shroud of uneasiness that came over him. He got to his feet as the radio barked for Dispatch.

Startled, Sarah jumped. "Ten-four, sheriff's department. Go ahead."

"Sarah, this is Shep. I need an ambulance at Wylie's Ford on Stony Creek, and I need it yesterday, do you read me?"

"An ambulance at Wylie's Ford, dispatch without delay." She flipped a lever on the switchboard, which alerted the ambulance crew, then came back to Shep. "On their way, Deputy. Did you locate the chief?"

The radio crackled, then went dead. Sarah looked at Matt. "I don't like the sounds of this," she said.

"That makes two of us," Matt agreed.

He hadn't given the professor much notice, but now that Sarah had mentioned it, it was all starting to make a sort of thready logic. Not only did Bentz know Abby, he'd been familiar with at least one of the murder victims. He'd arrived in August, a few days after Matt himself, and as head of the anthropology department at New York University, he would have been responsible, not only for the welfare of his students, but for selecting and staking out the site itself.

The more he thought about it, the more uneasy Matt became. He'd staked out the dump site, hoping to get lucky, and had got a couple of adventurous kids instead and, a few minutes later, the professor. His appearance had seemed perfectly orchestrated at the time, but what if it wasn't? What if he'd been as surprised to find an audience there as Matt had been to find Abby, and his calm had been an act?

Was there a connection?

Or did the professor just have the annoying habit of popping up where he shouldn't be?

All of his speculation got Matt precisely nowhere. And by the time he turned off the main highway onto Osgood Dean Lane, he still could not draw any concrete conclusions.

Bentz hadn't done anything wrong, at least nothing Matt could prove. He was just your average, run-of-the-mill intellectual. Not a social butterfly, not seething with testosterone, but more given to immersing himself in textbooks and fitting together shards of pottery than social interaction.

No family, no wife, no friends . . . at least none who were apparent. His only obvious connection to Abundance a beautiful ex-colleague who seemed to have garnered a stalker, and a dig site that had turned out to be a grave site. . . .

A dump site . . .

There it was again.

Maybe he should share his information.

Then, just as quickly, he abandoned the idea.

This thing with Abby was going nowhere. Maybe it

was best just to leave it alone. She couldn't take the pressure, and he didn't like being hurt.

J. T. was making arrangements for his sister Beth's memorial service when Shep came by Julianne's house with the news. Abby had stayed the night and was warming water for tea when the deputy knocked. "I just came from Rebecca's. Is Julianne home?"

As if on cue, Julianne appeared in the doorway to the dining room. "Shep, what are you doing here? Is something wrong with one of the kids?"

Shep took off his hat and combed his fingers through his short brown hair. "Not the kids. Maybe you better sit down."

"Just tell me, damn it."

"Seldom Levene went down to the creek this morning to do a little angling, and he found John washed up on the rocks. Seldom got some of the water knocked out of him, but I'm afraid it doesn't look good. He swallowed a lot of water before he washed up on shore, but he was lying half in the creek when they found him, and comin' out of the mountains this time of year that water's awfully cold."

"How bad is it?" Julianne asked.

"Doc Fife rode with him in the ambulance," Shep offered, smoothing the visor of his hat with his hands.

"Shep, for God's sake!"

"Water in the lungs, hypothermia, and a knock on the head. I called the hospital from Rebecca's. He's in a coma."

"I'll get my bag," Julianne said.

"There's nothing much you can do—" Shep began, but Julianne cut him off.

"I'm going," Julianne insisted.

Abby, silent until now, put her arms around her friend. "I'll drive you," she offered. "Rose is at the manor if you need someone to stay with the children."

Shep nodded his thanks. "If she needs anything . . ." he told Abby; then, looking strangely ineffectual, he planted his hat on his head and went out.

Sharing his suspicions about William Bentz with the sheriff's department had never been much of a viable option, but with John Rhys lying near death in the hospital, it had become an impossibility. Not only did Shep Margolis have his hands full trying to juggle the department while the mayor sought a temporary replacement for Rhys, the deputy's prejudice was so large that he wasn't about to hear anything Matt had to say.

On his own, Matt pooled his resources, making phone calls, calling in favors, and asking questions. A friend on the staff at NYU had reported that, although Bentz was a bit odd, in the five years he'd been on the faculty, he'd been squeaky clean.

Matt mentally sifted through the facts. Bentz had been at NYU for five years, with no unbecoming conduct immediately detectable. That did not mean, however, that he hadn't been busy behind the scenes. Bentz knew Abby, and Abby had a stalker . . . someone with a slight build. Bentz was small and could be characterized as slight. And, he'd been in the vicinity when it all started.

In fact, he'd been lucky enough to be there when the first body, the body of Millie Gray, was unearthed. Matt frowned . . . lucky? Now that he thought about it, it was downright uncanny that Bentz had stumbled onto the very spot where Millie Gray was buried. Catherine had given the professor carte blanche so far as the location of the dig site was concerned, so how strange was it that, when choosing a spot to set up stakes, he'd chosen the grave site?

Matt suddenly stilled. "Shit, Matthew," he said. "You've been looking at this all wrong. Bentz's students finding Millie's grave wasn't a blunder after all. He'd planned it that way." Matt shook his head. "You're startin' to lose it." Starting to lose it? Hell, it was already gone. This vein of reasoning was dead-end stuff. The only possible way Bentz could have known where Millie's grave was located was if he'd put her there in the first place. Millie had been dead ten years. In fact, she'd disappeared on prom night of Abby's senior year.

Bentz was probably thirty, close to Abby's age. If he'd been here, Abby would remember it. Remember him. Wouldn't she?

He glanced at the phone; then, thinking better of it, he took up his jacket and truck keys instead and went out. It would be dark in an hour. A little field research was definitely in order. Maybe he could straighten this thing out on his own.

Nothing could convince Julianne to leave her brother's side, so Abby made the drive back from Kingston alone. But the sight of John lying pale and still in the intensive-care unit had left Abby feeling stressed and edgy. At five minutes past six that evening, Rose knocked on the library door and caught Abby seated behind the old rosewood desk, a pen poised in midair, staring at nothing in particular. "Miss Abigail? Are you all right?"

Abby glanced up, smiling what she hoped was a reassuring smile. "Yes, I'm fine. I was just jotting down some notes. I thought I'd revise my résumé before sending it out again. Who knows? There might be a private college out there somewhere willing to overlook my

recent debacle at Sullivan in lieu of my dedication."
She sighed. "Or maybe not. Yet I won't know for certain
until I've exhausted every available avenue. Then there's
the paperwork for the historical society. All in all, I
thought it would be best to keep busy."

Rose's worried expression softened, and she smiled.
"Is John Rhys gonna be all right? Miss Catherine'll be
mighty upset if anything happens to him."

Abby put down her pen. "They say it's too soon to
tell."

"If you'd like, I can stay," Rose offered. "Patricia's
safe at home with her parents, and I was just goin' to
my sister Ada's for videos and popcorn—or maybe you'd
like to come join us. No sense in you rattlin' around in
this big old place all alone."

"Thank you for the invitation," Abby replied, rising
from her chair to kiss Rose's cheek, "but I don't mind,
really. In fact, I welcome the solitude. I've got some
thinking to do."

Rose pursed her lips in disapproval, but she didn't
argue. "All right, then. If you're sure. But if you change
your mind, all you've got to do is call."

"I'll remember," Abby promised.

"I'll lock the door on my way out," Rose said. "But
don't you forget to reset the alarm." In a moment, she
was gone, leaving Abby alone with her thoughts.

She thought about calling Matt, inviting him over.
Yet she wasn't quite sure he'd come, or what she would
say if he did, and she didn't want to risk another argument. It was all so damned complicated, and the only
way out seemed to be to make a clean break, to walk
away.

Sinking into the leather armchair behind the rosewood desk, Abby tented her fingers in front of her face,
resting her brow on her fingertips. She closed her eyes,

trying to imagine life without him in it, but the prospect
was empty and dull. Then she remembered how it felt
to hear his laugh, his lazy drawl, the warmth that washed
over her when he touched her.

Tires crunched on the gravel drive. Shaking free of
her thoughts, Abby walked to the front door, expecting
to see him emerging from the battered black truck, but
there was only the red gleam of taillights in the distance,
and a long, white florist's box lying on the porch. Disappointed, intrigued, Abby opened the door, retrieving
the box, taking it to the kitchen. Placing it on the old
porcelain sink, she untied the red silk ribbon and lifted
off the lid.

Inside, lying on a bed of gauzy black, were ten perfect
long-stemmed red roses. Abby searched the box, but
there was no card enclosed. Locating an appropriate
vase, she filled it with water, lifting them from the box.
. . . But one of the thorns caught on the gauze and
dragged it from the box.

Abby disentangled the fabric, then went deathly still.

It wasn't packing material; it was a woman's wrap,
vaguely familiar. An unearthly chill crept slowly up her
spine, as if a bloodless finger traced a path along the
vertebrae. She'd seen it before—she was sure of it—
but not for many years. Ten, to be exact.

Abby stepped back, the fabric slipping from her nerveless grasp, pooling in a silken puddle at her feet. Her
heart was beating with heavy, sickening thuds as she
backed away from the blood-red roses and black silk
fabric lying scattered over the charcoal-colored slate of
the kitchen floor.

"Breathe, Abby. Breathe," she said. She snatched the
garment up as she spun, running from the kitchen,
pausing when she reached the hallway.

Had she heard a thump just now? Like the thud of a casement sliding back into place?

Without even thinking, she took the cell phone from the pocket of her Irish knit cardigan and dialed the carriage house. "Please be there. Please be there, Matt. Please be there."

Three rings and the machine clicked on. "Party Central," Matt's voice drawled. "Sophie, if that's you, I'm hard at it. Anyone else, you know what to do."

Abby clicked off and laid the phone on the table as she passed it, gathering her courage. "It's a coincidence; it has to be a coincidence." But the excuse just didn't gel. *How could it be a coincidence?* she wondered, entering the library, going directly to the desk and opening the drawer. The shiny stainless steel of the 9mm pistol Matt had insisted she take winked lethally in the lamplight. Lifting it out, she placed it on the desk blotter, then sifted through assorted papers and correspondence until she found what she was looking for.

It was a photograph of Millie and her prom date, Steve Faraday, and beside them, Abby, John, and Julianne. Steve was wearing a dreadful cream-colored tuxedo with a bright-red cummerbund, and Millie, looking dramatic in black, had a rose in her teeth and was camping it up for the camera. Slung low over Millie's arms was the gauzy black silk wrap, the same wrap that now shimmered dully in an unkempt pile on the top of the desk, the small tag hand-sewn onto the hem that proclaimed that it had been made especially for Millicent Gray, shattering any doubt Abby might otherwise have clung to.

It wasn't a coincidence, or a prank.

It was real.

Millie's killer was taunting her, just as he'd taunted her at the Pumpkin Fest. He was homing in on her, letting her know that he knew about her connection, her closeness, to Millie. That he knew about *her*. He'd invaded her bedroom, rifled her belongings, spied on her and Matt. He'd bought her roses . . . and only he knew what came next.

Outside the library, lightning flashed, and a smattering of raindrops were hurled against the glass. Thunder followed, so deep and so powerful that the floorboards trembled underfoot. Then the wind kicked up, howling around the eaves, flinging the French doors wide as it swept through the room.

Gasping, Abby ran to close and lock them, then leaned shakily against the paned panels, willing her racing pulse to return to its normal rhythm. When she glanced up, he was standing in the doorway. She was so startled, she nearly screamed. "Oh, William," Abby said shakily. "You gave me a fright. How did you get in?" Then, just as quickly, "I must have forgotten to lock the door. Careless of me."

His olive-drab safari-style jacket was spattered with raindrops across the shoulders, and the wind had ruffled his straw-colored hair. It was the first time she'd ever seen William Bentz with a hair out of place, and she almost laughed at the absurdity of her observation.

"I'm not interrupting, am I?" he asked lightly. "Or were you expecting someone?"

Abby frowned. "Actually, I am—expecting someone. In fact, he should be arriving momentarily." It wasn't quite a lie. She kept hoping that Matt would show up. "What are you doing here? Did you have business with Aunt Catherine?"

"Are you certain you don't know?" Bentz asked, his strange version of a smile tilting up the corners of his thin mouth. "Or are you merely pretending for my benefit?" He cocked his head, his eyes flat, his manner detached, as if he were viewing a lab rat instead of a human being.

"I'm afraid I don't know how you mean . . ." Abby sighed and, breaking off, rubbed her temples, where the stress of the past hour had begun to gather. "William, can this wait? Aunt Catherine's away, but I'll be sure to tell her you dropped by."

"That's considerate of you, only it isn't Catherine I want, Abigail," he said, making no move to leave. "It's you."

"I don't underst—" Abby began, then broke off abruptly as he pulled his hand from his pocket and held it out. A thin gold chain was laced between his fingers, its half heart lying in the center of his palm. "How did you?" It was her necklace, the same necklace he'd taken from her jewelry box upstairs and taunted her with at the Pumpkin Fest; the necklace Matt had returned to her. Then, it dawned on her. "It was you," she said, her incredulity barely registering, but she saw from his frown that he took offense.

"It seems I overestimated you. I thought somehow you would be quicker than that, that you would present more of a challenge. I had no idea when I chose you that you would be such a disappointment."

"Chose me?" Abby laughed. "For what?"

"Why, to play the game, of course. It's more than the others got."

"Others?"

"Shelley La Blanc, Victoria Lane, Beth Langtry."

"You've lost your mind," Abby said. "And I want you to leave, *now.*"

"My, how authoritative you sound," Bentz countered

smoothly. "But you don't make the rules this time. I do. Will you come with me willingly? Or must I persuade you?"

Abby sent a rapid glance at the desk. The drawer was open, the pistol lying in plain sight, just fifteen feet away . . . but could she reach it? She moistened her lips with her tongue. "Why are you doing this, William?"

"That's number two," he said, clucking his tongue. "No leaping ahead. You've got to play sequentially. What came first, Abby? The killer or the crime?"

"I don't understand."

"Of course you do. You minored in abnormal psychology. Humor me. Answer the question."

"All right. Killers aren't born, they're made," Abby replied, stalling for time. "Data indicates that psychopathy may have its roots in the home environment. Children from dysfunctional or abusive families are sometimes emotionally stunted—unable to respond to normal stimuli. Unless checked, it can develop into a lack of conscience, which seemingly is irreversible."

Bentz smiled. "You see, you *have* done your homework. That should be worth at least thirty seconds."

"The roses were the last clue," Abby murmured, pacing a little as it dawned on her what he wanted. "Or were they the first? The addition of Millie's wrap was chilling. You have a keen eye for detail."

"I thought you might like it."

"*Like* is hardly apt. Have you had it in your possession all these years? Since Millie's disappearance?"

"I believe the experts call it a souvenir," he said. "I call it a fond remembrance."

"An item taken off a victim by the murderer."

"Another five seconds. Shall we play a little longer, or end it? I don't wish to bore you."

"No. I want to understand." He flexed his hands, a

gesture of acquiescence. Abby breathed a little easier. "This seems surreal. You were here in Abundance ten years ago?"

"For a year. I was seventeen when my mother and stepfather came here, and we left that same summer. But it was long enough to leave its mark on me. I've been many places since, but I've never forgotten Abundance, or you, for that matter."

"Matt said the killer was a local man, someone familiar with the area." She swallowed, then prepared to press on, hoping to stall, hoping to buy whatever time she could, precious moments she did not want to forfeit. *Oh, God, Matt,* she thought desperately. *Where are you?* "That night—the night we staked out the dump site— your being there wasn't a coincidence, and you weren't following your students. You didn't know they would be there, did you? You didn't expect anyone to be there?"

"Twenty seconds more. Perhaps you won't disappoint me after all."

"You killed Shelley, and you planted her belongings in Matt's truck," Abby said softly.

"Shelley La Blanc was a trial run. I needed to see how sharp Sheriff Rhys was. Sad to say, but he never presented much of a challenge, jumping to all the wrong conclusions when I was just trying to get your attention. First the watch, then the wrap. It reminded me of Millie's. I just couldn't resist adding it. I suppose you could call it an afterthought. A good guess. You're getting better. Another twenty. Just a few more tries."

Abby glanced at the desk, and the pistol lying on it, half-hidden beneath some papers. If she could just get closer without attracting his attention . . . He had taken a piece of nylon rope from his coat pocket and was toying with it, wrapping it around both hands, smoothing it out again.

Abby felt her panic rising.

He was going to kill her.

She stepped back, yet not far enough. "You planned very carefully," Abby observed. "The watch, the roses and scarf. You're at ease with killing—Millie was your first victim, but Shelley wasn't the second, was she? And the attack on Julianne—you were responsible for that, too."

"And the sheriff," he reminded her. "He stumbled across my SUV. I was scouting out a location, a place where you and I could be alone, but he ruined it for us, so now we'll have to return to my original plan."

He took a step closer, the rope wound around both hands, with a good fifteen inches between ... just enough to close around her throat. Abby's stomach clenched, and her palms grew slick with sweat.

Was the safety on or off? Could she really pull the trigger? "Why now, William? You waited a decade."

Bentz's eyes were chillingly devoid of expression. A cat growing increasingly bored with the death throes of a mouse would have shown more compassion. He shrugged. "This is where it all began. Millie's death was something of an accident. I asked her out, and she laughed at me. So I followed her that night and waited for her lover to leave. I wanted to frighten her, to pay her back, but she died instead. And her death fascinated me. It was intensely profound. Beautiful. The experience was life-altering. I'm a changed man because of it."

Abby swallowed convulsively. She had a second or two, but no more than that. If she didn't act quickly, he would kill her, just as he'd killed Millie, Shelley, and Beth. Her body was blocking the gun from his sight.

With her left hand she reached back, her fingers brushing the cold steel, closing around it, but her fingers were damp with nervous sweat, and as she snatched it from the desk, it slipped from her grasp and bounced off the hardwood floor, skidding to a stop midway between her and the professor.

Chapter Fourteen

Drop a pebble in a pond, and the ensuing ripples were liable to wash right over the toes of your brand-new sneakers, Matt thought, slumped behind the wheel of his truck four doors down from the small white house at the corner of Which Street and Maycomb Avenue. Or, more appropriately in the professor's case, his ultra-conservative black wingtips, though the ripples ruffling the normally calm waters of Abundance lately were more like a series of tidal waves.

Once the bodies began cropping up and the parents got wind of it, Bentz's students had packed their duffle bags, one by one, and departed for parts more familiar. And Bentz was left to clean up the dig sites alone.

Unless this whole mess was cleared up quickly, funding for similar projects would likely be withdrawn, leaving the professor in an unenviable position next semester. If not for the fact that Professor Bentz was about as endearing as a case of athlete's foot, Matt might

have had a little empathy for him. As it was, the absence
of Bentz's protégés made his work just a little bit easier.

Sliding down in the seat, Matt slipped on a pair of
sunglasses and adjusted his ball cap so the visor was at
his nape. Then he watched the house while pretending
to nap, and he waited.

The sun went down in a blaze of golden glory, indigo
dusk settling in soon after, but the lights didn't come
on in the house William Bentz rented. Instead, the front
door opened and Bentz emerged, a small canvas bag
under his arm. Masked by the hurrying darkness, Matt
watched him open the driver's door of an ancient Ford
Pinto and place the bag inside. Then he climbed in,
flicked on the headlights, and drove slowly away.

You'd think a professor at NYU could afford better wheels.
The moment Bentz was out of sight, Matt stepped out
of the truck and made his way to the house. The front
door was locked, but the back door had a loose lock
plate. Matt took a credit card out of his wallet, forcing
it into the crack, and was halfway through a long list of
inane excuses for getting caught jimmying Bentz's lock
when the door creaked slowly open.

The rear entrance opened onto a small mud room,
amazingly free of mud. In fact, Matt thought as he made
his way into the kitchen, the place was spotless,
orderly—neurotically, fanatically so. Not a dish, not a
knife or a fork in the sink, and the stainless steel was
scoured to within an inch of Bentz's bland little life.
There wasn't even a water spot.

"He's a psycho, all right," Matt muttered. "Probably
not the sort to store human heads in the fridge. Too
messy." But he opened the door and peered in, just to
be sure.

There weren't any heads, no body parts in evidence,
but there was a six-pack of low fat yogurt and some

bottled water. He checked all the cabinets, the drawers, and under the sink. He peered into the broom closet, the oven, then methodically rifled the other two down-stairs rooms.

But he found nothing. Nothing to indicate that Bentz had a personality, let alone a freakish obsession that drove him to kill young women. Matt looked in the hall closet; then, taking out his flashlight, he went upstairs.

The stairway was narrow and the wood old. The treads, worn and paint-chipped, groaned underfoot. If there was evidence to be found anywhere, it would be in Bentz's bedroom, the room with the external lock. If his suspicions were based on even a grain of truth, hav-ing his students in the same house would have been risky, and he would not have taken any chances that they would accidentally stumble onto something.

Matt plied his penlight and held his breath. The first door had an old-fashioned hook-and-eye closure, barely enough to hold the door closed, let alone keep the curious at bay. The tiny beam slid to the second door, and a brass circle winked back at him. Matt whistled low. "Hello."

Recently installed, it couldn't be slipped with a credit card, and until now he'd never had a need for the tools of the trade of a second-story man. He grasped the knob, bracing a hand on the panel above the lock, and applied pressure.

Solid. As a rock. But the door frame showed signs of age and heavy use. Matt stepped back, gauging the distance and force required, then forcefully planted a boot directly under the lock. He felt the blow right up to his kneecap, but it didn't deter him from a second attempt. Another kick, and the jamb splintered. A third, and the door swung inward.

The bedroom was as neatly kept as the downstairs

rooms. An array of dress-casual clothes hung in the
closet; neatly buffed shoes were arranged on a shoe rack
underneath, a shoeshine kit beside them. His possessions were spartan: a stack of text books, a few biogra-
phies, a comb and brush that were so meticulously kept
that they looked new.

Matt surveyed it all with a gnawing sense of dissatisfaction. There was nothing in the drawers but neatly folded
boxer shorts and V-necked T-shirts; no crepe-soled
shoes on the shoe rack, not a clue that Bentz was anything other than what he appeared to be: an anal-
retentive academic with a personality as interesting as
plain, fat-free yogurt.

Matt kicked the footboard of the bed in frustration,
but the punishment was more than the old iron frame
could withstand. The footboard fell back with a clang
and a thump, the bed frame collapsing, the mattress
shifting on the box spring, drawing Matt's attention to
the edge of a large rectangular object jutting out from
under the old chenille spread. Flipping back the bed-
spread, he grasped the object and slid it from its hiding
place. It was a cardboard portfolio, battered and beaten,
the string that Matt now untied, a little frayed.

With the penlight clenched between his teeth, Matt
dumped the contents onto the sloping mattress. There
were locks of hair, odd pieces of jewelry, news clippings,
and something that looked like a page torn from a high
school yearbook. . . . But it was the headline of a clipping
half-buried beneath the rubble of the professor's life
that grabbed Matt's attention and held him in thrall:

*"WHISTLE BLOWER: SEX SCANDAL UNCOV-
ERED AT PRESTIGIOUS NEW YORK UNIVERSITY.
ASSISTANT PROFESSOR OF HISTORY AT J. T.*

*SULLIVAN UNIVERSITY ABIGAIL YOUNGBLOOD
RESIGNS AMID A FLURRY OF ACCUSATIONS."*

The contents of the story were lost on Matt as he
quickly shuffled through the pile of clippings. They all
had to do with Abby.

Matt's pocket buzzed, and he nearly jumped out of
his skin—one more reason *not* to carry his cell phone.
He answered, "Monroe."

"Matt," the voice on the other end of the line said.
"It's Jimmy. Listen, I did some checkin' up on that
Bentz guy, but I hit a dead end. I can't find anything
on him prior to nineteen-ninety. It's kinda weird, like
he didn't even exist."

Matt was staring at a yearbook photo of Abby when
the photo beside it caught his eye. The young man had
straw-colored hair, and thick-lensed glasses with a wad
of tape holding them together at the nosepiece. William
B. Wright's stare was every bit as blank as his current
incarnation's.

"You get that?" Jimmy asked. "Matt, you there?"

"Yeah," Matt said. "Yeah, I got it. Thanks, Jimmy. I
appreciate it."

He pocketed the phone and picked up the yearbook
pages, still a little mesmerized by what he was thinking.
He was looking at the kind of kid who would have
gone through life without a great deal of notice, so
unremarkable that he would have barely made a ripple
in the rich fabric of Abby's life—or those of her friends,
for that matter. In fact, there was a good chance that,
ten years later, she would not even remember him.

But he remembered her, Matt thought, glancing at
the clippings.

More than remembered.

For some oddball reason, known only to the professor,

Abby had become his obsession, his focus, and suddenly
Matt couldn't get back to Gilead Manor fast enough.

Abby dove for the weapon but miscalculated the distance. She landed hard, her chin striking the old pun-
cheons, and for a moment her vision swam in a swirl
of black and a multitude of pinpoint stars. Time slowed
to a crawl while she struggled to shake off the effects
of the blow. If she blacked out, she would never survive
the night. Bentz would win his maniacal game and go
on to devastate other lives. Head spinning, she thought
about Millie, Shelley, Beth, Matt . . . and Bentz.

He hadn't bothered to grab the gun.

Why didn't he grab the gun?

Her senses screaming back to full consciousness, Abby
lunged for the weapon, and at the same time, Bentz
swooped, wrapping the ligature around her neck, twist-
ing it tight. "You really didn't think it would be that
easy, now, did you?" he asked.

Abby clawed at the rope, but she couldn't pry it loose.
It was a controlled strangulation. She could breathe,
but just barely. Blood pounded in her temples, and
there was a whooshing in her ears growing louder and
more threatening with each passing second, like a distant whirlpool rapidly approaching. The closer she got,
the more certain it was to drag her down. Bentz was
behind her, beyond her field of vision.

It made sense, Abby thought. He chose his victims
carefully. He preyed upon the vulnerable, the unwary,
taking them by surprise so there would be no risk of a
struggle.

If it was the struggle that made him most wary, then
she would take it and use it, and pray that it worked.
Letting a slow sigh escape her, Abby squelched all of

her fight-or-flight instincts and forced her body to go limp.

She sensed his pause; then his grip on the ligature gradually eased. Blood rushed to Abby's head, filling her with a giddy relief, but she resisted the urge to suck in a breath of air and instead breathed slowly. Bentz got to his feet and moved into her field of vision. Abby could see him through her slitted lids, his khaki-colored trousers, matching socks, and crepe-soled shoes. Her heart was pounding so violently that she feared it would seize up and stop beating completely. Every fiber, every cell of her being screamed for her to move, to run, yet somehow she managed to lie very still, to wait.

Then, as he bent to retrieve the pistol, Abby made her move, leaping up, flinging herself at him. She hit him low, at the knees, bowling into him. Bentz fell headlong into the desk, striking his head. The open drawer toppled, burying him under an avalanche of old papers, photos, and receipts.

Abby heard him curse, saw him struggle up, but he rapped his head on the underside of the desk and abruptly sat down again. She didn't wait to see if he recovered, didn't stop to search for Matt's gun amid the debris of Catherine's life. Instead, she pivoted and ran from the room.

She made it as far as the hallway. If she could just get outside, she could lose herself in the darkness, find some place to hide until he gave up looking for her. But as she grasped the doorknob, his fingers clamped down on her wrist.

"You can't leave now, Abby. There are things I want to show you, things that will fascinate you."

"Damn you, William! Let go of me!" Abby tried to knee him in the groin, but he moved just in time, his hip deflecting the blow. The fact that she fought back seemed to make him angry. His fingers digging into her arm, he pushed her back, away from the door, then shoved her into the hall table. Abby staggered against it, stumbled, and fell, the ginger jar lamp splintering beside her.

"You might as well submit, Abigail," Bentz said. "If you persist in being so combative, the time you have left is going to be very unpleasant."

"All right," Abby said, closing her hand over a jagged piece of ceramic, getting slowly to her feet. "I'll come with you. But first, where are we going?"

"A special place, just for you."

"What kind of place?" Abby asked. Every second delayed increased the chance that someone would come to stop him.

"You've heard of it, but I doubt you have seen it. In fact, I'm the only one in generations to have figured it out."

"William, you aren't making any sense," Abby said impatiently. "Figured what out?"

"Why, the Youngblood family secret, of course. They've been so busy garnering respect over the years that they lost touch with their own legacy. Rather foolish, wouldn't you agree?"

With one hand, he stuffed the rope into his pocket. With the other gripping Abby's arm so hard it hurt, he propelled her down the long central hallway, toward the old section of the house, and the room that had survived the electrical fire days before. "The catacombs," Abby said. "You found the entrance." Somehow, Bentz had managed to uncover the secrets that had been lost to posterity.

"You'll like it there," Bentz replied, producing a small flashlight. "It's wonderfully private, and the one place we won't be disturbed." He opened the door and

shoved her into the room. It had once been the library—
an office of sorts for the original owner of the house,
Lucien Deane, Abby's great, great, great, great, great
uncle, but it was too hard to heat, and it hadn't been
used in years. Even now, there was an unnatural chill
in the room—not just the cold of a closed off room but
something else, a dank draft that smelled of must and
age, and earth.

Bentz turned to her, his eyes curiously bright. "Think
of it as a sort of immortality. Your name will go down
in the annals of Abundance's history, not to mention
the history of the house you love so much. And your
soul and mine will be forever linked, just like Millie's,
just like Beth's, just like all the others."

"You really are insane," Abby told him. She tried to
break his hold on her arm, but his fingers dug into her
flesh like talons. The grasp of a madman, or of someone
so inherently evil it defied imagining.

"We all have predatory instincts," Bentz replied,
touching with his free hand an ornamental carving
flanking the mantel, then another on the opposite side.
"The only thing separating you from me is a lack of
fear. The consequences of my actions don't concern
me beyond the moment, and I have never been afraid
to explore my darker side."

Abby laughed derisively. "It isn't just dark, William.
It's loathsome. You are the lowest sort of life form on
the planet. In fact, the algae on Fisher's Pond are ele-
vated far beyond you."

The ancient mechanism creaked and groaned behind
the wall, giving way by inches; then it stopped. Bentz
calmly reached out, pushing the portal open with a
protesting groan of metal hinges.

Cold, dank air swept into the room and over Abby.
It smelled of perpetual wetness, cobwebs, and other,

unidentified things she didn't even want to think about. She shrank back from the odor, the chilly damp, and from everything waiting for her beyond the black rectangle of the open door. "How did you know about this?"

"I collected things as a boy and hid them away in the cave deep in Vanderbloon's Woods."

"But the cave has been sealed off for years," Abby said.

"Where there's a will," he said with a smile. "I found a way in. This is where it all began, Abby. Come, let me show you."

Abby shook her head. "I'm not going down there."

"It's your choice." He took the pistol from his coat pocket, pressing it to the hollow under her ear. "A few more moments of life, or death right here, right now."

Abby swallowed hard. His size belied his strength. She couldn't overpower him without a weapon, and she couldn't break his hold. He had her precisely where he wanted her, and there was no way out.

This would be difficult enough for Catherine and Rose. She didn't want them to find her here in the mansion. With Bentz silently urging her on, Abby stepped through the door, into the bleak unknown.

Matt's old truck had a well-worn quality that was deceptive. With a three-hundred-fifty-horsepower engine and a four-barrel carburetor, it could almost sprout wings and fly. He had his foot jammed against the floorboard and had just passed sixty when the red-and-blue strobe of the patrol car flashed on and the black-and-white shot from hiding and straddled the road. He had the crazy urge to ram the car broadside and knock it out of the way. But before he could act on the impulse,

Shep Margolis stepped out of the driver's side door, positioning himself dead center in the target zone.

Matt stomped on the brake and the truck slid sideways, skidding to a stop a few feet from the deputy. Matt leaned out the open window. "Get the fuck out of my way, Margolis!"

Hitching up his polyester trousers, the deputy stalked to the driver's door. "Well, well, if it isn't our resident hotshot."

"Abby's at the mansion, and she's alone," Matt said. "There's a good chance that Bentz is planning to show up there."

"That's too bad, boy. Outta the truck."

"Damn it! Will you listen to me? William Bentz is the one you're after," Matt told him. "And Abby's his focus."

But Margolis wasn't feeling terribly cooperative. He laid his right hand on the butt of his revolver. "Like I said, out of the truck."

Abby could be in deep trouble, and not only did Margolis not care, he couldn't even get him to listen. Matt's frustration was boiling over; he swung the truck door open, hitting Margolis and knocking him off his feet. Then Matt shoved the gearshift into four-wheel high and hit the gas, tearing out around the patrol car, flinging torn-up turf and great clods of mud liberally over Margolis and his immaculately kept patrol car.

With two more miles between him and Abby, and the screaming black-and-white rapidly fading into the distance behind him, Matt floored the truck and hoped to Christ no other obstacles lay in his path.

* * *

"I can't see where I'm going," Abby complained. "If you don't want to be deprived of the pleasure of my company, I'll need a light."

Bentz took a book of matches from his pocket and at the same time shone the beam of the flashlight on an ancient lantern hanging on the head of a square nail. Abby took it down and opened the rusted door, lighting the half-burned candle inside it. It was almost as decrepit as the passageway, and it took several tries for the wick to catch.

Flame blossomed, and shadows leaped off the walls. The walls were dirt, shored up with wood, and the wood was rotting. Bentz nodded toward the lantern. "Don't attempt to use it as a weapon, Abby. You'll only succeed in angering me and needlessly making things harder."

"Is that why you beat Shelley? Because she fought you? Because she made you angry?"

"She got what she deserved." Calmly. Without a ripple of remorse or a flicker of emotion. Abby felt a chill sweep over her that penetrated to her marrow.

How would she ever get away?

Pleading with him would do no good. He had no conscience, no soul, no humanity, and though she'd heard of them, she was not familiar with the catacombs. Except for the questions Matt had raised in his research, she hadn't thought of them in years.

Would anyone else think of them? Would anyone think to look for her down here, or would her fate—like Millie's remain a secret until someone stumbled upon her bones in a decade or two?

Every step she took pushed her further away from her family, from her loved ones, from Matt.

Away from her life.

"I may need to keep the matches. This wick doesn't look very promising."

"Go on," Bentz directed. "But step carefully. Some of the steps are falling away."

Abby held to the makeshift handrail, but it appeared to have been added some time during the last century, and posed almost as great a danger as the treads themselves. Her mind was racing, but her attention was by necessity riveted to the crumbling stone underfoot.

Thirteen steps wound downward, then a landing, then thirteen more. She could feel the debris underfoot: pebbles, grit, and small chunks of mortar that had broken away and lay waiting to gouge a tender instep. Two treads from the bottom, she slipped on something small, hard, and round. Her foot flew out from under her, and she almost fell.

Abby cried out, the sound magnified as it was hurled back at her again and again. Then, as it faded, a chorus of high-pitched squeaks issued from the darkness below, accompanied by the furtive movements of the rats.

Sick with fear and desperation, Abby clung to the rail.

The beam from Bentz's flashlight flitted over the stone floor and a trio of rats that seemed stunned by the intrusion. Two scurried off into the darkness. The third, bolder than its companions, sat on its haunches and sniffed the air.

Abby shuddered. She'd wondered how Bentz had managed to get into the house without triggering the new security system. Now she knew. He hadn't entered from the outside. He'd used this passageway to emerge into the heart of the house when he stole her half-heart necklace, and he had used it again tonight. They had been at the mercy of his insane whim all along. He could have been in their midst while they slept, and they would never have known it.

That thought made Abby furious, and her fury burned away at the edges of her fear. "Do you really think that you can get away with this?" she demanded. "Do you think that no one will figure out that you are responsible for the killings?"

"I suppose that remains to be seen, doesn't it? Though I doubt I'll lose much sleep over it. Deputy Margolis isn't smart enough to figure it out, and Sheriff Rhys' chances of surviving his injuries are almost as slim as yours." Bentz motioned with the flashlight beam. The barrel of the pistol, trained on Abby, never wavered. "Get moving."

The catacombs were a subterranean maze of tunnels, carved from the rock by simple erosion over countless millennia. The slow *drip, drip, drip* of water was a constant irritant, and the air was clammy and cold. Water seeped down the slimy walls, forming puddles in even the smallest depressions in the stone.

Abby skirted the pools when possible and waded through when it wasn't, while she tried to imagine Bentz as a young man, making this underground hell his haven. No wonder he was so twisted.

They were moving deeper into the labyrinth. There was less moisture here, but the roof overhead seemed unstable. It creaked and groaned, an eerie sound that raised the tiny hairs on her arms and filled her with trepidation. Then, a thin trace of dust and stone crushed by the shifting earth trickled down, and it was silent again . . . but it was a waiting silence.

Somewhere in that quiet, Abby thought she heard a muffled thud, like the slam of a door far overhead. But it was only wishful thinking. No sound could penetrate the insulation of the rock and enter the caverns, and no sound would issue out.

No one would even hear her screams.

As the grim reality of her situation gelled deep in Abby's conscious mind, something snapped inside her.

Bentz was close. So close she could feel his presence behind her. Planting her feet solidly, she spun, ducking slightly as she swung the lantern at the professor, bracing herself for a bullet and hoping it didn't come. The lantern hit the flashlight, knocking it from his grasp. She had the brief impression of flying hot wax, Bentz flinging an arm over his eyes, and then the flashlight beam and the candle both winked out, plunging the cavern into total darkness.

Matt skidded to a stop outside the mansion and flicked off the key just as the patrol car topped the knoll half a mile back. He checked all the doors. The front entrance was locked, and so was the door to the kitchen. He plied the knocker and called Abby's name, but everything was silent and still.

Too still. It gave him the creeps.

Impatient to find her, he headed for the French doors and peered in. The desk drawer had been pulled out and lay upside down on a pile of papers. Matt banged on the glass. "Abby! Abby! It's Matt!"

Then, when she didn't answer, he put a shoulder to the door, splintering the latch and stumbling into the room.

A lamp had been overturned, its shade knocked off, and the bare bulb had set the papers to smoking. Matt righted the lamp and threw the damaged papers outside where they couldn't cause any harm. He'd worry about retrieving them later. First, he had to find Abby.

He made a rapid search of the mansion, grabbing up the fireplace poker as he ran, starting with the upstairs, then just as quickly coming back down. Next he went to the kitchen.

Blood red roses were scattered over the gray slate

floor and looked as if they'd been thrown aside. The florist's box and lid lay neatly side by side on the old porcelain sink.

Reaching down, Matt picked one up. There were ten in all. One for every year since Millie's death. One for every year a killer had roamed free.

Matt dropped the rose and exited the kitchen, continuing down the hall to the oldest portion of the house. Maybe she'd managed to get away and was hiding somewhere. But with every step he took, the sick feeling in the pit of his stomach intensified, became harder to ignore.

What if he couldn't find her?

Forcing air into his lungs, Matt tried to think rationally, but he couldn't quite get past the thought that it was happening again. He was caught in a recurring nightmare, in which a guy who got off on control had someone he cared about at his mercy, and he was powerless to help her.

He was trying to figure out where to go from here when the cold draft coming from the third room on the left got his attention. He flicked on the light, but the bulb must have burned out, so he followed the flow of unnaturally cold air. It led to the fireplace, which had been sealed off to prevent heat loss some time ago. But the draft wasn't coming from the fireplace. It was coming from the wide crack just beside it.

Matt stuck his arm through the opening and found the rusted lever. He pulled it down, and the wall panel creaked open ... just enough for him to squeeze through.

The slim beam from his penlight was beginning to fade, but it allowed him to descend the stone steps without breaking his neck. He had a quick glimpse of uneven stone walls coated with thick green slime and glistening with moisture. Then the batteries died, and the beam faded.

He was standing in the labyrinth of tunnels designed as an escape passage during the early days of Gilead Manor's construction—the tunnels he'd been reading about but had been unable to find. They had played a big part in the history of the Youngblood family but eventually, they outlived their usefulness and were sealed off. Or so everyone had believed. Obviously, some of the information he had garnered was wrong.

But was he off base about Bentz's bringing Abby down here? he wondered. Time was precious. Every second counted, and he couldn't afford to be wrong. One misstep, one miscalculation, and Abby would die.

He was just about to turn back, to make his way to Millie's grave site, when the sound of metal striking metal split the silence. Someone swore—a man's voice—and then running footsteps echoed through the shaft.

Matt plunged through the darkness, as quickly, as noiselessly as he could, the echoing of the footsteps the beacon that urged him on.

Abby could hear Bentz cursing as he searched for the flashlight. Holding her breath, she backed away, using the rough stone wall as her guide. She came to a jutting triangular-shaped stone and felt her way around it into a second tunnel that opened onto a cavernous room. "Abigail?" Bentz's voice sounded eerie in the larger chamber. "You may as well come out. There is nowhere to go. No way to escape me."

The dim beam of his flashlight flickered past her. Gasping, Abby flattened herself against the stone wall.

She saw him cock his head. The beam swung to the left and shone full in her face.

Abby stumbled back, her hands, thrust out to break

her fall, colliding with a pile of loose slate. Desperate now, she clutched the piece of broken ginger jar like a weapon. "Stay away," she warned.

"It won't work. You can't get away, and no one can help you now." Bentz took the rope from his pocket, winding it around his fists, drawing it taut between as he advanced, and at the same time, Matt appeared behind him. "Come to me, pretty Abby. Come to me."

Matt swung, the end of the poker connecting with the back of Bentz's head. The professor crumpled.

Sobbing, Abby staggered into Matt's arms. "Oh, Matt. Thank God you're here," she said. "I was afraid I'd never see you again."

He gazed intently down at her, holding her face between his hands. "Are you all right?" Then, at her nod: "You sure?"

"Yes. Let's get out of here," she said, but when they turned to leave and she saw that William Bentz blocked the exit, her whole world disintegrated. A trickle of blood streaked the side of his face, but the threat from the pistol he trained on them was real enough to give them both pause. "Mr. Monroe, how good of you to join us," he said to Matt. "That wasn't a very friendly greeting—I owe you something for that." He adjusted his aim and squeezed off a shot.

Matt dropped to his knees with a ground-out curse, blood welling from the wound in his left thigh.

Abby crouched beside him. "Matt? Oh, God. Matt?"

"Behind me," he gritted out, "The back of the cavern. It's supposed to open into Vanderbloon's Woods. Maybe you can find a way out."

Abby shook her head. "I won't leave you."

The dim illumination of Bentz's flashlight focused on Matt's face. Beads of sweat had appeared on his forehead and upper lip, and he seemed abnormally pale. Abby took off her sweater, wadding it up, pressing it hard to the wound to stop the bleeding. "It's not that bad, Abby," he assured her. "For God's sake, just go."

His shallow breathing betrayed his lie. Bentz had come closer, and now he stood over them. "Perhaps you'd like matching wounds?" he said. "A little something to take your mind off the hole in your leg."

Matt's expression was murderous. "Come down here and say that, earwig."

Bentz seemed thoroughly intoxicated with the power of his current position. He had the pistol. Matt was bleeding his life away on the cold stone of the cavern, and Abby was terrified that he was going to be torn from her forever. It must have been an incredible high for the slight, almost effeminate professor, Abby thought, holding their lives in his frail-looking hands.

Less cautious now, he leaned over Matt, the muzzle of the pistol aimed at Matt's heart. "Say goodbye, Abby."

"No!" Abby screamed as Matt's hand snaked out, seizing the pistol, forcing it up and away. It went off with a roar, the bullet striking the roof, ricocheting, then embedding itself in Bentz's shoulder.

He staggered back into the black depths of the cavern as the roof overhead made a strange pinging sound, and then as Abby watched in stunned silence, the cavern ceiling seemed to open up, and several tons of slate and stone dropped from the ceiling onto William Bentz. From the edge of the pile, a pale hand protruded. As the cloud of dust from the cave-in settled, it twitched once and then relaxed.

Abby clung to Matt. The sound of footsteps rang through the catacombs, then Margolis's shout. "Shep! In here," Abby called out. "We're in here. Shep, we need an ambulance."

* * *

The bullet had missed Matt's femoral artery by half an inch, but it shattered the bone and required surgery. Matt was entering the dawn of his second week in the hospital and was just restless enough to attempt an escape when Nurse Strand came in with his release forms. He scrawled his name everywhere it was required, then, with a sigh, succumbed to the wheelchair escort out of the building.

Sophie, his agent, was waiting at the entrance, all but hidden behind a huge vase of fern-sprigged chrysanthemums. "Matthew, what the hell am I going to do with you? I send you to the Catskills for the peace and quiet, and you unearth a serial killer."

"I didn't find him, exactly. He sort of found me." Matt waited out Sophie's tirade, then stated flatly, "I haven't finished the manuscript, Sophie. But before you explode all over the hospital foyer, all I need is a few more weeks. Looks like I'll be spending a lot of time on my keister, so there won't be any reason for me to procrastinate."

"You'll have all the time you need," Sophie assured him. "We can talk about it on the way back to the city."

"I beg your pardon?"

Sophie smiled. "I planned to surprise you, but I suppose this is as good a time as any. There's a vacancy in my building. As a matter of fact, it's directly across the hall from my apartment. You need to be back in New York, Matthew. Your editor called me yesterday. They'd like to reprint your backlist, and publicity is pushing for public appearances. They want to milk this latest escapade for all it's worth. It's going to go over really big with your fans."

Matt was about to decline when the yellow Jeep CJ7

pulled up to the curb a few feet away. The passenger's door opened, and the blonde at the wheel offered him a seductive smile. Reaching up, she lowered her sunglasses, peering over the top. "Excuse me, but aren't you Matthew W. Monroe?" she questioned in a low, sexy voice very unlike her own.

"As a matter of fact, I am," Matt replied.

"*The* Matthew Monroe?"

Matt flashed her his most devastating grin. "The one and only."

"Who is that?" Sophie demanded suspiciously.

"I'm his biggest fan," Abby said with a smile meant only for him. "Would you like a ride home?"

"That would depend," Matt said, pushing out of the chair on his good leg. "Is that all you're offerin'?"

"For the moment," she said.

"Then I accept, as long as you promise to take things slowly."

Abby got out to help him climb in, then handed him the crutches. He gave the gaping older redhead manning the wheelchair a halfhearted salute. "Sophie, I'll call you. You can count on it."

Much later, Matt sat on the bed at the carriage house, with a new notebook computer on a wheeled bedside table, pillows at his back. He'd worked most of the afternoon, taken a short nap, and was just settling back into the chapter when he heard her come in.

It was funny how attuned he was to everything about her: her scent, her voice, her walk. She was the genuine article, a class act from the top of her head to the tips of her toes, and the worst thing about finishing the book was the thought of giving her up. Yet whether he was dreading it or not, he couldn't delay any longer.

He listened to her cross the living room, her steps

slow, and he frowned. "Abby? You all right out there? Abby?"

"Coming." The house lights were being switched off, one by one, and the soft glow of candlelight replaced them. The suspense was killing him. Pushing the table out of the way, he reached for the crutches propped by the head of the bed, and at that same instant, Abby came into the room.

A change had come over her since the ordeal, but it was so subtle that Matt couldn't put a finger on it. Her silky negligee had spaghetti straps and was the unrelenting black of night. With the gown puddling around her slim bare feet and her honey-blond hair falling softly around her bare shoulders, she barely resembled the woman he'd first encountered in the carriage house a few short weeks ago. "Sorry, lady, but I think you've got the wrong residence."

She positioned a fat candle on the dresser and lit it with a match. "Are you sure you want me to go? I'm here to give you a back rub, and a front rub, and if you like I'll even cook you breakfast."

Matt narrowed his eyes. "Breakfast? It's barely eight P.M." It was crazy, but she fixed him with a look from those pale-green eyes, and his heartbeat accelerated just a little.

She shrugged, sitting down beside him on the bed, resting her hands on his shoulders under his open shirt, kissing the corner of his mouth. "There's a lot of time between now and then, which is good, because we have a lot of catching up to do."

Her mood, Matt reasoned, probably had a great deal to do with the fact that John Rhys had come out of his coma that morning, and that Catherine's and her brother's combined efforts had borne fruit, and Gilead Manor had been declared a historic landmark. Money for restoration would no longer be a problem. The fact remained, however, that Matt didn't really care what had triggered it, but he couldn't help feeling the slightest bit wary. "Is this for real?" he wondered. "Or am I gonna wake up and hate the fact that you're not really here?"

Reaching down, she retrieved the toothbrush from the foot of the bed where she'd placed it. It was still in the box. "Can you make room in your bathroom for this?" she asked, then paused to take a deep breath, still holding his gaze. "More importantly, can you make room in your life for me? If you can, I'd like to hang around and see where this thing between us goes."

Reaching out, Matt took Abby's hands, leaning in to kiss the hot curve of her cheek; then, with whispered encouragement, he allowed her to press him back into the pillows. Far above the bed where they made love, the moon rode high in the black sky, silent witness to the profound stillness of the Catskill night.

ABOUT THE AUTHOR

S. K. McClafferty is the voice of award-winning novelist Selina MacPherson. In addition to nine published novels, McClafferty enjoys painting, gardening, and stonemasonry. The author lives in Western Pennsylvania with her husband of thirty years and Shetland sheepdogs Faelan and MacPherson's Fair Fiona. Readers may contact the author through the publisher.

Romantic Suspense from

Lisa Jackson

__Treasure
   0-8217-6345-8 $5.99US/$7.99CAN

__Twice Kissed
   0-8217-6308-6 $5.99US/$7.50CAN

__Whispers
   0-8217-6377-6 $5.99US/$7.99CAN

__Wishes
   0-8217-6309-1 $5.99US/$7.50CAN
